# BATTLECRY

---

## THE BATTLECRY SERIES - BOOK ONE

## EMERALD DODGE

# ALSO BY EMERALD DODGE

**The Battlecry Series**

Ignite (Prequel Novelette)

Battlecry

Sentinel

Mercury

**Enclave Boxed Sets**

Of Beasts and Beauties

**The Oceanus Series**

Sea of Lost Souls

House of the Setting Sun (coming soon)

Valley of the Shadow (coming soon)

Crown of Sorrows (Prequel Novelette)

**Other Works**

Novenas for Mothers

Novenas for Students

Novenas for Singles

*This book is dedicated with great love to my husband Alexander Dodge—the boy in the cafe. You told your parents after our first date that I was an author. I used to think that you were just overexcited, but now I know that you believed in me long before I did.*

# 1

The eighteenth bomb exploded.

Flattened against a wall beside a stinking dumpster, I crouched and maneuvered my finger beneath the fabric of my mask to remove a piece of shrapnel caught there. I was so grateful the media couldn't photograph superheroes.

A nineteenth bomb exploded down the street.

I straightened and peered around the corner. The bombs didn't frighten me. I'd faced worse in my six months as a superhero on my city's team. Adrenaline surged through me during battles leaving no room for fear. My teammates were out there. A volley of explosions had forced us to scatter fifteen minutes before. They now hid somewhere among the twisted wreckage, abandoned ambulances and police vehicles, smoking shells of cars, and shards of glass. Before I made any decisions, I had to know their whereabouts and condition.

I sprinted across the broken road. The blood rushed in my ears so loudly I could barely hear the maniac's yells from where he stood on top of the overturned armored car. Civilians huddled sporadically around the scene, clinging to each other. Others were pinned beneath rubble, trapped there when the man's fireballs exploded and threw out shrapnel.

My quick glances towards the armored car revealed that I stood the closest to the masked bomber, since I couldn't see anyone else. It was up to me to do something, even though I was just as vulnerable to fireballs as the rest of my teammates. I didn't mind the death-inviting responsibility. My teammates were, with one exception, far more likable than me. My death wouldn't make that much of an impact.

I'd already counted four burned bodies. If the gathering clouds overhead emptied themselves on us, we'd have storm damage to deal with on top of bombs and mangled people pinned under rock and twisted steel.

Skidding to a halt behind a cement planter in front of the ravaged bank, I crouched as low as I could and surveyed the scene. Craters and broken cars covered the wide downtown avenue. Large enough to accommodate traffic for Saint Catherine's population of a quarter million, it was now a daunting battlefield.

Skyscrapers loomed large above me, though they provided little shade against the late-morning sun that blazed down despite the increasingly ominous threat of a storm. The summer heat, Georgia's defining seasonal attribute, pressed me from all sides. Not for the first time, I wished my fighting clothes were any other color besides black. I wiped sweat off my face with a gloved hand and peered around the planter.

I'd been smart to change locations, because I could now see three of my teammates, busy climbing over wreckage. My fourth teammate, our leader Patrick, was nowhere in sight, but I knew that he'd never be far from the Destructor. At least, I thought that was the name the bomber had shouted at us over the screaming of civilians when Patrick had ordered him to identify himself.

I'd had to suppress the urge to laugh; since when did supervillains have codenames like us? And if they were going to pick codenames, why pick one so *dumb*?

The Destructor lobbed another explosive at an unseen person in the distance. Not risking a melee, I picked up a tennis ball-sized rock and waited for the right moment. A rock thrown at just the right spot would knock him down long enough for me to take him out. Between my enhanced strength, speed, and agility, I wouldn't miss my target.

He whipped around and looked directly at me. "Did you think I wouldn't notice you?" he shouted as another blazing orb appeared in his hand.

I ran, my speed allowing me to barely escape the blast. Shards of glass and stone soared past my head, and a searing burn on the back of my neck followed by a wet trickle alerted me to a fresh wound. I'd have to deal with it later.

I dove behind a car with bloody handprints on the door. I peered through the window— he was looking my way. There was no hiding now.

Beneath his red-and-black mask, his eyes gleamed with the anticipation of my death. For a fraction of a second I felt both insulted that he was trying to kill me and invigorated that something was finally happening, though both were stupid reactions at a time like this, or any other time.

"Come out and fight," he said with a snarl, another glowing ball already in his hand. "A dead little girl would brighten my day."

I pursed my lips, since I knew better than to correct him. If he thought a twenty-year-old was a "little girl," then he'd already underestimated me. I needed him just cocky enough that he'd make a fatal error.

The Destructor jumped off the armored car and sauntered towards me, bandying his fireball about as if it were a beach ball. I slowly unsheathed the knife on my belt. Just a few yards closer, and I could throw it into his shoulder with such accuracy that I could sever the nerves without damaging an artery. He'd have quite a time hurling fireballs if he couldn't move his shoulder.

He stopped and tossed a fireball from halfway across the street. Once more, I ran for cover.

I was fifteen yards from the car when it exploded.

The blast threw me into a crumbling brick wall that promptly collapsed, unable to withstand both the shockwave and my weight. I tumbled a few times and the knife sliced my leg. I lay face down on the ground for a moment. A ringing sounded in my ears. Adding insult to injury, it started to rain.

"Battlecry, you okay?"

I heard the words from somewhere but the flashing lights in my vision distracted me from figuring out who said them. Weirdly, my dislike of my codename was the first thing I thought of while my vision cleared. I much preferred to be called Jillian.

The ground trembled, followed by walls of dirt and stone springing up between the Destructor and me. Earth-moving—Reid's power. It had to have been him who'd spoken. With shaking arms, I pushed myself off the ground. A sharp pain ran through my right shoulder, and I winced. Likely it was a sprain—it wasn't the first time I'd received such an injury. Fighting would to be that much more difficult for the next few weeks.

"I'm okay." I flashed the thumbs-up to where he stood on a levitating piece of pavement. He returned the gesture and, after straightening his blue mask and cracking his knuckles, flew away in the direction of a large car pile-up.

Screams filled the air again. Around the earthen wall, the Destructor bore down on a group of three injured businessmen huddled against the side of an overturned hot-dog cart. Cursing, I unsheathed another of my knives and prepared to charge him.

The Destructor threw his fireball. It sailed through the air in a perfect arc with a horrific hissing noise. The businessmen closed their eyes.

The fireball hit an invisible wall and disintegrated into thousands of sparks.

Patrick was here.

He emerged from behind a pile of rubble, his inhuman fury visible even from a distance. I swallowed the lump in my throat and returned behind the dirt wall, listening to Patrick and the Destructor trade curses. Every time the Destructor attacked, Patrick shot back an enraged response and I held my breath, my whole body tensed and ready to run far, far away. But I didn't run—I stood in my little enclave, clawing at my brain for a plan.

Footsteps a few feet beyond my hiding place made me look up.

Marco rushed in. "Hiding, B? I'll join you," he said, panting. "That guy nearly turned me into pudding and now Patrick is working on him."

An ugly gash marred his face, and blood dripped onto his ripped tunic. One of his sleeves had been completely torn off. He looked every inch the hardened fighter the public expected us to be, instead of what he really was: a seventeen-year-old who'd lied about his age to the police when he'd registered with the city.

"I'm not hiding," I snapped. "I'm planning. And don't call him his real name right now."

Patrick caught the Destructor's volleys and crushed them in psychic force fields—apparently the rain made the bombs more manageable. Sweat beaded on his forehead as he directed all his physical strength into his telekinesis. The only one of us who went unmasked, he looked even angrier than before. Rumbling thunder overhead completed the picture.

"Planning," I repeated, more to myself than Marco. *You're a super-hero, Jillian. Do something.*

"Plan something fast. *Atropos* is furious that this is taking so long."

I couldn't help but smile at Marco's tone when he said our leader's goddess-themed codename. "What makes you say that?"

Already Marco's presence had lifted my mood, but his words worried me.

Instead of speaking, he merely tapped his temple.

Ah, Ember. The team telepath had told him.

"Great." There was more acid in my voice than I intended. "Can you blind him?"

Marco harnessed solar power and could redirect the heat and light. One good blast of concentrated sunlight would end the fight... although he rarely unleashed his power like that in public because of the risk of blinding a civilian or one of us.

Marco shook his head. "No, too many people are around, and even if there weren't, it's too dark from the cloud cover. I've used so much of my reserves already cutting through rock and steel that I'm practically going cold."

I held the back of my hand to his forehead—he did feel cooler than usual. My heart sank. This fight was probably going to drag on for hours.

"We need to get in the air." I glanced up to see if I could spot my skinny twenty-two-year-old teammate on his flying pavement.

Marco lowered his voice. "Em told me Atropos said he needed to get people out of the rubble."

I frowned. "Where is Ember, anyway?"

*I'm helping out with the rescue effort.* Ember's mental voice filled the back of my mind in the strange whisper-echo tone of telepathy. *And now that I have your attention, Patrick's got some orders for you.*

*Of course he does.* The rain started falling harder, which didn't help my mood. *Have you been eavesdropping on me? I hate that.*

*Not now, Jill. Please. And I was in Marco's mind and heard your question.*

*Fine. What does Patrick want me to do?* I crossed my arms, hoping the attitude came across.

*He says go to the top of the Bell Building and signal when you're up there. I'll give you the rest of the orders when you're on the roof.*

*No! No more open-ended orders. Remember last time? I got shot because he didn't tell me a gang meeting would be going on.*

*Stop being an idiot! This kind of crap from you is why he's the way he is. And besides, the bullet only grazed you.*

I told her where she could put his orders.

*Jill, listen to me. I get that you don't like not knowing what you're running into, but please think of the rest of us. You're not the only one on this team.*

My resolve crumbled and was replaced by guilt. Ember didn't deserve my anger. *Okay, fine.* My shoulders sagged, causing a searing pain that took my breath away.

*Thank you.* A long pause followed—she'd slipped out of my mind for a few seconds. *The Destructor's not thinking about you at all. If you act fast, you can probably get to the entrance of the Bell Building without attracting his notice.*

I explained to Marco what I was about to do, then took a deep breath. With only a glance to double-check that my way remained clear and unseen, I started the hundred-yard dash, darting behind cars, massive upturned pieces of steaming pavement, and other large items that littered the street. The weather worked in my favor; the rain acted as a curtain of sorts and the howling wind, thunder, and cracks of lightning disguised my footfalls.

I jumped through the shattered glass doors of the Bell Building into the cool dimness of the marble lobby. Though glass and bits of marble littered the floor, it remained relatively untouched. Even the hidden speakers still worked, playing a tuneless melody that offices seem to prefer.

A snuffling noise came from behind the reception desk, and behind it was a woman curled up next to her desk chair, weeping softly.

"Where's the stairwell?" I demanded, trying to project authority with sopped clothes and hair plastered to my face.

She pointed a shaking finger to a door at the end of the foyer. I thanked her and ran to it, gearing up for a sprint up twenty-five flights of stairs.

I arrived on the roof, panting and wincing from the burning pain in my shoulder. I stumbled to the edge and located Patrick below, a dark little figure surrounded by tiny floating items. He had moved to the top of the armored car. The Destructor was desperately trying to land a hit on him, but Patrick's telekinesis wasn't allowing it. Dozens of fireballs sailed through the air and dissolved into steaming, fizzling sparks when they hit Patrick's shield.

"Hey, Atropos! *Atropos!* I'm up here!"

He didn't turn around. The storm drowned out my shouts.

I flicked open a pouch on my belt with an aggravated sigh, pulling out a small flare and igniting it. After waving it for a few seconds, Patrick noticed me. He shouted something to Reid. For a moment I couldn't tell what Reid was doing, but then—

"Oh, hell," I breathed.

The ground rumbled and shook. A small patch of earth sprang up under the Destructor, six feet wide but soaring hundreds of feet into the air—far too quickly for the Destructor to jump to the ground. My team hurried from their locations to the base of the tower to watch.

Ember's presence tickled the back of my mind once again. *I picked up from him that he's afraid of heights when he was standing on the armored car, so we're lifting him up to throw him out of his comfort zone. Patrick wants you to give him a beat down.*

The mental image of me kicking the Destructor in the stomach over and over again while he begged for mercy flitted across my mind. That wasn't my fantasy but Patrick's, relayed by Ember.

Of course. How many times had Patrick used me as the team's muscle? Sure, Reid could control lava, Marco could harness the *sun*, and Patrick himself could move things with his mind. Heck, even Ember was one of the few superhumans lucky enough to have two powers, telepathy and control over animals. Our leader had made it clear to me that I was useful for my fists and nothing more. I ignored the leaden weight in my chest and geared up for the fight, my feet automatically sliding into a defensive stance.

The earthen tower reached the roof and stopped. The Destructor huddled on it in the fetal position. Ember had downplayed his feelings about heights. He wasn't just afraid, he had a phobia. Beneath my surging adrenaline lurked something almost like pity, because a trembling, sniveling adversary just wasn't respectable.

Still, I'd rather have jumped off the Bell Building than reveal my true feelings to a supervillain. I stuffed down my pity and worked my face into a steely glare.

I jumped from the roof onto the muddy tower, my boots skidding on the wet pavement and only stopping an inch from his head. He yelped.

"Scared?" I sneered. I lifted him by his shirt with my one working arm, the blood pounding in my ears. "Good."

I threw him off the tower onto the roof and then jumped after him. He scrambled backwards and held up a hand. "Don't come any closer! I'll—I'll blow us up!"

"You'd have done it already," I said coolly. Energy manipulation like bomb-making virtually always required the Super to have working hands, so without a word I stomped on the hand clutching the ground with my steel-soled boot while simultaneously crushing the hand he was holding up with my own vise grip. Despite my pity, the crunches and his cry of anguish were highly satisfying.

I mentally reviewed the steps I was supposed to take next. Punch, kick, maim, the usual. But this pathetic man was down, and doing anything else just seemed... *mean*. I looked at him while he cradled his useless fingers and marveled at the irony of someone so powerful being so weak at the same time.

"You disgust me." I put my hands on my hips, ignoring his sobs. "I've been told to kick your head in, but I think you've learned your lesson. The police will be here in a few minutes. Have fun in prison."

I turned to go to the edge and signal the all-clear. The moment my back was to him, he swiped a leg under my own and I fell.

My injured shoulder took the brunt of the fall, and my head bounced against the ground. He awkwardly ran towards the edge. My groan turned into a growl of anger. That had been a rookie mistake.

"Get back here!" I yelled, jumping up and blinking away white spots in my vision.

He glanced back at me, eyes wide, his fear of heights battling his fear of me. I bridged the gap between us and grabbed his wrist just as he went over the side of the building.

"Let me go," he pleaded, crying again. "I can't spend the rest of my life in the Supers' prison! Have some mercy on a fellow Super." His wide eyes were slick with terror, but the shooting pain in my shoulder reduced my previous pity to dust. I just wanted this disgusting man out of my sight.

"You didn't show any mercy to the people down there," I replied with some difficulty, as he wriggled and pulled against me. Normally pulling a man up with one arm wouldn't have been a problem, but the pain in my shoulder compromised my strength. A deafening crash of thunder preceded even more sheets of rain. Rivulets of water ran down my arm onto his, making my grasp slippery. A few more minutes of this tug-of-war and the Destructor would get his wish.

*Patrick says drop him.*

"Shut up, Ember!" I yelled into the storm.

*Patrick will catch him.*

*Yeah, right.* Powerful as Patrick was, he struggled to catch falling people—as we'd witnessed during a suicide two months earlier. Gritting my teeth and cursing the Destructor's ancestors, I ignored Ember's further protests and with a burst of effort pulled the Destructor back over the edge. A quick punch to the temple knocked him out cold.

*He's down.*

Adrenaline drained out of my system and left a cold creep in my veins, the same creep I felt after every mistake and poor judgment call. Though I could feel Ember in my mind, she said nothing. When the police arrived on the roof, I didn't leave the scene until they asked me to.

Back on the street, Patrick was surrounded by soaked teenage girls holding umbrellas and a copy of a tabloid that had done a feature on "Saint Catherine's Heroic Heartthrob." After signing autographs, he fielded questions from reporters. Their ability to converge at a scene just minutes after an incident never failed to amaze me.

One particularly aggressive woman pushed her way to the front and stuck a microphone in his face. "Atropos, how did you feel when you were fighting the Destructor?"

He ducked his head, grinning sheepishly. "Well, every fight is a thrill and a challenge. I didn't have any time to be scared for myself, though. I'm always one hundred percent concerned about the safety of my team and the citizens of Saint Catherine."

Another reporter pushed his way to the front of the throng. "Atropos, our readers want to know what it's like being the leader of a superhero team."

Patrick's crooked grin made several girls giggle. "It's the best job in the world. My team loves me, I love them, and we're a well-oiled machine." His eyes flickered towards me.

Nobody else seemed to notice his momentary glare, though Ember clutched my hand. *I'm here for you no matter what happens.*

The reporter referred to her notes. "Our viewers voted on our final question: any tips for prospective superhero leaders out there?"

What a stupid question. You were born into our life or you weren't, and leadership was for men in elder families only.

He laughed. "Sure. Lead with a firm hand, and you'll have the respect of your team and your city."

The rest of us looked on in the rain while Patrick fed the crowd his smooth replies. We made sure to never stop smiling for the public in case they looked our way, just as we'd been told for years.

After all, if we didn't smile, people might guess the truth about us.

## 2

_____

"Jeez, Jill. What did you do to yourself?"

Marco examined my shoulder.

My cousin and I were in the sick bay, a cramped room with peeling white paint, lined with wooden shelves of medicines, pain relievers, bandages, and other supplies. The only furniture was a chair and an examination table made of a material that always stuck to my skin.

"I didn't do it to myself." I was unable to keep the bitterness from my voice. "A bomb knocked me into a brick wall and then that freak gave me trouble on the roof."

He prodded my shoulder and frowned deeper. "Well, you were right, it's a sprain. You're going to be in a sling for a while. I don't like the look of those cuts in your neck and leg, either." He took an arm sling off the shelf and handed it to me. We'd made Marco the team's official medic, simply because he had read more first-aid pamphlets than the rest of us. He'd even understood a few of them.

"That's just excellent," I muttered, putting the sling on and securing it. "Every team needs a useless member."

Marco casually redid my attempt to secure the sling. "Stop that. Nobody on this team will ever be useless."

I sighed, then pointed to the ugly gash that marred his light brown face. "Does that still hurt?"

He playfully smacked my hand away from his face. "Yeah, but I'm going to have a cool scar to brag about, so who cares?"

The front door slammed. We froze.

"Maybe all the swooning girls improved his mood," I whispered. Patrick's stomping footsteps through the house caused my heart to pound.

"In my office, *now!*" Patrick's harsh tones made my mouth go dry. His tone made him sound much older than twenty-five.

Marco visibly swallowed. "Maybe a missile will hit the house in the next sixty seconds," he whispered back. He helped me off the table and gave my shoulder one last worried glance. "Let's go."

We walked to Patrick's office and were joined outside the door by Ember and Reid. Ember's long red hair still smelled of smoke and death, and her skin was even paler than usual. She wouldn't meet my eyes. Reid's mouth formed a thin line, and his gray eyes contained the same hard apprehension that curdled in my stomach.

I took a deep breath and opened the door. We all filed in.

Inside, Patrick, tall and blond and terrifying, sat on the edge of his desk with his arms crossed, a look so chilling on his face that I had to fight the urge to step back. "Shut the door."

Everyone flinched, but he spoke only to me.

I closed the door as quietly as I could, trying not to seem fazed.

Patrick looked directly at me. "Jillian, we're going to talk about what happened today."

I gathered my nerve. "We fought the Destructor and won. Because we followed your orders."

Everyone nodded and murmured agreement. Patrick's eyes narrowed. I struggled to keep my breathing steady. Already my fight-or-flight instinct was screaming at me to escape.

"If you followed my orders, why didn't you drop the Destructor?"

The question cut into my core. My eyes itched with tears, but if I let them fall, he'd say I couldn't control myself.

"Because, um..." My gaze darted around the room as I tried to stifle the shame that my team had to watch what was coming. "Because..."

Patrick abruptly stood and took a step towards me. Everyone else moved back. "Because what, Jill?"

My mind was racing. I couldn't pick out a coherent answer. Patrick was my leader and I had to listen to him. As a member of a non-elder family in the camp, my position in life was to be under another person's authority at all times. No exceptions. To defy the authority of my leader was unthinkable—practically as unforgivable as defying an elder directly. The turmoil of being at a loss for words began building up inside of me.

"I was worried he wouldn't make it," I finally blurted. "A lot was going on and it was a long fall, you know."

An invisible force slammed me into the wall.

"How many times do I have to tell you that you *do not have permission to question my orders*?" He strode towards me. "You *stupid*, insignificant piece of crap! I let you stay here and this is how you repay me? This is how you treat me? Who are you to question what I'm capable of?"

"I didn't mean it like that, I swear!" The words struggled to come out through the pressure on my chest and neck. I couldn't control the tears any longer, and my fear transformed into naked humiliation that my team was watching me not just get punished, but cry about it like a child.

"Then how did you mean it? Were you questioning my authority?" His fist clenched.

Reid moved to stop him, but pulled back his hand after a second, doubt and fear warring on his face.

"I'm sorry," I managed to whisper as I hung my head, tears dripping down my nose. "I just... I didn't want him to die."

"What have I told you? Nobody cares about what you want!" The invisible hand of Patrick's telekinesis threw me into a bookshelf, where several heavy tomes of *Leadership and Wisdom* fell on top of me and made my shoulder light up with excruciating pain.

I squeezed my eyes shut, willing myself to stay still. If I kept quiet, there was no way he could think I was fighting his discipline. Marco rushed over to help me up. His hand brushed the laceration at the back of my neck and I could tell that it had opened up again.

"You're going to make her shoulder worse," Ember said, her voice shaking.

She crashed into the desk. "Now *you're* questioning me?"

My chin lifted against my will, forcing me to look into his hard blue eyes. New tears appeared. The telekinetic force grabbed my collar and hoisted me to my feet. The chalkboard we used for strategy notations floated over and landed next to me. My fingers plucked a piece of chalk from the air.

Patrick crossed his arms. "Draw the chain of command and explain it to us. I want to hear from your own mouth that you know our law."

I gulped and started sketching, struggling to control my trembling hand. "The chain of command is like an umbrella," I began, using the same words my teachers had used over the years. "Elders are at the top, followed by team leaders, then your father and mother." I drew a crude likeness of an umbrella and sectioned it horizontally, labeling the lines. The umbrella analogy was very old, created when people in the camps still had umbrellas.

"Go on." He gestured for me to continue.

"If you go out from under the umbrella, you'll be exposed to danger. If you mix up the parts of the umbrella, the umbrella won't work and you'll also be exposed to danger."

Patrick nodded. "Tell me the core character traits of a good superhero."

Those had been drilled into me since I was three. "Obedience, joy, loyalty, and silence."

"Tell us how you will model all these traits during our next mission." His voice was suddenly softer.

I breathed easier now that his ire appeared to be fading. "I'll obey you without question. I'll do so happily because you're my leader, and I'm loyal only to you. And, um, I won't talk much?" Silence had always struck me as an odd concept to call a "trait."

Patrick's face relaxed and he rolled his neck. "You guys all know I don't enjoy these types of meetings. But I carry the burden of leadership. If you don't obey, it is my responsibility to discipline you." He looked at Ember. "Em, we're going to have a discussion tomorrow about interrupting me during discipline sessions."

She gulped and nodded. Even though I could still feel the tingle in my injuries from his punishment just minutes ago, I had to quash the desire to beg him to not hurt Ember, too. Was I demented?

With that, he turned on his heel and walked out of the room. I'd survived.

We were all slow to move.

"At least he only wanted the four traits. I'd have been screwed if I had to list the principles under pressure," Marco said, erasing my drawing on the board and sliding it back to its storage place.

"I can review them with you," Reid offered, gently brushing chalk dust off my arm. "Cautiousness, deference, deci—"

Ember bent down to help me pick up the books that had fallen. "Spare us. That's the last thing we need right now. Jill, how're you doing?"

"My shoulder hurts," I mumbled, trying not to sniffle. "I'm going to go to the clinic." The free clinic downtown was our answer to injuries that basic first aid couldn't address. Most of their patients came in with gunshot wounds and knives sticking out of them, so they didn't ask questions about things like broken bones, sprains, or serious burns.

"Are you well enough to walk?" Marco started to fuss over my injuries again, but seeing the hard look I gave him, he stepped back. We finished putting away the books in silence, and I hobbled to my room.

Before I headed to the clinic, I would need to change into civilian clothes. As I undressed, I laid my uniform out on my bed: gray mask, bulletproof vest, khaki pants, utility belt, combat boots, and black gloves, undershirt, and hooded tunic. Gazing down at my battered, bloody uniform, I briefly thought about what it would be like to never put it on again. I was blessed with powers and the chance to defend innocent people with them, and here I was, disobeying my leader and daydreaming about abandoning my team. Loyalty, I reminded myself.

I pulled on a pair of worn jeans and comforted myself by putting on a pretty blouse speckled with blue flowers, the latter with some difficulty because of my sprain. After gently unwinding my regulation waist-length hair from its messy bun, I sat on the edge of my bed and brushed it.

I caught a glimpse of myself in a windowpane. Bruises and cuts crisscrossed my thin, pale face like splattered paint, though they couldn't distract from an obvious black eye, a leftover from a fight a few days prior. My thick hair was such a dark brown it was almost black, and it was matted with dirt, blood, and who knew what else. It was painfully clear that I wasn't pretty on the outside and, as Patrick was fond of reminding me, I was too obstinate and impulsive to be pretty on the inside.

After braiding my hair tightly in two sections, I scrubbed my face and put on foundation over the black eye, which didn't really conceal it. I topped off my disguise with thick-framed glasses that slightly obscured my dark brown eyes. I took a moment to gaze at my reflection, and all I could see was an unfortunate young woman, as forgettable as she was powerless.

Before I left base camp, I signed out in our log, writing my name, the date, time, location I was going to, and how long I expected to be gone. With any luck, my outing would be unremarkable.

## 3

The downpour mirrored my mood while I walked towards the clinic. I mentally dared every hypothetical mugger and rapist to try me, but I walked down the street in miserable safety. I kicked a soda can into the gutter.

I'd said I'd be gone for an hour. The clock was ticking.

When I arrived at the double doors with the large red cross on them, I only paused for a second before continuing on my way down the street. I didn't know where I was going. I passed the park where I'd once stopped a shooting, the office building where I'd chased a man who could chew metal and spit it out like bullets (three people died that day), and the road that led to the bridge where just six months ago I first met Patrick, Ember, and Reid. An ice storm had encased the city—Marco and I had been dispatched to help the other three, and our team had finally become complete.

Soaked to the skin and shivering uncontrollably, I turned down Davis Street, a fancy neighborhood filled with boutiques, specialty bookstores, and ritzy little restaurants that catered to the city's wealthiest.

As I approached a coffee shop called Café Stella, a customer opened the door with a jingle, and the swirling aromas of coffee and spices enticed me to enter. My hand met the door handle.

There was no way to justify this act of rebellion. What if a teammate saw me? But the café looked so warm and cozy, I decided to step in. Just for a minute or two. Patrick couldn't punish me too harshly for just wanting to step out of the rain.

The café was almost empty. The glass counter off to the side held rows of glistening pastries filled with chocolate and jams. Two glass jars on top of the counter were labeled "biscotti" and "amaretti." Other jars showed off types of cookies for which I had no name. Behind the counter hung a chalkboard listing the café's offerings. With a stab of embarrassment, I realized I didn't know most of the words. What the heck was a macchiato?

The digital clock on the microwave reminded me that I had forty-five minutes left.

"What would you like, sweetheart?" The middle-aged man behind the counter smiled at me. His name tag read Lee. I bit my lip.

"I've never had fancy coffee before," I admitted. "What's your most popular?"

Actually, I'd never had coffee, period. It wasn't available in the camp where I'd grown up, and if it had been, we probably wouldn't have been allowed to drink it. Elder St. James often lectured to children that anything that alters the mind, besides medication, was dangerous, though he never explained why. The coffee smelled so good, and the old lady in the corner who sipped on a large mug seemed to enjoy it.

He thought for a moment. "If you've never had a specialty drink, I'll start you off with a latte. It's just coffee and milk, so if you want something more, I can give you some syrup or chocolate."

He poured my coffee and gave it to me with a wink. I handed him my money, donated by a thankful almost-victim of an armed robbery, and sat in the corner on a squishy loveseat, grateful for Patrick's generosity. He allowed us to keep three percent of any money donated to team members. Because I didn't spend often, I'd accrued about twenty dollars in six months.

Before I indulged in the coffee, I took one last glimpse around me to make sure nobody was watching.

A fashion and entertainment magazine rested on the table next to the loveseat. I turned it over so as to not be tempted to look at it, because looking at media not sanctioned by the camp elders was a very serious infraction, far more serious than sipping coffee. Coffee just temporarily intoxicated the mind. Most, if not all, movies, television, books, music, and magazines could pollute it forever. If I thought hard enough, I could probably trace my character flaws to some rock song I'd overheard while grocery shopping with Ember.

I settled back into the loveseat and started flipping through memories, looking for a song or image that had left a bruise in my psyche. I took a sip from my latte. It was bitter, but I decided I liked it.

The door of the café opened again with its friendly jingle.

"Hey, Lee!"

I looked over to see a handsome young man about my age walk in with a thick book in his hand.

Lee looked up from cleaning a coffee pot and grinned. "Benjamin! How are you?"

Lee and Benjamin shook hands and chattered for a few minutes. I didn't normally listen in on civilian conversation, but Benjamin's deep voice and bracing northern accent were pleasant to listen to.

Lee pointed to the menu. "So what'll it be? I've got all the usual stuff and the new seasonal menu. Three new pastries, too."

Benjamin waved his hand. "Just my usual order, thanks. I'll take a chocolate croissant, though."

"You got it." Lee got to work, and I couldn't help but notice that Benjamin's "usual" involved a lot of chocolate syrup.

After Benjamin paid for his order and took it from Lee, he looked around for a place to sit. I returned to mentally reviewing all the civilian songs I'd ever heard—it wasn't a long list.

Far in the distance, many blocks over, wailing sirens made me pause in my thoughts and turn my ear towards the door. No explosions or gunshots... probably just an accident. Civilian authorities preferred that we wait until called in for those.

"Do you mind if I join you?"

I startled and looked up.

Benjamin stood next to me, smiling pleasantly. He gestured to the empty spot on the loveseat. "Not to be weird or anything, but the loveseat is the best spot in the place."

I doubted that. An identical couch sat in another corner near a pretty girl with spectacular hoop earrings. She'd been shooting glances at Benjamin since he'd come in.

I scooted closer to the arm of the loveseat, my own automatic smile stretching my face as I made room. "Er, no, that's fine. Make yourself comfortable." I certainly wasn't comfortable. Speaking with normal people outside of strict superhero business was so forbidden I half expected to spontaneously combust.

He sat. "Thanks." He stuck out his hand. "I'm Benjamin."

I awkwardly shook his hand with my left, a thrill shooting up my arm when he touched me. "I'm Jillian. Sorry about the sling."

He did a double take. "No apologies necessary. If you don't mind my asking, what happened? You look like you went through a harvester. Er, I mean, you look fine," he said sheepishly.

His embarrassment was touching. "Don't worry, I know I look bad. I got hurt at work today."

Benjamin's face hardened for a moment but then smoothed over. "I'm sorry to hear that."

I lifted my left shoulder in a shrug. "It happens."

We sat in silence for a few seconds. I tried to rework my face into something other than a grin. He seemed to search for a topic of conversation.

I glanced at the microwave. Thirty-three minutes.

Finally, he said, "So, first day of hurricane season. Scientists are saying we're overdue for a big one. Do you think it could happen this year?"

"Don't they say that every year?" I murmured into my latte.

He nodded. "Yeah, I guess they do. So, are you a student down at the university? I'm thinking about going there myself, and I wouldn't mind an insider's perspective."

"Sorry to disappoint you, but I'm an assistant gym teacher at one of the city schools." My usual lie came out easily. The job was ordinary and explained bruises.

He nodded and sipped his chocolatey drink. "You're braver than I am. I'm not sure I could work at a job that beat me up like that. What did you do, fall down some bleachers?" His words were polite and friendly, but I thought there was a tiny speck of sarcasm in there, too. He reminded me of Marco.

"That's exactly what happened." I was purposely neither enthusiastic nor dismissive. It was best to let civilians think what they wanted to think. The conversation was focusing on me far too much for comfort, so I pointed to his book. "What are you reading?"

A woman outside the window answered a phone call. After a few seconds, she gasped and took off running in the direction I'd heard the sirens.

Now I was intrigued, but I had to wait for the call to report to the scene—I was technically supposed to be at the clinic, much too far from the sirens to hear them.

He held it his book. "A nursing textbook. I'm thinking about quitting my job and applying to the nursing school down at UGSC."

"Nursing. Wow." I was impressed—The University of Georgia at Saint Catherine was the largest university in the region. "I don't know much about it, but I've heard that it's hard. Lots of long hours and cranky civilians. I mean, patients." *Whoops.*

"It can't be harder than my current job." There was an edge to his words. He hadn't appeared to pick up on my mistake.

"What do you do?"

"I'm an errand boy for my parents' human resources consulting firm. And before you ask, no, the work isn't hard. Being with my family all day is hard." He sank back into the couch. "I'm actually supposed to be on a job right now, but I decided to ditch." He looked sidelong at me. "I'm glad I did, though. Normally the company here isn't so nice to talk to. Pardon me for being so bold, but I love your Georgia accent. It's thicker than others I've heard."

Heat crept into my face. How should I even respond to that? "I—

I'm also ditching. My boss would freak if he knew I was here. But I'm glad I came, too."

I'd never had a real conversation with a young civilian man before, and Benjamin *was* incredibly nice to look at. Every once in a while he'd turn his head and his mop of light hair would bounce slightly, shifting into his eyes. He'd shake his head a little to clear it away, and I'd see his crinkly hazel eyes once more.

Benjamin grinned. "So how about we waste more time? Tell me about your bad boss and I'll tell you about mine."

His wide smile warmed my stomach. Against my better judgement, and the microwave's half-hour warning, I started talking.

"My boss isn't really bad, just difficult to work with. He... Patrick is kind of controlling. He yells a lot and gets really angry when I make a mistake. He's just really hard to please. But it's usually my fault," I added quickly. "I mess up, a lot and there's so much on the line when I do. I deserve what he does." I picked at a spot on the couch. "You wouldn't believe how much I mess up at work."

Benjamin raised an eyebrow. "I can't believe that. And your boss shouldn't yell at you. Although...I'm being hypocritical, because my dad yells at me a lot and I never tell him to stop. But Patrick's not your family."

Patrick actually was a distant cousin of mine. "Sometimes I think about quitting but then I feel terrible. Besides, Patrick would be so angry; he hired me and I owe him everything."

Benjamin set down his cup. "Jillian, I don't know what this Patrick guy has been telling you, but you can quit your job. And you know, if he's such an ogre that you're afraid to give two weeks' notice, you may want to report him to the school board. That sounds like a really bad place to work."

This was the downside to my cover story; it only worked at the surface level. "It's not that easy," I said softly. I looked up at him. "Tell me about your boss."

The lights flickered. Lee stopped cleaning and frowned at them.

Twenty-nine minutes... but I didn't want to go.

Benjamin exhaled in a long breath. "I should start off by saying that my mom and dad are under a lot of pressure all the time. When things get bad, they lose control and start screaming their heads off. Dad'll get gruff, mom will say something nasty to my brother, he'll reply with an attitude..." He trailed off and sighed heavily. "And then everyone jumps on the crazy train." He stared off into the distance for several long seconds, lost in thought. After an awkward second, he turned beet red and ran a hand through his hair. "I—I'm sorry, that was a lot to unload on you. Um, let me go get you another latte." He jumped up and headed towards Lee, still red as tomato sauce.

Smiling into the latte I was still drinking, I worked through his words, looking for the part that was supposed to be "bad." Authority figures had a right to rein in their inferiors through any means necessary, and sometimes that included yelling, even hitting. It was just an unpleasant part of life, like hail or sickness.

Still, I sensed that Benjamin thought this was unusual behavior in some way, so I sipped my coffee and decided not to comment on his family drama when he returned.

When he sat down again with a new latte in hand, a few awkward seconds passed before Benjamin spoke. "So if you quit your job, where would you work? Could you teach something else?"

I shook my head. "I don't know what I'd do. This is all I'm good for." The pain in my shoulder flared and I winced. I'd have to go soon, whether I wanted to or not.

He reached out to touch my shoulder, then drew his hand back. "I don't believe that. Give yourself a chance."

I was tired of this part of the conversation, but I didn't want to stop talking to him altogether. His black t-shirt said the word Nirvana on it and had a bizarre yellow smiley face below. "What does your shirt mean?"

Two shrieking ambulances raced down Davis Street, followed by a firetruck and police cars.

He pulled the bottom of his shirt to straighten out the front. "Nirvana? They were a nineties grunge band. You've never heard of them?" He was surprised, but I didn't hear any suspicion in his tone.

"No. Are they your favorite band?"

I could hardly judge him for enjoying a band, since he was a civilian and had no limitations on what media he could consume. I wondered what Nirvana's songs sounded like. They couldn't have been too bad, if Benjamin liked them—he was just so polite. Nearly all civilian music could corrupt, but I'd always gotten the impression from our lessons that some music could corrupt faster and more completely than others. Nursery rhymes and traditional ballads were alright—I even knew a few. Nirvana, whoever they were, were probably on the safe end of the scale.

"Eh, not really. They're okay. The shirt was last year's birthday gift from my sister. She's visiting right now, and I wanted her to see me wearing it."

I sipped my coffee to hide my smile. I didn't know what I'd expected from talking to this young civilian man, but such thoughtfulness about his sister's feelings wasn't it. I was moved.

"What bands do you like?"

*Dang it.* "Um, there aren't any specific bands, but I've always liked singing with my family. We used to sing around campfires when I was young." Those days seemed very far away. "Singing while we played in the meadow... while we worked... while we ran through the trees. I love to sing." I hadn't sung in six months.

Benjamin's eyes shone. "Were you in musicals when you were in high school? I wasn't good enough to be on stage. I ended up doing debate and forensics, plus some other stuff. What did you do?"

I knew what "debate" was, but not the other activity.

However, before I could bluff my way through an answer, my phone rang. A quick peek at the screen showed that it was Marco. I mouthed to Benjamin to hold on a minute while I took the call over by the bathrooms.

"Hello?"

"Jill, come home. There was a break-in at a bank and Patrick is freaking out 'cause you're not back. Tell me you're close."

So there it was: a robbery. Didn't criminals in this city ever sleep?

"Of course I'm on my way home. I just left. Give me fifteen minutes." I hung up and returned to the couch. "That was a coworker." I hoped my anxiety wasn't written all over my face. "I need to go."

Benjamin jumped up, and I saw for the first time that he stood at roughly six feet, just like me. "I had a great time talking to you," he said, taking my trash. "I'll just come out and say it: would you like to meet me here again?" He looked hopeful and shy at the same time.

His words hung in the air between us.

Nobody had ever asked to see me socially before. Back home, my only friends had been other children in the camp. Here in Saint Catherine, I had to be careful. Everything about the situation felt wrong. Forbidden. I could think of a dozen reasons to say no, the first one being the risk of Patrick pounding my face in for breaking a cardinal rule.

"Yes, I'd love to," I blurted. "How about next week, same day and time? In fact, let me get your phone number." I dug around in my pocket for my phone.

He told me his contact information and I saved it, making sure to label his contact file "Snitch #5" in case Patrick felt like randomly searching through it as he'd done in the past.

When I was done, I stuck out my left hand. "It was great to meet you."

He shook my hand and a spark of electricity traveled up my arm into the back of my neck and down to my thigh. "And you, Jillian. I really hope you'll consider what I said about your boss."

I nodded and we parted without another word.

I was walking out the door of the café when I realized that my shoulder didn't hurt anymore.

## 4

I smelled blood the second I stepped through the front doors of the bank.

Nobody else on my team did, as they lacked my heightened senses. They walked through the revolving doors of Saint Catherine Citizen's Bank with their usual cool confidence and went straight towards the stairwell to the basement, which was sectioned off with red and yellow tape.

I was the last to enter, so they didn't see me throw my arm over my face to block the smell and take a staggered step backwards, gagging quietly. The closer I went to the gray marble staircase, the stronger the stench became. For decorum's sake I couldn't hold my nose.

I caught up with Marco while we descended into the dimly lit basement. He smiled at me absently, but then seemed to really take in my appearance for the first time since I'd changed back into my uniform half an hour earlier.

"Where's your sling? And your black eye? And all your scratches?" he whispered.

"I'm feeling better," I whispered back. "I'll tell you about it later."

Ahead of us, Patrick stopped at the bottom of the stairs and inhaled sharply. He turned to look at the rest of us. "Go to my right. Stay around the edges of the room."

When we got to the bottom of the stairs I understood immediately why Patrick had reacted so strongly and why the whole building stank of blood; it was everywhere.

Pools of thick, congealing blood fanned out from three bodies on the floor, each covered with bloodstained white sheets. My first guess was that the three victims had been shot point-blank in the head. I kept my face expressionless, but I felt sorry for the three people. They'd either died from massive head trauma or slow exsanguination, and neither of those options were ideal ways to die. The latter method especially made me uncomfortable to contemplate, for my grandmother, my namesake, had died after having her throat slit by a supervillain.

The police and technicians moved around the scene with calculated precision, snapping photographs and making sketches while skirting around the little red lakes to avoid soiling their shoes and contaminating the scene. A man in a pinstriped suit, whom I figured was the bank's manager, spoke with great animation to the police, turning to point to the vault and to another wall.

I'd been so preoccupied with the mindboggling amount of blood that I hadn't noticed the ever-so-slightly irregular three-foot holes in both the vault door and the wall. What on earth were we dealing with?

A plain clothes detective I recognized from two other investigations saw us and walked over, stepping over the blood as if he dealt with oceans of it every day.

Patrick shook the man's hand. "I'm Atropos, the leader of this team. Are you the official police-super liaison for this investigation?" Patrick threw his shoulders back.

I stifled the urge to roll my eyes. We all knew each other, so this was nothing but posturing on Patrick's part.

The detective quirked an eyebrow but didn't miss a beat. "Yes, I'm Detective Burbine. I believe we've met. My partner Detective Floriendo is speaking to the manager now." He took out a little notebook from his pocket and flipped it open. "We've got a doozy of a scene here."

"Tell me everything," Patrick said.

"According to the branch manager, one of the guards heard something, a sound," he looked down to review his notes, "—like 'a fly in a bug zapper'—down here, so one went to investigate. When he didn't come back, two more guards went down, and they also didn't come back. The manager didn't hear anything that sounded like a break in, so he went down to see what happened. He found a hole in the vault door, a hole in the wall that leads to the basement of an adjacent house, and the guards dead on the floor. So far it looks like nothing was taken, but we're still confirming that."

"Can you look at security footage?" I asked.

Patrick glared at me. I looked down at my boots.

Detective Burbine shook his head. "No, and that's one of the things that made us call you guys in. The cameras were turned off via a massive program override. So were the sprinklers. We've never seen hacking like that."

I didn't think that sounded like Super work, but I kept silent this time.

Patrick thought similarly. "What makes you think Supers did this?"

The detective pointed to the vault and the wall with his pen. "Only Supers could have blasted holes like that without making a loud noise...and then there's the bodies."

We all turned to stare at the sheet-covered bodies. The technicians were finished examining them, so we made our way around the blood to the nearest corpse and kneeled down.

Before Detective Burbine pulled back the sheet, he looked up at us. "I've seen a lot of stuff in my fifteen years on the force, but I don't mind telling you guys these bodies really give me the creeps." He uncovered the first body.

None of us had a problem with gore, but everyone flinched at the sheer strangeness of what was underneath.

My guess of a massive head wound wasn't far off the mark, except the man's head and neck were simply gone, as if someone had taken some kind of cosmic eraser and rubbed them away. The blood had poured out from the hole at the top of the rib cage, making a sight that was as fascinating as it was grotesque. Detective Burbine put the sheet back over the corpse.

"What do you make of this? The other two are just like it."

"I've...never seen this kind of thing before," Patrick said. "Has anyone else?"

We shook our heads.

The detective sighed. "Well, take a look around and get the information you need. Here's my card if you need to contact me later, since this is our first introduction and all," he said, waggling his eyebrows. He handed Patrick his business card. Patrick nodded curtly, a muscle flexing in his jaw.

Patrick pocketed the card and gathered us in a far corner as not to be overheard. He looked at Reid and Marco. "Go talk to the residents from the adjacent house and see what they know. Marco, make that smile convincing. Reid, at least try to act smart."

Both Reid and Marco turned pink but walked away towards the hole in the wall.

He turned to Ember, who tensed. "Find an animal, a bug, a bacterium, something, that saw what happened. I don't want to see you again until you have a witness."

Ember nodded quickly and walked off. He rounded on me and my heart rate increased. "I don't want to hear from you unless you have something exceptionally important to say. Just get to work looking for clues and get out of my sight." I nodded and took a few steps back, more than happy to get away from him.

I started with the vault, deciding to throw myself into my work to block out the memory of pure hate coming from Patrick's eyes.

The robbers had managed to cut a clean three-foot circular hole in the vault door, but their method wasn't clear. There was no tell-tale warping caused by intense heat from a torch or a laser beam. Blades of any kind leave obvious marks. The door simply had a giant hole in it. I stepped through the hole into the vault.

The interior of the vault held no clues. There was no debris, not trace of the missing part of the door anywhere. The safe deposit boxes were all closed. The table and chair inside were undisturbed, a fine layer of dust covering them. In fact, a fine layer of dust covered a lot of the vault. That seemed odd to me—didn't people go in the vault all the time?

I poked my head out of the vault door and called over to the bank manager. "Sir, when was the last time someone accessed the vault?"

"A patron came in to access her safe deposit box an hour before the break in."

I thanked him and went back inside the vault. So someone had sat in the chair and probably put things on the table. Why was there dust on it? And why was there dust on the floor and the boxes? Snapping on a latex glove from my utility belt, I knelt down to examine the area by the vault door where the dust was thickest. I ran a gloved finger over the floor and held it up to the light.

The dark gray substance that covered the vault was the finest powder I'd ever seen. I blew on my hand and it swirled into the air, nearly invisible. I sniffed my finger and detected a whiff of metal, like the graphite in pencil shavings. I frowned and sniffed again. No, it wasn't graphite. It was like the sharp, thorny smell of my knives.

I unsheathed the knife on my thigh, enjoying the sound of the action, and compared the scents. Yep, they were the same. The dust was steel, or something like it.

I looked from the powder to the door and back, searching for connections. Why was the steel dust coating the inside of the vault? How was it used during the break-in? Was it part of the process of making the hole? I looked closer at the door. Like the headless bodies, there was no sign of force on it. It was as if part of it had been erased from existence.

Then a thought occurred to me. I left the vault and walked over to one of the bodies. "Detective, can I see the body again?"

Detective Burbine lifted the sheet and this time I looked at the area around the corpse, especially the area where the head would have been. I put on a clean glove and swiped a finger on the ground next to the pool of blood. A faint powdery residue, similar to the vault dust but lighter in color, came up. I directed the officer to pull the sheet back further so I could examine the torso. As I suspected, there was more of the substance on the man's clothes.

A few minutes of investigation revealed that it was on all the bodies. I could see small piles of dust underneath the hole in the wall; it looked like fine sand.

I walked over to Patrick, who was talking to a computer technician working on the security terminal. "I need to talk to you."

Patrick paused in his conversation and stared at me in disbelief. "What?"

"There's something you need to see in the vault and on the bodies," I said. For once my confidence superseded my internal tremor.

He crossed his arms. "Well, what is it?"

"There's a kind of dusty residue around the holes and bodies. I don't know what it's from but I think it's connected to the robbery."

"Dust? You interrupted me to tell me you found dust?" I was sure that Patrick was about to launch into a rant about my investigative skills, but he saw the technician's shocked expression and dismissed me with a wave of his hand. I knew better than to push the subject, so I tried Ember instead.

She was crouched down in the corner and staring intently at something in her hand. I knew without looking that it was some hideous bug.

I glanced; yep, a large spider. Even though I'd grown up outside, I didn't care for spiders.

"She's friendly," Ember said, tipping the spider back on the ground. It went back into a crack in the wall. "But unobservant. What's the point of having eight eyes if you don't use them?" She brushed herself off and stood up. "The spider was the only living thing in the room that survived the robbery. I've been listening to everyone and nobody knows anything."

She inclined her head towards me. *But I heard from Patrick that he's planning to do a random phone search soon, though I didn't hear when.*

I was so glad I had the forethought to think of the label "Snitch #5.'"

"I need your help," I whispered to her. "Can you get something that can taste?" *I have an idea that'll make Patrick happy with the both of us.*

She looked surprised but nodded. "Just give me a minute." She walked upstairs and reappeared a few minutes later with her hands cupped over something. "I saw mouse traps upstairs when we came in. This little guy was in a break room cabinet." She opened her hand, and a small gray mouse poked its head out.

I held the finger with dust from the body up to the mouse. "Ask him if this tastes like anything."

Ember held the mouse up to my hand, and after a few seconds the little rodent bumped its nose onto my hand and stuck out his tongue to get a taste. Ember's jaw dropped. "He says it tastes like bones and meat."

"Are you sure?" This was exactly what I wanted to hear.

"Yes, I'm sure! It's a very clear thought, bones and meat. He's thinking of... yuck, eating other mice."

"Here's the other thing I want him to taste." I held up the glove with the vault dust. Again the mouse bumped his nose to the glove.

Ember frowned. "He doesn't like that one. It's not food."

"What is it, then?"

She shook her head. "Mice'll eat nearly anything. If he doesn't recognize it, it's probably inorganic."

I went and scooped up a little bit of the sand beneath the hole in the wall and offered it to the mouse.

"That's rock," Ember said. She kissed the mouse on the head. "Good boy."

She went upstairs to release him, hopefully outside and away from traps.

I was missing something obvious, something that was straining at the edges of my understanding. I looked at the vault, then to the bodies, then back to the vault. The mouse tasted bones... bones and meat and something... inorganic...

"Atropos," I said loudly, striding towards the vault. There was no way he could get mad at me for interrupting him, not now that I was about to make him look good by solving a mystery on his watch. "I checked out your theory, and I've figured out what happened to the door, the hole, and heads." The sentence sounded better in my head than it did out loud.

Everyone in the room stopped talking and looked at me. Patrick raised an eyebrow but said nothing.

I took a steadying breath. "They were disintegrated." I scooped up a handful of dust from the vault. "Firelight confirmed that the substance in the vault and by the wall and the substance on the bodies are completely different. The first two aren't organic, probably metal and stone. The dust around the bodies is bones and flesh. I'll bet you anything that we're dealing with someone who can reduce small areas to this stuff." I tossed the metal powder into the air.

For once Patrick just nodded, his face blank.

While the police collected samples, my team hovered around me. "Any idea who could do this?" Reid asked Patrick.

Patrick pinched the bridge of his nose. "No."

"I once heard about a supervillain who could melt stuff," Ember offered. She looked at Patrick. "We learned about her from your dad, remember? I'm pretty sure she's dead, though. Maybe she had a relative with similar powers. Disintegration is similar to melting, right? Or maybe it was a Westerner?"

Marco snorted. "Why would a Westerner come all the way to Georgia to rob a bank?"

"Do you have a better idea?" Ember shot back.

"Stop it," Patrick hissed. "We're in public. Either pretend to agree or don't say anything at all. And smile."

We instantly obeyed.

"A person who can turn someone's head to dust is memorable," I said through clenched, grinning teeth. "Maybe we should ask around. You know, hit up the usual sources."

*Dangle the bait...*

Patrick cut in. "Everyone, go get into civilian clothes and start making the rounds. Firelight, you're going to go to Northside. Helios, you have Downtown. Tank, you're on the river. Battlecry, you have Old Town."

*Gotcha.*

He was going to Saint Catherine's Island, the biggest of many islands in the city and his usual patrol zone. But it didn't matter where he was going, as long as it wasn't Old Town.

We said goodbye to the police officers and left the bank. I was unusually lighthearted since I'd contributed to the investigation and successfully lied to Patrick.

We went back to the dilapidated house we called base camp. The others ran to get dressed, but I was in no hurry.

I walked up the narrow stairwell to my bedroom and pulled off my uniform, replacing it with the jeans, blouse, and glasses I'd worn earlier. I grabbed the sling from my bedside table and while I fastened it, looked around my small bedroom.

I'd grown to enjoy the feeling of confinement that four walls and a roof provided, though my bed, with its squishy mattress and green wool blanket, made my back hurt. I didn't have any decorations in my room like Ember did, but if I ever personalized my room, I'd incorporate flowers into it somehow. Asters and borage grew wild in the open meadows back home, and once upon a time my brother Gregory and I had delighted in making flower crowns for our mother.

While I put my uniform away, I looked at the empty dresser top and thought maybe a sketch of Gregory would be nice, too. He'd been my favorite sibling, before he'd been murdered by the Westerners.

Marco and I walked in the afternoon sun towards our assigned zones. He kept glancing at me.

"Seriously, where did your injuries go? And if your shoulder is better, why did you put the sling back on?"

I elected to answer the second question only. "I'm wearing the sling to test out a theory."

I couldn't help but smile. I was still riding the high from my little victory at the bank and I was positive my next theory was correct, too.

"What theory?" He sounded skeptical.

"Don't worry about it." I used my big-sister voice, hoping he'd take the hint.

He didn't. "Come on, Jill. You're killing me. How did you heal so fast?" He widened his eyes in a clear attempt to pluck at my sensitive side.

"Nice try. Miracles happen, Marco. Even to a person like me."

He snorted. "What is that supposed to mean?"

"Nothing. Nothing at all." I wasn't in the mood for chitchat. My mind was already miles ahead of us, sitting on a loveseat in a coffee shop.

We parted ways at High Street. Marco headed downtown while I made my way back towards Old Town, where Café Stella was. When I reached Davis Street, I pulled out my cell phone and pulled up Snitch #5's number.

Patrick had been so eager to look decisive and important that he'd taken my suggestion to find leads and ordered it without thinking. Had he been a little more thoughtful, he would've remembered that my "usual sources" were hookers, dealers, and other denizens of the night. There was nothing I could do in early afternoon.

Except one thing.

My finger hovered over the call button while I asked myself if I was certain I wanted to do this. This wasn't a one-off decision. This wasn't an order in the heat of battle. This was open rebellion.

I pressed call.

## 5

"You're an inspiration. No, really." Benjamin lifted his chocolate coffee in the air.

"Shut up," I said with a laugh. "All I did was come to a café for the second time in a day."

"Yes, but in doing so you managed to ditch your evil boss for the second time in one day. This is the best 'screw you' I can think of that doesn't involve painting something on a water tower."

We were back on the loveseat in Café Stella, coffees in hand. Benjamin had bought me his favorite drink, which he said was called a café mocha, with extra pumps of chocolate and a small mountain of whipped cream. I also had a cheese Danish, a fat blueberry muffin, and two biscotti waiting to be consumed. My hands were already trembling from the sugar and caffeine.

"I had more fun today than I've had since moving to Saint Catherine," I said through a huge bite of Danish. It was the most delicious thing I'd ever eaten. "I hope you don't mind that I called."

He waved away the idea. "I don't have any friends in the city, so it was an unexpected pleasure. As you can see," he said as he gestured towards his nursing textbook, "I don't have a lot going on. The alternative was going home, which I'm trying to avoid."

I sighed. "I understand that completely."

"Bad home life, too? That sucks."

I wasn't sure whether the lump in my throat was from the Danish or my sudden nervousness. "I live with some unpleasant roommates."

I was unsure whether or not that was a lie.

"That's a rough situation." His eyebrows knit together. I had the distinct impression he was thinking critically about something, but I wasn't sure what.

My eye caught the corner of a magazine that was underneath a newspaper. I recognized the blond hair in the picture, and I moved the newspaper aside to see the cover. Patrick's image smiled at me underneath a blurb that promised an exclusive interview with "Atropos, Georgia's Sexiest Superhero."

Benjamin laughed. "Why the face?"

I'd made a face? "That superhero on the cover. I just don't like him."

"What? Why? Don't superheroes fight muggers and stuff?"

"They do a lot of things," I said dully. "They're important to the city. But Atropos seems unpleasant. I saw him in action today and he, um, was...really...*hard* on his teammates."

Admitting Patrick's personality flaw was difficult, because I knew he only meant to train us up to be the best superheroes possible. It was disloyal not just to criticize him, but to criticize him to a member of the public. He'd led so many victorious missions.

I exhaled deeply as if doing so would expel the guilt.

Benjamin perked up. "You've seen them in action? That's so cool! What were they like?"

The delighted excitement in his eyes was so endearing I couldn't refuse to answer. However, I would need to select my words with care. "Atropos is telekinetic. There are four others who serve with him."

"What are their names? Do you know their powers?"

I pretended to struggle to remember. "I'm pretty sure there are two other men besides Atropos. I thought I heard the black man call the white one 'Tank.' Tank moves rock. The other man is called Helios, and he makes light come out of his hand, or something like that. The woman with dark hair is super strong. The redhead's code-name is Firelight, but I don't know what she does." Ember's powers were too subtle for a random civilian to know.

Benjamin mulled over the new information. "I wonder why the leader calls himself Atropos."

"Atropos is one of the—"

"Fates. Yeah, I know, I've read a book or two." He rolled his eyes. "She cut every mortal's thread of life. What I meant was, why did he choose a goddess's name? Why not Ares or something?"

I blushed at his tone. I couldn't fault him, though; if someone tried to explain the principles to me, I'd be dismissive, too.

"It is odd that he chose a woman's name," I agreed, sipping my coffee. "I bet the appeal lay in the idea of being able to control life and death." Actually, I was pretty darn sure that was the reason.

"That is *so* cool. Do you know if they're any good?"

His excitement was contagious. "They're the *best*." I was unable to keep an indulgent smile from my face. "They fight all sorts of criminals. Violent crime has gone down thirty-six percent since they started patrolling. There have been three superhuman attacks in the city in the last six months and they stopped them all. They even...." I caught myself.

Benjamin just looked more excited. "They sound amazing. I'd love to know what the redhead's power is. Do you know of anyone who might know?"

"Your best shot is the reporters who cover their stories." I pointed to the magazine with Patrick on it. "But take their information with a grain of salt. They've all missed that there's someone in town with healing powers."

There was a pregnant pause.

Benjamin's eyes darted towards the door. "That's, uh, that's a cool power." His enthusiasm waned with each word.

I slipped out my sling and he paled.

"A few hours ago I could barely use my arm and now it's good as new. Isn't that amazing?"

Benjamin shrugged. "Nothing about a healed sprain says super-human healing powers."

"Sprains don't just heal themselves in a few hours. It had to be something extraordinary. My shoulder was purple."

"It may not have been a sprain. A tense muscle can relax after a while, and you said yourself that you had a good time earlier. Maybe the hot coffee helped you unwind?"

"Sure, maybe. But that's not the only injury I got when I fell down the bleachers." He froze. "I also had a large cut on the back of my neck and on my thigh. Can you explain how those healed in a few hours?"

He clenched his fist. "I'm sorry, Jillian, I just can't." His words were tight.

"Benjamin." My voice was soothing as I placed my hand on his, but he pulled it away. "I know super powers exist and I'm not afraid of them." I put my coffee down on the table. "And really, did you think I wouldn't notice?"

He turned pink. "Why are you interrogating me?" He wasn't angry, but he definitely wasn't happy, either.

"Because life can be hard for people with gifts. Because the world expects things from Supers. Because you're burdened with a secret, and I don't mind helping you carry that burden."

His jaw hardened. "You want to talk about secrets, Jillian? Let's talk about the shiner that was on your face earlier."

I touched my eye, momentarily lost for words. He'd seen it under the makeup and glasses?

"That? That was nothing. It was from falling—"

"—falling down the bleachers? That's a load of bull and you know it. It was green and yellow, so you've had it for at least a couple of days, unlike your sprain. So tell me, do you fall down bleachers often?"

"My job causes a lot of injuries. I told you that." I was aware that my tone was far from convincing.

"Uh huh. You're an assistant gym teacher... at which school?"

"James Oglethorpe High School." No hesitation.

"And what's the district superintendent's name?"

"It's, uh, it's..."

We both knew that he'd cornered me. I didn't even know what a superintendent was. *You're stupid, you're stupid, you're stupid.*

To my surprise, his expression softened. "I think you have the bigger secret, Jillian."

"What gave me away?" My voice was faint. Could it be that six months of a secret identity had been unraveled by an observant man in a café in the space of a few hours? Was I really that terrible a superhero? I held my breath.

"Speaking as someone with serious sibling rivalry issues, I know what defensive wounds look like. The secrecy, the fact that you've been injured more than once this week, the way you were hiding here at the café...it all pointed to one conclusion."

He took a breath as if he were about to jump off a high dive.

"Someone's been abusing you. You need to get out of the relationship." We stared at each other. Then, I laughed. His face was somewhere between angry and hurt. "Why are you laughing? I'm serious!"

"I know, I know." My laughter turned to wheezes. His conclusion wasn't remotely funny, of course, but I couldn't hide my relief. "I know you're serious." I wiped my eye with a napkin and took a few breaths. "I just wasn't expecting that answer."

He scowled. "What were you expecting, then?"

"I wasn't expecting relationship advice, that's for sure." I was deflecting as subtly as I could.

He took my hand in his. "You can trust me. There's a shelter not far from here where you can stay. I can find out how to file a restraining order. You don't have to stay in the relationship."

This was surreal.

He continued, "Let me help you, please. You deserve better than someone who hits you."

In my mind's eye I saw a dozen memories of Patrick disciplining me for a smart mouth, a defiant look, insubordination, being late to a crime scene, talking to reporters, and rushing to defend Marco, Reid, and Ember from his fits of rage. I clearly deserved the punishments I received, and as I sat in a café eating treats with a civilian instead of actually doing my job, I knew I deserved another.

I hated how cold my hand became as I gently pulled it free from his warm grasp. "There's just too much you wouldn't understand."

"Then please tell me. Help me understand."

I shook my head. "I can't talk to you about it, but I can assure you that I am not in an abusive relationship. There are people in my life who are difficult, but I'm okay. Please don't worry yourself over me."

It was difficult to say the words. They weren't lies, but something inside me strained to take them back. The lump returned to my throat.

He looked doubtful. "Can you at least tell me who gave you the black eye?"

I had a strange impulse to tell the truth. I wanted to tell him the entire story of how I'd received my black eye. I wanted to give him a detailed explanation of where my sprain came from, and the cracked rib two months ago, and the countless scars that crisscrossed my back. I wanted to lay all my secrets in front of this person whom I'd known for a single afternoon.

This kind of idiocy was why Patrick disciplined me.

I picked up my coffee from the table and stood up. "You have a good afternoon, Benjamin. Thank you for the coffee and pastries. They were delicious."

He sighed and stood up as well. "Just promise me something?"

"Sure."

He placed his hand on my shoulder, and though I wasn't injured anymore, I still felt a tingle where he touched me. "Call me if you need help."

I hesitated, but then I nodded. "I will."

I turned and walked out the door of the café, brushing a tear from my eye. I wiped at my eyes all the way home, though I didn't know why I was crying. Being a superhero was a marvelous honor, and I certainly didn't need Benjamin's help.

# 6

At twenty-one hundred, we gathered in the living room for the evening lesson. Ember sat cross-legged on the floor in front of me. I sat on the sagging gray couch, brushing her hair and listening to Patrick read an instructive story from one of the volumes of *Leadership and Wisdom*, a series that contained a moral tale for every day of the year, plus a few civilian stories and myths about heroes.

Reid sat next to Ember and glanced at her every few minutes; I was certain they were talking to each other telepathically. Marco sat next to me on the couch, knitting a scarf. The corner lamp was the only source of light, so the whole room had a dim, honeyed glow that I found comforting. It reminded me of the campfires back home.

After the story ended, Patrick closed his book with a snap. "Talk to me. What was this evening's reading all about?"

Reid answered immediately. "It was about the authority umbrella. Everything went down the toilet after the team in the story disobeyed the elder. Even though their leader was with them and all their fathers gave their blessing, the elder said no, but they still went after their enemy. They weren't under the umbrella anymore."

Leave it to Reid to regurgitate the lesson at a moment's notice. He could've passed as an elder's son.

Patrick gaze fell on me, making my stomach churn. "Jillian, what are your thoughts? Would you say they were justified in their disobedience?"

I shook my head, comfortable that I knew the answer for once. "No. The team had noble intentions, but their disobedience cannot be justified because they rebelled against the elder. That's against the natural order."

As the words left my mouth I realized what the whole point of the evening's reading had been: my concern for the Destructor's life didn't trump Patrick's wishes. This was truly basic superhero stuff, and I'd forgotten it—again—in the heat of battle. I looked away, too embarrassed to face him.

Patrick simply nodded and looked at Reid once more. "So what should the team have done instead of going after their enemy?"

Again, Reid answered immediately. "Considering the seriousness of the threat, I think they should've asked their elder what to do. The team obviously wanted to embody the principles, especially decisiveness and justice, but they forgot about deference and cautiousness."

I mentally geared up for the usual grilling about how we'd demonstrated the principles during the day, but Patrick just smiled. "That's right. Good job." He put the book on the coffee table—it wobbled from the book's weight—and glanced at the wall clock. "All right, it's late. Lights out in two hours. I'm going out tonight and I want everyone to be asleep when I get back, understood?"

I was thrilled to go to bed before midnight for once, though a tiny voice inside sneered, *Yes, Father.* I corrected myself immediately. *The fourth, sixteenth, and seventeenth principles: reverence, joyfulness, and obedience.*

We all watched as he walked out and down the hall towards his room. The whole lesson had taken no more than fifteen minutes. When we heard his door shut, Ember took the hairbrush from me, gesturing for me to switch places.

Reid stretched and rolled his neck a few times. "Did anyone else almost fall asleep during that story?"

Marco looked at him skeptically. "If you weren't paying attention, how did you pull those answers out of your butt? And did it hurt?"

Ember swatted Marco with the hairbrush. "Don't be jealous just because you were telling stupid jokes to me the whole time and didn't have a good answer like Reid did."

Reid gazed at Ember with such adoration that I was tempted to gag for effect.

Marco opened his mouth to argue but I interrupted, determined to keep the atmosphere peaceful. "What's Patrick doing tonight? I thought he seemed kinda rushed during the lesson."

The other three looked at each other and then to me. "I don't know," Marco said. The unspoken end of his sentence was ...*and I know better than to ask.*

Marco's vague answer notwithstanding, I'd successfully redirected the conversation away from argument. Marco picked up his knitting once more and started to undo a snarl. Reid recorded the day's activity in our logbook. Ember brushed my hair and hummed a soft camp tune to which I'd forgotten the words.

I closed my eyes and hugged my knees, letting myself dream up half-formed fantasies about Benjamin sitting with us as a member of the team, reading his nursing textbook and drinking a café mocha.

I felt Ember pause while brushing my hair, but I was too lost in my happy daydreams to care.

---

AN HOUR LATER, I stepped into the steaming, bubbly water in the bathtub and sighed, already feeling some of the day's stress melting away. Sinking into the water and closing my eyes, I tipped my head back, enjoying the sensation of my voluminous hair being weightless for once.

I was so relieved to see the end of this day. Had our fight with the Destructor only been that morning? Patrick's punishment overshadowed my memories of the bombs. Although the times with Benjamin had been thoroughly enjoyable, overall the day had been a low one.

Bubble baths were one of the few luxuries afforded to me and I fully intended to take advantage of one.

I sat up in the bath and flicked open the pink bottle of shampoo, inhaling the rosy fragrance. Shampoo was still a novelty to me; growing up we didn't really wash our hair. Boys and men cut their hair short. Girls and women brushed their hair often and kept it in braids or buns to protect it, but our hair was always limp and dull. If we wanted to wet our hair, we jumped into a creek or waited for rain.

Whenever Super teams returned to the camp for a visit I'd always marveled at how clean and neat the women's hair was, and I'd been delighted to discover their secret. I squeezed a large amount of shampoo into my hand—waist-length hair requires a lot of shampoo —and started washing. After rinsing my hair, I scrubbed the mud, blood, and sweat off of my skin. It took several minutes, but eventually the red and black streaks were gone.

I climbed out of the bathtub and wrapped a thick towel around myself. Humming Ember's camp tune, I opened the bathroom door to step into my bedroom.

I yelped.

Patrick was lounging on my bed, my phone in his hand. He looked me up and down and smirked. "So that's what you look like under your ugly uniform."

I clutched my towel tightly around myself, too horrified to speak. What was he doing in my room? Why was he looking at my phone? I was uncomfortably aware that I was wearing nothing but a towel, dripping water everywhere and shaking like a leaf. I wanted to crawl into a hole.

"Did... did you need something?" I asked once I'd found my voice.

Patrick tossed my phone on my bed. "No, I was just doing a random accountability search. Who's Veronica again?"

I swallowed. "She's a college student who moonlights as an escort. She passes me information about the drug trade on UGSC's campus. I met with her last month, remember?"

Patrick seemed to accept that answer, which was the truth. I had my fib about Snitch #5 ready, but Patrick stood up and walked to the door without a word. Before he left he turned and looked at me again, giving me a lascivious grin and then shutting the door.

I stood there in the bathroom doorway, unable to process what had just happened. I didn't like him seeing me so exposed and vulnerable. Marco had seen me in varying stages of undress over the past few months while attending to my injuries and I'd never felt overly modest. Yet something about Patrick's gaze repulsed me. I ran to my dresser, pulling out pajamas and dressing at top speed.

Instead of falling into bed, I grabbed my wool blanket and squishy pillow and curled up on the floor. The hard ground was familiar and homey to me, just what I needed in times of stress like this. If there was a bug on the floor, well, that was just like home, too.

I stared at the wall, shivering. I needed to think of something to rid my mind of Patrick's grin. I squeezed my eyes shut and thought about afternoon adventures with Benjamin. Soon some of my stress leeched away, though even memories as nice as those couldn't entirely relieve my anxiety.

My phone beeped a text message alert and with lightning-quick reflexes I grabbed it, daring to hope it was from Benjamin. Instead, I read a text from Marco, asking me again where my injuries had gone. I tutted at his careless text and deleted it, then put my phone down.

Thoughts swirled around my mind while I stared at the cracked ceiling.

*Call me if you need help.*

I refused to examine the sudden urge I had to reach for my phone again. I didn't need help. I was fine. Benjamin, well-meaning as he was, had seriously missed the mark about the source of my injuries. Unfortunately, I was just going to have to let him believe that my non-existent boyfriend was a bastard.

My mouth twitched at the idea of me ever having a boyfriend.

I rolled over and closed my eyes.

*Call me if you need help.*

What did he know? He was completely integrated with society, unlike the rest of us Supers. It was plain that he was from one of the families who'd rejected the harsh reality of heroism and opted for the softer life. He'd never understand what it took to fight crime. To grow up under the constant eye of stern elders and trainers. To be hungry every waking hour. To memorize countless rules, traits, principles, and life formulas so that I might be the kind of righteous hero the world deserved.

*Call me if you need help.*

Besides, there was nothing he could do. There was nowhere to go. And even if there was, I didn't need help.

I was fine.

## 7

"You're telegraphing."

A second after I spoke I blocked Ember's punch, causing her to let out a slew of curses. I grinned. "Easy there, Ember. True heroines speak joyfully at all times, remember?"

"Yeah, right," she muttered, wiping sweat from her brow. "How am I supposed to throw a punch without making it look like a punch?"

"Don't make a big show of winding your arm up." I demonstrated what she'd done wrong.

It had been three days since the battle downtown. We were at home, in the basement, in the fluorescent-lit training room. The walls were covered in blue padding, cracked and peeling from too many sparring rounds. A worn punching bag hung in the corner. Free weights were stacked neatly at the far end of the room. Ember and I stood in the middle, where we'd been practicing our techniques for an hour.

"How do you make this look so easy?" Ember shook her head to clear sweat from her eyes. "I haven't landed one on you yet."

"It's just muscle memory, Em. I've been training longer than you have. Plus, I've got the build for it. Now, show me your fighting stance again. Okay, good. Keep your eyes forward, chin down, move your hand here. Try to punch me one more time. Imagine I'm your least favorite person."

I slid into my defensive stance. She narrowed her eyes, breathed for a few seconds, and threw a solid punch towards my face. I moved my head to the side just in time, but then she swung for my chin. I ducked again but could not block her knee to my solar plexus. My lungs emptied with a gasp.

I stumbled backwards and coughed. "Good hits. I didn't expect you to try that combination. Very—very good."

"Are you okay?" Ember rushed forward, more shocked than I was, then stopped when I gestured for water. She just handed me a bottle and said, "When you're ready, I'd like to go over the moves we practiced last week."

"Self-defense from supine? Sure, no problem." I took a swig and handed her the water bottle. "Have some water, though. You're paler than usual."

Knee to my stomach aside, I was delighted Ember was taking such a keen interest in training with me. Six weeks earlier she'd knocked on my bedroom door and explained that she wanted to be a more competent fighter, and asked if I could show her some moves. I'd thrown my arm around her shoulder and told her that she'd be beating people up in no time.

Since then, she'd progressed steadily. I also found that not only did I enjoy teaching, I looked forward to spending time with Ember. I had more fun with her than I'd ever had with my sister Allison, who was five years older than me and had always preferred the company of older children.

When Ember had had her fill of water, she capped the bottle and put it back on the bench. "I know we've gone over it a bunch, but I want to make it effortless."

"Sure, but it will never be effortless. The best you can hope for is muscle memory." I threw a slow punch at her head, which she immediately blocked. We high-fived.

A minute later, Ember laid on the ground, facing up. I knelt down between her knees. "I'm going to go over the steps again with you, and then we'll practice."

"Without a weapon first," she said, her voice hard.

I raised an eyebrow but said nothing. Not for the first time I wondered if something had happened during a battle that I didn't know about, but when I'd asked her during our first training session she'd sworn that nothing had. "I'm just tired of being the only one on the team who can't defend herself properly," she'd admitted.

I put my hands on her shoulders. "Normally when an attacker comes at you like this, they'll try to get in low and close."

"So I straighten my arms." She put her hands on my shoulders and locked her elbows. "And make sure my hands are on their shoulders, not their chest. Otherwise they can turn and knock my arms aside. My thumbs shouldn't be in your armpits."

"Right," I said, smiling. "What's the next step?"

Ember slid into a comma shape, her left leg raising up and going on my right hip. "Good! Next step." She slid her right hand down to my wrist and lifted her right leg to my left thigh, giving her enough leverage to push me back and throw me off balance. "Good, good. Final step. You like this part."

Ember grinned, a devilish gleam in her eye. "I slide my hands down to your wrists," she said as she did so, "lift my legs up," she continued, raising her legs up so her feet were next to my face, "and start kicking the crap out of the guy."

"Which I'll thank you to not do." I let go of her and scooted backwards. "Again? Faster each time until it's seamless."

My phone beeped, alerting me that we only had five minutes until chore time.

"Dang it," I grumbled. "I wanted to pretend I was a knife-wielding maniac."

Ember unwound her tapes. "If it makes you feel any better, I know for a fact that many criminals in the city think you actually are a knife-wielding maniac."

Snickering, I collapsed onto the padded bench and motioned for her to join me. I leaned my head back against the wall and took a few deep breaths, then started unwinding my own tapes and inspecting my hands. I had a few abrasions and sore points from the training. An idle thought of holding hands with Benjamin passed through my head, but it whisked away as soon as it came.

Ember sat down and leaned back next to me. When I glanced sidelong at her I saw that she looked troubled.

"Hey, what's wrong? If you're upset about running out of time, we can always practice tomorrow. Actually, I bet I could get Marco to do the clothes mending for you. He owes me a fav—"

"It's not that, okay? Ugh, sorry," she said, putting a hand over her eyes. "I'm dealing with some stuff right now."

Though I didn't have any idea what she was talking about, I inched closer to her and put my hand on her shoulder. "Do you want to talk?" My voice was gentle. "What's going on?"

Ember looked at me, her eyes large and sad. "Do you ever think about going back home?"

For a minute I didn't know what to say, but eventually I responded, "Um, sometimes. I would've thought that you knew that."

Ember shook her head and looked down. "I try not to pry, I swear. Sometimes things get through, though...." She trailed off, and then looked at me again. "Thank you for teaching me like you've been doing. It means a lot. I don't know if I'll be able to use what I've learned when the time comes, but it makes me feel better all the same."

"Um, no problem." I was still confused by the abrupt change in tone our conversation had taken.

While Ember took another sip of water I studied my friend in hopes that I could determine the source of her distress. The fluorescent lights cast odd shadows on her face, highlighting how thin and frail she was. I hoped she'd never have to use the moves I was teaching her. I wasn't convinced she'd be able to fight off any attacker who meant business. She shivered.

"Are you feeling okay?" I asked, even more concerned.

Ember jerked out of her reverie. "Yeah, I'm fine. A little cold, maybe. Let's get out of the basement."

We went upstairs and busied ourselves with our daily chores. Ember sat down in the living room with a sewing kit and began the endless process of repairing minor tears and rips in our uniforms while she watched the news, the only live broadcast we were allowed to watch. Every few minutes I heard her gasp in pain and suck on her finger. She hated sewing. Elsewhere in the house Marco and Reid had their own chores. I assumed Patrick was in his room.

For an hour I mopped the kitchen, cycled the laundry, and dusted the downstairs. When I was done, I sifted through a stack of police reports while standing in front of a map of the city, putting a color-coded pin at the site of each crime. There was a conspicuous lack of pins in a one-mile radius around our house; it was the only crime-free area on the map besides Harris Neck Wildlife Refuge in the southwest. Even the many branches of Blackbeard Creek had pins. I ran my finger over the blank circle, viciously proud that the city's scum wanted to stay away from us.

I was studying the map for new trends in crime when Ember called to me from the living room. "Jill, you're on the news!"

I poked my head into the living room. Grainy security footage of me flying backwards into the wall played, though they'd blurred my face as mandated by federal law. Only Patrick ever allowed his face to be shown in the media. "Why is the news still talking about that? That was days ago."

Marco and Reid came down the stairs just then. "Jill's on the news?" Marco asked. "Turn it up."

Ember turned up the volume.

"Last week's attack marks the eighth superhuman attack this year against buildings owned by Bell Enterprises." A map of the country came on the screen; little dots marked various cities scattered around the continent. "Each attack has had a death toll. This week's bombing claimed six lives, including two children. The federal investigation is ongoing."

The channel went to ads, and Ember muted the television. "What could anyone have against Bell Enterprises?" she mused. "I've seen their name on a bunch of items in the sick bay." She started to count off on her fingers. "The hydrocodone, the antiseptic spray, the cough medicine..."

"Why have you been reading the backs of first aid supplies?" Reid asked, his voice teasing.

"For your information, I'm allowed to know stuff once in a while."

"I didn't mean it like that," Reid said with an aggravated sigh. "Which you should know."

"Oh, because I'm a telepath?"

I tuned out their squabbling and tried to recall where I'd seen Bell Enterprises' logo. I had a feeling it was in this room, and when my eye fell on an aerosol air freshener, I remembered.

Studying the back of the can, I turned to Marco, who'd picked up his knitting needles from a basket next to the couch. "I thought I'd seen the name somewhere. Bell makes half the stuff that comes in our supply shipments, right? So why would someone want to attack a company that makes medicine and air fresheners?" I whipped my head around to the arguing pair. "And shut up, you two," I barked. They were arguing now about something Reid had said four months prior. They made faces at me but fell silent. "We're talking about the attacks on Bell Enterprises."

Reid rested against the coffee table. "It's weird that supervillains are targeting a private company like that. Any idea why the forbidden families would join together against a business? They're not arms dealers or anything."

Marco put down his knitting needles and started to unravel a snarl. "Maybe they're being hired by a business rival. Or maybe the Westerners have branched out from murdering us to murdering the companies that make our medical equipment."

"That's... not out of the question," I said slowly. "They hate normal people, right? I can see them blowing up kids to make a grand point."

There was a heavy pause while everyone digested that idea.

Reid abruptly stood up and turned off the television. "Who wants dinner?" he asked, his tone light.

We jumped up and went to the kitchen, chatting in low voices about battles with the Westerners. If they were getting restless, we'd receive news soon that more people back home had been killed. The elders occasionally made noises about assembling strike teams to go after the Westerners, but the plans never came to anything. I liked to dream, though; a small part of me relished the idea of fighting the people who'd killed so many of my family members.

Reid hummed quietly over the stove while Ember and I set the table. Marco opened a bagged salad and divided it into bowls.

When I placed the fifth bowl on the table, I realized I hadn't seen Patrick in hours, nor had I heard the floorboards creak above us. "Hey, where's Patrick?"

Everyone tensed. "He left earlier in civilian clothes, but I don't know where he was going," Reid said, not looking away from the pot he was stirring.

I lightly elbowed Ember. *Ever thought of listening in to his thoughts and finding out where he's been going?*

*No.* Her mental tone ended the discussion. Suddenly, she picked up her bowl and silverware and put them away. "I'm not hungry," she said. She hurried out of the room, a green tinge in her cheeks.

Reid ladled chicken noodle soup into our bowls. "I'll bring her some soup later. Here, Marco. Jillian, pass me your bowl."

We ate in comfortable silence until the sound of the front door opening and closing alerted us that Patrick was home. A minute later our leader walked into the kitchen and a palpable tension settled around the table. He sat down next to me, to my immense discomfort. I hastily gulped down half my soup and immediately regretted doing so when it burned my throat.

"So what did everyone do today?" Patrick began.

Nobody said anything.

Patrick raised an eyebrow and Reid hastily answered. "Marco and I reviewed the security requests we got from City Hall. We made notes and left them outside your door."

Patrick looked at me.

I blew on a spoonful of soup. "Besides my chores, I coached Ember on fighting moves."

Patrick paused while lifting his spoon and frowned, though he looked more puzzled than angry. "What's the point in teaching her how to fight? She's a telepath." He shook his head. "I don't even know why my father released her into public service," he murmured to himself.

"She expressed a desire to be more useful," I said delicately. "She doesn't want to be a liability, so I've been teaching her some basic self-defense techniques."

He appeared to think about that for a second, then said, "I'd hate for something to happen to her on the battlefield. Thank you."

I couldn't recall the last time Patrick had thanked me for anything. A wonderful lightness filled my chest. Maybe, just maybe, I'd found the way I could slip into his good graces.

To my satisfaction, he continued to speak to me. "So what moves did you teach her today?"

"We went over basic sparring techniques, focusing on opponents without weapons. We also rehearsed escaping from an attacker in the supine position. That means—"

"On your back. Yes, I know." Then he paused, looked up, and turned around towards the direction of Ember's room, his face inscrutable. His eyes narrowed a fraction, but then he smiled. He turned back around and faced us. "Thank you for dinner, Reid."

We all sat in our chairs, unsure of what to do or say. Patrick cleared his dishes and walked out of the room.

The atmosphere of the kitchen relaxed and we finished our meal in silence.

## 8

---

Thirty minutes later Ember came out of her room and joined the rest of us in front of the crime map.

It was a patrol night, so we had to decide where to patrol based on where I'd put the pins. We each had our own assigned zones, but for safety's sake we didn't have routine patrol routes within them. Patrols focused mainly on deterring street crime, but as mundane as street crimes could be, they could also be dangerous. We always planned out our patrols.

Patrick didn't care for the daily monotony of putting the pins on the map and interpreting the results, so the job fell to me. I always felt a rush of self-importance when I advised my teammates where they should patrol, though of course Patrick had the final say.

With my team assembled around the kitchen table, notepads in front of them, I began my briefing.

"First off, Marco. Downtown, especially the business area, has been quiet since the Destructor, but that's probably because nobody wants to go there. In the last three weeks there have been four sexual assaults in Varina Davis Park, so maybe start your patrol there."

Marco straightened in his chair. "Four in three weeks? Are we talking about one guy or a bunch of them?"

"Accounts varied," I said. "You can go through the police reports later for the details." I turned to Reid. "The major patrol points along the river have seen a decrease in crime since you helped bust the heroin ring." I smiled at him, proud of my friend. "There were two purse snatchings on Spanish Moss Lane last week, so I suggest you patrol there tonight." He nodded and made notes. I looked at Ember. "Northside has had a drop in sexual assaults but significantly more muggings than usual. There have been reports of gang activity in vacant lots, but those are unconfirmed."

Ember grimaced. "Sounds like I've got my work cut out for me."

Reid patted her shoulder and gave her a sympathetic look.

I turned to Patrick. "The Island has had one murder, three muggings, an armed robbery, and two sexual assaults since our last patrol brief." I never interpreted information for him, nor did I ever offer suggestions, lest he think I was giving orders. I'd only had to make that mistake once.

He smiled and nodded. "Sounds like I'm needed there tonight."

I pointed to Old Town on the map, where I'd secretly stuck a few extra pins at random. "My zone has had a rise in muggings, mostly concentrated around Davis. I think it's important for me to increase my presence there."

More like increase my amount of alone time so I could text Benjamin.

Everyone waited for Patrick, who mulled over the information. He made a note on his notepad, then flipped it shut and stood up.

"Here's tonight's roster." He rolled his neck. "Reid, since the river front is so quiet, you're going to be with Marco. Stop by the river to check on things, then spend the rest of the time at the park. I'm going to be on the Island." He smirked at Ember, whose eyes widened. "And since Ember is so worried about getting her ass kicked, you girls will patrol together in Northside."

I mentally shouted bitter curses. I'd tried so hard to make it seem like both Old Town and Northside needed patrols; why was he pairing us? My plans for texting Benjamin dissolved into nothing. I wanted to bang my head against a wall.

After the guys filed out to get ready, I looked at the map and started to plan our patrol. I turned to ask Ember where she wanted to begin.

She slapped me. Hard.

I stumbled backwards, clutching my cheek and stunned into silence.

Ember was trembling, though from rage or hurt I couldn't tell. Her face was white but her eyes were damp.

"Wha... what was that for?" I was too shocked to be angry.

"*That* was for telling Patrick about my training." She choked on the last word. "And if I thought I could, I'd slap you again for throwing that tantrum when you heard you had to patrol with me." A fat tear rolled down her cheek. "I thought we were friends."

I was so stupid. Of course she wouldn't want Patrick to know, because any sane person would want to keep as much of their life hidden from him as possible. She'd succeeded for six weeks until I'd opened up my fat mouth.

I crossed the space between us in one step and pulled her into a fierce hug. "I'm sorry for telling Patrick." My voice was muffled by her hair. "I really didn't know it was supposed to be a secret."

"You are the densest person I've ever met, Jill." She sniffled.

I didn't doubt it. "My complaints about tonight had nothing to do with you, I swear. I'm sorry you had to hear that." I pulled away from her and looked into her red-rimmed brown eyes. "Though I don't know why you were in my head."

Ember wiped her nose with the back of hand. "I've told you, sometimes I pick things up by accident. Emotions like anger come through easily. So do fantasies, unfortunately." Her teeth clicked together.

"Ew. Gotta say, I'm glad I don't have your powers." I focused on the patrol map, determined to not think about Benjamin and the fantasies she was almost certainly alluding to.

Ember rolled her eyes. "You have no idea. I'm sorry I slapped you, though. Just...don't talk to Patrick about me again, okay?"

"I won't. Promise." I gave her a brief side hug and then we went upstairs to prepare for patrol.

---

EMBER and I stood on the corner of Atlantic Boulevard and Ayrlee Avenue and readied ourselves to cross into the rough, depressed part of town called Northside. Our hoods were pulled up, casting our faces into shadow so if anyone glanced at us, they wouldn't see our masks. However, anybody could see that we were two young women walking down a city street after midnight. The chances of being hassled were high.

Instead of walking around looking for trouble, we decided to do the wait-and-see approach to crime fighting, taking off our masks and letting our hair down so we looked like neighborhood girls. We perched on trashcans at the mouth of an alley.

Chatting telepathically helped pass the time. We took turns asking each other questions.

I went first. *What do you do on patrol when you're by yourself?* I'd never patrolled with her, and I pictured her jumping from roof to roof, like I did in Old Town. It was occasionally awkward, but stealth was stealth.

She snorted. *Nothing like that. I talk with the residents a lot. There have been less crimes against prostitutes since I've made my presence known. Pimps know that if they rough up one of the girls, I'll rough them up. Some of the local teenagers have started thinking of me as a weird older sister.*

I could understand the sentiment.

*What do you think our families are doing right now?* Ember asked me while she twiddled her phone in her hands.

I checked the time on my phone. It was zero one. *Sleeping.*

Ember playfully punched my shoulder. *Okay, Miss Literal. What do you think they'll do when they wake up?*

I thought about my parents and living siblings back home, deep in the Chattahoochee camp, formerly the Chattahoochee National Forest. All superheroes were from former national forests; they'd been given to us by the government generations ago.

*Mom has a garden to take care of. Dad coordinates patrols around the border of the forest. Allison was married off to Samuel Dumont last year, so she's probably pregnant by now. Mason is on the hunting team, but he's also on the watch bill, so he'll patrol with my dad.*

*Sounds just like my home.* Ember's mental voice was wistful. She and Patrick were from the Oconee camp, a place I'd never been. She looked sidelong at me. *Your turn.*

I decided on a question I'd been wondering since I started training her. *How do you usually fight crime around here when it's just you?* I munched on an apple I'd brought from the kitchen. Ember refused it when I offered her a bite. *No offense, but you're not the most intimidating fighter.* I tried to picture her "roughing up" a rowdy pimp, but couldn't.

Ember flashed a grin at me, the playful gleam in her eyes visible even in the gloom. *Watch this.*

She closed her eyes for about five seconds. In the distance, I heard the booming bark of a large dog. A few seconds later a huge, shaggy dog turned a corner behind a nearby pawn shop and bounded towards us.

"Hey, boy!" Ember said, sliding down off the trash can and kneeling to greet it. It licked her face, its tale thumping wildly against the sidewalk. She looked up at me. *I let the neighborhood strays do all the work for me when I'm alone.*

*He doesn't look so ferocious.*

Ember grinned maliciously. "Looks can be deceiving."

The dog's friendly demeanor vanished. A horrible rumbling growl ripped out of the dog's jaws and it glared at me, its hair raised and teeth bared. I knew it was waiting for a kill order from Ember. I scrambled to pull my legs up onto the trash can. *You've made your point, Ember.*

The dog instantly returned back its former friendly self and padded away, its tail wagging. I watched it trot down the street and across the road, where it woofed playfully at an old homeless man pushing a shopping buggy full of possessions. He kneeled to pet it.

A shadowy figure hidden in a doorway sprang at the poor man, brandishing a gun.

"We're needed across the street," I said, jumping off the trash can and pulling out my mask.

Ember jerked her head towards the mugging and I heard the dog bark loudly, then a terrified yell that made the hair on the back of my neck prickle.

Tugging on our masks, we sprinted across the street. The dog had the mugger by the leg, its fangs sunk deep into the fleshy part of his calf, while the homeless man crouched behind his buggy. Ember dashed up to the elderly man and hurried him away to safety, with the dog following close behind.

In the meantime, I had grabbed the mugger's weapon and hastily unloaded it, throwing the bullets down a storm drain. Ember began to dial on her phone.

The mugger, a man in his twenties, cried on the ground and held his bleeding leg. I pushed him on his back with my boot.

He wailed and glowered at me. "Oh, go f—"

"That's physically impossible," I interrupted. "And unoriginal. Come up with a better insult. Oh, by the way, the dog is rabid."

It wasn't, but I liked seeing the man's eyes widen in horror.

Thunder rumbled overhead, mixing with sirens in the distance. I looked up at the gathering black storm clouds slowly blotting out the few visible stars and sighed. Patrolling in the rain was unpleasant.

The police pulled up and took over just then. After I told them what had happened and the would-be mugger was shoved into the back of a police car, I elbowed Ember. *Call it a night? We stopped a crime so we're allowed to go home now.*

Ember nodded. *Man, I'm tired. I'd give anything to be able to sleep until noon.* She grinned crookedly at me. *Any more questions about how I fight crime by myself?*

I laughed. *No, I'm convinced that you've got this. When you know as much as I do, you'll be unstoppable.*

We teased each other back and forth all the way home, the clouds eventually opening up and emptying their contents on the dark city.

# 9

When we arrived at our broken down house, the rain had started in full force. We stumbled in the door, wringing out our hair and tunics.

Marco came down the stairs, still in his black and green uniform, and greeted us. "Reid and I caught two men picking up underage hookers. We spent a while talking to the cops," he said quietly, offering us a towel each for our hair. "So we decided to call it a night. When we came home Patrick was still in his room. I don't think he left."

We nodded in thanks for the information and headed down the hallway towards the stairs. I passed the double doorway to the living room.

Patrick and Reid sat on the couch watching a recorded program made by Patrick's father, Elder Campbell. He was in an empty room, railing about something in front of a blank blue screen, the usual background for these videos. The Elders sent us programs like this to watch every once in a while, and even though they were mandatory, they made lively entertainment over dinner.

I leaned against the doorway, curious what this program was about.

Elder Campbell was recounting the story of how the original Battlecry, my grandmother, and her entire team had been murdered on the same day. After a minute of listening, I straightened, heat creeping up my neck.

"...but no matter what they *thought* was right, they were in direct defiance of their true authority: Elder St. James! Though they *called* her the leader, Battlecry wasn't a leader! Though they *called* her the authority, Battlecry had no authority!" Elder Campbell pounded the podium in front of him. "And so they were outside their umbrella, they were outside their natural protection, and they opened themselves to attacks from every kind of enemy imaginable." Elder Campbell looked directly at the camera, his blue eyes cold. "They took the word of a foolish woman over the wisdom of their elder and it led them to destruction."

I shook with barely-contained rage. My grandmother was a hero.

I internally cursed this man who'd twisted my family history into lies. The first Battlecry had valiantly led her team back in the years when women were still allowed to be leaders. They were all captured by supervillains and tortured for information about the camps, but they never broke.

Though I'd never seen the video of her death, I'd heard from my mother that she was defiant and strong to the end, even though her torturers had made her watch the execution of her team before brutally killing her.

Where did this... this *jackass* get off by saying that my grandmother had been responsible for her team's deaths? I had a sudden fantasy of pounding Elder Campbell face until it was a soft mess.

I was so engrossed in my vitriolic thoughts that I didn't notice that Patrick had turned around until he snapped his fingers to get my attention.

"Yes?" I said, struggling to keep my tone respectful.

He took out his wallet. "We're almost out of food. You girls are going to go get some. Bring back the receipt." He tossed his card to me, but I didn't move to catch it.

The clatter of the card on the ground seemed very loud to my ears.

Patrick squinted. "Did you hear me?"

I slowly bent down and picked up the card. "Yes," I said, my voice neutral. "We'll go right after we change."

Why hadn't I caught the card? I hadn't even thought about whether I should catch it, I just didn't. I supposed I was still upset from Elder Campbell's vicious lies about my grandmother and experienced a lapse in judgment. Still, it was just a card. The fact that I was even thinking about the deeper meaning of this, as if I had failed to catch a suicide jumper—*like Patrick didn't,* a tiny voice inside sneered— struck me as unhealthy.

As we climbed the stairs to our rooms, Ember's telepathy poked at me even though she was only a few steps behind.

*Why are you acting like this? He's thinks you're copping an attitude. That video has him all worked up into a frenzy.*

*So I didn't catch something he threw at me. That's hardly an attitude.*

I caught a mental image of her slamming me into a wall by the throat. *Jill, do not make that man angry. He's about to have a meltdown and he doesn't care who gets the brunt of it. You have to start submitting to him. He is the* leader.

I shot back with an image of me kicking her off me into the opposite wall. *I didn't catch a card. Get your head screwed on straight and think about it. All I did was not catch a stupid card.*

Ember's real-life face was incredulous. She stomped down the hall and into her bedroom. I went into mine, my anger melting away.

A dizzying array of emotions washed over me as I sank onto the bed and pulled my boots off. Ember was right; I was going to get hurt. Why couldn't I ever act like I was supposed to? I never said or did the right thing. I ran off to cafés to meet cute civilians while I was on the job.

Benjamin's face swam to the surface of my thoughts. I saw him sitting across from me in the café, holding a café mocha and frowning in concern. *Jillian, you didn't catch a card. Big deal.*

"Shut up, Benjamin," I hissed, punching my mattress. "Just shut up."

I threw my boots across the room and fell backwards on the bed, too weary to even sit up anymore. What were my other infractions? I regularly daydreamed about leaving my team when things got hard, and now I had wished harm on an elder. An *elder*. And then I'd gone and been disrespectful to that elder's son. This was why I wasn't allowed to make decisions for the team, why Patrick was always getting after me and correcting me, and why I added up to a terrible superhero.

Ember's knocks on my door pulled me from my misery, and I told her to give me one minute more. After I hastily pulled on a faded jean skirt and a green embroidered blouse, I opened the door. "Let's just get this over with."

It was still pouring when got to the front door, so we decided to walk to the convenience store several blocks away, instead of across town to the only grocery store that was open at half past two in the morning.

Ember grabbed the old black umbrella leaning in the corner by the front door, but it wouldn't open. "I guess we'll have to just get wet," she said with a shrug.

"That's okay. If we obey the authority above us, we'll always be under the protection of *that* umbrella."

I dodged her punch.

The sleepy, pimple-covered cashier didn't pay us any attention while we picked out what little healthy food there was in the cramped shop. Ember, who was experimenting with veganism, inspected food labels with increasing disgust until she simply grabbed apples from a small fruit basket on the counter. I selected several sandwiches, boiled eggs, milk, cheese, and spotted fruits from the refrigerated food case in the back of the store.

When Ember joined me while I was choosing sandwiches, I looked from the pile of food in my arms to Ember's sad little apples. "I'll literally pay you to eat something substantial for once. Your thighs look like my wrists."

"Spend twenty-one years listening to the death traumas of animals during hunting. You'll feel differently about your turkey and cheese sandwiches."

I shrugged and strode to the register. Just as I'd handed the cashier Patrick's card, I remembered that Marco liked a certain brand of lemonade that I'd seen in the cooler. Lemonade was one of the few beverages besides water, milk, and herbal tea we were allowed to drink, so I liked to make sure it was in the refrigerator as much as possible.

"I'll be just one second," I said to Ember, walking back to the cooler to get a bottle.

My hand was on the bottle of lemonade when the store's doors burst open with a bang. Two men with hoodies and black wool face masks ran in, guns drawn. One of them shoved Ember into the potato chip rack. The cashier's arms shot up and he backed away.

Both men aimed their weapons at the cashier, who was too terrified to move. "Open the register! Now!"

My mind took in the situation at top speed: *I'm at far end of store. Ember is at the register. Three cameras, no, there's a fourth. Only one civilian. Two guns, no knives, we aren't in uniform. Gotta think gotta think.*

The cashier opened the drawer.

Ember rotated her arm back, winding up for a punch.

Two shots punctured the silence.

I grabbed a can of dog food from the shelf and threw it as hard as I could towards the shooter nearest me. It hit him in the back of the head and he dropped. The other man raised his gun, scanning the shop for the perpetrator. I took advantage of his confusion and grabbed another can and kept low as I raced around the newspaper shelf and tackled him from behind. I hit him several times in the head until I heard a satisfying crunch near his temple.

Everything had happened in less than ten seconds. The two men, who were probably brain damaged if not dead, lay at my feet. The cashier trembled behind the counter.

I pointed towards the backroom. "Go! Hide in there and don't come out." He ran.

I looked down and my chest tightened.

Ember lay in a pool of blood, gasping and choking with a terrible gurgling sound I knew I'd hear again in my nightmares. Her skin was an ashy gray color that couldn't mean anything good.

"Oh God, oh God, oh God," I whispered, falling to my knees beside her. "Em, stay awake. You have to stay awake." I lifted up her blouse to see the bullet wounds. There was a perfect bloody hole above her navel and another below her right breast.

A catalog of faces flew through my mind. I didn't know what Patrick's presence would do here, but it wouldn't help. Since he was sitting on Marco and Reid at home, my mind settled on the only other person I could think of that would be of assistance. I pulled out my cell phone and called Snitch #5, daring to hope that he'd answer his phone at this time of night. After four rings:

"Hello?" His sleepy voice was the most beautiful sound I'd ever heard.

"It's Jillian. I need your help *right now*." I hated the squeak that ended up in there.

"What's wrong?" Some of his sleepiness had already cleared away.

"My cousin's been shot." My emotion began to brim over into tears. "The Shop Mart on Colonial, by the bail bondsman and tattoo place. Please hurry."

"I'm right by there. Give me less than two minutes."

How had I never seen him out and about if he lived in my neighborhood?

I shook my head quickly to clear my thoughts; I had to focus. Ember sputtered on some blood and I squeezed her hand. "Soon. Help will be here soon."

Though he'd told me he'd be just a few minutes, it surprised me when he ran up to the door in less than sixty seconds.

He saw Ember and gasped. "Have you called 911?"

I faltered. None of us were in the habit of calling emergency services when things went wrong; we usually called each other. If any calls were being made, it was the police calling us or us calling them after we'd stopped a crime. However, I knew that a normal person would call the police in this case, so I lied to Benjamin again.

"They said they'd be here as fast as they could."

Benjamin kneeled down next to Ember and lifted her limp hand, his fingers feeling around for her pulse. "She's fading," he said quietly.

"Can you help?" I wiped my face as his eyes flitted towards a camera on the ceiling. "Don't worry. Nobody will ever know about you. I can make the tapes disappear." And I could, if I asked Captain Drummond.

He looked doubtful. "How?"

Ember's breathing slowed.

"Benjamin, please! You have to trust me!"

His jaw hardened but he nodded. "Okay." He placed his hands on Ember's belly.

Ember cried out and arched her back.

"Is she in pain?"

"No," he murmured. "She's feeling the relief."

The bullets popped out of her torso and the wounds shut themselves, leaving no trace.

"Whoa," I breathed. "Just... whoa." I put my hands around Ember's shoulders, helping her sit up.

She took a shaking breath. "What just happened?"

Benjamin and I stared at each other and I mouthed for him to leave. He gave me an unreadable parting look that lasted for the longest second of my life, and then he was outside and out of sight before Ember could process anything. I stood up and offered Ember a hand.

Ember kept touching her stomach. "Was I *dead*?"

I shook my head. "No, my friend saved you. He's got a handy talent."

Sirens in the distance—presumably the cashier's doing—alerted me that we needed to take our leave, too. Stepping over the two gunmen, I hastily grabbed the lemonade for Marco and we left the store with our bags, though we hadn't paid.

When we passed an alley, Ember flattened herself against the wall and gestured for me to follow. She checked to see if we were alone and then whirled around at me, her face livid. "Jill, tell me everything. What happened back there?"

I didn't see a point in lying to a telepath. "You were shot and probably dying. I called my friend because he has healing powers. End of story."

Ember goggled at me. "So not only are you crushing on a civilian, you're crushing on a civilian Super. Jill, you're so freaking stupid I could kill you right here and now."

Though her insult to my intelligence hurt, I ignored it to address her claim. "I am *not* crushing on Benjamin." I instantly regretted using his name. So much for protecting his identity.

"Oh, shut the hell up," she hissed, pinching the bridge of her nose. "Don't you dare lie to me. I am a telepath, for God's sake. I hear your ridiculous daydreams about his hair or hands or lips or whatever every damn day. I hear you wish you could see him, and talk to him, and text him. Hell, I'm surprised I haven't caught you dreaming about him."

Invisible walls closed in around me as I realized the veracity of her words. Still, I tried my one last chance at redemption.

I cleared my throat and swallowed. "So what if I have a crush on Benjamin? He's just a civilian. I know it'll never go anywhere, so what's the harm in meeting with him to chat and have coffee once in a while?"

Ember slammed her fist into the bricks. "Because you don't know his allegiance! Nobody is born with superpowers that doesn't come from one of the superhuman groups, Jill. You *know* that. We all have an agenda."

I was resolute. "Not him. He's from one of the obscure families. He's not like us. His parents own a human resources consulting firm! You don't get more ordinary than that."

"And you're an assistant gym teacher."

"What?"

"That's your cover story. What if the consulting firm is his? What if he's not from one of the obscure families? What if he's from one of *those* families?"

"He's not," I said, an odd high pitch in my voice.

"What's his family name?" There was a dark edge in her tone that I didn't like.

"I don't know."

"Jillian Johnson, what is his family name?" The anger in her words alarmed me.

"I don't know, I swear! I never asked."

"Find out, and find out soon. If he's from one of the forbidden families, I swear to God, Jill...."

I straightened, my hands curling into fists. "Will you tell Patrick?"

Ember blinked at me, shocked. "No. No, I would never do that. I'm annoyed at you right now, but I don't want you to *die*." She put her hand on my shoulder. "Jill, I'm angry because I'm worried, okay? You're playing with fire. Maybe this Benjamin guy really is just a civilian, but there's every chance he's actually a homicidal maniac from one of the forbidden families. He could try to hurt you. Or worse, Patrick could find out somehow and he *would* hurt you. So I think you really should act like Benjamin is from a forbidden family."

"I won't stop seeing him, but I promise to be very careful," I said in pacifying tones. "I'll stop daydreaming about him, too."

She huffed at me but said no more.

## 10

W e entered through the laundry room door so Ember could shuck her bloodstained clothes without notice. Ember and I were assigned laundry duty, so we weren't worried about one of the guys finding bloody clothes. After she put on pajamas from the dryer, we went to put the food away in the kitchen.

The adrenaline from the evening had worn off and a deep fatigue trickled through my veins. I barely noticed when Patrick strolled in halfway through our emptying of the bags, only realizing he was there when he picked up a shopping bag and started digging through it.

He poured the contents of the bag onto the table with a tremendous clamor. "Took you long enough. I hope you got more soup."

"Oh," I said, suddenly nervous. "Um, I forgot you liked that. I'm so sorry." He shot me a dark look. "I'll go back after sunrise and get some."

He made a dismissive gesture. "Don't bother. You'll just get the wrong type anyway. Where's the receipt?"

My breath hitched. We hadn't paid for our groceries, so there was no receipt to show him. "We, uh, we forgot to get it."

He closed his eyes and breathed deeply. "And let me guess," he said, opening his eyes. "You're sorry about that, too?" Shaking his head, he picked up the bottle of lemonade and read the label.

Without thinking, I said, "Please don't drink that. I bought it for Marco."

The bottle hit me on the side of the head so quickly I didn't have time to process what had happened before I was on the floor. Blood poured from a fresh wound on my scalp. An annoying, logical part of my brain chastised me for letting my guard down around a known threat.

"Please don't," Ember begged while backing away. "She didn't mean it."

"Don't you *ever* tell me what to do," he growled, his fingers tightening around the bottle's neck.

I peered up at him through the blood dripping down my face. I was still in shock. He gazed down at me for a long second and then threw the bottle at the wall. Ember and I flinched.

Patrick stalked out of the kitchen, crunching on the glass as he went.

Ember fell to her knees next to me and put her arm around my shoulders. "You need to stop the attitude. For your own good."

"Let's... let's go... to the clinic. Down the hall. Yes, the clinic is down the hall." My disjointed words sounded far away, as though another person were speaking them. Pretty little red and green stars flashed in front of my eyes, disappearing when I tried to focus on them.

Ember patted my hand and guided me to the sick bay, calling for Marco when we passed his room. He poked his head out and swore when he saw me clutching my bleeding wound.

While Marco worked on my bandages, Ember gave me little tests like "count the fingers" and "name your siblings." My memory recall was fine but she didn't like how I reported seeing lights.

"I want to take you to the clinic." She took a step back and looking me up and down. "You're a mess. Or even the ER? We don't have to tell them we're on the city team. Nobody would have to know that we checked into a hospital. Or maybe I could ask a civilian to admit us? I think there's a loophole in the rules about that."

"No." I slid slid off the table, swaying on my feet. "Hospitals aren't allowed and I...I just want sleep."

Ignoring their protests, I left the sick bay and wobbled down the hall to my room. I didn't bother to undress before I curled up under the covers of my bed. The hard floor would hurt my head too much.

As the shock abated, hot tears dripped onto my pillow. What on earth was wrong with me? Why, *why* couldn't I just joyfully submit like all the others? Why did I have to earn Patrick's anger so much?

The events of the evening overwhelmed me and I burst into sobs. Angst over the video and the card, Ember's near-death, and Benjamin's face all fought for dominance as the thing I was crying about the hardest. Then I realized I was wallowing in self-pity, which made me cry even more.

I whispered relevant principles to myself in an attempt to focus on anything besides the pain of the wound. "Deference. Reverence. Contentment. Gratitude. Humility. Deference. Reverence. Contentment. Gratitude. Humility. Deference. Reverence. Contentment. Gratitude. Humility. Deference. Reverence. Contentment. Gratitude. Humility. Deference. Reverence. Contentment. Gratitude. Humility."

I dried my eyes and blew my nose, and after a few deep breaths I'd pulled myself together. Just when I was on the edge of sleep, my phone vibrated. I peeked at the screen.

*It was nice seeing you tonight, gunshots aside. Meet again sometime?*

Smiling, I deleted his text before I tapped out a reply.

*Yes. :)*

---

## 11

"Tell me what happened. Don't leave out any details."

Captain Hannah Drummond of the Saint Catherine Police Department sat across from me on a park bench under a shady weeping willow in Varina Davis Park. The breeze made her brown hair swirl around her shoulders.

Children ran around us with balls and toy airplanes, too involved with their play to notice or care about us. As it was, we both wore civilian dresses and hats, and were completely unremarkable, exactly how I liked my dealings with the official police department liaison.

I took a breath, though deep breathing made my aching head wound flare. "Firelight and I went to the convenience store last night around zero two thirty. Two men ran in and held up the cashier. Before I could do anything, one of them shot Firelight. I didn't know if they'd shoot anyone else, so I incapacitated them." Captain Drummond nodded and made a note on a little pad of paper. I remembered my promise to Benjamin and switched to fib mode. "I called my brother Mason because he has healing powers. He healed Firelight."

Captain Drummond scribbled something on her notepad. "Is Mason a registered superhero?"

"No, ma'am. That's why it's so important for the security tapes to be destroyed. I'd hate for him to be tracked down by people who want to exploit his power. He was simply visiting me to see how I'm doing. I hadn't seen anyone from home in over six months." I leaned closer. "After our younger brother died, things just weren't the same. My leaving hit him hard."

I hated to manipulate Captain Drummond like that, but I knew sharing a personal secret softened people. She wouldn't pry.

As I predicted, the police officer closed her pad and placed it in her pocket. "This all looks fairly cut and dry, so you don't have anything to worry about. I'll have to verify your story with your family history on file, but I don't think there'll be any problem. Thanks for calling me right away, Battlecry."

We exchanged goodbyes and she left.

I'd written in the logbook that our meeting was about the mugging, not the robbery. Little lies like that became easier every day.

Indeed, instead of immediately getting up and returning home, I sat on the bench for a few minutes and simply enjoyed the day. Sunlight drenched the park, sparkling off the pond's ripples. Sunbathers with earbuds lay on blankets in the lush emerald grass, oblivious to everything around them. Young couples pushed strollers with chubby babies on the bike path. A father bought his preschool-age daughter an ice cream cone from the snack stand and her face lit with anticipation.

I closed my eyes and inhaled the sleepy scent of the Georgia summer, imagining that sunshine and peace could intoxicate me. A curious contentment seeped through my veins; there on the bench in my sunhat and blue floral sundress I was unremarkable, and all the more accepted by the surrounding people because of it.

"Jillian?"

I opened my eyes.

Benjamin stood a few feet down the path next to a pretty young woman who looked so much like him it was amusing—she had the same sandy blond hair, friendly hazel eyes, and an identical contagious grin. They even had the same build, with long, lean limbs. The lines bracketing her eyes hinted that she was, perhaps, a few years older than him.

I smiled my first real smile of the day. "Benjamin! What are you doing here?"

"I was about to ask you the same thing. We're here for the free concert." He pointed to a pavilion in the distance where men were unloading instruments. "Are you here for the World's Biggest Hat competition?"

He indicated my straw hat, which I wore to conceal my head injury. Even though the chance was now before me, I didn't dare ask Benjamin to heal it since not only were we in public, but he'd want to know how I received it.

The young woman smacked his arm. "Benny! Don't be mean." She offered her hand. "I'm Eleanor, Benny's older sister. He's been showing me around the city. I've never been here—my family moved to Saint Catherine after I'd left for the Rockies." She cocked her head and smiled. "You must be the new friend he mentioned. I think your hat is stylish," she added, smiling beautifully. "Very Scarlett O'Hara."

Her voice was lilting and endlessly sweet, like how someone would talk to a small child. I had no idea who Scarlett O'Hara might be, but the way she said it made it appear a compliment.

"It's nice to meet you, Eleanor. How do you like Saint Catherine?" Being friendly to her required no effort.

"Oh, Saint Catherine is the most beautiful city. I've never seen such a charming place to live. Old Town is my favorite with all its little cafes and boutiques. In fact, I heard that Benny met you in a cute bohemian place not far from here while studying for his nursing classes." She beamed at her brother. "When he was little he ran around with a toy doctor's kit and listened to our heartbeats."

Benjamin cleared his throat. "El, what are the chances you could get us front row seats if you went to get them right now?"

Eleanor winked at me. "I think there's a strong possibility I can do that. See ya soon." After winking at her brother, who made a face, she walked away.

When she'd disappeared over the hill, Benjamin turned to me. "So... can I buy you an ice cream?"

I chewed my lower lip. A nap with a cool rag over my eyes sounded equally appealing. On top of that, I'd written in the log that my meeting with Captain Drummond would take about an hour, which left me about thirty minutes before I had to return to base camp. But who knew when I'd have a chance like this again?

Pulling my hat down a little lower, I nodded. "I can't stay long, but I would enjoy that." We walked to the ice cream cart, exchanging a coy glance along the way. I examined all the novelties and flavors for sale, unsure of what to request. "What's the best flavor?" I whispered. "I've never had ice cream before."

Benjamin did a double take. "Are your parents dentists?"

Once again, I was unsure how to answer him without revealing far too much about my upbringing and heritage. I opted to laugh and point to a picture of a neon ice cream novelty shaped like a cartoon character I often saw on children's shirts. "I'll have that one."

We walked around the lush beds of daffodils and tulips with our ice creams in silence for several minutes. The sweet creaminess of the dessert was wonderful, and I decided to have it again if I could.

Finally, Benjamin turned to me. "So are we going to talk about what happened last night?"

"My cousin is visiting me. We were in the wrong place at the wrong time."

"What were you two doing at the Shop Mart at that time of night?"

I decided to bring up the subject that always deterred Marco from getting too nosy into my private affairs. "She needed tampons."

Benjamin didn't blush like I thought he would. Instead, he took a bite out of his ice cream. "Fair enough." He was quiet for a moment. "Have you thought about what I said at the café?"

"It's like I told you. Nobody's abusing me." I avoided his gaze. My aching head wasn't from abuse, but Benjamin wouldn't see it that way.

Benjamin stopped walking. "You never did tell me who gave you the black eye, and I'll never stop wondering. I can't just ignore injuries. Maybe it's because of what I can do. When I see a person's pain I need to fix it. For example, I can tell you have a pretty bad headache right now. I can't fix headaches, though. I'm really sorry."

He was right; my head throbbed, causing the persistent buzzing in my ears to ebb and flow in a way that was impossible to ignore. Sitting on the bench wasn't so bad, but walking around was becoming increasingly difficult.

I sat on the stone ledge of a fountain and patted the spot next to me. "You're not wrong," I admitted. "My head hurts pretty badly, so let's just enjoy the beautiful day. No more talk about unpleasant things, okay?"

His eyes tightened for a moment, but he said nothing more. I pointed to a family picnicking under a shady tree. "I've seen families do that before but I don't understand the appeal. What's so special about eating on the ground?"

Benjamin studied them. "I suppose eating like that seems novel if you're used to eating at a table. Did your family never picnic when you were a kid?"

I flushed, aware that I'd revealed something about myself that I hadn't intended. "No, we didn't picnic."

Benjamin looked thoughtful. "No picnics, no ice cream. Gotta say, your childhood doesn't sound like a lot of fun."

"Tell me about yours. Eleanor seems nice. Is she visiting for a while?"

He laughed, though with a derisive edge. "A least a couple of weeks. She's here because she dumped her idiot boyfriend, Dean, and decided to put some distance between them." He rolled his eyes. "She's got two graduate degrees and joined MENSA for fun. He had to repeat eleventh grade and works on a lube rack. Her dating him was an act of charity." He bit off another chunk of ice cream. "You know what she told me? Get this: on one of their dates she asked him how he felt about euthanasia. He said he didn't have any particular opinions on Chinese kids." Benjamin shook his head. "Like I said, he's an idiot."

Men-suh? Yooth-in-asia? I'd never heard the words, but I understood that Benjamin expected the average person to know what they meant, and that he valued intelligence. That right there would pose a problem for me, since I was dumber than a sack of rocks.

I hurried the conversation along. "I think you mentioned having a brother?"

"Yeah, an older brother, Beau. I don't know what to tell you about him except that he addressed me as 'buttface' for two years straight when we were kids."

I almost choked on my ice cream. "My sister, Allison, cut off my hair when I was sleeping once," I said when I'd recovered. "And I'm not even sure where to begin with my brothers and their rivalry. Gregory and Mason tried their best to kill each other over the years."

Privately I remained thankful that my brothers' powers, respectively superhuman eyesight and the ability to talk to ants, were so useless in combat.

While we talked, the sun came out from behind a cloud, causing Benjamin's hair to shimmer brilliantly. I was struck by his handsome features, which were so different from what I grew up seeing at Chattahoochee camp. His face lacked the underfed, scarred combination with which I was so familiar, instead radiating robust health and wellness.

I wondered if he thought I was attractive, but immediately disregarded the thought. Bruises and mismatched secondhand clothes attracted nobody.

"Maybe I can meet your siblings someday," Benjamin said, his tone hopeful. "Or you can come over to my house. My siblings can usually manage some courtesy if I bring a friend home. Well, just Eleanor. I'll tell Beau to buzz off. And my parents are so thrilled that I pulled my nose out of my books long enough to meet a girl, they probably wouldn't mind if you robbed us on the way out."

"I'd like that," I said slowly. "Meeting your parents, I mean. Not robbing y'all. Maybe one day we can arrange something."

"How about this Friday? There's a great magic show in town right now. I'll take you out to dinner and a show, and then bring you home to meet my parents. Would that be okay?"

I blinked. Courtship. He was trying to initiate *courtship* with me. I couldn't deny it anymore. It was one thing to sit in a café for a few hours and drink coffee and eat pastries, but it was another thing altogether to court me. All the men in my life had made it perfectly clear that I would never be anybody's first choice for courtship, what with my rebellious temperament.

Benjamin must have mistaken my shock for displeasure, because he backpedaled rapidly. "Or, we can hang out at the park or Café Stella. Or not, if you don't want to. I-I've just really enjoyed our time together and I'd like to get to know you more. But if you don't want to hang out, we don't have to. I can leave right now. " Spots of pink appeared in his cheeks, which I found endlessly endearing.

"I didn't say no," I reminded him when I'd recovered my ability to speak. "I was just surprised. Nobody's ever seriously courted me before."

He cocked his head to the side. "I'm starting to think your family is pretty old-fashioned. I've never heard anyone refer to dating as 'courting' before."

"We're... we're different."

Benjamin got up to throw away our trash, leaving me alone for a few seconds. Several yards away, under the shade of a tall oak tree, half a dozen elderly couples had arranged themselves in front of a young woman in exercise clothing. She leaned down and plugged her mp3 player into a small radio, then scrolled on the screen until she found the song she was looking for. Sweet, peppy music filled the air, and then a man's crooning voice began to sing. I wasn't sure, but I thought the song might've been an old one.

The couples began to dance, their feet shuffling in a slow, practiced rhythm. I watched them, charmed.

"The retirees' class would listen to Frank Sinatra," Benjamin said when he returned, smiling and shaking his head.

"Is it a dance class? I love dancing."

It was true; dancing was a longtime pastime of mine, though I had few chances to dance in Saint Catherine. Back home my friends and I would join hands around campfires—dutifully lit by Marco— and sing songs about heroism, our feet moving in time with the beat. I even knew a few couples dances.

"You do? I wish I could say the same. I can't dance to save my life. I was abandoned by my date at senior prom for an hour because I embarrassed her on the dance floor."

"People who say that are usually thinking about it too much." I stood up and held out my hands. "Let me show you." Headache be damned.

He paused, then let me pull him off the bench. "I'm telling you, you're wasting your time." He was smiling, though, so I put my hand in his and nudged his other hand down to my waist, eliciting a luscious tingling all over my body.

I gazed into his eyes. "Don't think about your feet. Just feel the music and let it move you."

"Did you get that from a headphones commercial?"

"What? No. I don't watch television."

"You're a bigger nerd than I am."

We were moving in time with the music, swaying back and forth a little. I pulled him closer, our faces inches apart.

"And you're a better dancer than you think," I said quietly. "Your prom date was stupid. I wish I'd been there to dance with you."

On top of the thrill from Benjamin's hand on my body was the thrill of actually knowing what a prom was; Ember received two invitations to proms the month previous, so we'd looked up the word in Patrick's dictionary. I imagined Benjamin in a sharp black suit, whirling around a room with a dark-haired girl in a glittery blue dress, having the time of his life.

"I wish you'd been there, too. I would've been dancing with the prettiest girl in the room."

I stopped dancing. I was pretty to him?

The sun came out from behind another cloud, causing my headache to announce itself with a pain so breathtaking I broke away from Benjamin and stumbled back to the ledge, all thoughts of proms and fun forgotten.

"It's my head," I gasped.

Benjamin kneeled down beside me and raised his hand to my head, but pulled it away with a pained expression. "Did you get hurt at work again? Was it your boss?"

At that moment, my phone beeped the alert that my hour was up. "I didn't get hurt at work, but I have to go now." I was unable to keep sadness from my voice.

"You're the hardest person to hang out with, I swear." He ran a hand through his hair.

"It's not you, I promise. But I really do have to go." I stood up and immediately sat again, the head wound's negative effect on my balance increasing. "Head rush," I explained, then stood up again more slowly. "Say 'bye' to Eleanor for me!"

I wandered away, the pain stabbing me above my ear and the world teetering around me. Before I reached the road, I looked back. Benjamin sat on the ledge around the fountain, staring at his phone.

My phone beeped and I glanced at the screen. *Wanna find out if you like picnicking? I'm going to set one up tomorrow and I'd love it if you came.*

I typed back a reply. *Sure! Text me where and when. We'll see about Friday.*

Then I deleted the texts on my way home.

## 12

"Tell me why we're doing this again?" Marco's brow furrowed.

I put a thumb drive into the port on my laptop and pulled up the correct file. Marco sat next to me on the couch in his bedroom with his own laptop, in the process of downloading files from a different thumb drive.

"I got a tip today that other Supers are in the city and I want to cross reference their names with known Supers," I explained. "These files are the latest information we have on all the families in the country."

I wished the files were on paper. One of the hardest adjustments to living in the city was using technology in our daily life. Though the camps had allies that used things like telephones and computers—the same allies that kept tabs on Supers and made files such as these—most of us lived a wire-free life. It had taken several weeks for me to shake the fear that I'd press the wrong button and cause my laptop to burst into flames. Months ago, Patrick had caught me poking around the metal box of switches in the laundry room. He'd dragged me away by my hair, screaming that I'd kill us all by messing with electricity, and since then I'd been hesitant to deal with electronics.

I liked my phone, though.

Marco tutted. "This folder's a bunch of photos. Am I looking for someone specific?"

I frowned. Marco couldn't help me if he didn't know what Benjamin looked like. "What's in the other folders?"

"Um, there are documents in this one. I don't know what they're about." His eyebrows knit together. "Why did you even ask me to help you? I don't know what or who we're looking for."

"I want this done as fast as possible," I answered without looking up from my screen. "And we'll take a look at the photos when we're done. In the meantime, just go through the documents and look for references to anybody with healing powers, or anyone named Benjamin, Eleanor, or Beau."

"What's the surname?"

"I don't know."

I'd forgotten to ask Benjamin, like an idiot. Marco didn't know it, but the whole point of this research was to cross-reference Benjamin's family with non-superhero families, especially the forbidden ones. The blacklisted family names were drilled into me so I'd be able to identify threats when they were introduced: Rowe, Peery, Snider, Hensey, Trent, and Edge. However, they were all psychopaths and murderers, so I wasn't worried that Benjamin was one of them.

Still, due diligence and all.

I went back to my thumb drive. File after file of dense records were in the folders, each one detailing the lives of people long dead. Occasionally I'd see a family name I recognized, such as Johnson, St. James, or Harris and I'd swallow sudden homesickness.

After twenty minutes of fruitless searching, I found a subfolder I hadn't gone through. I clicked it open. A brief glance at the files' contents made me tap my cousin's shoulder. "Marco, look at this."

The folder contained hundreds of dossiers. Each family had their own subfolder, some containing dozens of names. Some dossiers had names, gender, birthdates, power, and a picture. Others simply had their gender and approximate age. For fun I did a search for my own name and found my file. My surly face glared at me from the computer screen and I couldn't help but crack up, though I abruptly stopped when my head throbbed again.

"What day of the month is it?" I asked, wincing.

"Um, the fifth, I think. Why?"

"Did our medical supply box come yet? It usually arrives in the first week of the month, right?"

Marco thought for a second. "Uh, yeah, it did. I put the box in the sick bay but I haven't opened it."

"Get me some hydrocodone, please." I gingerly touched the side of my head. The pain was becoming nauseating.

"Don't you think that's overdoing it a little? Hydrocodone is strong stuff. I don't think you're supposed to take it when you have a concussion. The elders were only able to get us drugs without prescriptions because they told Bell Enterprises we wouldn't abuse them."

"Just give it to me. I know what I'm doing."

I moved my head side to side to see if the buzzing would go away. It didn't. I knew narcotics weren't recommended for head injuries, but I was in too much pain to care.

Marco left and quickly returned with the little pill bottle and water. After swallowing four pills, I returned to perusing the files.

He hummed while he worked, and I couldn't help smiling, because he was still the same kid at heart that I'd known since childhood. My cousin had been my brother Gregory's best friend and a frequent tagalong when my brother and I did our daily chores growing up. His presence was one of the few comforts I had at base camp.

I wish I'd insisted that we do our research in my room, though. I didn't care for Marco's decorations, which were posters of past superheroes, all of whom were long dead. Mighty men and women in various candid action shots were displayed around us, tall and proud as they defended the American people from evildoers. It was as if they could see me, knowing my true purpose and judging me for it.

I slid down a little lower on the couch.

Searches for "Benjamin," "Beau," and "Eleanor" came up empty. I searched for "healing powers," "human resources," and even "blond."

The last search gave me hits for a known superhuman named Fortuna who worked out of Las Vegas, but there was no information on her except that she was a probability manipulator—whatever that meant—who frequented casinos and cleaned them out. I showed her dossier to Marco and we both agreed that whatever her power was, it was cooler than our own.

Finally, I opened the six folders containing the most current information on the forbidden six families. If Benjamin was one of them, his information would be in one of those folders.

One by one I looked at the mugshots, police sketches, photographs, and grainy security pictures of the people who'd turned their backs on righteousness and embraced villainy. I was surprised by how few of them there were. I would've thought that after a century they would've had more members, but if our reconnaissance teams said this was all there was to know about the forbidden families, then this was all there was to know. Elder St. James had once told me that of all the groups of Supers, the forbidden six families were the most surveilled, the most spied upon. There were probably cameras in their bathrooms.

Benjamin wasn't among them, nor were his siblings.

I closed my laptop and pulled out the thumb drive, idly turning it over in my hand.

So... he wasn't a supervillain. But what was he? It wasn't impossible for him to be unknown to us. With so much focus on the supervillain families, other people were bound to fall through the cracks.

Deduction time. I knew enough about our kind and his family to guess which superhuman groups he wasn't from.

He definitely wasn't from mine, the superheroes. Everything about Benjamin spoke of ample food and medical care. He apparently enjoyed eating outside on the ground, as if he hadn't grown up in a furniture-less shack like everyone on my team had.

The Westerners, Gregory's murderers, were insular and antisocial. I was comfortable supposing that Benjamin wasn't one of them.

I'd established he wasn't from the forbidden six families.

That left the one mysterious group that I knew almost nothing about: the people who'd purposely slipped into obscurity, intending to hide their powers from the public.

I closed my eyes and drifted back to when I was in Café Stella with Benjamin. I saw the excitement in his eyes when I described my team and our powers. He so eagerly wanted to know more about us... he could only be from a family of people who didn't have regular contact with other Supers. I'd guessed so earlier, but now I was certain.

The thought threw me for a loop, but I liked the idea of a super-human family that didn't cast themselves into the heat of battle all the time. It sounded so weird, but an inviting kind of weird.

Children could run around and play instead of beating each other up.

Mothers and fathers could get jobs and raise their children in a house with a roof and bedrooms.

There would be enough food to truly satisfy, not just stave off starvation.

My mother wouldn't have had to bury three babies because of a lack of medical care.

Suddenly I didn't want to ponder this alternate life anymore. I turned to Marco, who was smiling at his screen. "What are you looking at?"

He turned the laptop around and showed me a black-and-white photo of stern-looking people in seriously old-fashioned fighting clothes. The women wore skirts and one of the men wore suspenders. Two of the men had facial hair, which was forbidden to all men from the camps, even the elders.

One of the women stood in the center, just a little more prominent than the others. She looked a little bit like me, with thick, dark hair and bushy eyebrows that dominated her face. A glint of strength in her eyes, visible even decades later, dared me to challenge her.

"Who are they?" I asked.

"Some of our ancestors. Our camp was founded a few years after this was taken. The lady in the middle is Christina St. James, our grandma's grandma. You know, the first superhero in American history."

Of course I knew it. I looked at the faces of people who were long dead and wondered if they'd be proud of me.

Marco's phone beeped and he shut his computer. "Patrolling time. I convinced Patrick that you should be with me because of your head injury. Ember is going with Reid. Meet you at the door in five?"

I nodded and pocketed the thumb drive.

The pills kicked in while I was lacing my boots. Luscious, numbing warmth radiated out from my stomach to the tips of my fingers and toes, causing me to fumble with the laces. In the recesses of my brain I knew I shouldn't patrol while under the influence of a narcotic, but it was hard to care. Marco was a good fighter and I'd be safe with him.

---

## 13

P atrolling was more difficult than I'd anticipated.

After I stumbled over a curb for the third time in thirty minutes, Marco guided me by my elbow over to a bench at a deserted bus stop in the industrial part of town.

"Sit here for a while and take deep breaths. I can't believe I let you have the pills."

"My head doesn't hurt anymore," I mumbled, the words struggling to form in my throat.

"Oh, I bet nothing hurts anymore for you." He rolled his eyes.

I closed my eyes and let my head loll backwards, the motion causing a pleasant *whoosh* sensation. I did it two more times until Marco's warm hand caught my head. "You're going to make yourself sick if you keep that up."

I sat up and let my eyes focus on the area around us. The Bell Enterprises' Industrial Complex was across the road, fenced off with an old chain link fence. Beyond the fence was a massive campus of parking lots, warehouses, and a huge chemical plant. It was deserted, lit up only by floodlights on the buildings and a few streetlights in the parking lots. I stared at the guard building at the gated entrance of the Complex. Something was wrong with it, but my mind struggled to process what it might be.

I pointed to the little shack after thirty seconds. "Their security sucks." I cracked up. "No wonder they're always getting attacked."

Marco stiffened and he scanned the parking lot, focusing finally on the guard building. "There's nobody in there. That's really weird. With all the attacks you'd think they'd have heightened security. In fact, something here stinks. Where is everyone?" He stood up, pushing me back down when I tried to stand. "You stay here and take deep breaths. I'm going to check on the guard."

Humming to myself, I watched him melt the lock and push the gate open, then peer into the guard shack. He froze, then turned and sprinted back to me.

"The guard is unconscious in the shack. The screens with the security feeds are all showing snow. Not a single camera in this facility is working, as far as I can tell. It's just like what happened at the bank. The guard was intact, though."

"The fence isn't," I said with a giggle, pointing to a hole in the fence about twenty feet down the street from us. "Poof! Gone, just like the heads."

Marco's eyes followed my finger. "Someone's *cut* the fence. The piece they took out is on the ground. We should check that out once you're done laughing about homicide."

Hoisting me up by my elbow, he dragged me over to the hole in the fence, where we bent down for a closer look at the loose flap of chain links. It had been cut recently; we could see small fibers attached to the jagged metal. We were dealing with another attack on Bell Enterprises. Marco rolled up his sleeves to let in as much ambient light as possible. "We might have to bust some heads. Are you up to this?"

I responded by twiddling a knife and promptly dropping it.

Marco glanced back at the bus stop and then shook his head. "Just stay behind me, okay?"

"Back up," I grunted.

Marco took a step backwards. "What is it?"

"No," I groaned. "Call for back up."

Uncertainty passed over his face. "Um... I... I'd rather not have to explain to Atropos why you're stoned senseless. I wasn't really supposed to give you the pills."

"I'm *not* stoned senseless."

He pinched my nose, hard. "Can you feel that?"

Instead of bothering me, the childish gesture made me laugh so hard I stumbled backwards, tripped over my feet, and nearly fell.

Marco looked again at the bus stop, then back to me. "Please, *please* try to focus, okay?"

I nodded, solemn. "Focus. Right."

We worked our way through the fence with little difficulty and moved into the shadows of the warehouses, pressing ourselves against the walls to stay as small as possible.

"Over there," Marco whispered, indicating warehouse fourteen. "I just saw a moving light. Could be a flashlight, and that's suspicious." We ran as stealthily as possible through the lot and up to the side of the building. Flattening ourselves against the bricks, we listened for any sound from within. There was nothing but silence. "We need a plan," Marco whispered. "Any suggestions?"

"Superhero stuff," I slurred.

"I can't believe I didn't think of that," he muttered. "Okay, I've got an idea. I'll open the door and stun them, and then we'll both run in and grab everyone. Be fast about it, though. I only have one good flash left in me."

"Make a noise so they look at you."

"They might not be on our side of the warehouse. If I make a noise right off the bat, I risk giving away that we're there. We should surprise them."

"No, we don't know where they are." Beneath my drugged torpor, fear stirred. I didn't like barreling into blind fights.

Marco made a noise of disgust. "You know what, this conversation wouldn't be happening if we had the whole team. I'm calling the others. If Atropos puts my head through a wall, oh well." He pulled out his cell phone.

"No no no!" I snatched his phone away. "We can do it your way. Don't call anyone. Please."

Marco's eyes darted back and forth while he debated with himself. "Okay, I won't call for backup." He slowly turned the handle to the warehouse side entrance, his hand raised.

I remembered to close my eyes just in time.

Marco's light flooded the warehouse, shining through my eyelids. If the thieves—or whatever they were—were looking towards the door when he made his little show, they'd be temporarily blinded. I ran in, blinking away little spots in my vision.

Unfortunately, the two men inside hadn't been facing the door.

The warehouse was filled with row upon row of metal shelving lined with barrels. Some barrels were labeled with innocuous strings of letters and numbers, but a few had large black-and-yellow biohazard symbols printed on them.

The two men were standing next to one and had removed the lid. From what I could see, they were taking a sample; plastic cups with lids and labels were scattered around them. Curiously, while they both wore nondescript gray garb, their faces were hidden in masks like myself and Marco. I was intrigued; I'd never encountered costumed criminals who committed such a mundane crime as corporate espionage.

The shorter of the two slowly put down his little plastic cup. "Easy there, man. We're not going to cause trouble if you don't."

"You're breaking and entering," Marco said, his voice deeper than usual. "Put your hands on your head and kneel with your ankles crossed."

The order always sounded more intimidating when Patrick said it.

Neither of them complied.

"Are you the team leader?" the taller one asked, his voice considerably lower than his partner's.

I couldn't see under the short one's hood, but his head movement made me think he was looking back and forth between Marco and me.

Before Marco could answer, the shorter one spoke again. "Neither of them are the leader, idiot. Haven't you seen him? He's all over the tabloids every week. They call him Atropos." He pointed to his partner. "And that's Cyber, by the way. He thinks his codename is cool. What do you guys think?"

"Shut the hell up," Cyber growled.

There was a second in which nobody moved, but then Cyber bolted towards the door.

Marco was faster. A ray of heat flashed from his hand towards the man's knee and the would-be escapee howled in pain, stumbling forward.

Not wasting a second, I clumsily ran towards him and tackled him.

Marco raced towards Not-Cyber who... disappeared?

He reappeared behind Marco half a second later, sitting on another barrel. He hadn't teleported; rather, he'd run so quickly he'd blurred. "I'll go quietly if you can catch me," he teased, before reappearing a second later by a pillar yards away.

Cyber wasn't so jovial. He lacked super strength and was injured, but I was injured and intoxicated, which made for a painful stalemate. I pinned him down with a knee, but with a yell he threw me off balance and swept his leg under my own. I fell, aware of how stupid a move that was.

Out of the corner of my eye I could see Marco vainly chasing after the other man. He'd let Marco barely brush his fingers against him and then reappear ten feet away, laughing uproariously.

I landed a knee in the tender flesh of Cyber's groin and he roared again in fury. With surprising strength, he punched me in the stomach, and although it didn't hurt much, I was winded. I vaguely noticed that his hands didn't feel like normal human hands; they were harder and heavier.

In the two seconds I took to recover my breath, he whipped out a switchblade.

Cyber swiped at me with an angry shout, and I barely jumped

away from the blade in time. I grabbed his arm, intending to twist it and make him drop the knife.

He backhanded me across the face and I stumbled into metal shelving, dazed.

I charged at him and ducked away from his knife, but he grabbed me and in one motion sliced my neck under my ear. The hydrocodone couldn't mask the searing pain. I fell to the ground, my hand pressed to my gushing neck.

Swift realization hit me: I was going to die.

Cyber stared down at me, his chest heaving. Slowly, so slowly, he walked towards me.

"Cyber, stop!" His partner appeared in a blur and pushed Cyber's arm away. "We already have enough bodies at scenes to deal with. We don't need a dead hero on our hands on top of everything else."

Cyber snorted. "You weren't singing that song in Baltimore."

The shorter one tensed. "Just go."

Cyber gestured at me with the knife. "She's already dead. She'll bleed out in the next few minutes. Let's just finish them off. I thought you were into that angel of mercy crap."

I felt a sob in my chest. It fought against the pills and lost. *You're a failure.*

I already felt measurably cooler than usual. Snatches of thoughts appeared and vanished in my brain. *Where is Marco? Is he okay? What is going on? The floor is cold. There's a bug under the shelf. Someone... should really... clean.*

Each thought was stupider than the last. I tried to focus on the conversation above me.

"Take the product and *leave*. You've done enough."

"You're a baby," Cyber snapped.

Even in the midst of exsanguination I thought that was an odd thing for a hardened criminal to say to his partner in crime. The reply, a string of profanities, was more the usual.

Cyber stormed off and out the warehouse door.

To my surprise, the remaining man kneeled down next to me and gently pulled me into a sitting position against a barrel. I could see Marco lying on the ground in the distance. He was breathing.

"What're you doing?" I mumbled. I no longer had the strength to fight, but I still tried to pull away.

"Easy, easy, don't move," he said quietly. He pulled out a cell phone. "I'm going to call an ambulance. You'll die if I don't."

"No, don't. Don't." I wanted to die like my grandmother. Her life blood had spilled out, too. And like her, I wasn't afraid of death. I wished I could've lived longer, and that my final months had been happier, but I wasn't afraid.

He paused, and then nodded. "Is there someone else you'd like me to call, then? Or text?"

How weird. He was obviously a criminal and criminals were soulless. This was a fact of life that had been hammered into me from birth and I wasn't comfortable with it being defied in my last moments. However, he was offering me an unexpected last chance to send a message and I intended to make the best of it.

"My phone." My voice was failing. "Text snitch... five. Tell him... I'm sorry I can't... be there tomorrow."

"I hope this person misses you." He slipped my phone from my pocket and tapping out the text. "It's nice of you to send a final message."

I was unable to reply but I enjoyed his kind voice. I hoped he wouldn't hide my body. Gregory's body had been washed away and the lack of closure still hurt.

The coolness had turned into fuzzy warmth that was creeping from around the edges. I felt disconnected from my body.

He put the phone down. "There, it's sent."

My sight was dimming. When I approached the edges of my consciousness I heard a text alert. Another oddity—my phone was always on silent when I patrolled. Even there, dying in a pool of my own blood next to a masked thief, I felt a stab of annoyance that I couldn't see what the text said.

However, the man glanced at his own phone. There was a brief silence before the phone slid out of his hand and clattered to the floor.

He pulled off his hood and mask, sandy blond hair spilling out.

Benjamin stared down at me, shock and horror written on his face. "Oh my God."

The last thing I was aware of before the world went dark was warm hands on my cheeks.

## 14

I opened my eyes and blinked up at the high ceiling of the warehouse, shivering and wincing against the brightness of the fluorescent lamps.

Several feet away from me Marco sat up and rubbed his head. "What happened? Where'd they go?" He poked at his temple. "I could've sworn he hit me right here but there's not even a scr—holy *cow*, where did all that blood come from? Are you okay?"

I was sitting in a large pool of congealing blood. A familiar tightness gripped my chest; nobody lost that amount of blood at once and lived. I touched my neck and felt smooth skin. "I'm—I'm fine," I choked out.

Marco was still staring. "Where did that blood come from? Wow, you must have really injured that guy. He should be dead."

Dead.

The realization hit me like a wrecking ball: I'd almost died, and Benjamin was a criminal. A supervillain. I leaned over and emptied the contents of my stomach.

Marco just laughed. "I wondered when the pills would make you do that. Too bad you didn't barf all over the big guy."

When I was done, I heard a strange whooshing sound and

focused on it, then realized it was my own hyperventilating. I crawled to my feet, sticky blood clinging to my fingers and clothes.

Marco got up and walked to the barrel Benjamin and his partner, whom I assumed was his brother Beau, had been looking at when we first came in. He pulled out a little flask from his utility belt and scooped some of the liquid into it.

"If you're feeling better, come over here and take a look at this stuff. I don't know what it is, but I want to know why they were looking at it. Can you call the team and ask them to rendezvous at the bus stop across the street? Battlecry? Hey, where are you going?"

I pushed the warehouse door open and ran out into the night, echoes of my footfalls bouncing around the deserted lot. Marco shouted for me to wait for him, but I was already sprinting. I slowed only to rip the broken fence back so I could duck under it, then I turned and fled down the street.

The world flew by as I ran past the police station where I had registered as a superhero. I rushed past the middle school that a disgruntled ex-teacher had tried to set on fire during an assembly. I ran past the alley where I met my first snitch who passed on a piece of information.

I continued my flight all the way to the bridge at the edge of the city, where Marco and I had been greeted by Patrick, Ember, and Reid only six months before. I dashed to the side of the bridge, slamming into the waist-high safety barrier. I gripped the railing and looked down at the dark stillness of Blackbeard Creek's main branch which, despite the name, was actually a large river.

My strength left me, and I sagged against one of the metal support beams, looking out over the dark water, sweat dripping down my face into my eyes. The bridge was silent except for my panting breaths, which turned into sobs. I cried for several long minutes, not knowing or caring if anyone saw me. When the tears stopped, I hiccuped and peered around.

A memory tugged at me—I'd talked down a jumper here once. While she'd been hanging off the edge, she'd told me her life wasn't worth living anymore.

I'd replied with the standard response: "There is always hope." Then I'd offered her my hand and the warmest smile I could muster. "Whatever it is that made you think this is the answer, it's temporary."

Did those words mean anything anymore? Had they ever meant anything? I'd learned them along with a thousand other platitudes in my training, the same training that had tried to teach me how easy and natural it was to joyfully submit to my leader, my father, and my elder. Yet, my whole life I'd struggled to joyfully submit to anyone who had authority over me. Since leaving home and joining the team, I'd failed to submit altogether. But why?

The memory of Benjamin's shocked voice in the warehouse rose up, unbidden. I let out another sob and sank to my knees. Somebody had to have forced Benjamin into a life of crime—that was the only way someone as kind and caring as him could've worked alongside the man who'd sliced open my neck and left me to die. Somebody had threatened Eleanor, perhaps, and coerced Benjamin into the criminal underworld.

Even in my fractured state I knew I was deluding myself. I'd heard his mocking laughter as Marco tried to stop him. Benjamin hadn't been concerned when Cyber pulled the knife on me, only when the situation had become messy.

Elder Campbell's dire warning had been correct: I'd wandered outside of my umbrella and it had led me to destruction. I was lucky to have met a villain as kind and gentle as Benjamin. Now that I thought about it, could a villain be kind and gentle? Was anything about Benjamin genuine? If I'd gone home with him to meet his parents tomorrow, would he have attacked me?

I cried myself into a new headache.

There was no point in lying to myself anymore. I wasn't a hero. I wore the mask and had the lineage, but I was a disgrace to my family and unable to bring honor to them. I questioned every order, thought about my happiness before the functionality of my team, and worst of all, I despised my calling.

There was only one thing left to do now.

Taking a deep breath, I climbed over the barrier. The only thing between life and death was the grip I had on the steel railing. I hoped Marco wouldn't miss me too badly. Even now, years later, he still suffered from Gregory's death.

A shining memory of my younger brother played in my mind: carefree and so alive, laughing wildly while chasing a rabbit for dinner, the other boys calling after him. He'd caught the rabbit in one of his snares that day and prepared it for us himself. I could still hear his laughter.

I hung my head, regretting my decision to think about my dead brother. He never would have wanted me to jump off the bridge. He'd be angry and ashamed of me for abandoning my duties.

Oh, what the hell did he know? He was dead, drowned by a Westerner. Maybe he'd be happy to see me, wherever he was. Where did people go when they died? I wanted to know.

An image of Gregory's unimpressed, are-you-kidding-me expression brought me back to reality. Committing suicide would only make me more of a failure. Besides, my stupid powers would probably have prevented me from dying from the fall.

Sighing, I glanced over my shoulder towards the lights of the city and wondered if I could run back quickly enough before anybody noticed I had taken detour to the city limits. I was weak and selfish and unworthy of my position, but I was a superhero. I had responsibilities. My suicidal impulse melted away, leaving nothing but blank misery. I climbed back over the rail.

I started the dreary walk back to base camp, swallowing my feelings yet again, not letting myself think about Benjamin or of the blood pouring out of my body earlier.

Whenever a surge of emotion threatened to engulf me, I stomped it lower and lower until I was more numbed than any pill could make me.

## 15

Base camp was just coming into view in the distance when Marco sprinted towards me. "Jill! I told Patrick you left to chase down the guys. He's furious at you for leaving me, so *please* tell me you caught them."

I was too numb to care. "No, I didn't catch them." I marched past him and into the house.

Patrick was waiting for me.

"Where the hell have you been?" He stomped up to me until his face was inches from mine. "You abandoned Marco! Do you know how many protocols you just broke? He could've died! You could've run into a trap! What were you thinking? Were you thinking at all?"

He slapped me, but I didn't feel the sting.

I closed my eyes and breathed. "Are you done?" I opened my eyes.

Ember and Reid were peeking around a door frame. Marco was behind me in the corner.

He sputtered. "Am I... what did you just say to me? Who do you think you are?"

Beneath the numbness, an intense ball of emotion started to spiral like a tornado, stripping away my inhibitions. Ember's voice prickled in my mind. *Jillian, calm down.* I forced her out with surprising ease.

"I think I'm the best-trained fighter on this team," I replied quietly. "As you are well aware."

"You could be God for all I care, but I'm the leader and you will submit to me. I am the authority, *you're* a bug. You're not even worthy to breathe the same air as me, do you hear me? You're just a—"

"Patrick, shut up."

Total silence followed.

As if in slow motion I saw him raise his hand and swing it towards my cheek again. Every ounce of my training, twenty years of ingrained teaching, screamed at me to accept the punishment of my leader.

I mentally squashed the ball of heat in my stomach until it diminished to a mere speck... but in the next fraction of a second, the speck exploded into fireworks of rage.

I caught his hand in midair and squeezed it until bones snapped, then I shoved him against the wall. Patrick howled and his knees buckled as I kept my iron grip on his broken hand.

I slammed him once more into the wall, throwing my weight into it and pinning him there. My teammates were yelling at me.

"Who do *you* think *I* am?" I hissed through gritted teeth. "I'm your teammate who is *sick* and *tired* of putting up with a pathetic excuse for a leader."

I punched him in the jaw.

"I hate being on your team."

I kneed him in the stomach.

"I hate looking at your ugly face every single day."

I felt his telekinesis weakly pulling at me, so I threw him down the hallway to distract him.

"And I *hate* that you've made me feel like *crap* just for breathing."

I kicked him in the gut.

I was tossed backwards into the living room by an invisible force, flipping over the couch onto the coffee table, which fractured under my weight.

I jumped up and vaulted over the couch. I tackled Patrick to the ground, aiming a punch for his face. He moved his head aside, and my fist hit the floor, the woodgrain splintering from the impact.

He kicked me off, the thrust bolstered by telekinesis. "Someone get her!" He held his stomach where I'd kicked him before.

I narrowed my eyes. I didn't know what I was fighting for anymore, but if I had to fight my whole team, I would.

Nobody moved.

Patrick's eyes, before filled with nothing but malice, widened in shock.

I lunged at him again, pulling him down to the floor, and this time he wasn't able to push me off. I unleashed a volley of blows to his face, neck, and torso. His telekinesis tugged at me, growing weaker every second.

Finally, it ceased and Patrick's eyes shut.

I looked down at my unconscious leader. He was breathing raggedly and oozing blood from his nose and mouth. I could hardly hear my own thoughts over the sound of blood rushing in my ears. A sharp pain in my hands made me gasp—I was clenching my fists so tightly that my nails had cut into my palms, and my right hand's knuckles were raw from striking the floor. I unclenched my fists.

There was a shuffling behind me and I spun around.

"Don't!" Ember held her hands up. "We're not going to fight you, are we, guys?"

Marco and Reid were flattened against the wall. Reid's eyes darted from me to Patrick and then to me again. "Go. Just go."

"Are you going to follow?" My hand hovered over one of my knives. I'd seen him watching the speech next to Patrick only days before, and he'd always been the one to give the best answers during the nighttime readings. I had no ill feelings towards Reid, but was he a threat? He was a rules man. "Are you going to defend your... friend?"

"Patrick is *not* my friend," he said, his voice hard. Reid matched my cold glare with his own. "*Hell* no, he is not my friend. As if I'd ever defend him."

"Swear it."

Reid put his right hand over his heart, the age-old sign of honor in the camps. "I swear. If we meet again, it'll be as real friends."

Patrick groaned.

I spun around, the adrenaline rush ebbing and leaving in its wake icy cold fear. I'd broken two cardinal rules now: don't fraternize with the forbidden families and never attack your leader. Without saying anything to my teammates, I sprinted up the stairs towards my room.

I felt Ember in the back of my mind. *Hurry!*

I changed into civilian clothes faster than I ever had before, dropping my uniform onto the floor. I grabbed my old pink backpack and stuffed clothes into it, along with my blue yarn bracelet and random items that were laying around my room.

I rushed down the stairs, where Patrick was still lying on the floor in the hallway, beginning to stir. Before I could stop myself, I fished his debit card out his pocket and then half-tossed him into his office and slammed the door.

Ember, Reid, and Marco stood by the front door. Ember handed me a plastic bag full of food. "The card's PIN is zero seven zero four. This is all we have that travels well. I'm sorry I couldn't find—"

I hugged her as hard as I could, and then the men were hugging us, too. I broke away. "Come with me." I took in their frightened faces. "None of you fought me off. He'll... he'll be angry."

Ember bit her lip. "You need to go now, Jill."

I slipped out the door and into the darkness. Before I was fifty feet from the house, the door banged open and Marco ran down the steps. "Jill!"

I turned around. He didn't have any supplies, so he clearly intended to ask me to stay. "Marco, go back inside. Save your breath."

He shook his head, tears spilling down his face. "Please don't go. Please. We came here together and it's gotta stay that way. We can fix this."

"This is best for all of us. I'm not fit to be on a team."

"But if you leave, you can't be a hero anymore. You could get hurt. It's not safe out there. Where are you going to go?"

I put my hands on his shoulders. Though he was nearly an adult, he seemed so small. "I've made mistakes that I can't fix." I hugged him once more and gently pushed him away. "I'm sorry."

I fled down the street and didn't look back.

## 16

The first thing I did was max out the debit card.

When Patrick's account information popped up, I squinted at the screen. Why did his personal account have over two thousand dollars? I didn't dwell on it; I took all of the account's contents and put the cash in various places on my person. After I secured the money, I set out looking for a good place to spend the rest of the night.

My initial impulse was to go to Café Stella, though I knew it was closed. My chest constricted painfully when I thought of the central figure in my memories there, and I vowed to never think his name again. To me, he would just be The Criminal.

My second thought was to go the shelter The Criminal had mentioned the first day we met, but that seemed too predictable. What if Patrick decided to look for me? After all, I had just thrashed him and stolen his money. I headed towards Varina Davis Park, which had plenty of trees, rock outcroppings, and ditches, but disregarded the idea. The park was too obvious of a hiding place. I kept walking, making my way to Old Town.

I had literally no idea what to do next. Being a superhero was all I knew how to do. My whole education revolved around that life. I couldn't go home to Chattahoochee camp—they'd beat me, or worse, haul me in front of a tribunal headed by Elder St. James. I couldn't go back to base camp, because Patrick would certainly kill me. I didn't know anyone in the city besides The Criminal, so I couldn't crash on someone's couch.

A new feeling washed over me: uncertainty about what lay ahead in my life. I'd always been under an authority umbrella. Now, I was outside of anyone's umbrella, lacking direction. Who was my authority now? Who would make decisions for me? Who would correct me when I was wrong? My new-found independence wasn't natural and I knew nothing good could come from it.

Still, I wasn't going back to either camp. I had to make a decision.

Was I a civilian now? If so, what did a young civilian woman do with her time? I knew they got jobs and went to school and spent time with other young civilians, but I had no idea what those activities entailed.

How did someone go about getting a job? Was there a test to take? How did people decide which school to go to? Could you show up one day and just listen to a lecture? A criminal I'd once met—I gulped—talked about "applying" to nursing school. What other kind of schools were there? Was I even smart enough to apply to school? I doubted it.

Fatigue set in. I walked for an hour, dragging my feet and scanning for a quiet place to sleep that would shield me from both bad weather and my old team, should they come looking for me.

I turned down a dark avenue that led into an upscale neighborhood full of town houses and community gardens growing roses and tomatoes. I passed James Oglethorpe High School, where I'd once told The Criminal I'd fallen down bleachers. He'd pretended to care.

A block beyond the high school, there was a darkened community building of some sort. While I watched, a woman walked out the front door and hurried to her car. Was the door unlocked? I went up to the building and pulled on the handle. It opened, so I went inside. Maybe there'd be a bathroom to sleep in.

The lobby of the building was dark except for a sliver of low, reddish light coming from a room off to the side.

Curious, I peeked in and saw a table displaying a burning candle inside a red hurricane glass next to an ornate sunburst decoration that I thought might be made of gold. There were several wooden benches in the room facing the table. *What a strange room.*

I sat down on the back bench and looked at the sunburst decoration. My tiredness settled on me like a blanket, and I slumped down on the bench, allowing the hypnotic flickering to pull me into a dreamless sleep.

---

I AWOKE to the deep *bong* of a bell somewhere above me.

The hard surface on which I slept tricked my sleepy brain into believing I was on the ground in my former room, so I wasn't expecting to fall when I rolled over. I landed painfully on the scratchy carpet with a yelp. Rubbing my elbow, I sat up and saw that I'd fallen off the bench.

The door opened. A spectacled man in a black dress peered down at me, his eyebrows raised, but he was smiling. "I came in here to wake you up. It was very sweet of you to take one of the early morning slots, but I think, perhaps, you were too ambitious?" He laughed.

I smiled and nodded, not understanding at all what he was talking about. He continued, "Now I feel bad. I thought I knew all the adorers, but I don't remember seeing you here before. Are you new in the parish?"

"Um, yeah." I grabbed my backpack. "Sorry about falling asleep."

I walked past the man and out into the main lobby.

Several dozen people were lined up at the far end of the room, which had a double doorway leading into a large hall filled with rows of tables and chairs, at which were sitting unkempt people in tattered clothes eating pancakes and eggs off paper plates.

My stomach growled.

A middle-aged woman hurried over to the man. "Father Kokoski, you've got a phone call from the hospital downtown. Mrs. Gruneisen's taken a turn for the worse and her family is being called in. They need you there as soon as possible."

He ducked into an office labeled *Fr. Peter Kokoski, F.S.S.P.*

I wandered over to the line that led to the table where cheerful women in simple dresses and head coverings served breakfast. While I waited for my turn, I looked around the room.

I finally recalled a lesson about civilian life from years before and decided I was in a church.

I'd never been in a church before. A display case in the corner held pamphlets about "sacraments," though I didn't know the term. A silver water dispenser with a spigot sat in the corner. Near the display case, next to a small statue of a pretty woman in blue, a large sign with an arrow pointed the way to the gymnasium.

A cork board on the far end of the room, beneath a horrible decoration depicting a half-naked man nailed to a cross was covered with pictures of children in green plaid uniforms. The sign above the cork board read "Sacred Heart Students Meet Bishop John."

When I got to the head of the line, the woman serving pancakes did a double take. "We don't get a lot of people your age here." She ladled syrup on my pancakes. "Are you okay, dear?"

I took my plate. "I'm just hungry. I won't come back again."

She shook her head. "Come back whenever you need to, sweetie." The endearment sounded as natural as my own mother's.

I blinked away sudden tears, uncomfortable with strangers being so nice to me. In a way she reminded me of The Criminal.

I took a foam cup of orange juice and searched for an empty seat with my plate in hand. I avoided eye contact with the many people who paused mid-chew to watch me walk past them. A woman wearing a threadbare shirt leaned over to her neighbor and whispered something. The other woman's eyes widened and she nodded.

*They know you're an outsider. They know you don't deserve a hot breakfast as nice as this.* I sat down at an empty table in the corner and propped my elbow up next to me, trying to shield myself from view. I ate my pancakes and eggs mechanically, too self-conscious to enjoy the delicious food heaped on my plate. As soon as I finished, I intended to leave the church and make my way to the edges of the city. I didn't know where I'd go, but as long as I was in the city limits I was in danger.

I peeked past my arm. Two old men at the far end of the row of tables were looking at me with curious expressions.

I went back to looking at my food, blushing furiously. I realized I was the youngest person in the room, but why were they staring like that?

An elderly man wearing dog tags and a patched field jacket slid into the seat in front of me, his plate piled with pancakes, eggs, and bacon. There was bacon? I couldn't help perking up.

Without a word he took the bacon from his plate and laid it onto mine.

I jerked my head up. "Sir, you don't have to—"

He held up his hand and shook his head. "Please accept it as a thank you."

I frowned. "A thank you for what?"

"For saving my life the other night," he said matter-of-factly.

I stabbed a piece of pancake, taking care to keep my breathing even. The Criminal saw me with actual battle injuries and got it wrong, but this old man figured me out in two seconds. I needed to get out of town.

"I don't know what you're talking about," I said calmly. "You must be confusing me for someone else."

"Battlecry." He sounded annoyed.

I raised an eyebrow. "Yes, I've been told that I bear a passing resemblance to her. But I promise you sir, I am not a superhero."

The man leaned on the table. "You and the other lady fought off that punk kid with the gun. He was trying to steal my coin can. I saw your long hair and the way you stand, like soldiers. When you walked through the room just now, I knew it was you." His eyes softened. "You don't forget it when someone saves your life. So, thank you."

I put down my fork. "Sir, I'm glad you were assisted when you needed it, but if I were Battlecry, why would I be here? Our city's heroes have their own home, and I'm sure they have breakfast every morning."

He stroked his beard thoughtfully. "That's a good question. Maybe you're undercover—"

"—in which case you're blowing my cover."

"—or maybe you're like every other person in this room, down on your luck for some reason or another. Could be you need help."

I leaned forward, my jaw clenched. "Well, there's your proof that I'm not Battlecry. Superheroes never need help from civilians."

He raised an eyebrow at me and then gazed out over the social hall. "Most of us have been mugged at least once. Pearl over there was hit in the head with a brick a few years ago, never did find out who attacked her. See that woman in green? That's Holly. Someone knocked her down last year and stole everything she had, and she was already homeless. Then he raped her."

I was too shocked by these sordid revelations to speak. He turned back to me. "Maybe superheroes never need help, but some people in this city do. There have been less crimes against the homeless and the needy since you guys moved in. We feel safer knowing the heroes of Saint Catherine are watching over us."

The tears were back. He handed me a paper napkin and patted my shoulder.

When I was done wiping my eyes, he continued. "What I've been trying to say, and what you won't let me say, is thank you. Y'all have made a difference to us. I don't know why you're here, but if you need help, there are people here who owe you their lives."

And with that, he took his paper plate and walked away.

I sat in the corner, my shoulders shaking from silent sobs. I didn't understand where these intense emotions were coming from, but ever since I'd unleashed my wrath on Patrick, a great wall in my mind had cracked and splintered. Now every feeling I'd ever ignored or denied was leaking through. The more they came through, the bigger the crack became.

I couldn't leave the city. Not after that speech.

*Sincerity. Responsibility. Endurance.*

For the sake of the principles, I had to stay here and do what I'd vowed on my honor to do: protect and serve the citizens of Saint Catherine. Maybe I was a severe disappointment to my peers, but around me were dozens of helpless, innocent people on the margins of society who relied on me.

I took a few deep breaths and stood up, then threw away my plate in the rolling trash can next to the table. I dug around in my backpack for a hair band, and when I found one I pulled my hair into a pony tail. Then I put on my backpack and walked through the crowd with my shoulders thrown back and my head held high, like a soldier.

Right before I exited the church I took out almost all of Patrick's money from its hiding places and wadded it into a container labeled POOR BOX.

Then I pushed open the door and walked into the sunlight.

## 17

After leaving the church, I made my way towards the edge of town. I left the upper class neighborhood where I'd spent the night and traveled north, towards Ember's patrol zone.

Nobody recognized me—after the incident with the old man at breakfast, I half-expected people on the street to stop and point—but a few times young men in cars would honk and yell at me.

At noon I stepped into a convenience store to escape the brutal midday heat. I'd kept about fifty dollars of Patrick's money, so I allowed myself to buy a cold drink. The air conditioning inside the store gave instant relief and I decided to linger for a while.

The young cashier kept shooting glances at me, though when I met his gaze he busied himself rearranging candy bars by the register. I made sure to not appear as if I were shoplifting.

I strolled past the magazines, pausing when I saw the one I'd seen in Café Stella with Patrick on the cover, advertising an interview with "Georgia's Sexiest Superhero." My hand automatically reached for it, but I caught myself. Maybe I'd left my team, but magazines were still forbidden to me.

Or were they?

I'd already broken two cardinal rules. What was a magazine

compared to fraternizing with The Criminal and thrashing Patrick? I checked to make sure nobody was watching me, then grabbed the magazine from the rack. To be safe I tucked it inside a gardening magazine. Gardening magazines probably weren't allowed either, but I'd rather someone caught me reading gardening articles than a magazine that proudly called Patrick "sexy."

I'd never read a magazine before, so I was unsure of what I'd find. I'd been warned at length about how corrupting civilian media could be, but Elder St. James had never said what, exactly, I could expect in a magazine such as this. I was terribly curious.

The first thirty pages were just pictures of women who looked like Ember: tall, beautiful, and extremely thin. I felt the urge to buy them all cheese Danishes, and vaguely wondered if Ember had skipped anymore meals since I left.

I flipped past the skinny women and found the table of contents. There were lots of promising articles about dating, makeup, hair, clothes, movies, and something called a "horoscope."

Patrick's article was on page seventy-eight, but I wasn't ready to read it just yet.

One article in particular caught my eye.

*Are You in an Abusive Relationship?* was tucked into the back of the magazine between an article about the risk of staph infections from bikini waxes—nothing in the description was familiar to me—and "bedroom tips."

I stared at the picture of a man standing over a cowering woman. Her hand was outstretched to ward off an oncoming blow. The Criminal's voice wafted through my mind.

*Jillian, someone's been abusing you. You need to get out of the relationship.*

I almost threw the magazine back onto the rack in my haste to get rid of it.

Breathing heavily, I marched to the cooler and grabbed a cold bottle of water, mentally slapping myself for even looking at the iced coffees. The Criminal drank coffee; who knew what I'd turn into if I kept up that kind of behavior? Picking up the magazine had been wrong. If I got hit by a bus after I left the convenience store, it would serve me right. I'd never read a magazine again.

The doors of the convenience store opened with an electronic chime, and the corner mirror revealed three pretty young women walking into the store. They were all dressed in cut offs and tank tops —much more sensible in this weather than my khaki pants and gray t-shirt.

One of the girls saw me by the cooler and waved. "Hey, Brianna! I thought you were working today!" She walked over to me, then did a double take. "Oh, sorry, girl. I thought you were someone else."

I felt my face turn red, as I'd never gotten used to interactions with female civilians my age. What was I supposed to say to her? Ember would've known. *Because she's a better superhero than you ever were. She takes the time to get to know the citizens. You* made friends with *a psychotic supervillain.*

"Um, that's okay," I mumbled.

I turned away, but she stayed put. "You look familiar." She studied me. "Do you go to King High School?"

"No," I said curtly. I didn't want this conversation to go any further, considering what had happened last time I talked to a young civilian.

Her companions rounded the corner of the aisle. I wondered if I could jump over the magazine rack and bolt without attracting too much attention.

"Hey Jasmine, who's your friend?" one of the other girls asked.

The third girl froze halfway down the aisle and swore. "You're one of *them*," she breathed, undisguised awe in her voice.

Did everyone in this wretched city know me? Why did I even bother wearing a mask?

The first girl looked at her friend, and then me. "Oh!" she exclaimed. "Ohmigod!"

The cashier looked up. I shushed and beckoned them to come closer, which they eagerly did.

"Ohmigod, I can't believe it's you," Jasmine whispered. "Why aren't you wearing a mask?"

"She's obviously trying to get a drink," the second girl replied. "Like, it's *hot* out."

"Ladies, please." I rubbed my temples. They giggled.

"I'm Imani," the second girl said. "These are my friends Jasmine and Shantrelle." I nodded at them in acknowledgment. "And you... you're *Firelight*." She said Ember's codename as if she hardly dared speak it.

"You idiot," Shantrelle said. "This is Battlecry. Firelight has red hair and a dog sidekick."

"But this is Firelight's neighborhood," Imani snapped. "I've seen her here before. She kicks ass. And she's got the long hair. This one time, Big John's guys were hassling me and Firelight ran up and I swear to God, she set a dog on them and it, like, tore their faces off." She looked at me, shy. "That was you, right? You walked me home and talked to me about how to tell Malik that I like him."

I pursed my lips, deciding whether it was even worth it to lie. "My codename is Battlecry," I said quietly. "But *please* call me Jillian when I'm not wearing my mask."

They gasped in unison. "I didn't know superheroes even had names," Imani said.

I raised an eyebrow—I'd never heard that superhero myth before, and it stung.

Jasmine smacked her shoulder. "Of course they have names. They're people, you know." She grinned crookedly at me. "You know Atropos, right?"

Her friends tittered and blushed.

"Yes, I know him. He's the leader." I could taste bile.

"You're so lucky," Shantrelle said with a sigh. "I wish I could live with him. I saw him fighting once. That man is ripped." She leered at Imani. "Maybe he'll save me from a burning building one day."

"I want him to save me from a different kind of fire," Imani said, laughing.

They broke into fresh giggles, but Jasmine stopped when she saw my humorless expression. "What's wrong?"

"Atropos is a jerk." My grip tightened on the water bottle. "Y'all deserve better suitors than him." Though I knew I was being rude, I pushed past them and walked up to the cashier.

The three girls followed me, peppering me with questions.

"Why's he a jerk?"

"Did you guys used to go out? Did you break up?"

"Why are you in Northside?"

"Is Firelight nearby?"

"Can I be your sidekick?"

"Does Helios have a girlfriend?"

I spun around. "Please, stop. I'm not allowed to talk to people, especially about, well, the things you're asking about."

"You're not allowed to talk to us?" Jasmine repeated. "Why?"

"Let me show you why." I slammed my bottle of water down in front of the startled cashier. My super strength caused the bottle to burst.

Swearing, I stormed over to the magazine rack and grabbed the women's magazine.

Holding it up in front of their shocked faces, I growled, "You see this guy? He's the reason I can't talk to you. When he says something is forbidden, it's forbidden. If he caught me talking to you right now, he'd beat me until I couldn't stand anymore. That's what your precious, sexy Atropos is really like." I threw the magazine down onto the dry part of the counter and glared at the cashier. "Ring up the magazine, too. I need something for target practice."

There was complete silence except for the low thrum of the coolers.

Instant regret replaced my indignation, for I'd broken yet another rule: never, ever reveal a leader's methods of punishment. Civilians were soft, uncomfortable with the stark reality of our lives.

"You can have the magazine and water," the cashier said. He pushed them towards me. "They're on me."

I looked into his eyes and once again was reminded of The Criminal.

"Excuse me," I muttered, grabbing the magazine and bottle and striding towards the doors.

"Jillian, wait," Jasmine said, catching up to me. Imani and Shantrelle followed close behind.

I didn't break stride. "Please forget you ever met me. I'm not supposed to be here."

Jasmine was undeterred. "Did you mean what you said? Back there, about Atropos beating you until you can't stand?"

I stopped and looked her straight in the face. "Yes. That was true. Tell all your Atropos-worshiping friends."

Her expression hardened. "I hope you kick his ass."

The corner of my mouth twitched. I nodded once, then turned and continued north.

# 18

I walked through dirty streets lined with abandoned buildings, into unkempt neighborhoods with cracked sidewalks and over-grown yards. Factories belching steam loomed over the small houses. The melancholy whistle of a train in the distance told me I was near the train yards, and the city limits.

This was my destination. I'd stay in the city, but I needed to be far away from Patrick.

The sun was low on the horizon when I found an ancient shed hidden in the brambles and long shadows of a thicket near the train tracks. I broke the rusted padlock and forced open the door, dodging a shower of spiders, dust, paint chips, and splinters. The shed smelled faintly of mildew and dust, but it was empty.

After removing the cobwebs with a stick, I laid down on the ground with my backpack under my head. Immediately, my thoughts turned towards the people I'd left behind.

What would Reid be doing right now?

If I had to say who the second-in-command of the team was, I'd settle on him, if only because he was the person who earned Patrick's wrath the least. Reid struck me of the sort of man my parents hoped

I'd marry one day: he knew every principle, embodied all four traits, and was quick to offer help when we needed it.

Patrick knew the same amount of information as Reid, but Reid's embracing of our teachings had always struck me as more genuine. I was tempted to resent him for never stepping in between me and Patrick, but why would he? Patrick had the right to punish me.

After a minute of thinking, I remembered that Reid was the primary cook of our little household. I wagered it was around dinner time—I didn't dare turn on my phone to check lest I be tracked—and he liked to make soup. I closed my eyes and inhaled, pretending that the musty scent was actually steam from a thick stew full of meat and vegetables.

Back home in Chattahoochee, meals like that were only available whenever the charity truck came, which wasn't often, but here in Saint Catherine we could buy cans of soups and stews, and bread rolls and salad and lemonade to go with them.

Yes, he would be cooking a big pot of soup, and Ember would refuse her bowl, possibly because she was crazy.

Ember. What would my sister-in-arms be doing right now? Talking to Reid, probably about me. Hiding up in her room. Throwing weak punches with bad form at the punching bag, with nobody there to correct her. Brushing her hair by herself instead of letting me brush it for her, and missing spots in the back because of it.

If plotting the crimes on the crime map now fell to her, she was probably getting ready to give a patrol brief. The only positive in the last possibility was that the amount of reading required for reviewing police reports would improve her literacy, as it had mine.

Marco was sitting up in his room, staring out the window and thinking that he'd just lost another Johnson cousin. I was certain of this.

And Patrick... Patrick was probably in pain from my attack, and thus ready and willing to inflict pain on the other three.

I curled up, guilt crashing down on me. Whatever was going on in that house, it was my fault. If Patrick hurt anyone, it was because of me. I rolled over and hugged my knees, trying to ignore the ache in my chest by focusing on the painful emptiness in my stomach and the annoying scratch-scratch of a rodent in the corner. Tomorrow I'd start fixing up my new home into something habitable.

Though I was exhausted, sleep was hard to come by. When I did sleep, I dreamed I was lying in a pool of blood.

---

I DEDICATED the next two days to making the shed weather proof, scrounging plywood, nails, tarp, plastic, and whatever else I could find from various junkyards and abandoned properties.

On the second day, while I was laying a small barrier of bricks around the perimeter of the shed to keep out rodents, I tripped over a low vine and stumbled into my pile of bricks. My pants tore at the knee, revealing a shallow, bloody slice in my leg.

Sitting on the ground, I poured a trickle of water over the cut and idly wished Benjamin could heal it for me so I didn't get an infection.

*Benjamin.* The rustling leaves overhead seemed to whisper his name.

It was the first time I'd allowed myself to think his name since I'd set out to make a new life for myself. Where was he right now? Did he hate me? Did he regret sitting down next to a sad, broken woman in Café Stella on that rainy day? Was he evil?

Part of me seethed. *Of course he's evil. He's a* criminal. *He was going to let you die.*

But that wasn't right—he'd tried to call an ambulance for me. I'd stopped him.

The same voice had an answer. *Because you gave up on life, like the quitter you are.*

I dabbed at my cut, wincing from both the pain in my knee and in my mind. Angry, cutting words raged against me, but beneath it all was the memory of Benjamin's hands on my face, healing power flowing into my body, and the question I'd refused to ask myself until now.

*Why did he save my life?*

## 19

I jerked awake. Something was lurking outside the shed.

On my feet at once, I tuned my ears to the quiet breathing of the trespasser. By its breathing alone I could tell that it wasn't human.

I cracked open the door and peered into the darkness, the poor visibility less of a deterrent to me than to other people.

Dim moonlight glittered brownish-yellow in the eyes of a large dog five feet in front of me. It sat politely, its tail thumping against the ground, as if it were expecting me. Hanging from its mouth was a plastic bag with the logo of the convenience store where Ember was shot.

My eyes met the dog's and I felt an almost infinitesimal tug in the back of my mind.

Ember had sent the dog to me and was controlling it from across the city. Intense pride washed over me. I'd never, ever tease Ember again, even if she couldn't fist fight worth a darn.

The dog gently placed the bag at its feet with a metallic clunk and sauntered over to me. I sank to my knees and embraced the shaggy animal, my heart swelling almost too much to bear. "Thank you," I whispered into its muzzle, hoping Ember could hear me. "I miss you, too."

The dog pulled away from me and nosed around the bag, eventually picking up, with its teeth, a small black item. I took it and turned it over in my hands, my face breaking into a grin. Ember had sent me a police scanner.

Curious if the bag contained anything else, I fished around and pulled out a few cans of food, a moist towelette from the sick bay, and a bottle of water. Crushed under all the cans lay a thin envelope.

I kissed the dog on the muzzle and ruffled behind its ears. "Go on now," I whispered. "Go on home."

The dog stared at me for a long moment and then wandered back into the brush towards the lights of the city.

I returned to the shed and sat on an upturned metal trashcan I used as a chair. By the light of my flashlight I tore open the envelope. Ember's messy, scrawling handwriting filled a torn piece of notebook paper.

*Jilly, Patrick is reely mad at you. He rote a letter to elder Campbell about you and says he will kill you if he sees you in the city and made us lissen to it. Marco told him thats murder and Patrick hit him and he fell. Reid told Patrick he cant act like he is an elder when hes not and Patrick punched him. He shoved me down the stares and I am scared to be alone with him. I miss you and I wish we coold patroll like last time becuz you make me feel braver. Pleez be safe.*

*Love, Ember Harris*

My fist clenched reflexively, crinkling the letter. I smoothed out the letter and read it again.

I had never felt more selfish than I did at that moment.

Determined not to break down, I folded the letter and placed it in its envelope before laying down on my makeshift bed.

Unbidden images of Ember tumbling, screaming, down the hard stairwell seared my imagination, making me sit up with a gasp.

Opposite the horror in my heart, fury wrestled for control. A brief thought of Patrick's fist connecting with Marco's jaw crashed over me, and the fury won.

Half-formed plans to storm base camp and rescue my teammates began to whirl around my mind. Every time I imagined punching

Patrick's face, the resultant rush urged me to picture the scene again from a different angle. The thoughts were so deliciously subversive. I let my mind wander farther down that path.

Fighting Patrick.

Making Patrick's eyes widen in fear again.

Feeling the crunch of bone beneath my first.

Beating Patrick. *For good.*

A shiver raced down my spine. I'd never deliberately entertained thoughts of facing another superhero in combat before. The elders couldn't hear thoughts, but if they could, such an idea would've been declared a thought crime. I paused, taken aback at the bizarre concept—could I commit crimes in my mind? Was my mind a place that could be, or should be, governed and policed?

For some reason, I thought of the women's magazine that sat untouched in my backpack.

Even if I defeated Patrick, what would I do?

My own question caught me off guard. Nobody else was trained to be a leader. Sons of elders became leaders. Sometimes nephews of elders became leaders. Marco and Reid had never been trained for leadership, though they weren't disqualified from leading if the need arose. Ember and I weren't eligible, period.

I chewed on my lip and stared at the ceiling. Crickets and cicadas outside called to their own kind in a familiar symphony that normally I would've found relaxing, but now I just found annoying.

I'd spent my entire life sleeping on the ground, listening to bugs. I'd run away from my whole world and here I was, sleeping on the ground and listening to bugs. I hadn't changed my life, just my location.

With a groan, I sat up and hugged my knees. My head felt foggy and slow as it worked through my late-night thoughts.

What was I doing here? What was my goal?

Closing my eyes, I breathed in deeply and exhaled slowly, as my cousin Christiana had taught me to do. Before she was killed during the skirmishes with the Westerners, she'd suffered from hearing voices and would do breathing exercises to calm down and tune them out.

I breathed in and out again, deeper this time, and one by one, I sifted through the shreds of thoughts.

*I am Jillian Johnson.*

*I am a superhero.*

*I almost died a few days ago.*

*I was saved by Benjamin, a criminal.*

*I left my team in disgrace.*

*I promised the citizens of Saint Catherine that I would defend them.*

*I am outside of an authority umbrella.*

*I don't care.*

At that moment, the tension in my body that I had been unaware of lessened a little. I lay back down and closed my eyes, and for the first time in many nights, I slept well.

---

THE NEXT MORNING, I cracked open a can of baked beans and turned on the police scanner. While I listened to chatter between units, I thought I heard a voice far in the distance.

I turned off the scanner and concentrated.

"Jill! Where are you?"

It was Marco!

I jumped up, unbolted the shed door, and threw it open. While clambering through bushes, I spied Marco in the distance with a garbage bag over one shoulder and no mask on.

"*Marco!*" I didn't care who heard me. I crashed through the rest of the thorns and broke into a run. When I met up with him, I hugged him so hard he let out a little "oof!"

"Jill, you're squishing me." He tried to pull away.

I squeezed him harder.

And then he'd dropped his bag and was embracing me with equal desperation, his whole body shaking with everything left unsaid.

I inhaled my cousin's scent, allowing myself to remember happier times in years gone by. In all those memories Marco was a constant—his sneaky grin, his silly jokes, his unfailing belief that I was admirable. I hadn't realized until just then that I *needed* Marco, and he very possibly needed me equally as much.

Marco was here and everything was going to be alright. I wasn't going to be alone anymore. I released Marco and gently pushed him back, taking in the sight of him.

My joy drained away.

Marco's lip was swollen and purple, as was the skin around his left eye. His right hand was bandaged, and I thought I saw a hint of bruising under his collar, as if someone had wrung his neck.

I swallowed. "Patrick?"

Marco sighed. "Yeah."

"Come inside and we'll talk."

Resisting the childlike impulse to take him by the hand, I led him through the bushes to the small shed. When he crossed the threshold, he stopped and stared at the little home I'd made for myself.

He picked up my homemade lantern, a metal can with tin foil inside to better reflect my flashlight's beam, and examined it. "This place is as least as nice as an elder's house. Did you do this in just a couple of days?"

I shrugged. "Not much else to do but fix it up." I took the lantern from him and put it in the corner. "Now tell me everything. Why are you here? Are the others on their way now?"

He sighed. "No, it's just me. I couldn't stay there anymore." He sank down onto the upturned trashcan and I kneeled down beside him. He looked at me, his brown eyes sad.

"After you left, things got ugly. Uglier than normal, I mean. Patrick would walk around the house and fly off the handle about everything. Reid did something, I don't know what, on the afternoon after you left and Patrick threw a pot of boiling water at him. It didn't hit him, but some of the water splashed into his eye and now his vision is blurry. And then later Patrick yelled at me for not arranging the sick bay the right way, and he punched me and tried to choke me, but then Ember came in and asked him to stop."

He furrowed his brow. "I guess he thought something bad at her, because she screamed that she'd report him to the elders if he did it. Later he threw her down the stairs."

I knew about that already, of course, but it was still horrible to hear. "Was she seriously hurt?"

He shook his head. "No, but I heard her crying in the kitchen. I went in to comfort her, and saw her putting stuff in the bag, and the dog at the door. I realized what she was doing so I asked her to tell me where you were. I got lost a few miles from here when the dog got away from me. That was...that was rough." He cleared his throat. "I thought it was my punishment for leaving the authority umbrella. I spent a long while wandering around Northside thinking I'd never find you." He looked me square in the eye. "I'm not going back."

I squeezed his hand. "Neither am I. We'll figure this out together."

I smiled weakly, my genuine happiness pricked with sudden guilt for leading him into my life on the edge. I had to be strong for him, though. He'd never know about my doubts.

Some of the emotion left his face and he opened the garbage bag. "So, where should I put my stuff?"

## 20

Though I'd told myself I would continue to protect the city, the police scanner and our masks were pushed under a pile of clothes in the corner of the shed and ignored after Marco joined me. Every day I glanced at the pile and told myself I'd know when the right time was to bring them out again, but before I knew it days slid into weeks.

Marco and I found odd jobs to do for a little money in the nearby neighborhoods. Elderly residents were happy to have young, strong people mow their lawns, weed their flower beds, and put together simple sheds and other construction projects. Sometimes we earned cash, other times we were paid with a meal and a shower. The edge of Northside was outside of our usual patrol area, so we remained blessedly unrecognized.

It was the most peaceful life I'd ever known.

Though we worked for people of all ages, the young women of our neighborhood were especially fond of Marco, and they made up a disproportionately large number of our clients.

The newly-married Mrs. Macudzinski, whose husband never seemed to be home, fussed terribly over him and asked him, and him only, to dinner on more than one occasion. He politely refused each time.

A flock of tanned teenage girls in impossibly skimpy bathing suits approached Marco en masse one afternoon and asked him to join them at the local swimming pool. When he actually hesitated in his answer, I smacked him and told the girls to get lost.

"You're the least fun person alive," Marco groaned a few minutes later, massaging his shoulder where I'd hit him.

"We may be outside of the umbrella now, but if I ever catch you abandoning a job to cavort with girls, I *will* write your mother." I picked up my pruning shears and turned back to the shrubs.

After three weeks of working every day, we'd saved up enough money to do something fun downtown. After much discussion, we agreed to see a movie together at a discount theater. It was our first movie and we were terribly excited. At the theater, Marco spent a small fortune on a box of brightly-colored gooey candies about which I couldn't bring myself to lecture him. When he offered me a handful I found myself savoring the sweet, bold fruit flavors.

I enjoyed the film, which was an action thriller with car chases and explosions. However, halfway through the movie, a scene played out in which the scarred, accented villain grabbed a young female bystander and held a knife to her throat, issuing an ultimatum to the frantic hero.

"Jill? What's wrong?" Marco whispered.

I was hiding my face in my hands and suppressing the urge to vomit. I heard a wet gurgling coming from the movie and jumped up from my seat, sprinting down the theater steps to the exit.

I didn't make it to the bathroom in time. I doubled over in the hallway and threw up. The skin of my throat tingled as if I'd just been touched there—I clasped my hand to it and squeezed my eyes shut.

*I hope this person misses you. It's nice of you to send a final message.*

"Whoa," a theater employee said behind me. "You sit down. I'll get one of the janitors. Dang."

Marco hurried out of the theater and put his arm around my shoulder. "C'mon, let's go home. You got a bug or something?"

I heaved again and Marco half-dragged me out of the building into the muggy night air. He pulled me down onto a bench and ordered me to put my head between my knees. I complied, and he started gibbering about food poisoning and the flu.

"It's not the flu." I slowly lifted my head up. "It was the movie."

"The movie made you sick?"

I briefly considered lying to him about why I reacted the way I did. After a moment's pause, I stood up and beckoned him to follow me home. "I need to tell you something."

While we walked under streetlights and past rowdy bars, I explained to him how I'd met Benjamin in Café Stella and begun a tentative friendship with him.

Marco didn't say anything until I told him about the fight with Beau and my neck wound.

"I thought there was an unusual amount of blood. I couldn't explain it, though, so I guess I just never thought about it."

"Well, I think about it. Anyway, stuff happened and he figured out it was me in time to reverse the blood loss. And then I went home and beat up Patrick."

Marco threw his head back and laughed until his eyes teared up. "That will forever and always be my favorite memory. So, have you seen Benjamin since that night?"

"No," I muttered. "I doubt I'll ever see him again. Besides, what would I say to him if I did?"

Marco smirked at me. "How about, 'wanna court?'"

"Did you not hear the part where he's a supervillain?"

"No, I heard that part. Did you know you smile whenever you say his name?"

That caught me off guard. "That doesn't mean anything," I snapped. "He's from one of the forbidden families and I can't be associated with him."

"You also can't beat up Patrick and run off. And yet, here we are."

I had no reply. We walked back to the shed in heavy silence.

When Marco and I lay down on the floor of the shed, now with a cheap blanket on it to insulate us from the dirty surface, he drifted off to sleep immediately. I listened to his gentle snores, yet more late-night thoughts swirling.

Deep in the recesses on my mind lurked disquiet, like an invisible splinter in one's finger, too small to detect from anything besides the constant throb. I strained to focus on it. It didn't have shape or form, like thoughts. It was a tiny ball of emotion, but unconnected to anything else in my mind.

I bolted upright. The splinter was unconnected to anything in my mind because it wasn't from *my* mind. Ember was casting her influence farther than ever before, reaching out across the void to send me a message, faint as it was. I focused as hard as I could on her pinprick connection.

Fear. Anger. Stress. A ghost of a shadow of a memory of falling, falling, falling. A call for help. Thunderous voices and breaking glass. And finally, one clear image: Marco, sitting on the couch, quietly unraveling a knitting project.

The connection blew out like a candle in the darkness.

"Marco! Wake up!"

Marco jerked awake and nearly blinded me with a ball of light. "What's wrong? Is it Patrick?"

"Sort of." I shoved my feet into my boots. "Ember just sent me a distress call. I'm going back to base camp right now and rescuing them. This whole split-team situation is a load of crap."

Marco stepped between the door and me.

I huffed. "What are you doing? Move."

"No. We're not going back."

I did not have time for this. "Marco, I'm not going to physically force you to move, but I will punch an escape hole in the roof. I swear I will."

Marco took a shaking breath. "If it's so bad there, let them leave like we did."

"Ember's in trouble! She probably can't leave. She—"

"She's in the same damned situation we both were until we *left*!" Marco's eyes glowed yellow, vapor-like tendrils of raw energy curling up and away from them.

"Easy there," I whispered, my hands up. "Your eyes..."

My priorities swerved from aiding Ember to preventing Marco's further power incontinence. I would not fare well if he unleashed the full potency of a Georgia summer day two feet from me.

The glow faded as quickly as it had come, and Marco sank to the ground, his face in his hands.

"Don't go," he groaned. "Don't go, Jill. Patrick will kill you and this will be for nothing. Ember and Reid and Patrick have been going at it since you left. Whatever is happening there now is nothing they haven't said or done before."

I kneeled opposite Marco and put my hand on his shoulder. This wasn't the Marco I knew. I struggled to recollect the last time I'd seen his eyes glow—Gregory's death, maybe. He never raised his voice at me. I'd been accused of unforgivable obtuseness before, but I wasn't so dense that I couldn't sense that my friend was deeply upset, and his newfound contempt for our friends was foreign to me. There was something beneath this outburst, something he wasn't telling me.

"Are you really only afraid that I'll get hurt? Or is there something else you'd like to talk about?"

He leaned against the shed door and closed his eyes. "Do you know how often Patrick called me a 'child' or 'stupid kid'? He'd make fun of me for being short, or for playing with civilian kids." His fist clenched. "I'm nearly eighteen. I've risked my life for this city. I've stared down the barrel of a shotgun. I've had to take criminal lives to save innocent ones. I... I...."

"You're an amazing superhero. One of the best. I'm so honored to serve with you. You're no more of a child than I am."

"But I'm the youngest." He jabbed his thumb at his chest. "And if this stupid kid can figure out how to walk out the door, then so can they."

His assessment of the situation didn't seem quite fair to me, but I couldn't put my finger on the reason. I didn't want to risk another glowing-eye incident, though, so I nodded once and laid back down.

After several heavy breaths, Marco stretched out on his bed, snoring less than two minutes later.

Sleep eluded me. I flipped onto my side and drew squiggles in the fine layer of dirt on the floor, trying desperately to ignore the heartache Ember's message had kindled.

What was happening at base camp? Poisonous fantasies of my friends being killed seeped into my mind, causing every muscle in my body to tense, ready to spring into action. An owl hooted above the shed, making me jump.

I needed air.

Taking care not to disturb Marco, I got up and opened the shed door, purposely leaving my boots behind so if he woke, he'd know I hadn't gone off to fight.

I wandered to the edge of the thicket, where I could see the city stretch out for miles, the lights like an ocean of orange and white fire-flies that fuzzed around the edges because of the Georgia humidity that rolled in from the Atlantic.

Somewhere out there in the ocean of lights, Ember and Reid were locked in a never-ending battle against the one person who should've been their greatest protector. I understood the final telepathic image forced through the connection, Marco's deft undoing of his knitting: Patrick was unraveling, falling apart at the seams and growing more dangerous by the hour.

My heart ached for my friends, and though I hated to admit it, for Patrick. He'd lost the respect of his team. A significant part of me wanted to throw down my knives and beg for forgiveness, but an equally significant part of me recoiled at the thought.

Why, though?

My parents had warned me before I was released into public service that Patrick had a reputation for a "lack of patience," even before he'd been given leadership of Saint Catherine's team. When I first met him, I thought he'd be firm, but fair, maybe like Elder St. James.

One month later, I'd abandoned any ideas that Patrick was like Marco's uncle. A reporter for the Saint Catherine Times-Mirror had pulled me aside after a fight to ask a few questions about life on the team. Patrick had interrupted and said I wasn't authorized to speak to the press, grabbing my shoulder and pulling me away. At first I thought he was protecting me from a threat I didn't yet understand and felt a twinge of gratitude and relief that I had such a proactive, vigilant leader.

Later, while I was curled up in my bed and sobbing over one of the worst beatings I'd ever received, I tried to reconcile Patrick's behavior to at least one of the twenty-nine heroic principles, the four traits, or any of the hundreds of lessons on superheroism I knew by heart. I couldn't then, and months later I still couldn't. Every time Patrick laid a hand on me, something in my heart punched back. This was, of course, why he punished me.

The cycle would've killed me, and the Elders would've reprimanded Patrick for being too heavy-handed, or too impatient, or something else just as inane. He would've been temporarily removed from his position, but before long they would've placed him exactly where an elder's son was destined to be: in charge of vulnerable people who weren't allowed to fight back.

Unbraiding my hair, I leaned against a large oak and gazed up at the sky.

When I was a small girl I'd come to understand that I could always see just a few more stars than the other children. I could distinguish between more hues in the brilliant fall leaf displays, and the blue-green-gold shimmer on a starling's wing was more impressive to me. My powers gave me a view of the world which few others could share. Now that I thought about it, perhaps it was this slight separation from my peers that was the source of my rebellion. If I were being honest with myself, I had to admit that my propensity for defying authority went back years.

Now, here at the dark edge of Saint Catherine, I felt once more that I was glimpsing something few others from the superhero camps could see, but this time I didn't know what it was. I scanned the southern horizon, where heavy clouds were rolling in, slowly obscuring the stars. Lightning flashed within, illuminating silvery patches for fractions of a second, as if someone were firing a gun inside. Low rumbles of thunder followed each flash.

I stood there for a long time, wondering if the stillness was the beginning of peace, or the calm before the storm.

## 21

The night's downpour blew itself out by daybreak.

The brilliant azure sky was dotted with fat, puffy white clouds that drifted south to north. The leftover damp from the storm gave a fine shine to green leaves, making them sparkle like emeralds. From inside an air-conditioned building, the day must have looked exquisite.

Marco and I started doing yard work for Mr. and Mrs. Hull at eight o'clock in the morning, and we were not impressed with the weather.

By early afternoon it was one hundred degrees, and the humidity was so high that it felt like stepping into my old bathroom after I'd run the shower for ten minutes.

Sweat slid down my back and into my eyes while I weeded Mrs. Hull's expansive rock garden. Even Marco, the natural sun-lover, took frequent breaks from mowing the lawn to step into the shade of a tall boxelder tree.

I joined him there during his third break and gave him a fresh water bottle, courtesy of Mrs. Hull.

He chugged half of it and dumped the rest over his head, sighing with exaggerated pleasure. "Was it this hot during the summers back home?" He took off his shirt and mopped his face with it.

"Yes," I said as I redid my ponytail to get as much hair off my neck as possible. "But we had more trees to stand under, and if it got really bad we could always jump into the creek."

He grinned and punched my arm. "Hey, remember that one stupidly hot day when I'd absorbed so much heat that when I tried to burn some off, I accidentally set the woods on fire?"

I burst out laughing. "I think everyone remembers that. Elder St. James ran around yelling, 'Put it out! Put it out!' and you were like, 'Why is everyone looking at me?'"

Mrs. Hull must have heard our laughing, because she opened her screen door and called out to us. "Dears, if you get too hot to work, you can come inside. I've got lunch on the table. Take off your shoes, please."

Marco whooped and tugged his shirt back on. Together we dashed up the brick steps and went into the cool, dark little house.

Marco and I sat down at the round wooden table, taking in the feast before us. Mrs. Hull had made thick sandwiches, each one stuffed with sliced meats, bacon, lettuce, tomatoes, and potato chips. They were held together by toothpicks that had colorful transparent paper on their tips, a detail so pointlessly cute that I loved it.

I grabbed the sandwich with a blue toothpick. Marco grabbed two sandwiches, though I guessed he cared more about the size than the colors of the toothpick ends. To Marco's complete delight, Mrs. Hull produced a large pitcher of lemonade from the fridge and poured us tall glasses. She set down a plate of chocolate chip cookies in the middle of the table.

After Mrs. Hull "blessed" the food—I made a mental note to investigate how this worked and why some civilians didn't do it—we started eating with gusto.

While I chewed, Mrs. Hull chatted amiably with us about her children and grandchildren. She complained that they didn't visit her as often as she would've liked, and I got the feeling Marco and I were a substitute of sorts. Mrs. Hull was the first elderly woman to show any kind of affection towards me. I had never known my grand-parents.

When Mrs. Hull paused to refill Marco's glass, I pointed to a sand-wich. "Ma'am, would you like me to bring Mr. Hull his lunch?"

"No thank you, sweetheart. Carl's medication takes away his appetite." She continued her story and I mused about how to get her to call me 'sweetheart' again. Halfway through lunch I stopped eating to wipe my sweaty face with my sleeve. Mrs. Hull pursed her lips. "Young lady, why are you wearing boy's clothes?"

I froze mid-chew. I wore Marco's clothes when we did odd jobs, as I only had two outfits at the shed. I was unaware of any civilian taboo against wearing nondescript opposite sex clothes in this context, but still my heart raced. Would she kick us out? Make us pay back the money we'd given her? Tell Patrick?

*Jill, you're panicking. Think.*

I smiled as prettily as possible. "I borrowed my cousin's clothes today because my work clothes are dirty."

She *hmm*ed and went back to tell us about her son's exciting job in the Army. I smiled along with her story, my heart slowly returning to its normal pace.

"Mary, turn on the news!" Mr. Hull yelled from the living room, causing Marco to choke on his lemonade.

I handed Mrs. Hull the remote to the little kitchen television and she clicked to the twenty-four-hour news network. A picture of emer-gency vehicles filled the screen.

"—stand-off has stretched into its third hour. Residents have reported to us that the suspect has a history of violent behavior. Police have tried to reach the suspect through a negotiator, but so far all attempts have been unsuccessful."

A picture of two pretty young children, a boy and a girl, in the arms of a smiling woman appeared in the corner of the screen.

The reporter appeared to be listening to a message from an earpiece. "We've just received official confirmation that the suspect's name is David Greene, and the hostages are his wife Irene and their children Joshua, four, and Victoria, six."

My eyes narrowed. I had opinions about adults who preyed on children.

"Oh my word," Mrs. Hull said, covering her mouth. "How horrible. Their father must be insane. Imagine, holding your own family hostage like that." She got up from the table and joined Mr. Hull the living room.

Marco's middle finger tapped out a light rhythm on the table. To the casual onlooker, it was a twitch. To me, it was a message: W-H-A-T-I-S-P-L-A-N

I considered our options. On the one hand, the police were on the scene already. If they required superhero assistance, they'd call the official city team, which we weren't part of anymore. I doubted they'd call for the team, though; superheroes were usually only called in by the police when there was suspicion, or proof, of Super activity. As fatal as a hostage situation could be, the police were trained to handle it.

On the other hand, I'd seen hostage situations go wrong, and any man who would hold his own family at gunpoint could not be negotiated with. What if the police were out of their depth?

My finger tapped out a reply: W-E-F-I-G-H-T.

He nodded, and I drummed out a little plan. While Marco bussed our dishes, I pretended to receive a text from "my mother." I walked to the doorway of the living room and frowned.

"Mrs. Hull, I'm so sorry, but my mother's car ran out of gas on the side of the interstate. We need to bring her a container of gas right away. We'll come back as soon as we can to finish up."

Mrs. Hull nodded without looking away from the television. "Of course, dear. Take your time. Carl and I aren't going anywhere. Drive carefully and make sure to wear your seatbelts."

We promised we would, and hurried out of the house. Once we were on the sidewalk, we sprinted back to the shed, not caring about the heat. We grabbed our masks and the police scanner from under the pile of dirty clothes. I tuned in to the Saint Catherine Police Department's channel and listened for the codes. The reporter had given the street name, Maple Boulevard, in the broadcast, but we didn't know the current situation.

Marco and I listened carefully to the scratchy voices.

"...movement from suspect... all units ten-zero."

10-0 meant "use caution." They were still in the standoff.

"Ten-four, CP."

"Movement from suspect."

I held my breath.

"Confirm...."

The scanner's speaker gave out a weak scratching sound and then faded into nothing. The batteries had died.

"Oh, that's promising," Marco muttered.

I sheathed my favorite knife. "Let's go."

Technically, I wasn't supposed to use my knives for anything less than a kill, but sometimes my hand slipped and evil people who threatened small children found themselves less a few fingers. Maybe my hand would slip today.

Marco and I were only ten blocks from the run-down street where Mr. Greene and his family lived. We hurried through the tired, crumbling neighborhoods of Northside, on the lookout for police cars.

After a few blocks of running, the streets lined with squat houses with trucks perched on cinderblocks in the front yards turned into vaguely quaint streets with row upon row of townhouses and no front yards.

When we turned onto Maple Boulevard, I realized immediately that approaching the home wouldn't be easy. Two dozen police cars were parked up and down the road, all facing the ordinary row house I'd seen on the news half an hour earlier.

I beckoned Marco to follow me to the next street over, Oak Terrace, where the houses' backyards bordered the backyards of those on Maple. Every yard was fenced—perfect for what I was planning.

In one quick motion I jumped over the fence gate of the house opposite the Greene home and pulled my mask on. Marco followed me over the fence and did the same. We sprinted to the back of the yard and huddled behind a woodpile while I peeked through the slats of the fence into the Greene's backyard. As I thought, there were a dozen heavily-armed police officers.

I was in the middle of formulating a distraction when a man's voice bellowed from the house behind us. "Just what do you two think you're doing?"

A middle-aged man with a bat ran out at us, cussing about thugs and trespassing. I held up my hand to stay Marco, knowing exactly what was about to happen. Sure enough, the man caught sight of our masks and froze, then lowered his bat to the ground.

"Oh... oh, it's y'all guys." He backed up, groping blindly for the handle to his door.

I held a finger to my lips and he nodded once. He mouthed something to me: *thank you.*

I smiled and turned back to look through the fence. None of the officers had paid any attention to the yelling man in another yard. Peering through the slats again, I tried to pick the best course of action.

The sun went behind a cloud for a brief moment, but it was enough to give me an idea. I held up my hand and communicated the plan using modified sign language.

It was simple: Marco would absorb the light in the backyard for a few seconds, allowing us time to break into the house. The police would be too busy trying to figure out where the sun went to see us. Sudden darkness wouldn't stop us; superheroes owned the night.

I held up three fingers. Marco sat on his haunches, ready to spring.

Three...

Two...

One...

In a fifth of a second almost all the light in the backyard disappeared. The officers, too well-trained to yell in alarm, whispered frantically and adjusted their helmets while we scaled the fence and ran along the edge to the door, where Marco deftly melted the pane of glass next to the lock.

I reached in through the new red-rimmed hole and unlocked the deadbolt, slipping inside with no fuss, and then hastily closed the curtains on the window. Marco released the light and the backyard lit up. The whole plan had taken no more than five seconds.

I didn't let our success excite me—we were now in a dangerous position. An armed maniac was somewhere in the house with three civilians. I didn't know where they were, what weapons Mr. Greene had, or what kind of training he possessed. For all I knew, he'd killed everyone already and was waiting for police to storm his house so he could go out in a blaze of glory.

Marco and I scanned the kitchen to get a better idea of the layout of the downstairs. The kitchen itself was gorgeous, by far the most luxurious kitchen I'd ever seen. Copper pots and pans hung from a bar on the ceiling above the stove, and matching utensils were in a vase next to the range. Ceramic jars labeled FLOUR, SALT, and SUGAR were lined up according to size on the counter.

I wished my mother could see the lovely cooking space. She made dinners over a campfire with a pot that had no handle.

*Focus, idiot. Principle twenty-three, self-control. Principle ten, attentiveness.*

Squaring my shoulders, I regrouped my thoughts and searched the kitchen for anything out of place, anything to indicate what sort of ordeal we could expect. The whole kitchen smelled lightly of roses, my favorite scent, and lemon cleaner. Photos of the Greene family papered the refrigerator, their beaming faces belying the ugly truth elsewhere in the house.

Marco tapped my shoulder and pointed to the honey-colored table on the other side of the island. In the center was a knocked-over crystal vase. Pink and white roses, plus the water they'd been in, were scattered all over the table. The discordant image stood out like a bruise. The hostage situation had probably followed a fight in the kitchen.

I searched for a clue as to why Mr. Greene would snap. My gaze fell on the fruit bowl on the island that had several pieces of torn up mail. I wasn't sure, but I thought they might be financial documents of some kind.

I picked one up, not fully understanding the information on the fragment. Red ink was bad, though. I knew that much.

Against my will, a swell of pity washed over me as a tentative theory formed: we were dealing with a desperate man whose world was collapsing. It didn't make me like him, but I wasn't comfortable anymore with my hand slipping.

The ceiling creaked and we froze. A male voice drifted down from an upper floor, the cadence of the speech making me think he was talking on a telephone. I sighed in relief; now we knew we were alone downstairs.

Marco and I tiptoed to the bottom of the stairs, which was the place where we would be at the biggest disadvantage. I decided to avoid the stairwell altogether because I didn't know which steps creaked, instead perching on the handrail and near-crawling up that instead. While it was considerably more awkward, it was silent.

Rolling his eyes, Marco did the same, though more slowly than me.

When I reached the top of the railing I lowered myself onto the landing and listened again. I could hear snuffling and whimpers from a room on my right that had been padlocked. The door had butterfly stickers on it, so I assumed the children were in there. The man's voice was coming from a closed room on the left.

I listened and discerned a few words about "payment" and "confirmation." He'd finally decided to talk to a negotiator.

I had to make a decision. As much as I enjoyed thrilling displays of heroics, the police had accomplished their purpose and talked down Mr. Greene. I bowed my head, ashamed that I'd so callously disregarded Saint Catherine's police force. Maybe they weren't superheroes, but they fought and died for the citizens, just like us. How easily I'd forgotten that while in the Hulls' kitchen.

I signed to Marco our new plan: *We need to go. Hide in attic until night. Family will be at police station for a long time.* He nodded and we tiptoed to the attic opening at the end of the hallway.

"No! I want confirmation that the money's been sent before I give you anything! I'm not a damned idiot!"

We whirled around. Mr. Greene's enraged words barely sounded human. What had happened in a few short seconds?

A woman's frightened wail cut to my core. "H-honey, p-please!"

The horribly familiar sound of a slap made me flinch. It was like listening to my childhood.

Marco's eyes displayed little emotion, just a hardness that aged him. He met my gaze and raised an eyebrow as if to say, *so what are you going to do?*

I took a deep breath and held up my hand, prepared to sign a reminder that if we broke down the door, we might accidentally kill Mrs. Greene. Before I could, my sensitive ears heard a small gasp.

"Davey, please don't do this," Mrs. Greene whispered.

"You made me do this, Irene. A man can't just stand by while his wife leaves him. I'm sorry I couldn't provide for you and the kids." His voice broke.

A small clink of bullets in a chamber.

A frantic plea to God.

I kicked open the door at the same moment Marco unleashed the payload of the sunlight he'd stolen from the backyard. Blinding whiteness filled the small room for a second, but I wasn't deterred. I'd already memorized where Mr. Greene was standing: in the center of the room, over his bound wife, holding a pistol to her head.

I threw myself at Mr. Greene, pulling his weapon out of his hands and slamming him into the wall in one motion. "Clear!" I yelled the usual signal to my team out of habit, remembering with a pang that my entire team was with me already.

Marco ripped off Mrs. Greene's bonds, helping her to her feet while murmuring comforting words. He led her out of the room.

Mr. Greene pushed against me and yelled a few insults about my parentage and sexual history.

I just rolled my eyes. It was always the same accusations. My former sympathy for Mr. Greene was nowhere to be found.

When he paused for breath, I grabbed a fistful of his hair and made him look at me. "If the negotiator promised you anything besides three hots and a cot in state prison for the rest of your life, I'm sorry to say that he lied," I said cheerfully.

"All you freaks need to be taught a lesson. Learn your place."

I laughed and threw him to the ground.

"I suppose you'll be the one to do that?" I cooed, taking my butterfly knife out of my pocket and twiddling it around my fingers like a child's play thing. In fact, I had played with butterfly knives when I was a child. "Please, tell me what you have in mind. I would love to see 'threatening a registered superhero' added to your rap sheet, which I should remind you is already about as long as my arm."

The sound of a window breaking downstairs alerted me that the police were in the house.

"Helios, we've got company!" I yelled to the next room.

"Okay!" he called back.

Tense male voices floated up the stairwell, followed by the foot-falls of boots. Within seconds the SWAT team appeared in the doorway.

The point leader of the SWAT team shouted at us from behind his helmet. "Drop your weapons! Get on the ground!"

I let Mr. Greene go and pocketed my knife, not taking my eye off the six firearms pointed at me. A man shouted an identical order in the other room. Marco would know what to do.

I sank to one knee with measured slowness, my hands up. "I'm Battlecry, a registered superhero with the city of Saint Catherine. I have the right to kneel and remain in possession of my weapons."

The SWAT team would've learned superhero laws in their train-ing, but it was always good to remind them. There was a long pause, and then the leader nodded once and signaled to the others to subdue Mr. Greene.

While the SWAT members handcuffed Mr. Greene and led him away, the team leader motioned for me to sit down next to him on the bed. After taking off his helmet, he pulled out a pad of paper and uncapped a pen. He didn't look happy.

I bit my lip. Now I had to explain why, exactly, two maverick superheroes were at the scene, and I had to explain it in such a way that Patrick wouldn't be alerted. *Think, think...*

"Okay, you're Battlecry, right? I'm Captain Harkins." He scratched his chin. "I normally only work with Atropos. Where is he?"

I had my reply ready. "The main team decided to split up into smaller tactical groups for certain types of missions, for the conservation of manpower. I'm sure you would know all about that."

Sometimes I thought my real power was inventing twaddle like that on the fly.

"I see." Captain Harkins made a note. "Tell me exactly what happened before you came here. I didn't send up a call for Super assistance, so there was a crossed wire somewhere. Did the department's superhero liaison, what's her name, Captain Drummond, call you guys in?"

I blinked, stunned. I'd expected a rant about interference, but Captain Harkins was ready and willing to believe that it was all an innocent misunderstanding.

I plunged ahead with that in mind. "I don't handle the requests from police. That's Atropos' job. But you know what, let me talk to Atropos first about the miscommunication, and then I'll get in touch with Captain Drummond and smooth this whole thing over. I'm terribly sorry about the confusion, and I don't want to cause anymore headache."

Captain Harkins held up a hand. "No, no, it's fine. We always appreciate you guys helping out with this kind of stuff. I just would've hated it if one of my men shot you. Can you tell me what happened after you entered the house?"

I filled him in on the brief showdown with Mr. Greene, glossing over how we entered the house, because the police generally frowned on us using our powers to deliberately hinder their missions. "Then you guys came in, and now here we are."

Captain Harkins flipped his notepad shut and tucked it into his pocket. "Got it. Thanks, Battlecry. I'll be in touch with Captain Drummond."

"Oh, no," I said quickly. "Like I said, I'll call Captain Drummond. You don't have to do anything."

Captain Harkins gave me a quizzical look but nodded. "Okay, you can call Captain Drummond."

I shook his hand and walked out of the room onto the landing. Police officers were interviewing Mrs. Greene at the bottom of the stairs. Giggles floated from the other bedroom, where the kids had been imprisoned, and I poked my head inside.

Marco sat on the bed, with Joshua and Victoria on either side of him. In his palm was a small glowing ball of light, dim enough to look at directly, like an old lightbulb. He was moving it around in the air in front of the kids. Whenever one of them would reach for it, Marco made it dart in a different direction. The children were enchanted.

Victoria saw me in the doorway and squealed. "Firelight!"

She leaped off the bed and threw herself around my middle. I didn't have the heart to correct her, though I had a wild thought about buying a page in the newspaper, and putting my face there with the caption MY NAME IS BATTLECRY.

I knelt down to her level and peered into her shining brown eyes. "Are you okay, Victoria? Today must have been a scary day for you."

She gasped. "How do you know my name?"

I winked. "That's my superhero power. I can peek into a little girl's heart and find out all her secrets. For example," I said, looking over her shoulder at the room's décor, "I know that you like princesses, horses, and dolls."

Victoria broke into peals of laughter. "Yes! Wow, can you tell what I had for dinner last night?"

"I *could*," I said with exaggerated thoughtfulness, "But I'm so hungry myself I think I'm going to... eat a little girl!" I started tickling her and making chomping noises.

She shrieked and ran back to Marco, who was shaking with laughter himself. Joshua hugged him and said nothing.

Marco patted Joshua's head. "I gotta go now, kiddo. You remember what I told you about nightmares, okay?"

"Everyone has them," Joshua mumbled, his lip quivering.

Marco carefully pulled Joshua's arms off of him and gave him a brief hug. "You're going to be fine." He brushed away Joshua's tears with his thumb. "And if monsters ever do attack the city, my friends and I will stand between you and them. That's our promise."

It was easy to forget that Marco was only seventeen.

Victoria threw her arms around my neck. "Thank you, thank you, thank you!" She showered my face and mask with sticky kisses. "Firelight, can I see your face?" She put her hands on my mask and tried to pull it off.

I covered her hands with my own and gently pulled them away.

"I can't show you my face. It's against superhero rules." I pouted.

She gasped. "Superheroes have rules?"

"Superheroes have a buttload of rules," Marco grumbled.

I shot him a glare. "Yes, we have rules. They keep us and other people safe. Now, let's go find your mommy."

We took the children by the hand and led them downstairs to their mother, who paused while talking to the police and embraced her children.

They didn't notice when we slipped out the backdoor into the backyard, where we jumped back over the fence into the yard of the man with the bat. We crouched behind the woodpile.

"How long are we going to stay here?" Marco asked. "I'll bet my front teeth that my flash was caught on camera and aired. We should assume Patrick knows our general location now."

"I know, I know." I rubbed my forehead.

*Think, Jill. What would Patrick expect you to do, and what is the opposite of that?*

I had no idea what Patrick *expected* of me, as I'd never been able to put my finger on the pulse of his mental processes. His fits of temper and black moods came on at random. I concentrated harder.

The better question was, what would an unhinged, paranoid person think of my actions?

That was easy: he'd see me as the "leader" of a new superhero team. I snorted to myself—Patrick always did have a vivid imagination when it came to my motivations and schemes. He probably thought I was going to announce myself to the media as the new leader of Saint Catherine's superheroes, like I was an elder's son or something.

I started laughing, and Marco raised an eyebrow. "What's so funny?"

"Patrick probably thinks I'm a leader now." I pictured myself as a trainee back home, wearing the red sash that future leaders wore instead of the usual black. It made me laugh harder. Yes, Patrick was *definitely* going to make a mountain out of a molehill.

Marco didn't laugh. "Well, you kind of are."

I stopped laughing. "Don't be ridiculous."

"Jill, you came up with a plan to storm the house and rescue the hostages, led me here, and we carried out the plan. You worked with the cops and now you're the one thinking about how to get away. The only thing you haven't done that Patrick normally does is slap you around, be an ass to Ember, and make fun of me and Reid."

I sighed. Though he was technically correct, Marco's youthful naiveté was getting the better of him. "I'm not eligible to be the leader. You know that. You're actually in an elder line, so you should be the leader. I can help you."

"I don't want to lead," he said flatly.

That gave me pause. I'd never considered that a superhero wouldn't want to be a leader, at least on some level. "You don't really have a choice."

For the first time, a flash of anger crossed Marco's face. "You didn't have a choice about putting up with Patrick. You didn't have a choice about meeting with Benjamin. You didn't a choice about stuffing Patrick's head in a toilet—you know what I mean, don't give me that look—but you made a choice anyway. Maybe, just maybe, you can make a choice about leadership."

I hesitated. "How long have you been thinking this?"

"Since I left Patrick's team and decided you'd be a better leader."

"Marco."

"Yes, leader?"

I pinched the bridge of my nose. "This conversation is going in circles. We'll talk about it later, but until then, do not call me 'leader.'"

He saluted me. "Whatever you say, not-the-leader. Now, I believe you were in the middle of making a not-leader decision about what to do next?"

*Oh, right.*

The sound of cars and trucks on Oak Terrace warned me that our way home was densely populated and we would not be able to slip away unnoticed.

A shadow moving in one of the second-floor windows of the batman's house caught my eye, and I considered an option I hadn't before: hiding inside the house. One of our "buttload" of rules was that we couldn't ask for sanctuary from civilians. Hiding among unpowered people was dishonorable and weak.

Right now, it was also eminently sensible.

"Follow me." I got up and walked towards the back door of the house.

Marco smirked. "Interesting choice of words."

"No, that's not... oh, shut up."

I knocked on the glass door and within a few seconds the man from before answered, though without the bat, and gawked at the two superheroes at his threshold. "Can I, uh, help you guys?"

"Can we stay here until sundown?" I jabbed my thumb behind me towards the Greene house. "There's too much activity to make a quiet getaway, and right now we need to lie low."

He stared at us with his mouth open for another few seconds, but then gave himself a little shake and stood aside. "Yeah, um, come right in and make yourselves at home." After he closed the door behind us, he called out, "Penny! Kids! We've got company!"

A woman's voice replied from the upper floor. "Who is it?"

"Just come down and see," he called back. He looked at us. "Can I get you guys a, uh, drink? Or food? By the way, I'm Lawrence." He held out his hand.

I returned the handshake. "Hi, Lawrence. I'm Battlecry."

"I'm Helios." Marco shook his hand. "And if you don't mind, I'd love something to drink."

While Lawrence went to get glasses of ice water, Marco and I sat on the soft leather couch in the living room. Two sets of stomping feet came down the stairs.

"Dad, Mom says she'll come down when she's done folding laundry. And who's visiting, again?" A young teenage girl asked while she walked into the kitchen with her similarly-aged brother following close behind.

He looked around and jumped when he saw us on the couch. "Tatiana, look!" He pointed at us.

Tatiana shrieked. "Oh my gosh, Dad! Did you invite them? What are they doing here?"

Marco grinned and leaned back into the couch, but I sat straight up, still uncomfortable with such attention. I had a sudden craving for a café mocha.

Lawrence poured a box of crackers onto a plate and started slicing cheese. "It's rude to talk about people like they aren't there. Go introduce yourselves."

The two kids shuffled towards us, blushing furiously. The girl stopped in front of me and held out a trembling hand, her bangle bracelets clinking from how hard she was shaking. "I... I'm Tatiana Gonzales," she squeaked. "I'm your biggest fan, Battlecry."

"*Miss* Battlecry," her father corrected from the kitchen.

"Miss Battlecry," Tatiana said, blushing even harder.

I took her hand in my own. "Thank you, Tatiana." I injected as much warmth as I could into my words. "I've always wanted to meet my biggest fan. Your bracelets are very pretty, by the way."

She broke into hysterical giggles and hid behind her brother.

The boy stepped forward and offered his hand. "I'm, uh, Sebastian. I'm a huge fan, too."

Marco scooted closer to the edge of the couch. "Wanna sit down and talk? Battlecry and I are going to be here for a while."

They hesitated, but then sat down next to us.

Lawrence walked over with the cheese and cracker plate balanced on his head and two glasses in his hand. "Hey, y'all, check out my super balancing powers. I bet I could join your team."

Tatiana and Sebastian groaned and covered their faces in mortification. Marco and I just laughed, jumping up and taking the plate and glasses from him.

Lawrence settled down in an armchair and leaned forward with his elbows on his knees. "So, what brings the city's finest to our humble abode?"

I sipped my water. "We intervened in the hostage situation at your neighbor's. We can't give the details, but we need to wait for the cover of darkness to leave."

"But don't worry," Marco said quickly. "You guys aren't in any danger. We're in a funny situation right now. Just team drama, personal stuff."

"Is it about Atropos?" Tatiana asked.

There was a long silence.

I cleared my throat. "Why, uh, why do you ask that?"

Tatiana gaped at me. "You mean you haven't heard. It's all over your team's forums."

Lawrence frowned. "Sweetie, what are you talking about? What forums?"

Tatiana jumped up. "Hang on, let me get my laptop. I'll be right back." When she was in the hallway, she yelled, "Don't go anywhere!"

Sebastian smiled apologetically. "She's been obsessed with you guys since you stopped Mr. Harrison from burning down our school during the assembly a few months ago. She's got fan art of you up in her room. If you hang out here long enough, she'll probably ask you to sign it."

I was still trying to figure out the appropriate response to that revelation when Tatiana rushed back into the living room with her laptop, its power cord still plugged into it and dragging behind.

"Here, let me show you. It's all anyone talks about at lunch these days." She was almost breathless.

Lawrence caught my eye and mouthed an apology.

*Don't worry about it,* I mouthed back.

Tatiana tapped on the keys and concentrated at the screen. "I'm a member of the biggest fan sites, and this one person, Atropos-Hater101, joined them all a few weeks ago. They posted identical threads on the same day. The main Atropos fan club banned her right away, but some of the other sites allowed her to stay. Here, look." She turned the laptop towards me. "Before I show you the post, have you seen your site?"

The website's banner was an artful depiction of five black silhouettes, obviously my team and me, in front of a black and white panorama of Saint Catherine. Bold text below our silhouettes read:

## THE HEROES OF SAINT CATHERINE
## THE FRONTLINE IN THE WAR ON CRIME

Marco put down his drink. "*That* is freaking awesome."

Tatiana beamed. "I like the banner too. I hope you don't mind the silhouettes."

"We don't mind," I said quickly. "Now, what is this post you were telling us about?"

"It's right in here." She clicked a link to a subsection called *All Things Atropos*. The top discussion thread in the subsection was titled *Atropos is a Jerk!!!!* There was a little image of a flame next to it.

She opened the thread. "Read it."

"Listen up, because I just found something out about Atropos that you all need to know," I read aloud.

With growing horror, I realized I was reading Jasmine's account of the conversation I'd had with her so many weeks ago at the convenience store in Northside.

While I had forgotten the conversation almost immediately, she'd told everyone she could.

*My friends and I ran into Battlecry at a store today. She was acting super weird, and when we asked her some questions about Atropos, she freaked out on us and told us that he's a jerk. Turns out, he beats and abuses his teammates! Battlecry didn't even want to talk to me because Atropos might beat her until she couldn't walk. Those were her exact words!!! An* *asskicker like her was afraid to talk to some random chick in a store!!! We've all been worshiping this guy as a hero and behind closed doors he's the real villain. She told me to tell everyone—so spread the word! F\*\*k Atropos!!!!*

My heart rate increased. Never once had I considered that my furious parting comment to Jasmine, to "tell all your Atropos-worshiping friends," would inspire her to tell everyone *in the world*.

I didn't know much about the internet, but I understood that it was large and easily accessible to civilians. I had to assume that every civilian in Saint Catherine knew that Patrick wasn't as pleasant as he pretended to be. He'd be furious with me... out of his mind...

Marco stared at me, disbelief and anger warring for dominance on his face—he knew I'd messed up.

I turned the computer away from me, unwilling to read the replies to the post. "They're really talking about this at your school? Everyone?"

Tatiana nodded, eyes wide. "Yes, and that's not all. The post happened, and then you two disappeared from the public. Now there's rumors that Atropos killed you for telling someone."

"Nobody actually believes that, though." My voice was higher than usual.

"Miss Battlecry, are you alright?" Sebastian asked. "You don't sound good."

Tatiana nodded again. "A few people believe it. I heard that last week Atropos was booed at the scene of a car crash."

"Honey, where are you hearing all this?" Lawrence asked.

"I told you, on the forums. We can't take pictures of you guys, so whenever someone sees the team in action, they get on the forums and make a post about what happened. Last week someone made a post about how when Atropos showed up to help at a car crash, a whole bunch of women booed him and told him to leave."

"What else is on this forum?" Marco asked, sterner than I'd ever heard him. He understood the ramifications of what Tatiana was saying even if she didn't.

"Um, each of you guys have your own website, though Atropos' is the biggest. The team website is the most popular general forum, though. It has sections for sightings, fan fiction, a 'thank you' section where people can express gratitude for rescues and stuff, and smaller sections dedicated to each of you. Oh, and this one section about sex and romance and stuff, but the moderators won't give you the password unless you can prove you're over eighteen. We can't post fan art, though." She sighed. "Hey, by the way, can you sign my pictures?"

Both Marco and I had covered our mouths.

The doorbell rang. Penny yelled down the stairs for nobody to answer because it was a delivery she'd been waiting for.

Tatiana closed her laptop. "So, is it true, Miss Battlecry? Is Atropos really like that?"

"Yes," I whispered. "I guess there's no reason to deny it anymore."

Marco put his head in his hands. "Dammit, Battlecry. He probably would've let us live in the shed in peace if you hadn't gone and told someone. Now it's only a matter of time."

Lawrence's face was grim. "Battlecry, Helios, if this is true, I'm going to call the mayor's office. I voted for Saint Catherine to have a superhero team brought in because crime in the city was getting out of control, but I don't want a man like that in charge."

I heard Penny open the front door. "Why, hello! My goodness, what a surprise. Can I help you?"

"Good afternoon, ma'am. I'm Atropos, your city's superhero leader."

I froze.

"I'm looking for two of my teammates, whom I believe are in this neighborhood. Have you seen them?"

## 22

I wrung my hands. "He can't know we're here."

Lawrence grabbed Marco and me by the hand. Tatiana and Sebastian watched, hands over their mouths, while he pulled us towards a door off the kitchen.

"In here." He opened the door to the garage. "The car's unlocked. Get in, stay low." He closed the door behind us.

Marco and I opened the door to the car, a blue SUV, as quietly as possible. We lay down on the floor, still and straight as statues.

"Jill, I am going to burn your hair off when this is over. I am so angry at you, I... I...." Marco trailed off, breathing heavily. "God, do you ever stop and think?"

"Stop talking so I can listen," I whispered, concentrating as hard as I could on the conversation in the foyer. The low rumbling sound of two male voices were interspersed with a higher, female one. After a few seconds, the front door closed.

I hardly dared to breathe as the minutes passed. Why was Lawrence taking so long? Was Patrick inside the house?

Finally, the inside garage door opened, though I couldn't see who it was from my angle on the car's floor. Lawrence's face appeared in the window and he slid the door open. He held a pile of clothes.

"You can sit up. He's gone. I told him you two ran through my yard and headed south. My wife wanted his autograph, which is what took so long." He handed us the pile of clothes. "These are from our closets. I can drive you anywhere you want to go, but since he's looking for you, I figured you needed to be in disguises for a while. You might, uh, have to take off your masks." He put his hands in his pockets, shame-faced. "Sorry."

"Don't be sorry," I said. "You're right. The masks have gotta go."

Marco shook his head. "And what about the rules that you were so concerned about when Victoria wanted to see your face? That was, what, an hour ago?"

I pulled off my mask. "You know what? If this rule makes it so I can't get away from Patrick, then it's one rule I could do without. Everyone in town recognizes me anyway."

Marco paused, but then pulled off his mask.

Several emotions flitted across Lawrence's face, chief among them surprise. "You're so young." He glanced back and forth between us. "You guys look like you're still in high school."

"I could be," Marco admitted. "I think I'd be starting my senior year this fall."

Lawrence made a noise of disgust.

Tatiana ran down the steps into the garage, a sparkly blue headband in her hands. She opened her mouth to say something to her father, but when she saw my bare face she stopped, simply gazing at me with undisguised wonder.

"You're so pretty," she murmured before giving her head a little shake. "I brought you my favorite headband." She thrust the accessory at me.

Blushing, I accepted it and took my hair tie out of my hair, shaking my ponytail loose. I placed the headband on my head. "How do I look?"

"Like a woman with a headband," Marco snapped. "We're wasting time."

I was going to have to make up with Marco somehow, though I

couldn't envision any kindness that would undo the damage of a civilian turning people against Patrick because of something I said.

Lawrence peered out the small windows in the garage door. "Helios is right. I can't see Atropos, but we need to assume that he's still looking for you nearby. My wife doesn't know you're here, so you'll have to get changed out here. We'll leave in five minutes. C'mon, Tati, let's give them some privacy."

They went into the house, and Marco and I started putting on our new clothes. My new pink ruffled blouse and denim knee-length skirt fit well and were cute, though they clashed loudly with my boots.

Marco's clean-cut appearance in his new jeans and white collared shirt triggered a childhood memory, and I giggled before I could stop myself.

He scowled. "What could you possibly be laughing about right now?"

"You look like the charity people who came with the boxes when we were kids." I gestured to my own conservative outfit. "We both do."

Marco's lip twitched, but he crossed his arms. "I'm still mad at you," he muttered.

I leaned over and hugged him. "We're going to be okay. I don't know what we're going to do, or how we're going to do it, but we'll get away from Patrick and this whole thing will smooth over."

Marco sighed and returned the hug. "I guess I'm not really that mad at you. I'm just kind of scared of Patrick. I know he's pissed at you for making his fans turn on him."

A few seconds later Lawrence returned to the garage, this time clutching car keys. Tatiana and Sebastian hung back in the doorway, grim-faced. "Are you guys ready? I'll take you anywhere you need to go."

I hadn't given any thought to where we should go. The shed, tucked away from witnesses, was an unsafe choice. If Patrick were to somehow track us down, I wanted the confrontation to be public.

Perhaps there was some place in the city where we could bide our time until nightfall by studying the forums. "Is there somewhere we can use the internet?"

Lawrence nodded. "The public library has free internet terminals. Which branch would you like to go to?"

"Is there a small, out-of-the-way branch anywhere? I don't want to deal with a lot of people."

My father once told me that libraries were "temples of false knowledge." Now here we were, unmasked in front of a civilian, hiding from the leader I'd beaten up, and considering doing online research—another privilege reserved for leaders—at a temple of false knowledge.

Lawrence smiled. "There's a smaller branch about five miles from here, the John Mosby Library. It's where the kids go after school. Lie down again and I'll take you there."

We obeyed and laid on the floor of the SUV while Lawrence started the ignition and opened the garage door by pressing a button on the visor. He backed the vehicle out into the road, and then we were on our way.

Lawrence scanned the street as he drove. "I don't see Atropos anywhere. Hopefully he went south, like I said you guys had." The SUV accelerated. "We're on the freeway now. You guys should probably sit in the seats and put on the seat belts, unless you're invulnerable to car crash injuries."

After we clicked our belts in, Marco leaned forward. "We're really grateful for everything you've done. If there's anything we can do to repay you—"

"This *is* repayment. The twins were in the auditorium at the middle school when Brian Harrison set that fire. The fire marshal said that if Battlecry and Firelight hadn't acted so quickly to stop him and evacuate the school, people would have died. The way I see it, you saved my children's lives."

I reached forward and put my hand on his shoulder. "That's what we're here for."

Lawrence took an exit off the freeway into a pleasant, affluent neighborhood with large, stately homes, manicured lawns full of brightly flowering bushes, and wooden swing sets in the backyards.

Women walked down the sidewalks with small dogs, and a man stood in his driveway, waxing a shiny black sports car.

A lightness flooded through my chest—as a general rule, wealthy areas had little street crime, so we were less likely to be recognized.

We finally pulled into the parking lot of a small two-story stone building with lush weeping willows on the grounds and a bench with a colorful flowerbed arranged around it. Sculptures of children sitting and reading books were arranged here and there around the greenery, forever frozen in childlike contemplation. I'd never been to a library before, but if they were all like this, I wanted to go more often.

Lawrence drove to the main entrance and turned around in his seat, his eyes sad. "I'll let you guys off here. Are you going to be okay?"

My heart was beating harder now that I had to get out of the car. "Yeah. We'll hang out here for a while and then go back to where we've been holing up."

His expression darkened. "I'm calling the mayor's office and telling her what you guys told me. If that doesn't work, I'm calling my representative in Washington. I know you don't want me to, but I'm not going to have a scumbag like Atropos lead my city's superheroes. From what I've seen, you're the better candidate, Battlecry."

Marco smirked.

My face was warm as I offered my hand. "You're very kind. I hope to see you again, though I hope it's in a safer situation." I paused. "And you can call me Jillian."

Marco stuck out his hand, too. "And I'm Marco. Marco St. James."

For some reason, giving our names just felt right.

We climbed out of the car and waved to Lawrence as he drove away. When his car disappeared into the neighborhood, we turned and went through the swooshing double doors of the library.

The cool, quiet atmosphere of the library wasn't what I expected of a temple of false knowledge, though I honestly couldn't have said what I did expect. Something threatening, maybe.

Instead, middle-aged women sat behind low desks with computers, scanning piles of books and chatting quietly with each other. An elderly man pushed a cart stacked with books and movies, humming quietly to himself. In a corner marked Imagination Zone sat a dozen small children at the feet of a man holding up a picture book. He read a line from a page with dramatic flair, and the children gasped and tittered. Their mothers sat behind them, all absorbed in their own novels.

There were rows upon rows of books in every direction. I stood rooted to the floor, slack jawed.

To my right were a dozen waist-high rows, above which hung a sign that said Reference. To my left were ten-foot high stacks with black lettering, each word a different subject, or so I assumed. On the far left wall was a section called Biography, and even though I didn't know what 'biography' meant, energy surged through me—I could find out what it meant. On the far right wall was a long shelf with magazines and newspapers, and the energy doubled in strength.

There was so much information available to me. This was what it was like to be Patrick. No, this was what it was like to be Elder St. James.

A child's laughter from above caught my attention, and I remembered that there was an entire second floor of possibilities. If this was a small branch, what was a big one like?

A large stairwell in the middle of the first floor ascended to the second, leading to a small area that overlooked the larger first floor. I could see a section marked Fiction, and beyond that a sign that read Computer Room.

"I'm going upstairs," I said to Marco, who also hadn't moved. He nodded and continued staring at the shelves of books.

I squared my shoulders and headed for the stairwell. Out of the corner of my eye I saw Marco wander into the stacks and pause at a shelf marked Arts and Crafts.

I pushed open the door of the computer room and sat down at a computer terminal, my fingers trembling. Was it really this simple? Could I actually access the whole internet? Even Patrick couldn't do that, I was pretty sure. From what I'd been told, the elders only approved a few dozen websites, and they received a monthly report about where Patrick went online.

The computer's screen had a picture of a globe with the word *Internet* underneath. I clicked that one, holding my breath.

**Please Enter Patron ID**

I swore so loudly, a young mother nearby threw me a dark look and covered her toddler's ears.

I stormed out of the computer room and over to the young woman at a round desk marked Information. "I need a patron ID."

The young woman, engrossed in her data entry work, jumped in her chair. She stared at me from behind thick-framed glasses similar to the ones I used to have for disguise. "A patron ID?"

"Yes. I need one." Screw politeness.

She looked left and right around her desk for something, then fished out a piece of paper from a pile of folders and pamphlets next to her mug of coffee. "This is the application. Fill it out and bring it to circulation desk downstairs. They'll issue you a library card, which will have your patron ID on the back."

I grabbed the application from her and scanned it, immediately noticing a huge problem. "This says I need a piece of mail or government-issued ID."

"Of course. We use it to verify your address."

"What if I don't have one of those?"

She eyed me warily. "You're free to browse our selection, then. You just can't use a computer or check something out."

I slammed the application down on the counter, not caring that I was acting like a child. Resisting the urge to stomp, I wandered over to an empty table and threw myself into a chair. Within moments I'd slumped down in my chair and shut my eyes.

What a stupid day.

Focusing on the hum of the air conditioning system, I willed my frustration to ebb away. "Be like Marco," I murmured to myself. He was always so darn cheerful, except when I screwed up and basically dared Patrick to try to kill us.

A woman's scream shattered the silence.

I bolted to my feet, my eyes darting wildly for the civilian in trouble. After a second, I relaxed my stance. The few patrons on the second floor hadn't moved, though the woman at the information desk was glaring at me.

*Dang it.* I'd fallen asleep and gotten worked up over a dream.

Sitting down again, I began making a list of priorities for my time here. Since I couldn't research the superhero forums, I had to make use of the library some other way. Were there any books about my ancestors?

I craned my neck to peer over the balcony and see if I could see a section in the stacks labeled Superheroes. I located it, but scowled when I saw that the shelf was in a small area sectioned off by caution tape. The piece of paper hanging from the tape read PARDON OUR DUST.

A man wearing thick gloves was digging around a hole in the wall, a large spool of electrical wire next to him.

I fell back into my chair and grabbed the lone book on the table, no doubt left there by some lazy patron. It was a children's introduction to science, and before long I had flipped to the chapter about electricity in an effort to determine what the thick-gloved man was doing to the wall. After just ten minutes of reading I knew more about electricity than my entire former team combined.

"Jillian? Is that you?" The sweet, lilting voice made me look to my left.

Benjamin's sister Eleanor strode towards me, her arms full of books. When I met her gaze, she broke into a wide grin so much like Benjamin's that my stomach fluttered. "Jillian!"

"Hi, Eleanor!" I hurried to meet her. Though she was probably a criminal, she had never been anything but polite and gracious to me, and I took some of her load out of her arms. "Here, let me help you with those."

"Oh, thank you so much." Her eyes were sparkling. She tilted her head towards one of the reading rooms. "I'm taking these in there."

"Are you, uh, here by yourself?"

A mischievous gleam replaced her usual twinkle. "I think Benjamin's downstairs. Would you like me to go find him?"

"No!" My voice was far too loud, and she raised her eyebrows. "No, thank you," I said, more genially. "That's really not necessary."

"I won't, then." She smiled. "But I was sorry to hear that you and Benny had an argument. He's been unhappy for weeks." We were at the reading room she'd indicated. "Let me get the door for us." She turned the knob and pushed the door open and grinned again. "Well, I guess I was wrong about that."

Unsure of what she was talking about, I walked past her into the reading room, stopping mid-step.

Benjamin sat at the little table, absorbed in a textbook. Note cards were scattered around him. "El, do you have another pencil? Mine broke." He glanced up at his sister.

Our eyes met.

---

I DUMPED the books onto the table with a crash and turned to dash out of the room, down the stairwell, and possibly several miles down the street. Benjamin stood up so fast his chair fell over. "Jillian, wait."

He reached for me, but I flinched back.

Eleanor took this all in, still smiling. "How about I leave you two to smooth things over." To my shock, she winked at Benjamin and walked out, closing the door behind her with a sharp bang.

I backed into the wall, not daring to blink. Bile rose in my throat —Eleanor had known he was here. Of course she had. She'd known and she'd lured me into a trap because she was one of *them*.

Benjamin held up his hands, palms out. "Jillian, I'm not going to hurt you, I promise."

"Is your brother here?" I hissed.

"No. I swear, it's just me and Eleanor. She insisted that we had to study here because it has the best reading rooms or something like that, though now I see what her real purpose was." He wrinkled his nose. "God, I hate it when she does this."

"Does *what*?"

He sighed. "She's a probability manipulator. A powerful one. She must have sensed some kind of possibility that you'd be here today and done whatever voodoo it took to make sure we'd meet." He righted his chair and slouched in it. "I wonder if she made it so we'd meet that day in the park, too. *Damn*, I hate her sometimes." He covered his eyes with his hand.

"I'm going to go now." I groped behind me for the doorknob, but it wouldn't turn. "What? Hey!" I jiggled the doorknob.

"Oh, *come on*, Eleanor," he grumbled, staring up at the ceiling. When I kept jiggling the doorknob, he looked sidelong at me. "Don't bother. Even if you broke the lock, I guarantee you she's ready and waiting with some other highly unlikely hijinks to inflict on us so we'll have to talk."

"Talk? There's nothing to talk about. You're a criminal. No, you're a supervillain. I'm a superhero. I have nothing to say to you."

Benjamin leaned forward on the table, resting his head on his hands. "Did Atropos give you the black eye?"

My hand fell from the doorknob. "Boy, you don't let stuff go, do you?"

"That's not an answer."

"No, Atropos didn't give me the black eye. There, happy?"

"No." He gestured at the empty chair across from him. "I have a few more questions, and seeing that Eleanor will keep us in here until we, I dunno, make out or something, we might as well start talking."

I didn't move.

Benjamin ran a hand through his hair and looked away, his hard features melting into uncertainty. "Look, things went wrong a few weeks ago, and I just... I want to start over. I'm sure you have a lot of ideas about me and my family, and I don't think they're all accurate. I met a girl in a café and I really liked her. I still do. I just want to talk to that girl again."

I crossed my arms. "Why do you care about that girl if you know she's a superhero?"

Benjamin did a double take. "Am I not allowed to have a soul? *That girl* was bruised, wearing a sling, and obviously being beat up by someone, possibly her *boss*. I don't know what kind of monster you think I am, but I didn't stop caring just because I find out that your boss, Patrick, is actually Atropos. And don't you dare try to tell me that you got hurt fighting crime, because your face turned *white* when you talked about Patrick."

My mouth fell open. "You're a criminal. You're not supposed to care about... about abused women, especially superheroes. You're not supposed to be nice and kind and buy me coffee. You're not supposed to heal me when I'm dying. You're not—"

"Yeah, well, Atropos isn't supposed to be a violent dickhead." He stood abruptly, his jaw clenched.

My hand reflexively went for my favorite knife on my thigh, but was met with blank denim.

"And you know what?" Benjamin continued, his voice growing louder. "Superheroes aren't supposed to hide in cafes, so depressed about their horrible life that they'll tell the first 'nice' person they meet about how scared of their boss they are. Superheroes aren't supposed to call me when their teammate gets shot, but let themselves die on a cement floor when my punk brother slices their neck open!" He was yelling now, his hands balled into fists.

"What the *hell* do you know about us?" I screamed back, traitorous tears overflowing onto my cheeks. "You have no idea what we're like!"

His nostrils flared while he took a deep breath. "You're right, I don't. Like every other American, I used to think that all of you were virtuous do-gooders who deserved the praise we've heaped on you for a century." He snorted. "Now I'm beginning to see that we've all been duped."

"We may not be everything you expected, but *you* didn't catch *me* stealing from Bell Enterprises that night," I hissed.

His eyes narrowed. "Fine, you got me. What are you going to do about it, hero? Call the cops? Fight me? Have Atropos come and give me a black eye and a sprained shoulder?"

I ignored his jibe and instead let his epithet roll around in my head. *Hero*.

It's what he'd called Marco and me when we encountered him and Beau stealing from the barrels. He made the innocuous word sound like a slur. *Just like you do with* "criminal," I realized. The similarity struck me as significant, though I couldn't explain why.

My anger receded like a wave on the shore.

"I won't call Patrick or the police," I said softly, my arms falling to my sides. "I'm not on the team anymore, and I don't want to fight you." The old lump returned to my throat. "I'm sorry for yelling."

He dropped into his chair. "I'm sorry for yelling, too. I'm sure we scared some library patrons out there." He nodded towards the door. "Can we just talk for a while? At a normal volume?"

I slid into the chair across from him and put my hands on the table, and he copied me. All was quiet for a few moments, and then Benjamin spoke. "Is your name really Jillian? Or is your real name Battlecry, and Jillian is the codename?"

"My name really is Jillian. Jillian Johnson, actually. Battlecry is the codename I inherited from my grandmother."

He shifted uncomfortably in his chair. "You're related to *that* Battlecry? Whoa. I, uh, learned about her in school."

That gave me pause. What did civilians like Benjamin learn about superheroes in school? Propaganda, probably. Would I have to correct some twisted version of reality for him?

"Is your name really Benjamin?"

"Yep. Benjamin Trent."

I chuckled with dark humor. "Did you know that if you'd told me your surname on the day we met, I'd have never talked to you again?"

"Why?"

"The Trents are one of the six forbidden families that declared themselves to be enemies of superheroes decades ago. If Patrick ever found out that I'd not only met you, but had coffee with you, he'd have—"

"—beaten you until you couldn't walk?" Benjamin finished for me, somber. His fingertips brushed mine. "I read the post online. Did he give you those injuries, that day that we met?"

"Actually, no. Those were from a fight earlier that day. Remember the guy who blew up downtown? Although, during that fight I disobeyed Patrick. When we got home he tossed me around his office with his powers, which didn't help. It could've been worse, though. He could've broken a bottle over my head like he did right after the shooting at the convenience store." I swallowed bile. "That's why your brother was able to best me. I'm not a crap fighter. I was just whacked out on painkillers I took for the pain in my head."

Benjamin gaped at me. "What happened after that night at the warehouse?"

Ashamed of the true course of events immediately after I left the warehouse, I skipped to the showdown. "When I returned home Patrick started in on me and I snapped. I've been on the run ever since. Marco—you call him Helios—joined me a few days later."

Strangely, Benjamin looked relieved. "Atro... Patrick didn't hurt you after the warehouse fight? For knowing me?"

"He slapped me, but only because I ran off and left Marco by himself. He doesn't know about you. Why?"

"There's been some rumors online about him. A lot of people, um... a lot of people said that when you and Helios disappeared, it was because Patrick had hurt you. After I read the post everyone's talking about, I put the pieces together and realized that you and Helios disappeared right after you fought me and Beau." He blinked quickly. "I've spent the last few weeks thinking that maybe Patrick... *did* something because you knew me, or didn't stop us, or..."

I reached out and squeezed Benjamin's hand. He stopped talking and gave me a weak smile.

I smiled back. "I won't say I'm fine, but that night, Patrick was afraid of me for a change."

Benjamin's face lit up. "You kicked his ass? Isn't he telekinetic or something? You must actually be a pretty great fighter to beat him."

"I'm awesome. The whole team is. Well, awesome in different ways. Ember isn't so great at close quarters combat, but she's the strongest telepath you'll ever meet. She can even talk to animals." My enthusiasm waned as I thought of her final message to me from the previous night. "She and Reid are still with Patrick," I mumbled.

"Ember's a telepath?" He leaned forward. "Can she hear all thoughts?"

"If she listens in, yeah. She doesn't try to eavesdrop, but she says fantasies and emotions get through a lot."

He looked thoughtful. "That must get annoying. For you, I mean. And for her, I guess."

I shrugged. "At some point I just accepted that she'll eventually know all my secrets."

An unnamable emotion passed over his face. "Ember and Reid are Firelight and Tank, right? Why haven't they given Patrick the finger?" Benjamin screwed up his face. "What's his hold on you guys, anyway? Is it blackmail? Does he have dirt on you? Is he threatening you?"

"He's the leader."

Benjamin gave his head a little shake. "No, I get that. Why don't they fight back like you did?"

"He's the leader." I didn't see what was so difficult about this.

Benjamin studied me. "Huh."

"What?"

He drummed his fingers on the table, still looking at me oddly. "You changed when you said that. Your whole demeanor, your voice, everything."

I'd changed? I stroked my hair, self-conscious under his scrutiny.

Benjamin continued to gaze at me, wheels turning in his head. "I'm curious. Why is your hair so long? Don't get me wrong, it's beautiful. But it has to be a liability on the battlefield."

I couldn't help but preen when he said "beautiful." "Super-heroines wear their hair long *because* it's beautiful. Beauty commands respect and makes civilians trust us more."

"Uh... huh. Can you tell me some more about being a superhero?"

I racked my brain. Now that it was put to me, the many and varied rules I'd grown up with were hard to name. "Um, let's see. Well, only men in elder lines can be leaders."

"Elder lines?"

"Descendants of the people who founded our camps back in the 1930s."

"Why only men? I'll wager that you'd be a better leader than Patrick."

"Women are more emotional and prone to making poor battle-field decisions."

Benjamin squinted at me. "You just did it again. You went all weird and robotic."

"Robotic? I did not."

"Yeah, you did." He shook his head, chuckling without humor. "I wonder if it's brainwashing," he murmured, more to himself than me.

I'd never heard that word before, but I didn't like it. "Well, if I'm brainwashed, I like having a clean brain."

Benjamin stared at me, then burst into laughter. He doubled over, nearly wheezing. "Oh my God," he said between laughs. "Oh my God. Clean brain."

I glared at him. "What's so funny?"

He sat up, grinning. "You. You're funny, and you don't know why. I'm not telling you, though." He wiped away a tear, mouthing "clean brain" and grinning again.

"I don't understand why you find this funny. I know we're different than civilians, but our rules have produced every superhero in America. I get that *you* might not be so fond of superheroes, but we are a valuable part of American society. Tell me you understand that, at least."

Benjamin's hand fell on the table with a thud. "What I understand is that America knows nothing about what their bright, shining heroes are actually like and actually believe. Seriously, tell me more about your way of life. No matter what you'll say, I'll owe myself five dollars."

I crossed my arms. "I don't care for your tone."

He straightened and raised his hand in a placating gesture. "I'm sorry. Please tell me more about your culture."

"Just so you know, I don't expect you to grasp any of this."

"Agreed." He smirked.

I huffed. "You asked me out to the movies, that day at the park. You'd probably call it a date. Well, we don't date. We court."

His eyebrows shot up. "What's the difference?"

"Dating is just sex and stuff, right? Courting is where you go to your dad, ask him to go to my dad, who then asks me if I'm interested in getting to know you. If I say yes, we spend time together with a chaperone, and after a while we decide whether we want to get married or not. The elder has to give permission of course, and these days we check the family trees to make sure couples aren't too closely related. That's a new policy, though." I was descended from several cousin marriages.

Benjamin let out a low whistle. "If it makes you feel any better, I wasn't planning on having sex with you on our date. Maybe hold your hand, but that's it. I don't have sex with women until at least the second date." When he saw my expression, he rolled his eyes. "Jillian, I'm kidding."

I'd remembered watching my sister be publicly disciplined after our father caught her rolling around in the bushes with a young man when I was younger. Superheroes, who were out in the world and in the public eye, could look forward to even harsher punishment. Benjamin had no idea how unamusing his joke really was.

"Anyway," I continued stiffly, "When you bought me that ice cream, it was the first time I'd ever had it. We weren't allowed to eat stuff like that growing up. No candy, no ice cream, no cakes, cookies, pastries, or anything."

Benjamin's smile turned sly. "That's why you ordered all those pastries in the café. You were feeling adventurous."

"Rebellious would be a better word."

"Oh no, a superhero is eating biscotti. Someone stop her before she lands herself in jail."

I couldn't help but laugh. Putting it that way, it did sound a little absurd.

He drummed his fingers again. "Anything else?"

"Oh!" I slammed my hand on the table so quickly that he jumped. "I'm not allowed to even be here. Libraries are totally off-limits.

They're temples of false knowledge, though honestly this place doesn't seem so bad."

"Temples... of false ...knowledge." Benjamin stretched out the phrase as if he was unsure of what he was saying. "*Please* be kidding."

"Nope. Though, I'm starting to question whether Elder St. James has ever been in a library."

He rolled his eyes. "I wondered when you'd get there. By the way, if this place is a temple of false whatever, why are you here? I mean, I'm glad you are, and I applaud any effort to act like a normal person, but aren't you afraid you'll absorb some of the false knowledge and turn into a supervillain like me?"

I was certain he was being sarcastic, but I gave him a straight answer. "I won't look at any of the novels. The educational books shouldn't be too bad, though they might have something wrong in them about superheroes. Children's moral tales are probably okay, as long as they have a clear hero and villain. I also won't read any magazines."

"You can't watch television or movies either, can you?"

"No. Although, Marco and I went to a movie a little while ago." I looked down. As much as I'd enjoyed the movie, it was difficult to admit how badly I'd broken the media rules that night.

Benjamin gently tilted my head up, his eyes sympathetic. "Hey, how about all three of us get out of here and go see a movie? I'll buy you something healthy to eat so you don't have to worry about breaking three rules, just two."

"Three rules?"

"Going to a movie, eating junk food, and hanging out with a supervillain."

I smiled, biting my lip. "I really would like that..."

"But?"

"But Marco and I are hiding here because Patrick is looking for us. We, uh, operated on our own today in a way that was kind of, um, highly public. We need to wait for nightfall to go back to the shed."

He wrinkled his nose. "You live in a shed now? Why am I not surprised?" He pulled out his cell phone. "I'm looking for a cheap hotel room for you two. I can't stand by while you get hantavirus from a rat or something."

The deadbolt in the door clicked and the door swung open to reveal Eleanor. Benjamin and I stared at her, our faces identical masks of annoyance.

Eleanor held up a key. "What are the chances that this door would spontaneously lock itself and the librarian would lose her key until just now?" She shrugged and smiled.

"Zero," Benjamin snapped. "The chances are zero unless some blonde psycho does her witchery."

Eleanor *tsk*ed and pocketed the key. "'Witchery,' really. Don't be jealous just because my powers are more impressive than yours, Benny." While he floundered for a reply, she patted me on the shoulder. "I met Marco downstairs. He's in the arts and craft section looking at knitting patterns."

She walked out while I mouthed wordlessly at her. How did she know Marco's name? What did she know about us?

Benjamin dropped his head onto the table and banged it twice. "I hate my sister. I hate my sister."

I stood up. "Let's just go."

Benjamin sighed and collected his things, and then we left the reading room and walked out onto the second floor of the library. The setting sun shone through the high windows, casting beautiful fiery red and gold beams onto the walls.

Benjamin and I set his books down onto a table in the corner and wandered over to the balcony. We leaned on the rail and watched the evening library patrons mill around the first floor, too engrossed in our people watching to talk for several minutes.

Eventually I pointed towards a huddle of squishy chairs. "See him, in the blue chair? That's Marco."

Benjamin squinted in Marco's direction. "I thought Eleanor was joking when she said he was reading knitting patterns. What's that about?"

I smiled, my memories rolling back to happier times. "One winter when we were kids, charity people we'd never seen before came to

Chattahoochee camp with boxes of goodies for all the children. Everyone's box had something different in it. Some of the things inside Marco's box were a pair of knitting needles, yarn, and instructions. He knits whenever he can."

I indicated my blue yarn bracelet, a gift from Marco. I liked to think of it as my lucky bracelet, though I wasn't sure whether I actually believed in such things.

"Charity people? Are superheroes p—I mean, underprivileged?"

"Yes, we're poor. We're not allowed to have jobs, so money is hard to come by. At least half of our food came from the charity people, and almost all of our supplies. The boxes were the best thing they ever brought, even better than the food."

"What was in your box?"

I closed my eyes and relived the magical moment of opening my box, nearly a decade before. "A doll," I said quietly. "A beautiful doll with brown hair and a yellow dress. A purse with embroidered flowers. A pink, sparkly toothbrush with blue toothpaste that tasted like fruit. Soap that smelled like roses. A beading kit. Crayons, blank paper, and pencils. Hair bows in all the colors of the rainbow, a brush, and a little mirror."

That had been the best day of my life.

"Is Elder St. James the leader of Chatta... Chatta...."

"Chattahoochee camp. Yes, he's the leader. Our leaders are called elders. He's Marco's uncle, though Elder has so many sons that Marco wasn't trained for leadership."

Benjamin thought about that for a minute. "I'm beginning to wonder if anything I think I know about superheroes is true. We were told in school that leadership is based on capability, not maleness, and nobody ever said anything about any elders. None of the documentaries or books about you guys talk about them." He pursed his lips. "I hate being lied to. I hate feeling stupid."

As if Benjamin could be stupid. He was one of the smartest people I'd ever met.

I leaned back against the rail, my elbows propped up. "Tell me about the documentaries." Yet again I had no idea what he was talking about.

"There was a famous one that came out about twenty years ago called *The New American Heroes*. It covered the first superheroes, how you guys were ceded some of the national forests, all the laws enacted about superheroes, and stuff like that. There was even footage of, um, your grandma." He had the grace to look ashamed for mentioning my grandma's death video.

I put a hand on his arm. "You said there were books, too?"

Happiness returned to his features. "Tons. Histories, biographies, even books about how superhero fashion has changed over the decades. And then there's the novels."

I straightened. "Novels? What novels?" Why on earth would anyone write a novel about superheroes? What could they put in such a novel? We were so boring.

Benjamin beckoned for me to follow him down a long aisle. He studied the spines and tutted to himself as he searched. Finally, he kneeled down and pulled out a thick volume from the bottom shelf. "Here you go." He placed it in my hands.

The cover of the book, *Rescued by Danger*, showed a picture of an absurdly muscular masked man inside a burning building. Flames licked at his shins, but he didn't seem to notice, instead gazing down at the thin, unconscious woman in his arms. She was wearing a lacy black nightdress.

I squinted at the cover. "Who the hell is this supposed to be?"

Benjamin took the book from me and placed it back on the shelf. "The character's name is Danger. He's arguably the most popular fictional superhero in print. I think the *Danger* series has twenty books or so. It was made into a TV series a few years ago, though it wasn't very good. Bad writing and terrible special effects."

"*Most* popular." There were more? And if they were about super-heroes, could they corrupt me anymore than I already was? Somehow I didn't think so. And just how much superhero-themed media had Benjamin taken in? He spoke about the books, documen-taries, and shows as if he were quite familiar with all of them.

Benjamin nodded. "Oh, yeah. Superhero fiction is an enormous industry. You guys even have your own subgenre of romance novels. You should see those covers." He winked at me. "They don't court, if you know what I mean."

Heat crept up my cheeks. "Well, that's just silly. We've always courted."

Benjamin leaned against the bookshelf, arms crossed. "So, have you ever been courted by a handsome, eager young hero?"

I was amazed by how he could inject laughter into every word while keeping a straight face.

My cheeks were warm. "Yes, once. Sort of. He wasn't a hero."

He grin widened. "Do tell."

I scoffed. "There's nothing to tell. It was right after my brother died. This one boy, Matthew Dumont, started hanging around a lot. It turned out that my parents thought a boy's attention would help me with my grief, so they arranged it all with Matthew's parents. One day after about a month, he got too handsy. We had a huge fight. The truth came out."

The nausea I'd felt back then, when I'd discovered that Matthew's attention wasn't genuine, crashed over me, ever fresh. I held my fist to my mouth, trying to suppress the newly-visited humiliation.

Benjamin must have mistaken the gesture as an attempt to swallow sadness, because his brow furrowed as he spoke. "That's harsh, and I'm sorry to hear about your brother. Were you close?"

"Yeah, we were. But that was a few years ago. I've gotten over it."

Benjamin thought for a second before bending down and picking out another book, handing it to me with a small smile. "Danger lost a brother in the fight against the forces of evil, too. This is the first one in the series. I think you'd like it, when you stop laughing about how wrong all the details are."

I was beginning to suspect Benjamin had read all the Danger novels many times over.

The cover was emblazoned with the title *Codename: Danger* and presented the same muscle-bound man as before standing at the top of a skyscraper, surveying the metropolis below while he held on to the spire. Unless he could fly, there was no good reason for him to be that high.

I fanned the pages. "What are this guy's powers? Invulnerable to fire and flying? Does he have any more powers? Because I've never met anyone with more than two."

Benjamin laughed and threw an arm around my shoulder. "I'm guessing you don't have a card, so I'll check the book out for you."

Benjamin's arm around my shoulder was an unexpected pleasure. Suddenly shy, I glanced away, aware that his face was quite close to mine. He still shook his hair to get it out of his eyes, just like he had the day I met him. He grinned at me, kindling the familiar warmth in my stomach. My sensitive nose detected a hint of soap on his skin, and sunshine, and something deeper, more basic and organic. I resisted the urge to press my nose into his neck and inhale.

Instead, for one brilliant moment I let myself revel in my crush, casting aside the bald fact that I hardly knew Benjamin, and what I did know about him was that his family was eternally at odds with mine.

I pictured courting him back home, holding his hand while we walked through waving grass, sharing a tender kiss in the lacy shadows of the forest. I gazed down the chasm of my imagination, building a world where Benjamin, this handsome man who thought I was pretty, would be eagerly welcomed into my family as a brother and a son.

A woman's terrified scream from downstairs jerked me back to reality.

We dashed to the balcony and scanned for the woman who'd screamed. Library patrons were rushing towards the exit, but I couldn't tell what they were running from. I dearly wished I had my knives; they made me feel so much more prepared in situations like this.

Eleanor sprinted up the steps two at a time and grabbed us by our collars, pulling us away from the rail.

"You need to run," she whispered, glancing behind her as if she were afraid someone had followed her.

Benjamin grabbed my hand. "Why? What's going on?"

She looked behind her again. "It's him. It's Atropos."

"What?" I gasped, taking a step back. "How did—who told—"

Eleanor glanced behind her again. "No offense, Jillian, but all of you stick out. I knew you were Battlecry the day I met you in the park. It could be someone here saw you and spread the word."

I swore. "I'm going to find Marco. He's down there right now." I turned to Benjamin. "Will you come with me?"

Eleanor shook her head frantically, her eyes wet.

"Too late. Atropos found Marco first."

## 23

Rational thought stopped.

I planted a hand on the balcony rail and jumped over, dimly aware of Benjamin and Eleanor shouting something at me. I landed on top of a bookshelf, then lightly jumped to the ground. Blood pounded in my ears as the details of the library zeroed into sharp focus.

Patrick was here. If he'd killed Marco, he was going to die, simple as that. I'd killed before, and I had no qualms about killing again. I shrugged off my lack of knives; bare hands would do.

I whipped around the corner of a bookshelf and froze.

Patrick stood in the main aisle with his back to me. Marco hung above him like a grotesque puppet, his limbs twisted. Marco's face was a violent shade of purple as he clawed at his neck in a vain effort to remove the invisible hands that choked off his air supply. He saw me and gurgled.

"It's about time," Patrick said, his tone so icy that it cut through my fury. What did he plan to do here at the library, in public? How desperate was he for revenge? The memory of his fearful eyes when I attacked him so many weeks ago played across my mind.

He was afraid then—it was possible he was afraid still. I needed to exploit that fear, as he'd exploited mine too many times. I squared my shoulders. If Patrick wanted a showdown, he was going to get one.

But he was going to have to fight Battlecry, not Jillian.

"Drop him and face me." I raised my voice as if I were on the streets with a common thug. "Only a coward uses a human shield."

Patrick spun around. "A *coward*?"

Marco dropped to the floor in a heap. He was breathing, so I didn't spare him a worry. Patrick was working himself into a mania, which would make him dangerously reckless. But I had learned how to exploit recklessness when I had killed rabid animals in the woods back home.

"Yes, a coward." I didn't take my eyes off Patrick's face. "You attacked Marco to lure me out. That was a bad move, *leader*."

I needed to keep talking while I came up with a plan. Now that I was within feet of my furious, lethal, and highly unpredictable foe, I realized that jumping over the balcony and announcing my presence hadn't been the best idea I'd ever had.

Telekinesis prickled at my skin and clothes, though it was too indistinct to have any effect on me. I suspected that he wasn't consciously controlling his power anymore, instead letting it billow off him like fumes from a gasoline can.

He was going to explode if I didn't stop him.

"Well, say something." I put a hand on my hip. Several feet to my right was a janitor's closet with a fire alarm next to it. I casually took a step towards it. "Don't just stand there and glare at me. Where are your usual threats? I've missed them *so* much."

"I'll kill you for what you did to me," Patrick hissed, his face flushed white. The telekinetic fumes increased, just as I hoped they would.

I took another step to the right.

"Oh yes, it was so disrespectful of me to tell civilians about your leadership style. Or, wait a minute, I broke the silence, didn't I? Does that make me disloyal or disobedient?" The words poured out of me, laced with acid.

I took another few more steps to the right, stopping when I stood between Patrick and the janitor's closet. I'd charge him, and he'd blow me backwards towards the fire alarm. I needed to distract him for even just one second.

Despite my taunts, Patrick straightened, the corners of his mouth turning upwards in a humorless smile. "You're confident. I'll give you that. You gave the others confidence, too. I can respect the ability to inspire others."

*Wait, what?* Had he just paid me a compliment? I raised an eyebrow, unsure of what to do or say.

His smile grew wider. "It's too bad Reid and Ember aren't as durable as you are. Their little mutiny this afternoon didn't end well for them, Ember especially." He tilted his head back and laughed.

I launched myself at him.

As I suspected, he blasted me backwards into the wall next to the janitor's closet, but I hadn't braced myself for it.

I slammed into the wall at the same time that Patrick yelled in pain.

While the spots in my vision cleared, I made out Marco throwing bursts of heat at Patrick, who was chucking books back at him. Marco didn't look any worse for the wear.

Yards away, Benjamin stood behind a pillar, clutching a pair of scissors and watching the fight— he'd helped Marco up while Patrick was busy with me.

I pulled the fire alarm.

A head-splitting ringing filled the library, followed by the spluttering of long-unused sprinklers overhead. Several dozen nozzles began to spray water in every direction, soaking each person, book, and machine in the building.

The few civilians left in the library screamed again and ran around with their arms over their heads. Patrick and Marco both stopped and covered their ears, blinking confusedly at the sprinklers as I'd hoped they would.

I lunged at Patrick, tackling him with half a year's pent up fury. We tumbled for a moment, grappling with each other, until his fist connected with my temple and I fell on my back.

In less than a second he was over me, his hand around my throat, invisible weights pinning my wrists to the floor. Water from the ceiling sprayed into my face, blinding me.

I'd acted in anger, and now I'd paid the price.

Beyond us, I heard Marco's furious yell, and then the horrible sound of him being thrown back into a piece of furniture.

"Hey, I did this with Ember a few hours ago," Patrick said, panting. "It was fun."

Thoughts of disemboweling Patrick pierced through my mind, dragging a fog of rage over me. Pulling my hands up with immense difficulty, I gouged my nails into his skin, but he simply squeezed my windpipe harder.

My hands were forced back to the floor, and blinding rage melted into panic as I realized I couldn't get him off me.

I was not going to die on the floor of the library at Patrick's hands. I was not. I was *not*.

White spots sparkled around the edges of my vision.

I was not going to die like this. I was not going to die like this.

And then, out of nowhere, two hands seized Patrick's neck and pulled him off me.

The crushing weight on my wrists dissipated. I choked a breath and coughed for several seconds, then pushed myself up from the waterlogged carpet and searched frantically for my adversary.

Several feet away Reid and Patrick were throwing punches in the artificial downpour, snarling at each other with a hatred I'd never seen between them. Reid's lip was bleeding and the shadowy beginning of a black eye was apparent, but if he was in pain it didn't slow him down. He exuded as much physical power as any fighter I'd seen. I couldn't believe I'd ever thought of Reid as skinny.

But why was he here? My immediate guess was that he was defending me, but when had Reid ever stepped in between Patrick and me?

And then Ember was there, kneeling next to me and hoisting me to my feet, her mouth a grim line. "Up you get," she whispered. "Back here." She pulled me behind a bookshelf.

I opened my mouth to express how happy I was to see her, but stopped when I really saw her. A dried trail of blood beneath her nose told of a recent nosebleed. Thin red scratches on her neck disappeared beneath her collar. Her knuckles were torn and bloody, familiar to a hand-to-hand fighter like myself.

Hatred boiled in my veins. "What did he do to you?"

Ember scowled. "We'll talk about that later."

Before I could respond, the ground rumbled, the hallmark of Reid's abilities. I gasped—he was causing an earthquake while we were inside. The ground rumbled again—I had to get involved. This fight was getting out of control.

Ember tensed and stepped towards the fight, but I grabbed her shoulder. *We have to coordinate our effort if we're going to accomplish anything.*

Her jaw hardened. *Any ideas?*

*I know you hate doing this, but can you be our communicator?*

Surprisingly, Ember gave me a soft smile. *I don't mind doing it for people who ask nicely.* She cracked her knuckles. *So what's the plan?*

Reid and Patrick were locked in a dead heat. Reid was either trying to knock down Patrick via small tremors or he was suffering anger-induced power incontinence, like Patrick had a few moments ago. Marco was down. Ember wasn't terribly useful right now except for her telepathy.

So that left me.

Patrick had temporarily bested me because I'd moronically attacked him dead-on when he'd expected it. I squeezed my eyes shut in annoyance with myself, because of course he'd expected it. That's why he went after Marco initially. I'd flown into a rage, and then later on he'd bragged about hurting Ember, chipping at my control again.

I hated to admit it, but Patrick had played me like an instrument. He'd be expecting me to do something equally amateur again. I needed to move him into a corner this time. What was his weakness? I'd already pulled the fire alarm to distract him.

I scanned the library for a weapon.

My eye fell on the spool of electrical wire beyond the caution tape. An hour before, I'd read in the children's science book about the dangers of mixing electricity and water. I glanced at my feet, where water was already pooling in the indentations my boots left in the carpet, and then over to the circuit breaker box. I'd been surprised to read that it wasn't remotely dangerous.

The ground wobbled again.

*Ember, I need you to relay a message to Reid and Benjamin, and also memorize some lines.*

*Tell me.*

*Tell Reid to start directing the fight towards the circuit breaker box—*

*The what?*

*The metal box by the janitor's closet. Direct the fight towards that. When Patrick's not looking, have Benjamin heal Marco, then tell him to hide again.* I gave her some more lines I needed her to say, as well as lines to pass to the others.

She grinned. "Brilliant."

I sprinted around the shelves, taking the long way to the spool of wire. I grabbed the end of the spool and hastily unwound the entire line, then ran to the breaker box. I shoved one end of the wire into the breaker box, slamming the door on it so the rest stuck out like a strange rubber tail. I turned over a mop bucket and stood on it.

"Battlecry, *no!*" Ember's terrified scream made everyone's heads whip around and look at me.

"If anyone so much as sneezes, I'll fry every last one of us!" I brandished the other end of the wire and glared at Patrick. "Give me a reason."

He eyed it and took a half step back. I felt a small tug on the wire.

I jerked the wire away. "Telekinesis is a conductor, moron. If you lift this cable up, fifty thousand volts of pure electricity will surge directly into your brain." I pointed to the breaker box. "It's plugged right into the source."

"What's a conductor?" Ember asked, fearful.

"It's what's going to make killing you all very easy if I drop this. Believe me, I don't want all of you to die, but if that's what it takes to kill Patrick, that's what's going to happen. By the way, water is a conductor, too." I pointed to the sprinklers that were still gushing water.

Reid's eyes flickered to Ember, and beyond him Marco and Benjamin stood behind a pillar, watching Patrick. She'd filled them in on my performance.

Patrick eyed me. "You're lying." His words lacked conviction.

"She's not." Benjamin stepped out from behind the pillar, trembling. He held his hands up to Patrick and me as if to calm frightened animals. "I know you're all superheroes, but if the end of the wire touches the floor, we're all dead. No superpower can protect you from that much charge." He looked at Patrick with pleading eyes. "Please listen to her. I... I think she'll really kill us all." He leaned towards Patrick as if they were friends. "I saw her reading about bomb-making earlier. She's crazy."

"I really will." I narrowed my eyes. "Killing everyone here to kill you is a sacrifice I'm willing to make." Marco gasped. I softened my expression. "Even you, Helios."

The thought of Marco dying made my stomach twist.

Reid stepped forward. "That won't be necessary. I can raise an electricity barrier around Patrick to contain the power."

Patrick flipped him off. "Traitor."

Reid returned the gesture, then looked at me. "On your order." His eyes glowed a soft white, indicating his complete psychic hold on the earth below us.

I lifted my chin and stared at Patrick. "Easy way or hard way, dick."

*Ember, where are the emergency services?*

*Less than sixty seconds away.*

*Good. I can't bluff for much longer.*

Patrick took a deep breath... and then sank to his knees.

He'd surrendered.

I stepped off the bucket, my face not showing the elation behind it. "Cross your ankles and put your hands behind your head."

He gave me a dark look but put his hands behind his head. "My father will order your death for this," he muttered.

I kicked his ankle. "Then I'll zap him, too. I said cross 'em."

I wasn't afraid of Elder Campbell. Marco had left the team like I had, but unlike me, he hadn't assaulted Patrick before doing so. My former leader had had no right to attack Marco, and even an elder's son could expect reprisals for such an act. Elder Campbell would be angry that we'd defied his son's authority, but Elder St. James wouldn't let him do anything to us.

The sudden high whine of sirens outside the library comforted me; I'd only have to pretend to threaten my team for a minute longer.

I pointed towards the library doors. "Now would be the time to decide what you're going to tell the police. Two dozen civilians saw you ambush Marco."

Patrick said nothing, merely narrowing his eyes at me. Water poured down on the six of us for a few tense seconds, and then his face drained of emotion, smoothing over into a mask of resignation.

"Fine," he spat. "You win. Congratulations."

*Well, that was easy.*

The doors burst open and several firemen rushed inside in their full gear. In other circumstances I might have felt a twinge of guilt for summoning them when there was no fire, but now they served as uniformed witnesses to Patrick's surrender.

Confident that Patrick wouldn't attack us when city personnel were present, I took a step back and told everyone to watch him while I went to find the most senior police officer on the scene, and possibly the fire marshal.

One of the firemen walked towards me. Behind him was Captain Drummond in an elegant floor-length dress—I supposed she'd been called in to work after normal hours when word got out that Atropos had started rampaging around a city library.

Both of them opened their mouths to speak.

The lights flickered, then went out, plunging the library into blackish-blue shadows.

I spun around and looked at Patrick. He was watching a fireman flip switches in the circuit breaker box.

Patrick turned to me, grinning.

## 24

A hard, smooth weight pinned me down. I cracked open an eye and saw the darkened library, tilted and blurry.

My initial dim thought was that the library patrons probably didn't appreciate all the bookshelves being on the ground, nor the lights being out. Strange wailing sounds filtered in from all around me, and after a second I realized it was the sound of many people crying and moaning for help.

Why was it so dark? Why were the bookshelves on the ground? And why was I several yards away, next to a wall? Why were people crying? What was going on?

Blinking, I forced myself up, and the large weight slid to the side with a clatter. It was an upended table. After struggling to my feet, I surveyed my surroundings.

My first impression was that the Destructor had dropped a bomb in the middle of the first floor. The library was in ruins, the wreckage radiating out from a central point about fifteen yards from me.

Civilians, dead and alive, lay all over the ground, though most were lying prone at the base of solid, grounded objects like walls and desks.

The main overhead lights were out, leaving only a few emergency fluorescent lights which cast odd shadows over the wreckage. The sound of dripping was a ceaseless drumbeat in the background.

A woman in an EMS uniform hurried over to me, a medical bag in her hand. Her neck badge identified her as Sarah. Other EMS personnel attended to wounded civilians. I couldn't see my team.

Sarah took my hand. "Are you alright? Sit down, don't walk, you might have broken bones. Can you hear me? What's your name?" She looked over her shoulder. "I need help over here!"

"Battlecry."

"What?" She pointed a penlight at my eyes.

I turned my head away and shoved her hand down, annoyance finally overcoming my dull confusion. "My name is Battlecry. I'm one of the city's superheroes. What happened here?"

Sarah studied me for a moment, then clicked off her light. "What's the last thing you remember?"

Patrick on his knees. The sprinklers raining down on us. Turning to speak to Captain Drummond and the fireman. And then... and then...

"My team fought Atropos." My voice was faint. "He surrendered."

Sarah shook her head. "The call we got said a bomb went off, but Captain Drummond over there says Atropos sort of, well, blasted everything in the place. That was nearly twenty minutes ago."

She continued to speak, but I couldn't process what she was saying.

I staggered away from her, towards the ruined books, struggling to accept what I was seeing. Small water droplets fell on my face. I'd seen destruction before, in some cases much worse than a destroyed library.

But I'd never seen death and destruction of this level at the hands of a superhero.

Patrick Campbell, born and raised in Oconee camp, the proud son of an elder, had killed civilians to evade capture. I expected him to try to strangle me to death, but kill civilians? Never.

Captain Drummond was alive, sitting against a wall and speaking to another police officer. Though her dress was torn and she had countless scrapes and bruises, she appeared unharmed.

We made eye contact and she nodded her head towards the fallen bookshelves, where a dozen or so emergency workers were attending to the fallen.

As I walked over, I passed the crumpled body of the fireman who'd been standing next to Captain Drummond. Before I could reflect on how many people Patrick had killed, two emergency workers moved aside, allowing me to see what lay on the ground ahead of them.

"Let me by!" I shoved EMS and police out of the way.

Reid and Ember were laid out side by side, bloodied and unconscious, but still breathing. Marco rested against a pillar, his leg sticking out at an odd angle. He was holding an ice pack to his head. Beyond him was a surly Benjamin, sitting on a table with his arms crossed while an EMS man took his blood pressure.

He looked up, and though he didn't smile, his features relaxed somewhat.

I rushed to my best friend's side first.

"I don't... I don't know what happened," Marco stammered before I could speak, his face haggard. "One second I was standing next to that jackass, and then the next I was lying on top of a bookshelf with a gimpy leg." He sat up with effort and gestured at his broken limb. "God, I'm going to be useless for a while."

Relief flooded through me. He was injured, but not fatally.

I kissed his forehead. "Nobody on this team will ever be useless, remember? Can you brighten this place up a bit?"

Marco shook his head, stopping abruptly to grimace. "No, I used nearly everything when I was fighting. It's too dark outside for a recharge now, and stupid fake fluorescent lights make me sick."

"Then rest for now." I kissed his head again. He closed his eyes and breathed deeply.

Ember and Reid both had bloody lumps on the sides of their

heads, but their pulses were even and strong. I wasn't worried that there'd be any permanent damage—not if Benjamin was there.

Before I left their sides I put Ember's hand in Reid's. Skin contact facilitated telepathy, and while I didn't know if Ember could speak telepathically when she was unconscious, I knew that if she could, she'd want to talk to Reid.

Finally, I walked over to Benjamin, who was hunched over on the table, his right arm in a blue sling identical to the one I'd been wearing when we first met. The medic who'd attended to him was now helping a policewoman with a pencil sticking out of her torso. Dark bloodstains on both their uniforms reflected the dim light.

"What's the damage?" I lightly touched his sling.

He winced. "A sprained shoulder, believe it or not."

"Did you fall down the bleachers?"

"That's the official story. But just between you and me, I got tossed into a wall by some overpowered maniac."

"Been there, done that."

Benjamin laughed, then sighed. "Unfortunately, I'm the one person I can't heal. This thing's gotta heal on its own, which could take a little while. At least it's not broken, right?"

A flashlight's beam momentarily lit up Benjamin's face, and he jerked his head down.

I reached out my hand and brushed his cheekbone with the tips of my fingers, avoiding the cuts and bruises. "You'll heal. I promise. I'm glad you're okay."

The humor in his eyes melted away, leaving empty sadness in its wake. "I don't know where Eleanor is." He peered up at the balcony. "I hope she got out."

"I'm sure she did. I didn't see her when I walked over here."

Benjamin swallowed and nodded. "You deal with this stuff all the time, don't you? Being tossed around, dead people, carnage. I used to dream about being a superhero—can you believe that?" He snorted. "Every kid in America dreams that at some point or another."

"They don't know what they're wishing for," I whispered. "This is what my world's really like underneath all the glamour and rules."

His face darkened. "It's not like my world is any better." Bitterness laced every word.

*Uh huh.* "Before today, when was the last time you were thrown into a wall? Because I can name half a dozen or so times—"

"Don't be stupid. There are worse things than battle injuries."

I raised an eyebrow at his tone.

He pinched the bridge of his nose. "Damn, this is hard to say out loud. I can't believe I'm even thinking it."

I had no idea what he was talking about, so I elected to say nothing.

He took a deep breath and spoke in a rush. "Look. My mom killed those people at the bank a few weeks ago, and it's made me do some thinking. I... I think it might be better if I just didn't go home. Ever."

Benjamin's *mother* had killed the guards? I had trouble believing that the mother of people like Benjamin and Eleanor had decapitated three innocent people.

However, my disbelief warred with my raging curiosity about the peculiar crime scene. How had she killed the guards? What were the Trents trying to steal? Who was targeting Bell Industries, and why? And what did he mean, "didn't go home"?

And though I knew Benjamin's family were supervillains and that he himself had committed crimes, it was still difficult to wrap my mind around the idea that his family were killers.

And why was he telling me this *now*?

Benjamin must have taken my silence for surprise, because he continued. "Don't get me wrong, I care about my family, but... they're not... I mean, we've never really..." He trailed off and stared at the ground. "I just can't deal with all the murders anymore."

"Are you talking about running away?" I crossed my arms, still trying to make sense of what he was saying. It was an odd idea, since he was at least my age. He didn't have to run away, he could just leave. Or did supervillain families have different rules?

He glanced up just then, clearing his throat and looking at someone behind me.

I sneaked a look—it was Captain Drummond, walking our way with a distinct air of aggravation. "We'll talk later," I said in an undertone. "Can you heal the others?"

"Reid and Ember now, Marco later." He hopped off the table. We shared a parting look, then he wandered off towards Reid and Ember's motionless figures on the ground.

Captain Drummond walked up to me, her mouth a thin line. "You're coming down to the station."

"Am I under arrest?"

"No, but we're going to talk about what happened here."

"Captain, I don't—"

"Three of my men are *dead*, Battlecry. I want answers, and so help me, I'm going to get them. Now are you going to do this the easy way, or the hard way?"

I rocked back on my heels. "Hypothetically speaking, what's the hard way?"

She narrowed her eyes at me for a few seconds, then lightened. "That boy you were talking to... he's cute, isn't he? You two looked pretty cozy."

That threw me for a loop. What did Benjamin have to do with this? "He's a friend," I hedged. "He's not important."

"A friend? Interesting. A few weeks ago you said he was your brother. Mason, I believe."

*Oh, crap.* "Um, well, about that. See—"

"I watched him heal Firelight on the security tapes before I destroyed them. I have to say, that is an impressive power. Unique among Supers, even. I've never heard of another healer. Actually, wait, I have." She leaned towards me so our faces were inches apart. "Did you know that Bell Enterprises has hidden cameras in all their facilities that transmit their feed off-site? There was a break-in at the Industrial Complex a little while ago. Things weren't going well for you, were they? And then *Mason* very kindly removed his mask and healed you. Or should I say Benjamin Trent, known member of the Trent crime family?"

I felt as though ice water were in my veins. She had me. "I'll come down to the station. I'll explain everything."

She glanced behind her. Reid and Ember were sitting up, rubbing their heads and blinking. Benjamin was kneeling next to them and talking, probably explaining what had happened.

She smirked at me. "Get your team and get in a squad car."

## 25

Nobody in the police squad room gave much notice to the five battered young people who followed Captain Drummond into the conference room, though a police officer did ask Marco, who was leaning on me, if he wanted some aspirin.

If Benjamin was ill at ease among the police, he didn't show it, instead strolling through the precinct's headquarters as if he owned it. Ember and Reid, on the other hand, were tense and alert, their heads constantly swiveling.

Captain Drummond opened the thick door to the conference room, a gray, poorly-lit space that smelled of coffee and old carpeting. "In here. I'll be back in a minute."

I sat down next to Marco at a metal table with four chairs. The other three stood behind me, leaning against the wall. The wall opposite me was a mirror, allowing me to see them. Reid and Ember were visibly wary, but Benjamin's demeanor—hand on hip, blank expression—made me wonder if he'd done all this before.

Captain Drummond shut the door behind her, leaving us in silence.

"Why are we here?" Ember asked after a few seconds. "Jill, do you want me to listen to—"

"Don't say plans out loud. They can hear us." Benjamin nodded towards the mirror. "The good Captain is in the viewing room right now, probably with a detective. When she does bother to come back in here, I suggest we let Jillian speak for the rest of us. That'll keep things simple. We're not under arrest, so we don't actually have to talk to them."

Reid eyed Benjamin. "Who *are* you? How do you know so much about the criminal justice system?"

Benjamin shrugged.

Before Reid could pursue the topic, I interrupted them. Reid didn't know about Benjamin's sordid affairs, so I pulled out my trump card. "We'll do formal introductions later. Right now all you need to know is that this is Benjamin, and he saved Ember from dying of gunshot wounds last month."

I didn't care if we were being monitored. Besides, the Captain already knew.

As I expected, Reid gaped between Ember and Benjamin. Ember turned pink and nodded. Benjamin merely smiled.

"Since we've established that you can heal, *could you fix my freaking leg already*?" Marco said through clenched teeth. Beads of sweat dripped down his temples.

"Oh, sorry." Benjamin straightened. "I didn't want to do it at the library in front of all those people. A miraculously healed broken leg is harder to explain than two people waking up." He squeezed Marco's hand, and then let it drop. "There."

Marco rested his forehead on the table and breathed in and out. "*Thank you*. That's so much better."

The door swung open. Captain Drummond and a plain clothes officer crossed the small distance to the table and sat down, the former placing a thick file on the table in front of us. The Captain folded her hands in front of her. "This is Detective Yang. She's here as a witness."

Detective Yang inclined her head at my team but said nothing.

The Captain opened the file and flipped through the contents, pulling out three documents covered in yellow highlighting, sliding them towards me. "Read these."

My team, including Benjamin, huddled around me and read.

From what I could tell, they were witness statements for three different crimes. Each one described a house robbery on Saint Catherine's Island, the wealthiest neighborhood in the city by a wide margin. The details were fairly mundane—a break in, a masked burglar—but when I read the highlighted part of the first document, I had to reread it to make sure I'd understood it.

"The robber *flew* out the window?"

The only Super I knew to have been capable of true flight was the first superhero, my great-great-grandmother Christina St. James. She'd died seventy years previously. All other flight was technically telekinetic levitation.

Intrigued, I skimmed the next highlighted section: *He was tall and muscular, and when I told him I was armed the gun levitated out of my hand.*

And finally: *I screamed when I saw him, and I was thrown out of the room by an unseen force.*

Slow realization crept in as a memory fell on me, a memory of emptying Patrick's bank account and wondering at the large amount of money.

I looked up at my teammates, whose faces showed their own disbelief.

Captain Drummond gathered the documents and placing them back in the file. "Sound familiar?"

Reid shook his head. "That's impossible. There's no way Patrick is a criminal."

Benjamin barked a laugh.

Reid shot him a dark look. "No, really. Patrick is a lot of things I despise, but he's not that stupid."

Captain Drummond scribbled in her notes. "Patrick.... so that's his name. I've always wondered if you guys had real names."

"Why are you giving him the benefit of any doubt?" Benjamin asked Reid, glaring. "Or did you not literally stop him from strangling

Jillian earlier? What will make you see him for what he is? What does he have to do?"

For some reason, Reid looked at Ember, then back to Benjamin. "I don't know why I'm even talking to you. But I'm not giving him the benefit of the doubt. I guarantee you that I know him better than you do, and I'm saying that it's unbelievable that a psychotic control freak like Patrick would leave witnesses flapping in the wind." Reid looked away. "He has no problem hurting innocent people."

During their exchange, I simmered on one simple question.

"Why are we hearing about this just now? If you had proof that Patrick was committing crimes, we could've had him removed."

A nameless emotion stirred inside me, leeching into my veins as I weighed the implications of this knowledge. If Captain Drummond had come forward, we all could've been spared months of torment and "discipline." I wouldn't have had to flee my home and friends in disgrace. Everything could've... been different...

The emotion gained a name: rage.

"We didn't have hard evidence. Just descriptions of a possibly tele-kinetic man. The only person we knew of who matched the description was the city's superhero leader. That put us in a delicate position. Instead of passing it on to you guys and tipping our hand, we had to put together a case on our own. Today's display at the library confirmed that Patrick is operating outside the law."

"And you need us to take him down for you."

A chorus of *she knew, she knew, she knew, she knew* echoed around my head.

Ember placed a hand on my shoulder, and though she said nothing to me, I felt calmer knowing she heard my struggle.

"If it comes to that, yes. But for now I want to hear what you have to say about him and his activities. Word is that he beats up on you guys, though I find that hard to believe, considering that I've seen you all in action."

"Anyone can be abused," Benjamin said, his face twisted into a scowl. "And in case you didn't notice, he can throw people into walls with his mind."

Captain Drummond shifted in her chair. "Well, yes. Moving on. For the record, who is the leader now?"

Four pairs of eyes flickered towards me.

"I am."

There, I'd said it. I'd formally declared myself the new leader of Saint Catherine's superhero team, in defiance of all the rules.

"Figured," Captain Drummond muttered while scribbling in her pad some more. "So what happened in the library today?"

"Do you want the whole story, or the short version?"

"The whole story."

Folding my hands on the table, I pursed my lips and deliberated.

Captain Drummond was, from our perspective, a civilian, and civilians weren't privy to superhero business. They couldn't understand our mentality, and what they could understand they might scorn, for we were fundamentally different than them.

But I saw something in her face that made me wonder if I wasn't being fair to the police officer. The shadows under her eyes were so similar to mine, souvenirs of countless sleepless nights spent protecting faceless crowds from faceless threats. Worry lines crossed her forehead, left there by hours of stress. Beneath the bloody sleeves of her evening gown were well-toned muscles, honed in a gymnasium, ready to unleash on an attacker. She sat in her chair as straight and dignified as any superhero I'd met.

The rage subsided.

Captain Drummond, the leader of her team, had had to make a difficult decision. She couldn't have known the ramifications of not coming to us with the witness statements. If I were her, I would've naturally assumed that the whole team was corrupt.

*Ember.*

*Yes?*

*What does she really want to know?*

A pause. *She wants to know why her friends are dead and if she can expect any more deaths. She's really worried that this will turn into a Super versus police situation, and that we'll side with Patrick.*

*Does she think we're on his side right now?*

*No, but she doesn't know enough about us to feel comfortable. She likes you, but she's mad that you lied to her about Benjamin. Which is understandable.*

I sighed. "There's a few things you need to know about how superhero teams work, Captain."

Captain Drummond picked up her pen.

## 26

C aptain Drummond flipped her notebook shut and leaned back in her chair. "All that drama because you left the team?"

I'd been talking for an hour.

My team had listened in silence while I'd explained our whole story, beginning with meeting Benjamin and concluding at Patrick's escape from the library. When I'd reached the part about beating up Patrick, all of them snickered. Captain Drummond, ever professional, kept a straight face, but Detective Yang couldn't help a smirk.

I sighed heavily. "Like I said, I don't think anyone's ever revolted against their leader before. If Patrick hadn't committed bigger crimes and made me look better by comparison, my elder could very well haul me before a tribunal. There's still a chance of that happening."

The Captain thought for a few moments, then turned to Detective Yang. "Go get the newspaper on my desk, please."

The other officer nodded and left the conference room. Captain Drummond sipped from the mug of coffee she'd poured for herself halfway through my story, and I realized how tired I was. It had to be nearly midnight. As if on cue, Ember yawned and leaned against the corner.

Detective Yang returned with a copy of the Saint Catherine

Times-Mirror and threw it down in front of us. The headline screamed:

## ANASTASIA IS CATEGORY 2

Underneath was a satellite image of a large hurricane barreling down on the Atlantic coast.

Benjamin's eyes widened. "Category two? Wasn't it a tropical storm just yesterday morning?"

Everyone exchanged quizzical looks. Marco and I had been so off the grid we wouldn't have heard about a nuclear war. I suspected that Reid and Ember had been too busy with Patrick to watch for weather updates.

Captain Drummond nodded. "Nearly all projections have it making landfall on the Georgia coast." She crossed her arms. "So where are we? None of you are leaving this room until we've decided on a course of action."

"What do you mean?" I asked.

"What I mean is that there's a hurricane coming our way and a cop-killing ex-superhero on the loose. The department will take all the help it can get with evacuations and, if need be, rescues. But I want to know what you're going to do about Atropos. And don't tell me that you're going to handle him by yourselves. He killed three of *my* team today. We're doing this together."

I didn't argue. Instead, I looked sidelong at the door. "Could you give me a few minutes of privacy with my team, please? We need to have a chat before we make any decisions."

Captain Drummond and Detective Yang got up and went to the door. Before she left, the Captain turned around. "I'll be in my office next door." She shut the door with a snap.

*They're not listening to us.* Ember answered my question before I asked her.

I stood up and stretched. "Okay, guys, talk to me."

Reid pinched the bridge of his nose. "We need to leave the city. Patrick is either looking for us or getting ready to. The city has enough to deal with right now, between the scene at the library and the hurricane."

"There's no guarantee he'll follow us if we leave, though," Marco pointed out. "Leaving might very well give him free rein to loot after the storm."

I looked at Ember. "I'm still trying to figure out why Ember never heard what he was doing."

She glowered at me with bleary eyes. "If Patrick ever sensed me in his head when he didn't want me there, he'd dream up lovely little fantasies of how he really wanted to punish me, but couldn't. You want the details, Jill?"

I looked down. "Never mind. Sorry for putting this on you."

Reid tried to pat her shoulder but she shrugged him off, instead retreating to her corner to sulk. We all needed to go to bed, but we were going to have to muddle through this conversation first.

Marco grimaced. "Well, there goes my idea of Ember tracking Patrick down telepathically."

"So we can't really leave, but we can't exactly stay, either," Benjamin said slowly, thinking hard.

Reid cut him off. "No, *we* can't leave." He gestured at the rest of us. "You're not in this."

This was the part of the conversation I'd been dreading. Reid and Ember hadn't said anything earlier when I'd described my run-in with Benjamin and Beau, but I didn't need Ember's powers to know that they were thinking quite a bit.

I held up a hand to silence Reid. "Benjamin, at the library you were starting to tell me something, before Captain Drummond came over. What was it?"

Benjamin fidgeted, his unruffled exterior finally cracking a bit under the intensity of four superheroes staring at him. "Basically... I want to join the team."

There was complete silence for a second, and then Reid burst out laughing.

Marco kicked Reid's shin, causing him to wince.

Benjamin's cheeks turned a vibrant shade of pink. "I'm serious."

"Yes, I know you're serious. Tell me what your thought process is right now. Why do you want to join the team after everything I told you today? You didn't seem terribly impressed with us, honestly."

Reid's mouth fell open. "You can't really be—"

He stopped talking and spun around to stare at Ember, who was still seething in the corner. They traded almost imperceptible facial expressions for a few seconds before Reid huffed and leaned against the wall. "Please, tell us why you want to be a superhero," he said dully.

I would've given my right arm to know what Ember had said to Reid.

Benjamin scratched the back of his head and looked away from us. "When I saw my brother almost kill Jillian, I knew things had gotten out of hand. Not just at the fight, but in a bigger sense, too. I don't want to do this anymore. Mom and Dad are getting more reckless during jobs, like they don't care who gets killed, and now Beau's following their example. It never used to be that way."

"I wanna know why you didn't heal Jillian right away in the warehouse." Marco's tone brooked no argument. Though I trusted Benjamin, I was also curious about his defense. He'd offered to call me an ambulance that night, so why not just heal me?

"I didn't know it was *Jillian*. I would've been healing a superhero who could've possibly put my brother in the slammer. Not my noblest moment, but I had to choose between a stranger and my brother. But I couldn't just leave you to die." He sighed. "So I compromised by trying to call an ambulance. I figured you'd have a chance that way."

Reid and Ember listened with little emotion, but Marco snickered. "It must've been a nasty shock when you found out."

Benjamin's face hardened and he stared at the wall. "Yes, it was."

I had to be delicate. "It's really admirable that you want to trade crime for crime fighting."

Benjamin looked up at me. "But?"

"But you don't care for our ways. You made that clear today in the reading room."

"Neither do you."

"What I don't care for is Patrick's leadership. Yes, some of our rules are... confining, but they keep us safe. They give us structure. And you know what? They produce excellent superheroes." I gestured to my team. "All of us are products of the rules."

Benjamin rolled his eyes, though there was a hardness in his expression that hinted at more than mere sarcasm. "Why are you defending the system that you've worked so hard to get out of?"

That wasn't right. I'd simply broken away from Patrick's leadership, not the entire culture in which I'd been raised.

Or had I?

After all, I was a superheroine who not only had beaten up her leader, but had taken over leadership of his team. At this very moment I was entertaining the idea of taking in a member of the forbidden families, one with a checkered past, and telling him our most closely-guarded secrets. Did all of that add up to a full abandonment of my upbringing?

*Jill!*

Ember's impatient tone snapped me back to inside the conference room and I realized that I had drifted off into my own thoughts. My eyes itched with fatigue.

I planted a hand on the wall, bowing my head and rubbing my forehead while I thought. Sluggish bits of ideas churned in my mind while my team waited for a decision; their palpable impatience with me didn't help my thought process.

Patrick was a poor and ineffective leader, that much was obvious. He'd never bothered to employ the qualities of leadership that he should have. A change was warranted—but was *my* leadership warranted?

*Yes.* My automatic reply was fierce. *You left first, you made the decisions that led everyone here, and you're going to lead them against Patrick.*

*...No. You're overemotional and you have no idea how to lead people in combat. Let Reid do it.*

*Yes. You can lead.*

I was being ripped apart by my own brain. I squeezed my eyes shut and called on my training, imagining I was twelve years old and standing beside other children destined for public service.

*Principle three: decisiveness. I will choose a course of action when required and see it through. Principle twenty-eight: determination. I will defend my city no matter the obstacles.*

The age-old principles and definitions washed over me like balm, soothing my fractured mind. The principles were fundamentally good and right—they were worth supporting. They guided me when I didn't know where to go or how to act.

In a moment of perfect clarity, I saw the solution to the quagmire we were in.

I looked around at my team. "Okay, you know what? The problem here isn't with 'the system.' The problem is with Patrick and the situation we're in. Right now we've found ourselves in a tight spot, and we're making the best of it. We aren't the first team to encounter uncharted territory, and we won't be the last."

"What's your point, Jill?" Ember asked before yawning again.

Annoyance, likely born of tiredness, rose up in me. "My point is that the world isn't going to end if I'm the leader, nor will it end if Benjamin joins the team."

"No." Reid's defiant answer rang around the little room.

I was prepared for him. I looked Reid in the eyes. "This is my final judgment. Benjamin has proved time and time again that he possesses the qualities that, need I remind you, Patrick never did. He'll be a valuable asset to the team."

"I will not serve alongside a *criminal*," Reid hissed. "That's a mockery of everything we stand for. Marco is in the St. James line, but I'm actually of age, and I—I'm letting you lead because I didn't take responsibility when I should have. But I am drawing the line here."

*Oh, he did not just say that to me.*

"You're 'letting' me? Reid Fischer, let me make something perfectly clear."

His jaw tensed, and I geared up for a full rant about how he wasn't my father, elder, or anyone else with authority over me. I had an entire speech about how I was the leader now and that meant submitting to me, whether he liked it or not. That is what leadership is.

Then I saw our reflection in the mirror.

Four haggard people were positioned around the dark-haired woman in the center. She carried herself with quiet strength, and the gleam in her eye dared anyone to challenge her.

That woman was the great-great-granddaughter of the first and greatest superhero who had ever lived.

That woman was the granddaughter of the first Battlecry, who'd led her team until the bitter end.

That woman was me.

I was in a line of women far greater than I could ever hope to be, but I was living proof that those other women had existed. They'd led men and women into battle, Christina against literal armies. My grandmother Battlecry had given her life to protect other people, and her love for her team was so apparent that her enemies had killed them before her, knowing it would be the best way to torture her. I didn't know how to be a leader, but I supposed that their examples embodied some aspect of it.

I *was* going to lead my team and stop Patrick, and the whole world—every superhero, criminal, and civilian—was going to watch us. I didn't care how. I didn't care when. But we would, because we were born to defend Saint Catherine. Nothing was going to stop us—not elders, not rules, and certainly not infighting.

"Yes?" Reid said, ending my reverie.

"Do you believe in the principles?"

His indignation turned to confusion. "What?"

"Do you believe in them? All twenty-nine?"

"Uh, yeah. Why?"

"I do, too."

He studied me, working through what I was saying. "Okay. So?"

I closed the distance between us and put my hand on his shoulder. "I'm not trying to destroy our way of life, I promise. I'm trying to defend it." Reid stared at my hand, but he didn't shrug it off. "I'm your sister-in-arms. Please trust me." I was belatedly surprised by the amount of emotion I was able to put into my soft words.

"Jill, this is too much." He was barely audible. "Heroes are born, not made."

"Then what was Patrick? He's an elder's son and he chose evil. Benjamin is a supervillain's son and he's chosen good. If we can acknowledge that Patrick isn't a hero anymore, we can respect Benjamin's defection to our side."

"We don't *know* him, though. We don't know if he's truly chosen good. What if he just wants to find out our secrets and exploit them?"

"Ember can listen to his thoughts."

Benjamin made a face. "Does 'he' get a say in his defense?"

Everyone turned to him. Reid held out a hand as if to say, *we're listening*.

"Like Jillian said, Ember can hear my thoughts. All of you can beat the crap out of me. So if you're worried about me somehow over-powering you guys, or getting the drop on you, don't flatter me. As for whether I'm trustworthy, I'll just have to earn your trust. But I'd like to remind you that I've been in a position to hurt you all before and I didn't.

"I could've let Jillian die in the warehouse and killed Marco while he was unconscious. I could've let Ember die at the store, but I healed her at the risk of exposing myself as a Super. I could've told Patrick the truth about the wire. Say what you want about my criminal past, but the point stands that I've had plenty of chances to do harm to your team, once in self-defense, and I didn't."

Reid mulled over Benjamin's words. "Okay, you're not evil. But why do you want to be a superhero? Why *now*? Why not just leave your family behind and start over somewhere as a civilian?"

Reid's question was fair. Benjamin's request to join the team was unexpected, and I wanted to know why he was ready and willing to abandon his family for people who were, essentially, strangers.

Benjamin pointed to his sling. "I'm not positive, but I'll bet you anything there are rumors going around that we're dead. Patrick destroyed the library and there is already a body count. When Ember and Reid were laid out on the ground, I thought they were dead for a few minutes. That got me thinking that if I could get on the list of the dead, I could slip away unnoticed and never have to explain to my family why."

He gazed at me. "If you think you had backlash leaving your team, you've got another thing coming. We 'supervillains' aren't as unified as you guys are, but we have a few common beliefs. One of them is that family comes before everything. *Everything*. I can't over-state this. 'Family first. Family always.' That's our one real principle, and God help you if you forget it."

"You need protection," Marco said flatly. "We get it."

"But why would you want to risk retribution by joining up with a public team?" Ember asked. "You wouldn't stay secret long."

"Maybe, maybe not. You guys wear masks, or you used to. But I wanted to join the team because... because... I've always admired superheroes." He stared at a spot on the table, his face scarlet. "I might be the kid of supervillains, but I'm a healer. It's hard to parlay that into criminal enterprise. Whenever I'd hang out with the Rowe or Peery kids, they'd tease me because I was different. They played kill-the-hero, while I stayed on the sideline ready to heal the scrapes and cuts because I couldn't stand the violence. They called me Bleeding Heart Benjamin."

He looked up, but his eyes were distant and unfocused, a thou-sand miles away and years back. "In high school I joined up with JROTC, and even got myself an ROTC scholarship to Old Dominion University's nursing program up in Norfolk. I'd been born on the wrong side of the divide to be a superhero, so I figured the Army was the next best thing. They were eager to have me."

I was impressed, and a little fluttery at the idea of Benjamin in a soldier's uniform. The old sleepy warmth in my stomach returned. "The Army? What happened?"

"My dad happened." There was a lifetime of bitterness in his words. "He said no son of his would ever be the government's stooge, and a nurse on top of it. He made me refuse the scholarship and join the rest of the Trents in our little 'human resources consulting' business. I'd helped out before, but it became my job after high school. That was two years ago."

"You've been studying for nursing school, though. You've been planning to leave."

"Yeah. I was going to float some story about using my position as a nurse to, I don't know, steal pharmaceuticals or something. I hadn't picked a story yet when I met you at Café Stella last month."

"And then today you realized you had an unexpected chance to become a superhero?"

"Yes."

I turned to the rest of the team. "So now that you've heard his story, what do you say?"

I was convinced. I knew there'd be problems because our ways were alien to him—but he wanted to learn, and I wanted to teach him.

Marco shrugged. "I like him. A *real* medic would be a huge perk, plus he can tell us about the forbidden families."

I hadn't even thought of that, but now that Marco mentioned it, I imagined that Benjamin would be an unprecedented wealth of information on our superpowered foes.

Instead of answering, Ember placed a hand on Reid's cheek, gently turning his face to look at her. They gazed at each other for several seconds, until Reid closed his eyes and covered her thin hand with his.

"I know," he whispered.

"He won't," Ember said. "He's not like Patrick."

Reid brushed his thumb along her cheekbone, a terrible sadness lingering between them.

I had to look away.

Finally, Reid turned his attention back to Benjamin, who was examining his fingernails. "I know it's not up to just me, but I'll work with you if you swear to abide by our laws, as much as we do, anyway." He glanced at me. "We'll teach you the principles, the traits, everything. But you came to us, not the other way around. You're doing this our way."

"That's fine," Benjamin said. "Your way."

Reid turned to me. "Jill, are you sure your judgment hasn't been compromised by emotions?"

"I'm sure. I trust Benjamin with my life."

"Thank you," Benjamin said, smiling at me. "You know, we should make this all official. I'm a new member of the team, and Jillian is the new leader. Since those were democratic decisions, there should be a democratic swearing in."

"A what?" I asked. I didn't know what "democratic" or "swearing in" meant.

"What's a democratic?" Ember asked.

Benjamin let out a low whistle. "Wow. Um, it means voting. Never took a civics class, huh?"

I rubbed the back of my head, suddenly unsure. "Nobody voted for me. I just kinda assumed leadership."

Benjamin's infectious grin returned. "All in favor of Jillian being the leader of this team, say aye."

Four ayes echoed around the small room.

I bit my lip to contain my happiness. "Now what's this swearing in thing?"

"It's an official promise you make in front of an audience. You typically raise your right hand and take an oath to do whatever it is that you stand for."

The concept had appeal, but what would I say? "I promise to not be like Patrick"? I hoped that was implicit in my every word and deed up to that point. Marco echoed my thoughts. "What would go in this oath? The principles?"

"Please, not all of them," Ember said, shaking her head. "How about just the sixth, twenty-second, and twenty-third? Those right there are where Patrick screwed up the most."

"I like that," Marco said, a crooked grin lighting up his face.

Reid looked thoughtful, then turned to Benjamin. "You said you raise your right hand?"

"Yeah, and then usually you repeat after someone. I, so-and-so, will or won't do this and that."

Reid considered that. "Before we swear you in, we need to pick a codename for you. It's traditional for teammates to do it, but the leader gets the final word."

Only leaders could pick their own codenames.

"Mercury," I said without hesitation.

"Mercury," Benjamin repeated. "Why that?"

Camp education was thin at best, but we all knew the old myths, with their tales of heroes and mighty deeds. The enormous cast of characters found in myths had provided an almost endless list of codenames over the years. Most teams had at least one codename from mythology.

I pointed to Benjamin's feet. "Mercury had winged shoes that enabled him to run at superhuman speed. His winged stick, the caduceus, is also the emblem of the Army Medical Corps, I believe." Another part of my education: knowing all about the military.

"Plus, he was the god of thieves," Marco said with a snicker.

I tugged on his ear and he winced.

"I like it because it's one mythological name replacing another," Ember said. "I vote for Mercury."

The others echoed her vote.

I faced Benjamin. "If you don't have any objections, raise your, er, left hand, please." His right hand was in a sling, but I figured it didn't matter.

He straightened and raised his left hand, his face somber. I picked the words for his oath, which would be different than mine.

"I, Mercury, promise to defend the citizens of Saint Catherine against any and all who would do them harm, even at the cost of my own life."

Benjamin's eyes shone with an intensity that took my breath away while he repeated his oath. When he finished speaking, the other three patted him on the shoulder and back, murmuring words of welcome and appreciation.

Reid touched my elbow. "I'll give you your oath, if you want. Raise your right hand, please. I, Battlecry."

"I, Battlecry."

"Promise to take upon myself the singular burden of leadership."

My hand trembled, but my voice didn't. "Promise to take upon myself the singular burden of leadership."

"In doing so, I promise to support and defend all that is moral, equitable, and good." The sixth principle: justice.

"In doing so, I promise to support and defend all that is moral, equitable, and good."

"I will be answerable and accountable to my peers for all my actions." The twenty-second principle: responsibility.

Ember looked down, wiping a tear from her eye. I knew in my gut she was thinking about something Patrick had done to her, something he hadn't yet answered for, though I didn't know what. I would make him answer for it, though.

"I will be answerable and accountable to my peers for all my actions."

"I will guard my words, deeds, and thoughts with care." The twenty-third principle: self-control. My weakest area.

I swallowed. "I will guard my words, deeds, and thoughts with care."

"And I will never deliberately harm or attack my teammates," Reid added after a moment.

"Of course not," I said, shocked. Marco hid his grin, and I repeated Reid's addition to the oath. "I'll be the best leader I can be."

I lowered my hand and took a deep breath.

Battlecry was in charge of a team again.

## 27

"You want me to lie on official forms by saying Benjamin is dead." Captain Drummond sounded as if she weren't quite sure she'd heard me correctly. She leaned back in her office chair.

"That's right."

She and I were in her office, but the others were sleeping in the cramped dormitory intended for officers working overnight. My first act as the official leader had been to ask Captain Drummond for the beds. I, on the other hand, had to argue over Benjamin's future.

"Why on earth do you think I'd do that for someone whom I really should just arrest right now?"

*Don't slouch. Look professional.* "He's on my team now, which means you'll have to go to more effort than he's worth to lock him up. Besides, you'll never hear of him committing a crime again."

"Why should I believe you?"

"Because he's *on my team*, and if he's been on my team for thirty minutes, it's the same as if he's been on it for a year."

She glared at me. "You lied to me about him in the first place. As far as credibility is concerned, your name's mud."

"I lied to protect the man who saved my teammate's life," I growled. "Right now, you'd be wise to do the same."

She sat up straighter. "Are you threatening me, Battlecry?"

"No, I'm warning you. Benjamin is the newest sworn member of Saint Catherine's team. His family will want to know where he's gone. If you release a statement saying he's dead, they won't bother searching for him, nor have any reason to think the new superhero in town is their son. If you don't, his family *will* strike, and the city *will* be caught in the middle."

She breathed heavily for a long moment, then pushed herself out of her chair. Though the liaison was impeccably professional, I could see the weight of the day's events in her posture. She walked to the window and opened the blinds.

The tenth-story view was now a hazy nightscape, the city roads spread out like lace as they weaved around and over the many waterways of Saint Catherine. For a whole minute she stood there and gazed out the window, silently watching the late-night goings on downtown.

"They said I'd come to hate you, in the end." Her soft voice carried clearly through her darkened office. "When I received my assignment. They said there would come a day when I realized that I wanted you gone, but I couldn't afford to lose you. Superpowered handcuffs, I believe is the phrase."

I'd never heard that phrase. Handcuffs?

She turned to me, her face unreadable. "I want you gone. I want you out of my city, away from my citizens, and back to whatever backwoods camp sent you in the first place. I didn't vote for the city to bring in a team, and I didn't ask for this assignment. Police never want to deal with superheroes, and do you know why? Because in the end, the Supers run the city. It happened in Chicago, it happened in Mobile, and it's happening here."

"We don't—"

"Oh, shut up," Captain Drummond hissed.

I startled—I'd never seen her break her professional exterior like that.

She strode to her desk, grabbed a leaf of paper from a small stack on her blotter, and thrust it towards me. "Do you know what this is?

It's a letter of condolence to the newly-widowed Mrs. Keenan. Her husband, Patrolman Keenan, died today of a snapped spinal cord. He had two toddlers and a baby on the way. Atropos did that."

She pulled another piece of paper from the pile. "Sergeant Perez. Dead of internal injuries. She was engaged."

A third piece of paper. "Detective Kozak. Married, father of four. Died instantly when he hit a wall."

She slammed the papers down on her desk. "Atropos did that. Atropos, the leader of the superhero team we wanted so badly, did that. And now you are standing here, telling me I have to lie on an official document so a superpowered criminal *can get off scot-free*?"

"Yes."

I was sympathetic to Captain Drummond, I really was. But she had her team to look out for, and I had mine. Negotiating Benjamin's falsified death was my responsibility as the leader and I wasn't going to cave just because I was exhausted and she was yelling. And though it stung that she didn't like us, I wouldn't yield one inch, because we had every right to be in Saint Catherine until the day the mayor formally told us to leave.

"No. I'm not doing it, Battlecry. I swore to uphold the law."

"Then for the protection of my teammate, I'll have to remove my team from the city while he heals. If we have to be gone during the hurricane, then so be it, but I will not risk Benjamin's life by keeping him here when supervillains are looking for him. However, if you simply say that he's dead, we can stay and help you."

"I can't lie—"

"*Hannah*! People will die if you don't! What about this situation do you not understand?"

She sank down into her office chair, her energy gone. "What are you going to do about Atropos? When I said that we're going to handle him together, I meant it."

I chewed on my tongue. I still hadn't come up with a solid plan, but I had some ideas.

"You could send in a request to the Columbia team, or maybe Norfolk's. A few of them are from the Oconee camp, so they might be able to reason with Atropos. No, excuse me, they might be able to reason with *Patrick*." She raised an eyebrow. "He's no longer a super-hero and doesn't get the honor of a codename. Benjamin, on the other hand, does. He's Mercury now."

She threw me a disgusted look. "The last thing this city needs is yet more Supers running around, getting into battles and blowing up buildings. Give me something better."

I settled into the chair opposite her desk. "Well, my team doesn't know what Patrick is going to do next, and we don't have a way to figure it out. However, I'm comfortable saying that he's probably going to come after us. Maybe not this week, or even this month, but he will."

"Yeah, I figured that much."

"So why don't you officially say we're gone, too?"

She closed her eyes and rubbed her forehead. "What are you talking about?"

"Send him on a snipe hunt. Only EMS and cops know that we survived the library fight, right? So tell the press that we're, I don't know, at the Super hospital up in Virginia. He'll go north, and we'll train Benjamin down here in peace while he heals. If we're needed during the storm, we'll keep a low profile."

"And when he's done healing? What then?"

"I... I don't know. We can come up with a long-term plan after that."

"That's not good enough."

"That's what I have," I snapped, heat rising in my cheeks. I took a steadying breath. "Listen, it's in the middle of the night and we're both drained. If you will just make the statements about Benjamin's death and our hospitalization, it'll get the immediate Super problems out of your hair for at least the duration of the storm. Patrick is psychotic, but he's not stupid. He won't hang around in a hurricane zone if he thinks we're elsewhere."

"And the Trents? I don't see why they'd leave the city."

I pondered that for a few seconds. "Well, as far as they'll know, the police have their son's body. If you imply during the press release that you recovered evidence from the corpse, they'll probably leave to avoid arrest."

She sighed. "And where will you go in the mean time?"

I didn't bother hiding my grin. "I know a place for people who need help."

## 28

Father Kokoski said we could stay in the abandoned convent next to the church. The best thing I could say about it was that it was better than the shed.

When the front door swung open with a rusty creak, dust swirled on the floor, revealing the heavier mouse droppings mixed in with it. The dim foyer smelled like mildew, and I was certain I heard something large squeak within the walls.

While we watched, a large spider hanging from the ornate light fixture overhead curled up and scuttled back up to its web, which held the imprisoned corpses of several large flies.

Marco raised his hand and a dim orb of light appeared, casting a soft yellow glow.

The priest nodded in thanks. "It's a bit of a fixer-upper, but it should be big enough for all of you. There's some flood damage on the first floor from Hurricane Camden a few years back, but I think we got rid of all the black mold. If you see any, just stay away. Why don't you all take a look around and get situated? I'll call the utility companies as soon as I'm back in my office, and then I'll get you some supplies. I'll be back in an hour or so."

I shook his hand. "Thank you so much. We couldn't be more grateful."

After Father Kokoski said goodbye and shut the front door, Benjamin kneeled down to examine a fist-sized hole in the wall near the floor that exposed the wiring behind it. "This place should be condemned."

I let out a long breath. So this was where we were going to hide from Patrick. Could the broken windows, cracked ceiling, and rotting woodwork provide any kind of protection?

Was he outside right now?

Ember caught my eye. *I've been listening for him, Jill. He's not there, although Benjamin's thoughts are...odd.*

I looked over at Benjamin. He saw me looking at him and smiled pleasantly.

"We'll continue this conversation later," I murmured to Ember. "Let's just take a look around."

Beneath the gloom and decay of the convent were hints of a formerly comfortable residence.

The kitchen was open and spacious, with a large range and refrigerator. The downstairs living area was large enough to function as a training room, if we stayed long enough to convert it. Down a side hallway were a grimy bathroom and two small rooms that I mentally set aside as the new sick bay and a storage room. The bedrooms upstairs were small, but functional.

I took the smallest bedrooms for myself and my office, and let the others argue over the rest. There were two bathrooms, so I assigned the larger of the two for the men.

After the tour, we all stood in the living room. Benjamin put his hands in his pockets and blew out a breath. "So, any ideas what to do until the priest comes back?"

I sat down against the wall. "How about we start training Benjamin?"

Benjamin perked up. "That would be great." He sat down on the floor, and then the others followed suit, arranging themselves in a loose circle.

I leaned my head back. "Okay, so, being a superhero. As far as I know, you're the first modern superhero who wasn't raised in the camps. Your training is going to be way different than ours."

"There are three camps, right? That's what we learned in school."

"There was three originally. Now there's six: Chattahoochee and Oconee in Georgia—"

"Patrick and I are from Oconee," Ember interrupted. "Jill and Marco are from Chattahoochee."

"I'm from the Coeur d'Alene camp up in Idaho," Reid said. "I grew up on the banks of Lake Pend Oreille."

"And the other three are in Arkansas, New York, and Virginia," I finished. "The Arkansas camp is the newest, I think. The Virginia camp is where superheroes retire after they turn forty-five. All camps are in former national forests, and we live in little shacks and huts. No indoor plumbing or HVAC or anything. Our lives are tough. That's the bottom line of being a superhero, so get used to it now."

Benjamin snorted. "Don't get all sentimental on me."

"I'm serious. We're up at all hours, we fight with our bare hands, and we're always under someone's authority. Come to think of it, that's a good place to start your training. The entire superhero chain of command is called the 'authority umbrella.'"

"We use the analogy of an umbrella because it keeps us safe," Ember explained. "And yeah, we make fun of the whole 'umbrella' thing sometimes, but having a leader to look out for you really is the best way to live. Above the leader is our parents. Then there's the elder."

"Leaders have hard limits about what they can and can't do," I said. "For example, I can't be courted by someone on another team, because it would divide my team loyalty. The rest of you can court anyone you want, though. I'm not really sure what the logic is there. And of course, we can't commit crimes."

"You also can't attack your teammates," Reid said quietly. Ember fiddled with her braid.

Benjamin raised an eyebrow. "I want to know what you consider an attack if beating you guys up all the time doesn't count."

"You know, you're part of the authority umbrella now," Marco commented, pointing at me, his eyes still closed.

Benjamin asked a question to which Reid replied, but I wasn't paying attention.

Marco's comment had dislodged something in my mind. I was the leader, voted in and obeyed as such. But was I part of the official camp authority structure?

The answer was an immediate and forceful "no." Even though my ancestresses were among the greatest heroes to ever serve the American people, that was the past, before we had the principles. Though there was no argument that I was leading—here I sat, the leader— there wasn't a place for me in the official hierarchy of the camps. I could wear the king's crown, but to them I would never be king.

Then again, why did the camps have to know? If I never told anyone of the mutiny, I could go months without having to explain what happened to Patrick. Our lives in Saint Catherine were almost autonomous; we didn't have to communicate with nearly anyone from the camps if we didn't want to, though we had to accept regular deliveries of camp media like *Leadership and Wisdom*, the speeches by Elder Campbell, and other similar items. Nobody back home had a phone.

A strange thought popped into my head: *Do I even want to be in the authority umbrella?*

I didn't understand my own intrusive question. Of course I wanted to be in the authority umbrella, because that meant I could lead and guide my team, protecting them from the consequences of mistakes. Being a leader was so much more than giving orders—it was giving your life for other heroes.

It was standing in front of the people who stood in front of the innocent. It was making sure my team got sleep, food, and housing even though I had no idea what was going to happen tomorrow. It was all the things Patrick had never done.

Images of Patrick yelling and raging swirled with a memory of a woman with dark hair and defiant eyes, and then I was standing on a flat rock back home, overlooking the deep creek that ran through it

and contemplating the best way to catch fish, because Gregory loved
fish and Mom wanted to hang them from trees to entice Gregory to
return from the depths of the forest...

"Jill, wake up."

Marco's gentle hand was on my shoulder, his ever-radiating heat
tangible even through my clothes. I was lying down with my head on
a wadded-up hoodie, though I couldn't recall lying down. When had
I fallen asleep?

Marco smiled, his warm brown eyes crinkling. "You've been
asleep for hours. Father Kokoski brought us tons of supplies, so we've
been setting up while you slept. Lunch is ready."

He helped me up and we wandered into the kitchen, where a
transformation had taken place.

The surfaces were now dust-free and lined with box upon box of
clothes and supplies. Stacked in the corner were five squishy, worn
sleeping bags, topped off with wool blankets. A collapsible card table
and mismatched folding chairs stood in the middle of the kitchen.

Reid stood at one of the counters, cutting peanut butter sandwiches in half. Ember distributed little plastic containers of applesauce to each spot at the table.

Benjamin tossed me a juice box. "Hey, look who's up. Hungry,
fearless leader?"

"Starving." I sat on one of the folding chairs. The rest of the team
joined me. Reid doled out the sandwiches and we began to eat.
"Where did Father Kokoski get all this stuff?"

I sincerely hoped he hadn't spent his own money on us, or worse,
money from the poor box. There were people in the city who needed
it more.

Marco answered. "He said the clothes are from the thrift shop the
church runs. The food is from their food pantry. A bunch of stuff is
from the camping supplies the church's Boy Scout troop keeps on
hand. Everything else was stuff from around the church."

Reid pulled an envelope from out of his pocket and slid it towards
me. "He wanted you to have this. It's money for any miscellaneous
purchases. We agreed that you should be in charge of it."

I peeked inside the envelope. There was at least five hundred dollars in it. I'd never held so much money that I hadn't stolen, though I couldn't help but feel that I was, in a way, stealing from the homeless population. "Why is he being so nice to us?"

I could understand gratitude for saving the life of his loved ones, as Lawrence had expressed just yesterday, but as far as I knew, I'd never assisted Father Kokoski, nor had any member of my team. Someone would've mentioned rescuing a man in a black dress.

Benjamin folded his arms on the table. "I told you yesterday—people think superheroes are virtuous do-gooders. I have to admit, you've got an amazing PR strategy going on. Schools teach an extraordinarily sanitized version of your lives. There are documentaries, books, TV shows, movies, all this crap about how wonderful you guys are." He sipped his juice. "But nothing about the cult."

"What's a cult?" we asked in unison.

"I don't know if 'cult' is really the right word, but I can't think of a better one." He chewed on his lip while he thought. "It's like... a group of people who are totally controlled by someone, and they usually believe weird stuff about themselves, like they're superior or have special knowledge or something."

"That doesn't sound remotely like us," Ember said, affronted.

"Okay, fine. Why can't you guys read books or magazines?" His tone bordered on challenging.

Reid held up a hand to Ember, who was turning red. "Most civilian media can corrupt us. Superheroes have to be pure of mind and heart. God knows where Patrick went wrong, though."

Ember deflated and shook her head. "Patrick was always a mess. A couple of years ago, he asked his father if he could marry me someday. Elder Campbell said no because we were too closely related, and I kid you not, Patrick threatened to leave the camp and live as a civilian. His father dragged him to the center of the camp and beat him in front of everyone."

"He wanted to marry you?" Marco asked, before he mimed vomiting on the floor.

Reid scowled at the table top. I'd never heard this story before, but I suspected he had.

"Yeah. He never bothered to actually court me, though. He was never interested in anything I had to say or how I felt. Well, except once." She turned to Reid. "We arrived a week before you came, remember? When we got to the base camp, Patrick just kept walking around the house, touching everything and saying, 'oh my God, oh my God.' When he saw a bathroom for the first time, he turned to me and asked the strangest question." She screwed up her face into an uncanny mockery of Patrick's permanent scowl. "'Ember, did you know that civilians lived like this?' He looked like a kicked puppy."

Everyone except Benjamin cracked up. I wasn't surprised that Benjamin didn't see the humor; he didn't understand the strangeness of Patrick revealing any sort of weakness or ignorance.

However, I *was* surprised when he frowned and said, "I feel sorry for him."

There was complete silence at the table for several long seconds.

"We're not going to kick you off the team for saying that, but *what*?" Marco stared at Benjamin like he'd just grown a third eye.

"Don't get me wrong, I think Patrick is a terrible person, and I'm not excusing his actions one bit, but I can't help but see why he'd be upset. You guys grew up in totally avoidable poverty, and it sounds like Patrick's dad is a dick. It must've been difficult coming to civilization after, what, twenty-something years of being beaten and starved and finding out that hey, indoor plumbing is a real thing, and his father had kept it from him for no reason."

"There is a reason, though," I insisted. "If you knew our history, you'd understand."

Our complex history, starting before World War I, would take many days to lay out. How could I quickly explain the current philosophy without explaining the dark days of the 1960s?

And if I explained the great upheaval of the first Battlecry's generation, I would have to ultimately explain the rise of the superheroes in the first place. Until Benjamin knew all this, he'd ask these questions. I'd have to be patient.

Still, I was uncomfortable with, well, not how *often* Benjamin asked questions—as I enjoyed teaching him—but how he asked them. His questions usually sounded more like he was interrogating us, with an air of judgment, a speck of sarcasm that made me feel that he knew something I didn't.

I'd allowed it when he wasn't on the team. Now that he was, I was going to put my foot down.

Benjamin took a bite of his sandwich and chewed, his eyebrows drawn together. "Help me understand."

I was ready. "The short version is that after my grandma died, there was a lot of unrest in the camps. People couldn't figure out why we'd been humiliated so badly, or how a team as strong as Battlecry's had been defeated. There was this one guy—"

"Garrett Williamson," Ember said, nodding. "He was from Oconee camp. We call him Elder Williamson, even though he wasn't actually an elder. He died when we were all kids."

"I remember the memorial," Reid said thoughtfully. "We burned an effigy of him in his honor, even though he wasn't a superhero and hadn't died in combat."

"Anyway," I went on, making a face at my interrupting teammates. "Garrett said he knew why Battlecry's team had died: we'd gotten soft with our comfortable lives. Superheroes had to be hard, like the Spartans from the stories. He took the principles that Christina St. James had compiled and fixed their definitions, wrote down the four traits, and came up with our new laws and way of life. No buildings, no women leaders, no medicine, no civilian media, no nonessential education—"

"No dancing, no red if you're a woman," Reid said calmly.

*Wait, what?*

"What the *heck*?" Marco burst out.

Ember and I looked at each other. I'd never heard those rules, and Ember's open mouth indicated that she hadn't, either. Reid's quizzical expression only deepened my own confusion.

Benjamin leaned back in his chair, watching the scene unfold.

"What do you mean, no dancing or red for women?" Ember sounded disgusted.

Reid's gaze darted between us. "Isn't... isn't that how it is in every camp?"

"Oh, yeah, these are the faces of people who know what you're talking about," Marco retorted, pointing to the rest of us.

"What's wrong with dancing?" I demanded. "Or red?"

"Well, dancing tempts people to lust. It's just wiggling your body around. Women can't wear red because it's the color of passion, and men are more likely to be inflamed by passion than women."

Ember slammed her hands on the table and jumped to her feet. "My hair is red. Do you think I'm some kind of whore because I was literally born wearing the evil, inflammatory color?"

"Holy sh—no! That's not what I meant!" He jumped to his feet. "Please, Ember, that's really not what I meant!"

Benjamin watched this all with interest. "I suppose now would be a bad time to tell you that your new leader loves to dance. We danced at the park." The corners of his lips turned up. "That was nice. Less wiggling, more standing close and enjoying each other's presence."

Reid stared daggers at Benjamin, then looked at Ember and me, his hands held up in a placating gesture. "Obviously my camp has different rules. You all can dance, and I don't care. I'm sure there's something you can't do that I can."

"Yeah, lead," Benjamin grunted. "But since Jillian broke that glass ceiling, maybe you should ask Ember to dance with you and see if wiggling your body really is as bad as you think."

"I doubt Reid wants to dance with a red-haired wanton woman," Ember replied silkily. "Dancing while being in proximity to that much scarlet? Who knows what you might do, all overcome with passion." She practically spat the last word.

Red flags flew up all over my brain—Ember and Reid weren't talking about dancing or rules. There was something more to this conversation, something prowling at the edges of my comprehension.

"Stop it," Reid ordered, though his voice trembled. "Just stop."

Ember's mocking expression hardened into the steeliest glare I'd ever seen on her face. She squinted at Reid, undoubtedly throwing a silent barb at him.

Whatever she said, it was enough to make him turn and almost run out of the room.

Benjamin rose partially from his chair. "What was that? Do you want me to go get him?"

Ember threw herself back into her chair. "Screw him. Let him sulk. He deserves to feel like a turd after..." She trailed off, breathing raggedly. She banged her fist on the table, startling us. "Patrick used to say that my hair was a distraction to him during combat. He said one day I'd get what was coming to me for tempting men. My hair is an 'eye trap,' apparently. He was always thinking about... about..." She grabbed her spoon and tried to finish her applesauce.

When it was halfway to her mouth, she broke down, her spoon clattering to the floor.

"Ember!" I turned my chair so I could hug her, but she shoved me away.

"D-don't t-t-touch me." Her voice was shaking so much I could hardly understand her. "*Reid!*"

Reid sprinted into the kitchen door. "What is it?" His eyes darted towards Benjamin.

Ember fled to him, throwing herself against his chest and sobbing without restraint.

He wrapped his arms around her, stroking her hair with such tenderness that once again I felt as though I were witnessing something not intended for my eyes. A flash of a memory, barely tangible, seared through my mind: terror. Ember had projected complete and utter terror.

"Someone needs to explain," I said, my tone underlining that it wasn't a request.

"You do it," Ember groaned. "I... I can't. I don't want to think about it."

Reid grabbed a sleeping bag from the pile. "Why don't you lie down." He guided Ember into the living room. "Just shut your eyes and rest for a while."

She nodded, sniffling and wiping her eyes. They disappeared into the living room. Marco shrugged at me, his eyes wide. Benjamin simply sat with his hand over his mouth.

Reid returned a minute later and quietly cleared away our dishes. When he was done, he sat back down in his chair, his shoulders slumped.

"I have Ember's permission to tell you this. God, I feel like a piece of crap for what I said earlier."

I doubted that's what he needed Ember's permission to tell us. "We're listening."

He cleared his throat, not taking his eyes off the table. "I'm sure you guys were wondering how Patrick found you after your little stunt with the hostages."

I had wondered, but between the events later that day and Eleanor's hypothesis that we'd been recognized, I hadn't spared it an extra thought.

"When Patrick saw Marco's flash on the news, he knew you were still in town, and operating on top of it. He looked for you in that neighborhood, but he couldn't find you. When he got back to base camp, I was at the convenience store, but Ember was in the kitchen." His eyes darkened. "He cornered her and demanded she tell him where you were. She said no. He got so angry at her that he... he tried to..."

I felt the slightest tremor in the earth.

Benjamin leaned forward and put his good hand on Reid's shoulder. "We understand. Go on."

"She sent out a cry for help. It was a scream."

"Oh," I breathed. "I heard that in the library. I thought it was a dream."

Bizarre guilt washed over me; while I'd been happily reuniting with Benjamin, Ember had been trying to fight off Patrick. I imagined how that fight would go, and no matter how generous I was to Ember in my head, I couldn't avoid the fact that six-foot-four, muscular, and telekinetic dominated five-nine, frail, and telepathic in every scenario.

I didn't have a mirror on hand, but I was certain my face was green. I was going to kill him, and I was going to start with very specific dismemberment.

"I ran home as fast as I could. She actually was able to land some good hits on him, and managed to kick him a few times in the face. But it wasn't enough, and she was so terrified, she told him you were at the library. But even that didn't stop him." He looked at me with pleading eyes. "Jill, please, don't be angry at her. She loves you so much. She must have been out of her mind with fear."

"Believe me, nobody's angry at her." Marco's words were low with barely-contained fury. "I'd rather Patrick have a round with me or Jill than Ember."

"Like I said, he didn't stop when she told him where you were. I got him off her before he could actually rape her, but it was a very clear attempt."

I stood up, then turned on my heel and left the kitchen, striding past Ember's still form in the living room, heading to my new, empty office.

The blank space offered nothing to distract me from my homicidal musings, so I gazed out the window into the convent's muddy fenced-in backyard, unconcerned about being spotted.

I watched squirrels scamper around the shady trees, forcing myself to give them names and stories, anything to take my mind off of the memory of Ember's scream.

"Jillian?" Benjamin's voice pulled me back to my ugly reality.

I turned to see him standing in the doorway. "What do you want?"

"Marco thinks you're going to sneak off and look for Patrick."

"And you're here to stop me."

"Like I could. But I would rather you didn't go."

"Why? You don't think I can take him?"

"You're sleep-deprived, emotionally compromised, and weaponless. So... no."

I went back to looking at the squirrels, my forehead pressed against the cool windowpane. "Tell Marco I'm going to stay here like a good little girl."

"Tell me yourself." Marco strode into the room, stopping only when he was next to me. "You have a history of barreling head-first into fights against Patrick. You were thinking about going after him back there, weren't you?"

I let out a disgusted sigh. "Yeah, well, when has that ever worked out for me?"

Reid joined us. "To be fair, it worked once."

I cursed under my breath—I wanted to simmer in my Patrick-hatred alone. Why were they all here, anyway? Were the men all going to lecture me on being overemotional and impulsive?

And why was Reid holding a pair of scissors?

"We'll do that later," Benjamin said, eyeing the scissors. "Let's focus on the issue at hand. She's upset enough right now."

"Don't talk about me like I'm not here," I growled. "Someone had better tell me what's going on."

Benjamin held his hands up. "I'm sorry, that was rude. We just want to make sure you won't run off and try to fight Patrick on your own."

I put my hand on my hips. "Here I am, not running off. Are you going to post a night watch while I sleep tonight?"

Wait a second... what was this "we" business?

"Have you guys been talking about me?"

Their exchanged sheepish expressions confirmed it.

"Are you kidding me? You guys all got together and talked about how I would probably go off half-cocked and get my ass handed to me? And when did you even have this conversation?"

Marco stepped forward. "We never said that. When you were sleeping, and Ember was setting up your bathroom, we got to talking about how you'd be a better leader than Patrick. Honest! But we all agreed that Patrick's identified a weak—"

"A tendency of yours," Reid said quickly. "You're really protective of people close to you. And when you left the kitchen just now, we were worried that you'd sneak out the window."

The craving to slowly push a butterfly knife into Patrick's forehead was nearly all-consuming. But something had changed in the last twenty-four hours. I'd witnessed my best friend being suspended in the air, twisting and gasping for oxygen. I'd endured taunted hints that Reid and Ember had been hurt or even killed. All to manipulate me, and I'd fallen for it each time.

My hands fell from my hips. "I promised to exercise self-control when I said my oath. I meant it. I might need help sometimes, but I meant what I said." Sunlight glinted off the scissor blades in Reid's hand, diverting my attention. "What are the scissors for?"

Once again, the three of them shared significant glances.

I crossed my arms. "What is it now?"

"I think you should tell her," Reid said to Benjamin. "She likes you best."

"No, she likes Marco best."

"Actually, right now I hate all of you just about equally. The next person who acts like I can't hear you is sleeping in the bathtub tonight. Marco, talk."

Marco rubbed his head, reminiscent of Benjamin's nervous tic. "When you were sleeping, we also got to talking about how we're going to shop and stuff while we're in hiding. Civilian clothes are great and all, but...."

"But?"

"But you and Ember's hair sticks out too much."

Reid's grip on the scissors tightened, and understanding crashed down on me like a bag of bricks.

I backed away from them. "No. Hell no."

"Jill, please think about this," Marco begged. "It's for everyone's protection. It'll grow back."

"I'm always going to think you're beautiful," Benjamin said. "And we're not asking for you to shave your head, just cut it, so your hair isn't the first thing people notice. Maybe shoulder-length, like Eleanor's. Don't you think she's pretty?"

I backed into the wall. They couldn't cut my hair if I was pressed up against something, right? I wasn't going to let them cut my hair like I was a dishonored daughter of the camps.

Superheroines who slept around had their hair cut. Camp girls who embarrassed their families had their hair cut. My hair was my glory, my most prized physical feature. My curves were unremarkable, my eyebrows were ridiculous, and my fingers were thin and knobby. But my hair? My hair was my one stunning feature, several luscious feet of dark brown beauty.

But as I stared at the three gaunt-faced young men in front of me, taking in their pleading expressions, I could not help but remember the fifth principle.

*Diligence. I will spare no effort in the defense of civilians or my teammates.*

I hid my face in my hands and stepped away from the wall. "Just do it. Quickly." I slowly turned around.

Gentle hands—I couldn't tell whose—gathered my hair together. There were a few sharp snips, and then I felt something I hadn't felt in years: ends of my hair brushing my shoulder blades. My head was already noticeably lighter.

"We'll talk to Ember when she wakes up," Marco whispered. Reid made an assenting sound.

I kept my face in my hands to hide the most embarrassing tears I'd ever cried. I hadn't been allowed to prepare for this loss, and it was a heavy loss, indeed. I had little in the world, but I had the respect of civilians, and Elder St. James had always let the girls know that their beauty had everything to do with that respect.

"Jillian, will you look at me?" Benjamin's voice lifted my spirits, though not by much, because I was keenly aware that the one person whose attraction I desired more than anyone else's was literally standing on locks of my hair.

I raised my head and met his kind gaze. He didn't look repulsed.

"Let's give them some privacy," Reid said, pulling Marco out of the room and shutting the door behind them.

Benjamin caressed the ragged ends of my hair. "You look really good. I think your hair has natural wave."

"I'm ugly now," I mumbled.

"You haven't seen yourself yet. I can see you, and I say you look magnificent, so there." He was still playing with my hair.

"You're just saying that to be nice."

"Oh, really?" Benjamin pulled his hand away. "You seem to think I grew up in your camps, with your weird teachings about beauty. Well, I didn't. I think you're hotter this way."

I was about to tell him off for making fun of our teachings again, but then I realized what he'd said afterward. "You think I'm hot?"

Nobody, not even Matthew, had ever described me as "hot", and that was a word we had at the camps.

Benjamin rolled his eyes. "Have you seen you? You're a tall, dark, ass-kicking superhero. Of course you're hot."

Then he grabbed me around my waist and kissed me.

## 29

"Are you punishing me?"

Ember stood in the corner of the living room with her head pressed firmly to the wall, much like I had a few hours before. Her wild eyes darted from the scissors on the floor to the front door. I didn't need telepathy to know that she was considering fleeing the convent, possibly back to Oconee camp.

"No," I gasped. "Never. After all we've been through, how can you think that of me?"

"Hair-cutting is for... for *whores!*" She grabbed her hair and stuffed it down the back of her shirt. "You're doing this because Patrick tried to rape me."

Her accusation stabbed at my heart. I kicked the scissors into the kitchen.

"Ember, *no*. Look at my hair. I cut it because our long hair is too noticeable. My new haircut means I can better protect all of you. Don't you want to help me do that? This is something we can do together to help our team."

"Why doesn't Benjamin have to cut his overgrown mess? He's in hiding, too."

She had a point.

"Benjamin, can you come down here, please?" I called loudly. The guys were upstairs, no doubt pretending they couldn't hear the drama downstairs.

A door opened and shut, and then Benjamin appeared, tromping down the stairs. "What's up?"

"Ember raised a good point about haircuts." I gave his hair a significant look. "We're not the only ones who can cut their hair."

Benjamin sighed. "Yeah, I figured this was coming. Where're the scissors?"

I pointed to the kitchen and he went to retrieve them. I turned back to Ember. "I'm not going to force you to cut your hair. But would you consider doing so if Benjamin did?"

She made a face at me. "Swear that this isn't about what Patrick did."

Instead of answering, I approached her slowly, pulling her into a hug. "I swear. Listen to my thoughts. We're going to stop him, Em. We'll make him pay for what he did. Cutting our hair makes it so we can live in peace until the time is right."

Ember wrapped her arms around me, and we stood there in the dim living room until Benjamin, standing in the doorway, cleared his throat.

We broke apart and Ember wrinkled her nose. "You first."

He pulled a folding chair into the living room and handed me the scissors. "I don't care what it looks like, just as long as it doesn't look like a dog chewed on it."

I ran my fingers through his thick, wavy hair and pouted. I'd tangled my fingers in it while we'd kissed, pulling him closer to me, delighting in how he looked and felt nothing like a camp boy.

Though I couldn't recall moving, I'd ended up against the wall, Benjamin's muscular body flush with mine, his hot breath in my mouth, his heady scent swirling, our hands roaming...

Ember smacked me upside the head.

I blushed furiously. "Um, yes, I'll give you as best of a cut as I can.

I've never done this before, so don't expect anything spectacular." I snipped an experimental lock, then another. It wasn't so bad. Soon a dark blond ring of hair encircled Benjamin, and the hair left on his head had a ragged, uneven texture that, unfortunately, did kind of have a chewed-on appearance.

"All done," I squeaked, grimacing. "Your turn, Ember."

Benjamin stood up and touched his hair, tugging on it. "It doesn't feel so bad. I bet I look good. Do you need me to make any other sacrifices to the superhero gods?"

*Get Reid*, I mouthed. Benjamin ran up the stairwell. After a few seconds, I heard Reid and Marco's hysterical laughter.

"The power of a crush," Ember muttered, sitting down and slumping forward on her knees. "Just get it over with. Your length."

"Can do." I pulled her hair out of her shirt and carefully measured where I needed to cut. Like me, she covered her face with her hands.

I worked quickly, mindful of how much each snip of my own hair had assaulted my ears. Her beautiful red hair fell on my feet, leaving a ragged shoulder-length style similar to mine.

She swished her hair around. "My head is so light. How do I look?"

"Gorgeous," I said, grinning. I was so lucky Benjamin had met me first.

Reid's footfalls on the stairwell made Ember freeze momentarily, then gather her hair in her hands behind her head. "Don't look at me!"

I gently removed her hands from her hair. "He's going to have to look at you sometime. It might as well be now. After you're done, let's go out and test our hairdos. We need to buy more supplies, and I need to stop by the shed and get our things."

I left the living room to give them some privacy, trusting that Reid would have the grace to shower Ember with praise, though of course she'd know if he was lying.

However, I didn't think he'd have to. I didn't know the depth of their feelings for each other, but I detected something more than mere infatuation between them. I recalled Reid's barely-controlled fury with which he faced Patrick in the library, understanding now that at least part of that fight had nothing to do with me.

## 30

A fter a late dinner we congregated in the living room to begin training exercises.

Marco and Reid sparred, reviewing basic hand-to-hand moves. I placed a sticky note on the wall and began the slow process of teaching Ember how to throw my knives, which had been rescued from the shed. Benjamin, who couldn't participate in physical training because of his sprain, sat against the wall and watched us for a while before deciding to read the newspaper I'd purchased while shopping for supplies.

Benjamin wrinkled his nose as he began to read. "The Times-Mirror is such a sensationalist rag. Give me the Washington Post any day."

"What's it say?" Marco asked through his mouth guard, blocking Reid's punch with is forearm.

Benjamin began to read with overdramatic enunciation.

"...our city's heroes, saviors of so many citizens, bravely fought against their much-praised former leader, Atropos, in a heart-pounding fight to the death at the John Mosby branch of the Saint Catherine Library. Though the reasons for the showdown remain unclear, unconfirmed online rumors indicate that a massive rift in the team has been forming for months, primarily concerning Atropos' treatment of his teammates. Anonymous sources report that when the smoke cleared from the battle, team heavyweight Battlecry emerged as the new leader of the beleaguered crime fighters."

Benjamin rolled his eyes. "And then there's a million quotes from dippy Atropos fangirls defending him, or trying to excuse his actions. This one chick here says she doesn't believe the rumors that he beat you guys up, and even if they were true, he's probably *very* sorry. Ugh, gag me."

I didn't want to hear about Patrick. "Any news about Hurricane Anastasia?"

Ember hurled her new hunting knife into the wall, missing her target by three inches. She'd already improved since we'd begun training ninety minutes before.

Benjamin flipped to the weather section. "Oh! Here's some good news. It's been downgraded back to a tropical storm. It'll make landfall tomorrow, but NOAA doesn't think it'll be too bad. The city might get some flooding in the lower areas, but I doubt we'll be called in for rescues or anything."

"This entire city is a 'lower area'," I reminded him. "We're at sea level, and there are more creeks, rivers, and marshes around here than dry land, I think. We might not have to do rescues, but there will be displaced citizens for a while. Could be that crime rises because of opportunistic scumbags."

Reid signaled for Marco to stop, then pulled out his mouth guard. "If that's so, we'll have to let the police handle it unless they ask us for help. We're in hiding, remember? I know it's hard, but we'll have to ride this out."

I yanked the knife out of the wall. "I know," I grumbled.

Ember took the knife from me. "If the storm does get bad, do you think they'll call in other Super teams? Who's nearby these days?"

I plopped down next to Benjamin and grabbed a juice box from a small pile next to him. "I don't think they'll call in another team, unfortunately. Apparently the cops aren't big fans of us."

"It would be nice to see another team, though," Reid said, a hint of wistfulness in his words. "My brother Reuben serves in Baltimore. I haven't seen him in years." He sighed. "I miss him."

"I grew up in Annapolis, so Baltimore's team was always in the news," Benjamin said. "Which one is he?"

Reid sat down on the floor near us. Marco and Ember followed suit, settling down and opening their own juice boxes.

"Obsidian. He can manufacture a shadowy substance and turn it into weapons."

"I know who you're talking about," Benjamin said, nodding. "What were his teammates' names, again?" Curiously, his gazed dropped to his juice box and he began to read the nutrition facts.

Reid thought for a minute. "The leader is Imperator. The others are Obsidian, Tiger, Argentine, Valkyrie, and, darn, what's-her-name, the newish one?"

I scowled. "Artemis."

Her real name was Berenice Grantham, and she'd grown up in Chattahoochee camp with Marco and me. She was several times stronger than me, but lacked my speed, senses, and reflexes. She'd always been a bully, and when she'd been called into service she'd driven her thumb into my eye one last time by stealing the codename I'd always wanted.

Patrick probably would've given me the mocking codename Battlecry no matter what I'd asked for, but I never was able to shake the feeling that Berenice had stolen something from me. She probably thought my assigned codename was hilarious.

"Even if the city requested another team, they wouldn't go so far afield as Baltimore," Reid pointed out. "More likely they'd call in the Columbia team. I met their leader a few years ago when he visited my camp for one of those courting swaps. His name is James McClintock."

Marco swore so colorfully that the four of us paused simultaneously and stared at him. Such language was more commonly heard from me, or Patrick.

Ember sipped her juice. "I assume there's a story there. I'm all ears. I gotta hear this."

Marco's demeanor changed in the blink of an eye, going from defiant to defeated, his shoulders slumping. He scowled at the mouth guard in his hand. "James is from the Ozark camp."

"So?" I asked. I'd met a few people from the Ozark camp and hadn't seen any reason to toss profanity their way.

Marco looked at me then in a way I'd never seen him look at me. Disgust, anger, and hurt warred in his eyes—hurt was the most apparent. My simple question had obviously been the wrong thing to say.

"Do you know why the Arkansas camp was founded? Do you *really* know?

"Ozark camp was founded in 1969 because the other camps were getting overcrowded," Reid said slowly.

Marco threw him a look of sarcastic pity. "Yeah, 1969. Six months after the elders lifted the ban on interracial marriages. Take a wild guess where the dissenters decided to move."

Benjamin leaned towards Marco. "Are you telling me there's an entire camp of superheroes in Arkansas built around racial purity? Holy *crap*."

Ember, Reid, and I stared at Marco in shock. I'd never heard that version of events, nor did I want to believe it. Ozark camp was home to several of my Johnson relatives, though I'd never met them. But I also trusted Marco.

"How have we never heard this?" Reid asked, frowning. "James never expressed any bigoted opinions to me when I spoke to him."

Benjamin laughed without humor. "That's not usually the sort of thing people volunteer." He turned to Marco. "But James said something to you, didn't he?"

"Yeah, when his team visited one winter. He was having trouble getting his fire started, so I offered to light it for him, and he told me to piss off. I asked him what I'd done wrong, and he looked me up and down and said I was *unnatural*. I asked my Dad, and he got real quiet and said the Arkansas families didn't think he should've been allowed to marry Mom."

I pictured my Aunt Grace and my Uncle Harold as I'd frequently seen them growing up: holding hands, watching their five children at play or training, their pride evident to all. The thought of not being allowed to marry someone because their skin tone was different was almost ludicrous to me.

Now, a Super marrying someone without powers? *That* wasn't natural. The elders ordered people to be whipped over something like that.

"So let me get this straight," Benjamin said. "Ozark camp are a bunch of racists, and the Idaho camp is somehow even more legalistic than all the others. Do all the camps have their own unique weirdness? Does Oconee have human sacrifices?"

"Why, yes," Ember exclaimed with feigned surprise. "We capture sarcastic supervillains and roast them alive for the summer solstice. I haven't been to a roast since I left, though. I miss the screams."

Marco's indignation was replaced by amusement. "*Damn*, Ember."

I looked Ember in the eye. "If that comment was meant to offend anyone here, think again, because there's no supervillain in this room, and I won't stand for you to threaten the *family members* of people in this room." Ember opened her mouth to argue, but I shook my head. "This isn't open for discussion."

I turned to Benjamin, who straightened. "Stop with the sarcastic comments about us and our camps. We're all superheroes, but we're all human beings, too, with all the flaws and warts that entails. *You* may not be a supervillain, but if you want to make comments about terrible things our relatives have done, I'll tell you a story about three headless corpses I inspected last month."

Benjamin paled. "Sorry," he muttered. "But going back to Marco's story, though... I'm amazed that you guys didn't know about the racism in the camps. It's curious that the Arkansas camp is the racist one, though. I hate to say it, but this *is* Georgia. If any of the camps had a racist undercurrent, I would've guessed it would be the ones in the Deep South."

Marco, Ember, and I gasped at once. I gestured wildly between the three of us. "Did one of us give you that impression?"

Benjamin held up his hands. "No! No, please believe me, that's not what I meant. What I mean is that with the region's history, I would've thought that the Georgia camps would be the likely candidates for problems with interracial relationships."

We all looked at each other. I knew I wasn't the only confused person in the living room. What did our region have to do with racism? That was like saying something about the land and water in Idaho made Reid's camp stricter, which was patently absurd.

"I'm sorry, I don't understand what you mean," I said, rubbing my forehead. "People in Georgia marry different races all the time."

"Well, yeah, but there's always been more racial tension in the South than elsewhere in the country. The Confederacy and segregation and all that, you know?"

"What's the Confederacy?" Ember asked.

I also wanted to know, since I'd never heard the word, nor did I have any clue what he was getting at. I thought segregation might have something to do with superheroes living apart from civilians, but that didn't jive with what he was saying about Georgia or racism.

Benjamin didn't answer right away. Instead, he quietly took in our blank expressions. I got the distinct impression he was doing some careful thinking. "What do you guys know about the Civil War?"

"*Civil* War?" Reid repeated. "How can a war be civil? That's an oxymoron."

Benjamin stared at him, stunned. "Who was Abraham Lincoln?"

That was an odd question. Why would Benjamin quiz Reid on trivia? Civilian education was stuffed to the brim with unimportant information that clogged up their minds. Our educations were super-heroism-oriented.

Reid blinked. "I don't know. What does that have to do with what we're talking about?"

Benjamin whipped around and faced me. "Name five elements."

I chewed on my lip while I thought. "Is that a trick question? I've only heard of four. Earth, fire, wind, and air, right?"

He faced Ember. "Spell 'Virginia,' please."

"V...e...r...j...i...n...y...a."

Benjamin gazed sadly at Marco. "There's a major holiday this week. Do you know what it is?"

Marco shrugged. "We don't celebrate civilian holidays."

Benjamin went quiet then, nodding curtly and picking up his paper and reading in silence.

We all finished our juice and went back to training, finishing up a bit later.

Benjamin didn't even speak when the power came on and the rest of us whooped for joy. When Captain Drummond stopped by, wearing civilian clothes and sunglasses, he didn't say a word while he filled out his superhero registration form.

After she left, Benjamin bade us goodnight and disappeared into his room, slamming his door so hard that dust fell from the ceiling.

I sheathed my knife and turned to Ember. "Dare I ask what his problem is?"

She glanced at Marco and Reid, who were wrestling. Marco had Reid in an impressive hammerlock.

She turned back to me and spoke in a low voice. "No, I don't know what his problem is because he's been using evasive thoughts since the police station. I've been meaning to talk to you about this. You told him I'm a telepath, didn't you?"

I blushed. "I'm sorry. He was asking—"

"—and you told him without a second thought. Jill, I get that you like him, but has it ever occurred to you that this whole thing is one big fact-finding mission for him? He just asks and asks about us, and then when he senses me in his head, it's all boring thoughts. Or thoughts about you two kissing. Ugh."

I crossed my arms, my blush returning. "Just because you find his thoughts boring or distasteful doesn't mean he's hiding something. He's really smart. Maybe you just don't understand what he's thinking about."

"Every time I try to get into his head to see what's up, he immediately starts reciting anatomy terms, translating what we're saying into Latin, or worrying about his sister. I know that kind of behavior. Everyone back home did it when I was around."

"Gee, I wonder why."

Ember glared at the ceiling. "And now he's singing a song in his head. He's doing this on purpose, Jill. He's hiding something. I think his little outburst just now is connected to it."

"You're wrong." I let out a long breath and added, "But I'll talk to him about it later."

"Good luck," Ember muttered. She turned around. "Marco, let go of him. He's turning purple."

I wandered upstairs, my head spinning. The light nausea in my stomach at Benjamin's sudden mood swing didn't bode well. My instincts were telling me that something was seriously amiss with my newest teammate, and I had no idea what my investigation would reveal.

Additionally, Ember was adamant that Benjamin wasn't acting in good faith. Something had gone wrong earlier and the way he'd slammed the door had been just a bit... hostile.

*No, you're reading too much into it. Remember the card? It's not that big of a deal.*

Perhaps this was Patrick's legacy: reading too much into nothing. Who knew how long it would take before I stopped reading a thousand words into one angry sigh.

There was no light shining under Benjamin's door, so I slipped into my sleeping bag and closed my eyes.

The sound of the front door shutting made them open.

Patrick was here.

I jumped out of my bag and grabbed my knife. I was on the landing in the space of a breath, every sense attuned to my surroundings. He was here, and I'd kill him. I'd drive my knife into his brain so fast that he'd never know what hit him. He'd made a huge mista...

A wooden creak to my left made me jolt. Benjamin's door was open, slowly moving back and forth in the breeze from his open window. He wasn't in his sleeping bag.

I inhaled the swirling dust mote in the hallway, locking on to his spicy scent, and followed it down the stairs to the front door. My eyes narrowed as I pulled open the door and began to track the "ex" supervillain's trail.

# 31

Benjamin's scent pulled me nose-first into Downtown, where we'd met the month before. Leafy trees bedecked with Spanish moss arched over the silent avenues and boulevards, forming a ribcage of sorts that shrouded me in shadows as I walked down the sidewalk. The darkness was one of the reasons I enjoyed patrolling in the wealthy district—I could see my enemies, but they struggled to see me. I could appear like the boogeyman and disappear just as quickly.

The other reason was the rooftops.

I scaled a tree and hopped onto the first roof in a block of row houses. These weren't the rundown, fire-trap type homes that I'd seen in Northside. No, these were four-story mini mansions. Their tiny yards were mowed by hired crews, and across the street was a manicured dog park. Large luxury vehicles were parked in front of every house.

Benjamin had turned down this street—hence the rooftop escapade. From my new vantage point, I could see him as he checked behind himself every so often. His hood was pulled up, but the height, carriage, and gait were distinctly his. I silently hopped over the narrow gap between two houses and watched him detour from the sidewalk to a gnarled old tree in a community lot.

He stuck his hand in the hollow of the tree and removed a small box plastic bag. From the bag he removed a small box with multiple antennae, fiddled with it, and then tucked it into his hoodie's front pocket. When he was done with his task, he hurried across the street at normal speed and pulled out a house key.

I ran to the back of the house and saw what I'd hoped to find: a small balcony, probably connected to a bedroom. I swung over the ledge and hung there for a second, getting a feel for the strength of the eaves. When I was sure of their integrity, I lowered myself in a slow, measured way onto the balcony's rail, coming into a perch like a cat.

Through the window, I could see a man's bedroom, if the men's clothes strewn everywhere were any indication. Various posters of lady action movie stars papered the wall, leaving little doubt about whose bedroom I was looking at. A framed picture of Benjamin and a group of friends sat on the bedside table. I was right. They were all in evening wear, probably at the same prom where his date had ditched him for an hour.

A quick, forceful turn of the handle broke the lock of the balcony door, and I slipped inside. I wasn't sure what I was going to do when Benjamin came in, but I'd do something. How dare he come back here? Even if he wasn't selling our secrets to his family —acid bubbled in my stomach at the thought—he was jeopardizing everything I'd worked for by showing his face at his family's home.

Footsteps on the stairs caught my attention. I sat on the bed and crossed my legs. I really did want to hear his reason for being here.

Benjamin walked into the room, but he was looking over his shoulder.

"Didn't expect to see you here, Benjamin."

He yelped and fell into the wall, his hand at his side and grasping at nothing. "*Jillian!* I—how did—why are—"

"You have ten seconds."

He put a hand to his chest to steady his near-hyperventilation, his heart jackhammering against his ribs. "Ten seconds to what?"

"You know damn well *what*."

I stood, noticing how his eyes traveled up and down my form. He wasn't admiring me; he was sizing me up.

He worked his face into a glare, though his eyes betrayed fear. "I came to get one of my nursing textbooks, okay? I'm the new medic. Do you think I'm here to tell my family about you? Do you have that little faith in me?"

Defensive. Accusatory. Trying to throw me off by making me feel faithless. *Nice try.*

I kept my expression grim. "And you couldn't go to the library, a bookstore, or literally *anywhere else* because...?"

I had him.

He averted his eyes. "Fine. I did want my nursing textbooks, but some other things, too. Personal effects."

He retrieved a backpack from his open closet and began to walk around the room, shoving small items into the backpack: the picture from his bedside table, a leather-bound journal, a small shooting trophy from JROTC.

While he worked, I walked to the bedroom door and casually leaned against the wall, biding my time. Just how gullible did he think I was?

After a minute more, he shouldered the backpack and faced me, an ugly scowl plastered on his face. "You can escort me home now."

I slammed his bedroom door shut. He jumped.

Oh, I'm sorry," I said with exaggerated surprise. "Did that seem angry to you?"

He backed up. "What's going on?"

"You tell me." I locked his door. "You aren't going anywhere until you explain your little attitude this evening, and then we're going to talk about something Ember told me."

There was a long silence as he looked at me, probably calculating what I'd said and how he was going to respond. Finally, the straps of his backpack slid down his good arm and he sat on the edge of his bed. "I'm dealing with buyer's remorse. Hate me for it maybe, but it's the truth."

"What's buyer's remorse?"

He clapped a hand over his face. "What's buyer's remorse," he muttered to himself. "Of course you don't know. Well, Jillian, it's the feeling you get when you spend your entire life wanting to be a superhero, and then when you actually get on a team you find out that they're all... you know what, never mind. Let's just go home and forget the whole thing."

My chin quivered as the sickening slime of embarrassment crawled through me.

"They're all what?" My voice cut through the unpleasant quiet like one of my knives. "What's the end of that sentence?"

His sheer level of contempt had wedged itself into my brain, severing his words from my feelings for him and allowing me a level of objectivity I'd never been able to have regarding the boy I'd met in the café.

I realized right then what I'd failed to see before: Benjamin was smart, he *knew* he was smart, and had little respect for anyone he deemed unintelligent. He'd dismissed and derided Eleanor's ex-boyfriend, mocked Reid for believing something unusual, and time and time again used his cocky sarcasm when someone questioned his vast pool of knowledge.

"It's nothing," he said quickly. "Listen, we need to go—"

"We're all *stupid*? Finish what you were saying. We're all *what*?"

"Uneducated!" He jumped to his feet. "My God, what kind of upbringing did you all have? I mean... I mean... what kind of heroes don't even bother to find out what civilians are celebrating? What would you do when the fireworks went off, stand there like idiots and wonder what they are?"

He picked up his backpack and chucked it into the corner.

"I know what fireworks are," I ground out. "Don't you *dare* stand there and accuse us of being idiots just because we aren't as... as... as informed as you are."

He snorted. "Great, so you know fireworks. That'll help you fight crime. And if someone gave you a ransom note, could you read it? Do you even know what ransom *is*?"

"I can read and write." My voice was like steel. "And I know how to cauterize a hand after cutting a finger to send along with a ransom note. I know how to emotionally manipulate a police officer to make her do what I want. I know how to kick down a door so it'll open instead of splinter. I know how to calm children down when their father tried to kill their mother. I know how to protect the people in this city when nobody else can. My entire education revolves around that goal."

"Oh, give me a break. Your entire 'education' was designed to keep you pliable and weak. You don't even have a choice about what you can do with your life."

"I chose to lead a new team! I chose to stay here and take in a criminal—"

"There it is again. I'll never be anything but a criminal to you guys, will I?"

"And I'll never be anything but a stupid hick to you, won't I?"

Benjamin exhaled heavily. "I never said you were stupid. That's —that's not—"

"You called me stupid in the library. 'Don't be stupid. There are worse things than battle injuries,'" I mimicked.

"Don't twist my words. Yeah, I said that, but you know very well that I'd just been tossed around by Patrick and my sister was missing."

Okay, sure. But he wasn't getting out of trouble.

"Twist your words? Well, how's this? You called me an idiot when you called Eleanor's ex-boyfriend an idiot for not knowing what euthanasia was. Oh, that reminds me: when we were kissing, was that an act of *charity* on your part, too? Because you obviously seem to think that stupid people like me don't deserve attention from the likes of you. Should I feel honored that the great book-learned Benjamin Trent sunk to my pliable level?"

Something I said must have bothered him, because for the first time he looked uncertain.

"You're right. I... I was unkind when I talked about Eleanor's ex the way I did. And no, I didn't kiss you as charity," he added, embarrassed. "I did that because I wanted to, and I sensed you wanted to, also." He rubbed the back of his head. "I'm sorry for being an ass."

"I don't care."

And I didn't. I didn't care if he was sorry—he'd endangered all of us by coming back here for trinkets. He'd insulted me and mine even though we'd taken him in and given him his life-long dream. He'd made me feel special and then mocked me. Maybe he was cute and interesting, but I could do better than this, both personally and professionally. I had that much self-respect, at least.

His face fell. "What do you mean, you don't care?"

"I mean if you want to be surrounded my smart people so much, you can stay here. Tell your family that we held you against your will or something. *I don't care.* You're not coming back with me."

I turned to unlock the door, intending to leave the house like a normal person.

He was in front of me in a blur, his hand held up like a crossing guard. "No. I'm not letting you leave until—"

His face was against the door before he could squeak, his arm twisted behind his back in a submission hold.

"What did you just say to me?" Nobody held me against my will. Those days were over.

His breathing picked up again. "Okay, that was wrong of me. But hear me out." His words were slightly muffled from having his cheek against the wood. "If you leave me here, they won't accept me back without questions, and they *will* get the truth out before long. They're good at that. I was seen with you all, and then I disappear? My parents aren't dumb. I'm tainted by my association with you guys, and there will be consequences for me if we meet again. I have nowhere else to go."

I was about to reply when I noticed the goosebumps on his arms that made his hair stick up. His fear was real.

I let go and stepped back, watching warily as he straightened his sling. "Before we go back, I'm going to ask you some questions,

Benjamin, and I want straight, honest answers. Do you understand me?"

He swallowed hard. "Yes."

"Why are you so afraid of your family?" I'd seen him with his siblings on separate occasions, and they were certainly familial, if not overly warm. I doubted they'd kill him.

Yet, he took a shaking breath. "My family has a long and violent history with superheroes. There's a lot of emotion there. If it comes out that I was with you, that emotion will override any love for me."

I swung his computer chair around and straddled it. "What was your role in that history?"

This was the most important part. Harboring a supervillain could get us into trouble beyond his comprehension. Even if we weren't hauled before a tribunal, teams could unite against us if they suspected he wasn't bona fide. When the chips were down and we needed friends, nobody would volunteer to help us.

I'd already started coming up with a few cover stories that hinged on us supposedly not knowing who he really was, but all of them would be shot to crap if, say, the Baltimore team knew him. Considering that he used to live just miles from their territory, it was a plausible threat. I needed to prepare for every eventuality.

Benjamin sat down on the bed again and stared at his shoes. "I've been involved in fights against teams before. They'd show up on jobs sometimes, and it came to blows."

"The Baltimore team, right?"

"No. It was the New York City team and the D.C. team."

*That* was a surprise.

New York City's famously effective team was forty strong across five boroughs, the biggest in the country. This fresh-faced minivillain had faced them and lived?

And Washington D.C.'s team, the Patriot Fighters, were a showcase team that reported directly to the President and protected the White House. As far as I knew, they didn't actually patrol or engage in regular superhero activities. The chances of them locking horns with the Trents seemed slim.

"You've been busy," I said as I worked through his words, doubt swirling with the desire to believe him. "Have you ever killed a super-hero?" I wasn't sure what I'd do if he said yes.

He shook his head quickly. "No, I've never killed a superhero. Or even tried... unless you count the warehouse."

"I don't. Now tell me," I said, tilting my head towards him. "Are those jobs and fights the extent of your past?" I enunciated every word.

He looked me square in the eye. "Yes."

"Is that why you work so hard to keep Ember out of your head? So she won't hear you thinking about your fights against superheroes?"

He looked away. "Yes."

I crossed my arms across the back of the chair and chewed on my lip while I thought about what to do with Benjamin Trent. He'd jeopardized everything by coming here, and he hadn't even had the decency to tell us he was doing it.

However... what harm had *actually* been done except to my ego? He hadn't been seen. His family wasn't here. He was sitting in front of me, shame-faced and contrite.

I could meet him in the middle.

I stood. "Okay."

He drew his eyebrows together. "That's it?"

"Yeah, that's it. I just want to know what I'm dealing with and what I can expect. You and your family have racked up some enemies and there's a lot of bad blood." The corners of my lips curled upwards. "And now you have to choose between college grads who will probably kill you and dumbass heroes who will protect you. This must be hard."

"You're not dumbasses," he said quietly. "I just told you about my past and you'll still take me in. That's... I've been a jerk. I'm sorry. I have no excuse."

The contrition on his face tugged at my heartstrings.

"How about we go home and get some sleep. Bring your pillow, if you want. We can start again tomorrow morning." I got up and joined him on the bed. "I'm sorry for, er, twisting your arm behind your back a few minutes ago. I get a little reactionary sometimes."

He ran a hand through his hair and wheezed a laugh. "Maybe you can teach me how to do that? In fact, would you like to trade? You teach me, I teach you all? Nothing serious," he added upon seeing my affronted expression. "Just some facts and figures that'll make it easier to live in the civilian world."

Instinctual revulsion at the thought of civilian education clashed with a wild desire to be the best leader of the best team in the history of superheroes.

Images of my teammates thoroughly destroying opponents through scholarly cleverness and craft flipped through my mind, but beneath it all lurked the truth: they'd never get on board with it. Not right now, at least. Our lives were already so uncomfortably different than the norm. Exposing them to more would just be cruel.

"O...okay. But just me. I think our team has had enough fundamental shifts in the last few days. School might just send Reid over the edge. Marco doesn't like change either, and Ember doesn't really trust you yet."

"If you say so. It'll just be us, then. I like that. I think I know what we can start with, too."

He eased himself to his feet and walked over to the bookshelf, which was stuffed floor-to-ceiling with at least a hundred books. He pulled off a fat volume and held it up to me.

Upon seeing the cover, I went over to him, taking the glossy book and staring down at the picture on the front.

The cover displayed a battlefield strewn with bodies and carnage. The living and dead wore either blue or gray uniforms, and one of the battle flags was a red rectangle with blue crossed bars, the bars dotted with white stars. I'd seen the flag countless times since moving to Saint Catherine, but I'd never bothered to consider what it symbolized.

"*A Nation Divided*," I read aloud, running my finger along the title. "*An Introduction to the American Civil War*. Why do you have this?"

"When I found out we were moving to Georgia, I thought I should read up on the history of the state." He gestured to the bookshelf. "Take anything that looks interesting. We can go to the library sometime, too. We can study anything you want."

His hesitant smile pricked at the remaining aggravation, puncturing it like a balloon. This was the Benjamin I knew and liked so much, who was concerned about others and wanted to right the wrongs he saw in their lives. Fighting the urge to smile back at him, I turned to the shelf and studied the spines.

I grabbed a slim volume with an intriguing cover of constellations at the same time that he reached for one of the *Danger* novels. Our hands bumped, and he shot me a grin.

The sound of a car door shutting made me pause.

Benjamin looked at his bedroom door, then back at me. "Oh, no. Oh, God, no."

He blurred to the balcony door, his books hitting the floor after he was already there.

I set down my books on the shelf. "Is it your parents?" I'd fight them.

Instead of answering, he shut the balcony door and yanked the curtain across it, then ran to the bedroom door, which he unlocked. "Get in the closet. Don't even breathe."

Something told me to not argue with him about this. I stepped into the spacious closet while he turned off his bedside light and grabbed his backpack. He joined me in the closet, gently pulling me into the back corner with him, then arranging clothes around us.

The front door opened.

Benjamin hugged me to him, his hot breath in my ear. "It's Beau. I disabled the alarm when I came in," he whispered. "You didn't trip it when you came through the balcony, so I don't know why he's here. I thought they'd go straight to Maryland."

"Maybe he wanted personal effects," I whispered back.

He snorted.

Heavy footsteps on the stairwell made us freeze. A large man with a heavy gait was coming our way. He reached the top of the stairs, then walked past Benjamin's room and down the hall. Benjamin held me tight, his heart hammering through his chest in time with mine.

"He's going to his room," Benjamin whispered in my ear. "If he's staying the night, we can wait an hour and go out the balcony and be gone before he knows we were here."

But Beau's business in his room was brief, because the footsteps returned, this time coming back our way.

They stopped at Benjamin's door.

I closed my eyes and reached down for my knife, slowly pulling it out of its sheath on my thigh. Benjamin's hand found mine and he squeezed it. I had no idea what Beau was capable of. I needed to expect anything.

Benjamin's bedroom door opened.

# 32

Beau walked a few steps into the room, stopping where I thought the bookshelf was. He picked up one of the books that Benjamin had dropped, and slid it back into place.

A second later, he began to move around the room, though I couldn't guess what his purpose was. Could he smell individuals like I could? Was he looking for something? Mourning his "dead" brother by going to Benjamin's inner sanctum?

His footsteps stopped right outside the closet door. There was a tiny, almost imperceptible sound of metal clicking against metal as he grasped the doorknob. A knife? A gun? I angled my body so I could spring at him as soon as the door opened.

Benjamin's breath stopped.

"Beau! Come on!" A woman's voice called from downstairs, making us flinch.

"Yeah, I'm coming." Beau's deep voice was so similar to Benjamin's.

His hurried footsteps disappeared out the door and down the stairs, which he took two at a time.

"Did you get the sample?" the woman asked when he was at the bottom.

"Here. Sorry about that."

The woman sniffled. "What were you doing in Benny's room?"

Beau sighed. "Just... I don't know. Looking at it, I guess. It looks like he never left. His stuff's everywhere. Eleanor's room, too." There was a pause. "Mom, please don't cry. I'll make it right. You still have me." He sounded more exasperated than comforting.

"My eldest and my baby," Mrs. Trent moaned. "Those monsters. They weren't even committing crimes. They were just at the library... studying like... like good people..." She dissolved into sobs.

Beau must've ushered her out, because her cries faded and the door shut. A few seconds later, a car engine roared to life.

When the car was no longer audible, I pushed away from Benjamin. "They're gone. Could you hear what they were saying?"

I still hadn't totally figured out what constituted "normal" when it came to senses. I was positive Benjamin couldn't see me in the dark closet, but I could see him. It was a delicious feeling.

"No. I didn't even know they said anything."

"Beau came to get a sample of something, and then your mom called us monsters for supposedly killing you and Eleanor."

"Eleanor's not dead, though." He rubbed his temples. "Great. They're mad at you for something you had nothing to do with. That's going to make it *so* much easier when we finally fight them. Get ready for mom to disintigrate someone. She's not going to be satisfied until she's killed a superhero, I promise you."

"Disintegrate?" I reached over and flicked on the light. "What do you mean, disintegrate?"

Benjamin blinked against the brightness, then sat on a steamer trunk in the corner and patted the empty spot.

I sat, and he let out a long breath. "Now's as good of a time as any to tell you what you're going to be up against. Mom can dissolve small areas of solid objects. Dad can manufacture an *assload* of electricity. Beau is a technopath. He even cut off his hands and replaced them with cybernetic ones that he built himself. Like I told you at the library, Eleanor manipulates probability. She doesn't lose—ever."

A shiver crawled down my spine. Each one of the Trents had a power that I didn't care to face in battle, and now I absolutely believed that he'd fought New York City and D.C. My mind was swift to connect their powers to the crimes in which I knew they'd participated.

Mr. Trent's electricity had likely caused the "zapping" noise the guards heard at the bank, and obviously Mrs. Trent had disintegrated the wall, the vault door, and the guards' heads.

The massive system override at both the bank and the guard shack at the Bell Enterprises Industrial Complex pointed to Beau's interfacing with the computers.

These were highly capable and lethal career criminals—so much so that Benjamin regarded playing dead as preferable to crossing them.

Now we had Patrick on one side and a supervillain family on the other.

"Well, that's just excellent," I grumbled as I pushed myself up. "Let's go home now and get some sleep. It sounds like we're going to really need to train you as hard as you can handle."

"You got it." He fished a small brass key out of the pocket of a bathrobe and kneeled in front of the steamer trunk. "One thing, though. I want my textbooks."

He opened the trunk, then popped out a false bottom. Underneath it lay several medical textbooks, a battered poster that I thought might show a superhero, and a copy of *Codename: Danger*, which bore a sticker advertising that it had been signed by the author. He lovingly touched the novel before moving it aside to grab a small book about first aid.

I kneeled beside him and took *Codename: Danger* out of the trunk. "I think I'll read this. It might be useful to see superheroes through a civilian's eyes." Goodness knew I needed a laugh.

"You can skip turning three hundred pages and check out the babe in the mirror. You guys have cultivated one hell of an image. I can criticize it all I want, but it worked. I'll give you that."

I put my hand on his and he looked up from the pile he was

making. "With me, what you see is what you get. I'm not an image or fantasy. I'm just Jillian."

He gently removed his hand from mine. "Remember what you said at the table, that you're all human and flawed?" He looked away. "I guess you've seen my flaw, too. I really am a snob, aren't I?"

"A little bit, yeah."

He blew out a long breath and ran a hand through his hair. "I, uh, understand if you don't want to date me after what happened tonight. I won't take it personally, and I promise to always be professional. I really do want to be your friend, though."

His plaintive gaze flickered up at me, making my heart swell. He'd admitted his snobbishness and had fully disclosed the hard truth of his past, which couldn't have been easy.

I didn't want perfection, I wanted honesty. I wanted realness and the intimacy it produced. Most of all, I wanted it with him.

My fingers brushed his cheek, a warm smile stretching across my face. "We're good, Benjamin."

We leaned towards each other at the same time. Our lips met, and this time it wasn't a frenzied kiss of passion. His soft lips moved against mine lovingly, tenderly, and I sighed with contentment. His rich scent filled the closet, kindling all sorts of interesting feelings in me.

I pulled away, pecked his cheek, and then stood. "Shall we?"

"We could wait a little longer." There was a note of longing in his voice. "There's a pretty girl in my room and my parents aren't home." But he was piling books into his arms, too.

My hand was one the doorknob when I stopped and turned around, something he said just registering with me. "Beau cut off his hands?" That dude was *crazy*.

Benjamin rolled his eyes. "Yeah, when he was our age. Apparently it helps him talk to computers even more. I think there's some kind of implant in his head, too. He's basically a cyborg at this point." He opened the door. "Let's go via the window."

I eyed his sling. "Why can't we just go out the door?" Even if he could traverse walls and rooftops like I could, he was injured.

"Because," Benjamin said, checking if the coast was clear, "I jammed the wi-fi signal that the cameras use earlier, but Beau returned. He apparently didn't notice what I'd done, but I'm not risking it twice."

"How'd you jam the signal?" I opened the curtain of the balcony door. I wasn't entirely sure what "jam the signal" meant, but it sounded complex.

Benjamin pointed awkwardly at his hoodie pocket with the hand on his bum arm. "I keep a jammer." He shrugged. "Sometimes I gotta get away from Beau."

When we were on the balcony, he peered over the rail and frowned. "Three stories... it's too far of a fall, and I can't climb down when I'm injured. We'll have to go on the roof. If I turn over the planter and climb we can—"

I cleared my throat, already kneeling and holding out my hands so he could step on them. He placed his books by me and took a wobbly step on my hands, allowing me to lift him past the roofline and haphazardly push him over the edge.

After tossing the books up, I merely climbed up the drainpipe. When I was at the top, I swung myself over with feline grace— perhaps slightly fancier than I might've been otherwise—and scooped up the books.

He gawked at me.

I peered around for cameras. "Aren't you worried about being seen?"

He snapped back from whatever fantasy he was in. "Um, no. I used to sneak out the balcony a lot. I arranged the cameras so this route is a blind spot." He pointed across the rooftop roadway I'd used to come.

I tilted my head, a real smile spreading across my face. "Camera jamming, blind spots, sneaking across roofs... you're resourceful, Mr. Trent. I like that."

I thought he'd turn pink and look down, but instead he stared into the distance. "Like I said... sometimes I have to get away from Beau."

Instead of explaining that enigmatic comment, he rearranged his books in his good arm and stepped over the gap between houses and we began the journey home.

I hugged my books to my chest, a thrill of victory coursing through my veins.

When we were on the doorstep of the dark convent, I kissed him on the cheek and unlocked the door, then pushed it open.

"Let's go straight to bed," I whispered. "We can study at night, after they've gone to sleep. They'll never know anything."

"If you asked me," Marco said loudly, "I'd say us not knowing anything is the crux of a lot of problems. Wouldn't you agree, Benjamin?"

Benjamin and I froze in the doorway.

Reid, Marco, and Ember were leaning casually against the wall across from us, their faces a mix of hard disapproval, amusement, and sadness.

"We... were were... um..." My mind reeled as I tried to find a plausible alibi for why we were returning from a nighttime outing with forbidden books in our arms.

Ember pushed away from the wall. "For the last freaking time, Jill: do not lie to me." She jerked her head towards Benjamin. "Go to bed if you're going to start that up, Merc. I'll stay well out of your head from now on if you promise to not sneak out again."

"Fine by me." He zipped up the stairs and out of sight.

Ember held out her hand. "The books, please."

I surrendered them without protest, since I was almost certainly about to be kicked off the team. My last act as leader was *not* going to be a tussle over *Codename: Danger*.

Reid took a book and flipped through it, then looked at the other ones, the lines in his forehead deepening. "You sneaked out for a novel, a book about the solar system, and the Civil War. Why?"

"I was following Benjamin," I muttered. "He left to get some personal effects. We talked and decided it was best if I did some light reading to brush up on my civilian knowledge."

"Yes, I gathered that much when you were both on the sidewalk,"

Ember said. "And I also gathered that what you *really* meant to say just now was that you can't wait to share your books with us, and that you wouldn't dream of hiding something of this magnitude. You know, like our last leader did."

She and I stared at each other. Her judgmental brown eyes bored holes into my own, and I dropped my gaze, too ashamed to look at any of them.

"So, school," Marco said. "This'll be different. I wonder if the priest next door will let us borrow textbooks." He put his hands on his hips. "I'm already the best fighter on this team, and soon I'm going to be the smartest. Get over it now, guys." He waved us off and went upstairs.

Just like that, the atmosphere lightened. Reid handed me back my books with a significant warning look, and I accepted them meekly.

Yes, our lives were about to become very different. I'd been caught red-handed in a scheme that involved lying to my teammates, and I hadn't given the lie more than ten seconds of thought. I really was an idiot.

But I didn't have to be. Education would fill most of my head, and hopefully, common sense would fill the rest. Experience was the best teacher, and I had had no experience as a leader, just as a follower of a terrible man whose actions often forced me to live in secrets and lies. It was reflexive. It was time to shed everything I thought of as "normal."

I closed and locked the front door, then leaned my forehead against it.

When Patrick came back, we'd be ready.

## 33

I pushed play.

"Heroes," began the garbled, vaguely human voices. "You have three days before I kill all five of you."

I pushed stop and passed the phone back to Captain Drummond, then sighed. "I picked up at least two dozen distinct voices, but I don't recognize any of them."

All of the previous five death threats had been crafted with the same incompressible technique, but each employed a unique jumble of varying ages, sexes, and accents. If taken at face value, we were being threatened by hundreds of people, though I thought this unlikely.

Captain Drummond, clad in grungy civilian clothes that made her appear to be anything but a police officer, made a little note on her notepad. "Aside from the threats themselves, we don't have any leads. Our tech guys isolated the same electronic signatures, so we're positive that it's the same person as before, but other than that, zilch. Sorry."

Marco frowned. "That was a short message. He's usually more, er, creative."

Reid and Benjamin exchanged a dark look—last week's recording had detailed, among other things, how Ember and I were going to die. I'd had to physically pull Reid from the door to stop him from going on a crusade.

Captain Drummond flipped her book shut. "Yes, he is, and that's why I dropped by in person. Messages that break a mold usually don't bode well. Not only was this one shorter, it mentioned a specific date. You guys need to be on guard."

I'd noticed that. Something else stuck out to me, too. "All five of you,'" I repeated. "Common knowledge is that we're a team of four, unless you told people about Benjamin."

Captain Drummond shook her head. "By law we can't make digital copies of your registration forms. Mercury's form is under lock and key, and at my house, no less. Nobody knows about him except me."

"So who's number five?" I asked. "Patrick?"

"It must be," she said. "Or maybe our anonymous friend isn't as clever as he thinks. Maybe other teams are getting messages from this guy and he reused this one."

"Now that you mention it, that's a possibility," Reid said. "The average team is five people strong. 'All five of you' could refer to, what, sixty teams around the country?"

"I'll look into it," she replied. "In the meantime, don't get complacent."

"We won't," I assured her. "Thank you."

This was one of the larger downsides to being a superhero: every lowlife, scumbag, crackpot, and psychopath this side of Mars tried to flex their muscles by taking us on. We'd even received a bomb threat during my first month in Saint Catherine. Like most threats, it had come to nothing.

But these were different. I couldn't explain it, but I felt it in my bones. Something was coming.

Captain Drummond packed up, then headed towards the door. When her hand was on the doorknob, she turned to me. "I meant to say before...I like what you've done with the place." She gestured around the living room, which had had a facelift over the last few weeks.

"Thank you," I said graciously. "And thank you for helping us in the *doing*. The workout equipment, especially, has helped immensely."

She shrugged. "It's the team's money." She nodded her head once, then stepped out into the night.

Marco let out a huge sigh. "Three days, huh? What's the plan?"

"For the moment," I said slowly, my hand still on the lock, "Just go back to what you all were doing. I need to think. Whatever you guys do, though, don't worry."

They didn't need telling twice. Reid and Benjamin gravitated back to the small training room in the far end of the convent. Ember curled up on the couch and took up the spool of yarn she'd been holding for Marco, who picked up his knitting needles and launched back into reading a world history book aloud, balancing the book on his knee.

The quiet sounds of clicking needles, Marco's warm voice, and the soft *whumps* of fists colliding with a punching bag mixed together to create a perfect domestic idyll. For me, anyway.

I walked upstairs and down the hall to my office, shutting the door quietly and pulling off my boots. Critical thought was easier when I was barefoot.

I sat in my rolling chair, then opened my desk drawer and removed the most important sheaf of papers, which I'd wedged into a folder marked TEAMS. I'd printed them out just this morning, but hadn't had time to review them yet. Better now than ever. I flipped open the folder, an online article about the Billings team facing me.

*Okay, focus. Billings. You're going to read about Billings.*

The faceless threat-maker was Patrick. Of course it was. Everyone else in the world thought we were in Leesburg, but the sender knew to contact the Saint Catherine Police Department. They knew we were in the city and were trying to flush us out. The fifth person alluded to in the message was Benjamin. Patrick had seen him in the library and... assumed he'd join the team? No, that wasn't right.

I flicked my own cheek. "*Woman*. Focus."

I needed to get through this stack. Work now, give myself an ulcer about Patrick later. That was the rule. I'd spent weeks researching each team in the country, scouring the data to find a team that would stand by our side when we faced Patrick, which was possibly in three days.

But as I turned over each sheet, the truth pounded into my brain: we were alone in this venture. As long as I was the leader, and as long as the team I led insisted on reading and learning, we were outsiders —and nobody was going to help outsiders.

Not that I was about to stop learning, though. I'd had six weeks of near-constant study under my belt, and with each passing book, I wanted to learn more.

Learning was like drinking sea water; the more I ingested information, the more I wanted it. The books were portals to new worlds and ideas, pouring width and breadth into my thoughts in ways I never could've fathomed before. Why, just last night I'd had a conversation with Reid about philosophy. We had spent hours talking about the nature of life and death while sparring.

As my mind grew, so did my desire to travel and explore. I wanted to see England, home of William Shakespeare. He'd written the most beautiful poem I'd ever read.

And the Rocky Mountains—no picture could possibly do them justice. I had to see them myself, feel the ancient stone under my feet, smell the crisp, piney air.

I needed to hold the sand of the beaches of the Pacific Northwest in my hands and let it cascade through my fingers.

But I could never leave Saint Catherine. The information in the folder was abundantly clear: there were teams in almost every major city in the United States, and they would not be understanding if we wound up in their domains. Superheroes existed to fight, not learn and develop.

However, that hadn't stopped me from trawling the internet to find evidence that maybe one person on one team was... like us, whatever that meant.

The Norfolk, Virginia team spent a lot of their time on or near Old Dominion University's campus—were they secretly attending classes? Or merely keeping students safe in the troublesome nearby neighborhoods?

The Texas teams were unanimously the most popular teams in the country. They were in parades, showed up at civic events, and even wore the Texas flag on their uniforms. They were flashy and personable, oh yes, but I knew enough about our methods now to see that it was all still a calculated ploy. Texans were proud of their state's history, and it followed that their teams would plug into that pride.

My finger brushed the face of the man pictured on the last sheet.

Piranha, or Milo Saur, was from my camp. He was one of the few superheroes who allowed his picture to be taken, which the fourth estate of Phoenix, Arizona happily did. Handsome, rugged, and lantern-jawed, Milo was extremely popular—which was why it was such big news that he'd disappeared overnight a month ago. The team had issued a formal statement that he'd gone missing on patrol.

But I knew the truth: Milo Saur was dead. The fact that no supervillain had gloated about killing him indicated that he'd done something to piss off the elders, and a strike team had zeroed in. He probably *had* gone missing on patrol, taken out by someone like my older cousin Kyle, who'd been chosen for strike team duty years before.

I wasn't a coward—*hell* no, I wasn't a coward. I was going to fight Patrick to the bitter end. But we couldn't call for help now, and if we ever left Saint Catherine for anything less than truly dire circumstances, a strike team would zero in on us, too. We could live here in peace as long as we continued to patrol.

Now that I knew about Milo, it was no longer a surprise that we hadn't heard from the elders about Patrick. They'd put off dealing with the naughty elder's son until they were sure we were still alive—since we hadn't been in contact with them—and when the focus was finally off of Saint Catherine and had moved to some other team's drama.

*Speaking of drama...*

My lips twitched as I stapled the print-outs from the Baltimore team's fan page. I'd found a new thread on Reid's brother's fan forums. Obsidian was extremely popular in Baltimore, and some giddy fangirl had showed up outside the team house with a sign that read, "Obsidian, will you marry me?" The ensuing declarations of love in the comments, along with rumors that Reuben that was already secretly married to Berenice, were highly amusing.

No wonder Benjamin had been obsessed with superheroes growing up. We were the best entertainment after television.

The distant rumble of thunder made me turn in my chair.

Far in the distance, lightning lit up the sky like a battle in the clouds. I put all but the Baltimore sheets away and walked to the window, which I opened. Muggy air flooded over me, filling my nostrils with the salty air that rolled in from the Atlantic. Overhead, churning storm clouds heralded another summer thunderstorm. However, this one would have extra firepower thanks to the system currently hurtling past the southeast.

I wasn't worried, though; the amusingly-named Hurricane Ben was slated to continue north and hit closer to Virginia. Still, the pressure tickled my sensitive skin, raising the hairs on the back of my neck.

I shut the creaky window and left the room, heading towards my bedroom. I was too keyed up to study, and reading my novels would be beyond me. I didn't want to interrupt anyone, so sparring wasn't an option.

The quiet fury brought on by the newest death threat, and the fear that underlined the anger, demanded action. My instincts mandated that I wrench open the door and scream for Patrick to come out and fight.

So, instead, I sat down at my early birthday present from Benjamin: an old upright piano. I had discovered that my peerless hand-eye coordination and an excellent memory added up to being a natural piano player.

My instinctual decisions, statistically, had been stupid. Patrick had repeatedly used them against me to great effect, and then I'd almost gotten kicked off the team two days into my position. If sitting around and studying had taught me anything, it was the value of calming down before I reviewed my options.

My fingers soared over the keys, weaving together a sweet melody I'd memorized. Occupying my hands helped me focus on the workings of my brain.

In a few quiet minutes, the tune wrapped around me, teasing out the answer I'd avoided all evening: we needed to get back out on the street *tonight*. If Patrick was planning an attack in three days, he was most definitely in the city. If we moved first, we had the upper hand. We could surveil, maneuver, and move in for the kill on our terms. Ember's telepathy would be the most important element in the mission. She hated scans of that magnitude, but what else could we do?

The notes dropped into the minor key.

Benjamin had never been in combat before. I had to consider his greenness, and plan around it.

We'd focus on his speed. While he didn't have super strength, running at full blast at someone would do the job. He'd picked up basic offensive and defensive moves during the week that he'd been healed, but he really was radiantly untrained in martial arts.

"Jillian?" His soft voice came from the doorway.

I brought the music back up into the major key.

He walked up behind me and began to massage my shoulders. "You only play this song when you're bothered. Talk to me."

"We have to patrol tonight," I murmured.

I turned around to say something, but the words were stolen out of my mouth when I was met by his naked torso. He'd been working out shirtless again, a new habit of his that cheered me endlessly. I gazed up at him, and he grinned down at me.

"Thank you for that," I said. He'd even wound tapes around his hands like a warrior. Yum.

He gently turned my head forward and began to massage the knots in my neck. "Do we have time for the menu planning before patrol? Reid and I were talking about some specific ideas for this week to incorporate more proteins."

"Was meat in any form one of those ideas?"

"Sweetheart, Ember's vegan, and she's dating the chef of the family. Ergo, we're all vegan by default."

"Goody."

"But to answer your question, no. Reid wants her to be able to eat anything he makes in peace. God knows she deserves peace. We all do."

I stopped playing and reached across my chest to catch his hand in mine. "He loves her very much."

I did not relish the thought of telling Ember to go back out while Patrick was out there. Not yet. There was literally no point in telling Reid to leave her side if she did go out—he'd disobey his own father in that matter. I'd seen the murder in his eyes when our anonymous foe had threatened to kill her, reminding me that I was lucky he was a trusted friend and not my enemy.

Benjamin combed through my hair with his fingers. "I'm more concerned about the brunette." His thumb grazed the nape of my neck, relaxing me more than the rest of the massage did. "You've got shadows under your eyes. Have you been staying up all night again?" He sat on the stool next to me and put his arm around me. "Tell me what's on your mind."

Damn him and his sexy northern accent. I could never refuse anything he whispered into my ear. I leaned into his embrace. "I don't want you all to fight Patrick. He's hurt all of you enough. I just want to meet him in the street and end it right then and there."

He pressed his warm lips to my temple. "He's never hurt me. I'll fight him for you."

I smiled. "My champion. Are you ready for your first mission?"

"Now?"

"Yeah, I think so. I'm working out the logistics of an impromptu patrol. It's going to be raining, so that impacts things. I didn't want your first patrol to be in inclement weather, but I don't think we have a choice anymore. Speaking of which," I said as I stood, "I need to tell

Captain Drummond that we're back in business. She might have preliminary measures in mind for Hurricane Ben, even if it's going to pass us."

"Oh, that reminds me... if Marco makes one more joke about that stupid hurricane, I'm going to kill him."

"Just ignore him. I've been doing that for seventeen years."

Benjamin snickered and pulled his shirt on, and we went downstairs to the living room, where our new laptop sat on the side table. I'd refused to put it in my office, since my teammates respectfully didn't enter that room without my permission, and I wanted computer access to be unhindered—and mine to be accountable. I sat down on the couch and put my feet on the table.

Marco, who was still knitting, glanced up at me. "I know that face. Are we going on a mission tonight?"

"Yes. I'll work on the details as soon as I email Captain Drummond. I think it'll just be Reid and me, though."

I typed in the address for my favorite weather website in one tab and my email server in another, then began to compose a message to the captain.

The phone rang. Benjamin picked it up. "Hello?" We never identified ourselves on the phone. "Oh, hi, Captain. Sure, here she is." He put his hand over the mouthpiece. "It's Captain Drummond, and she sounds, uh, stressed."

I held out my hand for the phone without looking up from the screen, though I did glance at the clock on the task bar. It was near midnight. "This should be fun. Captain Drummond. To what do I owe—"

"The storm has turned. NOAA just issued a warning about Hurricane Ben. It's heading straight at us, and now it's a category four. It's gone up two categories in twelve hours—we have to assume it'll be a five by the time it's here."

I caught Marco's eye and pointed to the television, which he immediately switched on.

It was already tuned to the 24-hour news network, which was displaying an enormous circling spiral of clouds barreling down on the southeastern United States. A red bar flashed across the top of the screen, information scrolling across in large black letters. The official seal of NOAA bracketed each end of the bar. Ember tossed aside the yarn and ran out of the room.

I stood, images of hurricane devastation in other cities rushing through my mind. "How far off is it?"

"We've got thirty-six hours."

"Do you need us for evacuations?"

Reid and Ember ran into the room, dressed in their sort-of uniforms: hoodies, khakis, and boots. Marco and Benjamin left, no doubt to get dressed themselves.

"If we've only got a day and a half, then the mayor won't issue the order. More likely we'll all be told to shelter in place. The interstate system hasn't kept up with the city's growth, so gridlock is a threat even in normal weather. If there's flooding, and there will be, people will die in their cars."

I swore. "Okay, I hear you. What do you need from us?"

"You're staying in the city?"

"Captain. Please."

"Then I need you to find a shelter during the storm and stay alive just long enough to help out during rescues. Hurricane Camden decimated the city a few years ago, which is one of the reasons why taxpayers demanded a team in the first place."

"Understood." I gestured at Reid to fetch me pen and paper. When he handed them to me, I hastily began to scribble down notes on how the team would help out during storm preparations. "What about the schools?" I asked distractedly, still trying to come up with ideas. "I'm sure the superintendent will—"

"It's a half day. I just got off the phone with my contact on the school board. Since there's no evacuation order, the mayor doesn't see any reason to cancel. What a moron. Um, forget you heard me say that, please."

I had a feeling that in another life, she and I might have been friends. "We'll be here no matter what. Moron mayor or not."

I thought I heard her laugh before she hung up.

Marco and Benjamin rushed back in, Marco hopping on one foot while he held up his other to finish tying his boot.

I passed the paper around. "This is it, guys. We've got the supposed death threat hanging over us, but that's in three days. We've got a major hurricane coming in less than half that time. The storm takes priority."

"That *would* stop someone from trying to kill us," Marco pointed out. "Even Patrick."

"Right. But right now, let's focus on this problem. It's midnight and raining, so there's not much we can do besides alert the local homeless camps and get them on their way to shelters, high ground, out of the city, I don't care."

Benjamin indicated the paper. "This says I'm with Marco. Why not you?"

"Because she wants you to focus, duh," Marco said, pushing Benjamin towards the door. "Let's go, Merc. Since I'm the senior teammate, you have to do everything I say. This'll be fun."

Reid and Ember kissed each other, then left, hand-in-hand.

I looked at the paper in my hand. I had a stop to make.

---

I DRAGGED my feet as I walked down the dark sidewalk, my boots sloshing through pools of water. Would it *ever* stop raining?

From the moment I'd left the house, for an entire hour, I'd been in the middle of a steady downpour. Great, livid flashes of lightning tore across the sky every minute or so, followed immediately by clashes of thunder so immense that they reverberated in my chest. Water ran in rivulets down my wrists and off my fingers. I probably looked like I'd climbed out of a well.

I turned a corner, the sudden familiarity of my surroundings causing my heart to throb painfully. I broke into a run, but this time the tired, squat homes of my former neighbors flew by as I sprinted towards the former base camp, not away. It was a strange, mental mirror image; the last time I'd been here, I'd not only run away from home, but I'd fled in fear.

I wasn't scared now. I was mad as hell.

I bounded up the steps and kicked down the front door. It flew open and splintered, sending dust everywhere. When my eyes adjusted to the darkness, I was both relieved and disappointed.

There were no footprints in the dust that led to Patrick. My sensitive ears detected no electrical humming from anywhere in the house —the silence was almost creepy, actually. Mildew, musty air, and the rotting food in the fridge mixed in my nose, but there was no trace of Patrick's scent. I'd been so sure he would've holed up here, especially with the storm coming. He was in the city. I just knew it.

The ceiling creaked. I whirled around and faced the stairwell.

"Patrick! Come out and face me like a man, you damned... yellow... baby!" I made a mental note to work on my trash talk after the storm.

Nothing happened.

A mouse squeaked. I whipped out my knife, then lowered it, breathing hard.

Maybe...maybe I was just paranoid because of the death threats. Maybe it really was just some nut job with a computer program and an ax to grind. We *had* received death threats before, and... and the last one had had the wrong number of people in it, since Benjamin wasn't on the team... officially...

I slowly sheathed my knife.

I dragged my fingers along the walls of the narrow hallway as I went room to room, double-checking that my worst enemy wasn't crouching behind a door. Each room was as empty as the last, though.

Bizarre disappointment washed through me, chased by embarrassment. I was dimly surprised by how much I'd been spoiling for a fight.

I stopped in the doorway of the kitchen, my hand curling around my knife's handle. The table and chairs were knocked over, macabre fossils of Patrick's attack. I gently pulled the table back into position and slid the chairs under them. Perhaps I couldn't turn back time and defend my friend, but I could do this, at least. It helped.

There was nothing worth looting, so I didn't bother. Our clothes had all been on the drab side, intended for blending in and being instantly forgotten. The only books were a camp-published dictionary and the multiple volumes of *Leadership and Wisdom*, all of which went into the toilet.

Before I left, I put the door back in its frame. When my foot was on the bottom step, I turned and looked at it.

"I'll be waiting."

Then I left the house for a second time. Unlike last time, I had a soft landing ahead of me in the form of a roof, clothes, food, and friends.

Though it was a long jog home in sopping clothes, I was energized when I arrived at convent. We were back in action. Benjamin was healed. I had a boyfriend. On top of it all, Patrick hadn't returned to the old base camp—and that was enough for me to decide that he might not return at all. Not anytime soon, at least. We'd get through the storm and be ready for the fight when it came.

Ember handed a towel to me when I walked in. "You're in a good mood." Reid was sleeping on the couch.

"We're the best freaking team, that's why." I was only *slightly* loopy from running across the city in a massive thunderstorm in the middle of the night.

"Shall we chant and do a hand stack before bed, then?" She rolled her eyes. "Go to sleep."

Marco and Benjamin blew in through the door, appearing as though they'd drowned twice over. Benjamin accepted a towel, kissed my cheek, and stumbled up the stairwell. Marco muttered something incomprehensible and followed him upstairs and into his own room.

Ember went to wake up Reid, but I put my hand on her shoulder. "I went to the old house," I said quietly. "He hasn't been there. He's coming back, but it won't be for a while, I think." I squeezed her shoulder. "We have more time."

She bit her lip, then nodded. "We went all over Northside and I didn't hear him. I...I don't think he's in the city, Jill. We made it no secret that we were back, and nobody bothered us."

"Good." I checked my watch. "We'll be up at zero nine tomorrow to start hurricane prep. I'm pretty tired, so if you get up before me, can you wake me up?"

"No problem."

I gave her a brief hug, then headed upstairs.

Tiredness crashed on me while I was donning my pajamas, and I sighed in relief as I slid into my sleeping bag. I'd definitely need a wake-up from Ember, who always helped Reid with breakfast.

I closed my eyes, finally at peace.

I awoke to sirens wailing near the convent.

"Wha?" I mumbled, sitting up.

What time was it? The morning light streamed through the window at a low angle, so I figured it was somewhere around zero eight.

As my sleep-fog cleared it occurred to me that there were a lot of sirens. And did I hear people running past the convent? Yes, those were definitely footfalls. Shouts, too.

Ember burst into my room, her eyes wild. "Jill, get up!"

I bolted out of my bag. "What is it? What's going on?"

She shuddered. "It's him. It's Patrick."

I grabbed her shoulders. "Where are the guys?"

She started to cry. "They're still asleep. I woke up when I heard... I heard their thoughts."

I gave her a little shake. "Whose thoughts? *Whose thoughts?*"

"The kids at the high school!" she wailed. "Patrick's killing them!"

## 34

I saw the school buses first.

Two dozen upside down public school buses circled the perimeter of James Oglethorpe High School like an obscene yellow belt, shoved up against the bricks. There was no room for firemen or anybody else to drop down and go inside the school.

Where the line of buses ended, upended cars, many with bodies inside, were jammed into the earth in front of doors and low windows, sticking up like jagged teeth. Every visible exit was blocked.

Inside the school, teenagers and teachers screamed for help.

"They smell gasoline, but the school isn't on fire... yet," I whispered to my teammates, who were huddled with me beneath a tree across from the school. "It's all over the school." I couldn't smell smoke, but the acrid stench of gasoline was overpowering. Patrick's intention was clear. My heart sank, and a distinct off-kilter sensation flooded through me.

He'd struck first.

Benjamin scowled. "This couldn't be more obviously a trap than if he spelled out 'trap' with burning letters on the lawn."

Hundreds of parents and emergency workers thronged around the school, hovering on the edge of the property. The screams from adults, mixed with the cries of the teenagers inside, caused a deafening clamor of hysterics. Emergency vehicles slowly pushed through the crowd, threatening to crush anyone in the way.

I watched the students on the upper floors bang against the windows. "Ember, is Patrick inside the school?"

One window on the north corner was empty—maybe an unused classroom. If we went inside the school, that would be our entrance.

Ember's fingers brushed mine. An image flashed across my mind of a classroom of terrified students staring at me. Behind them, there was a window through which I could see the school. A dead woman was on the floor, her neck broken and her glassy eyes staring at nothing.

*Patrick's in a trailer behind the school. He's holding a class hostage and he's thinking about killing them.*

Patrick's attack was clever; I couldn't send in my team without risking their lives in a firetrap. But his attack begged the question: why hadn't he set the school on fire yet? If he wanted to flex his muscles and *really* intimidate everyone, all he had to do was drop a match and watch the school burn. What was he waiting for?

I motioned for everyone to huddle around me. "You know what I need you to do," I said to Ember.

She wrinkled her nose. "Yeah."

"Are you up to this?"

"I don't have a choice."

"I'm giving you one right now."

She took Reid's hand. "Keep it short, okay?" She closed her eyes, then frowned. "Heads up, scumbag." Her eyes fluttered, then opened.

"Jill," she drawled. Or rather, Patrick drawled. "I'm honored." Ember had initiated telepathic communication with him.

Reid and Marco straightened. Benjamin narrowed his eyes.

"Get to the point, Patrick. What do you want?"

Ember laughed, though it didn't sound like her usual beautiful, high laugh. "I wanted to talk to you."

"So talk."

"Nope. I'm not saying anything more using the red-haired tele-phone. I'm in trailer five. Show up alone and I won't rip out the wiring in the gym. Imagine what that would be like... sparks, gasoline, and a giant wooden room. That's math I like." Ember cocked her head to the side. "Actually, bring Ember, too. The other two can go play boy heroes."

Ember shuddered, then shook her head. "I'm out of his head. Yuck." She cringed.

So this was my choice: going off with Ember to deal with a homi-cidal maniac and maybe the rest of my team dying, or ignore the maniac resulting in hundreds of people probably dying, including my team.

However, with Benjamin's healing and speed, the rescue process would be quicker, with fewer casualties. I still had some tools in my box. I could do this.

I pointed to the empty classroom. "Reid, the north window. Build a stairway and start getting students out through there. Don't let anyone pass within eyeshot of the trailers."

Marco blinked, stunned. "You're really going to talk to him. He'll kill you."

"He might not, but even if he does, we're not in a good position right now. Better my death than all the students. Get as many out as you can, in the shortest time possible." Reid nodded, grim. I put a hand on Benjamin's shoulder. "You ready for your first supervillain mission?"

He gave me a small smile. "Yes."

"Guys!" Marco said, glancing back and forth between us. "Didn't you hear me? Patrick will kill you, Jill!"

"That's a risk I have to take. Every mission has its risks." Frustra-tion was rising. I didn't have time for this.

"You don't know what you're walking into," Marco insisted. "Patrick's probably waiting in there to smack you around some more. He's a better fighter than you are."

The urge to smack *him* rose up, but instead I took a deep breath and turned to Reid. "You're in charge of your group. Get everyone out and then come to trailer five. Do *not* come in or indicate that you're there."

Reid nodded, then beckoned the other two men to follow. Benjamin and Reid disappeared into the crowd, but Marco trailed behind, glowering at me.

Ember and I dashed to the edge of the campus and made our way to trailer five. The other trailers' doors hung open, revealing empty classrooms filled with abandoned backpacks. My heart raced while I raised a fist to the closed door and pounded three times.

"Come in," Patrick's mocking sing-song voice called. Ember was green.

I pushed open the door.

Patrick sat with his feet on the teacher's desk, its rightful occupant dead on the floor next to it. A dozen teenagers stared at us. Some of them were weeping.

One rose partially from his seat. Sebastian Gonzales, Tatiana's brother, watched Ember and I walk into the classroom with a mix of relief and anxiety. The poor kid had had to endure a second attack on his school in fewer than six months.

"Sit down, Sebastian." Patrick waved his hand, and Sebastian was pushed down into his chair. "Class is over when I say it is."

I shut the door behind Ember and me. "We're here. Let the kids go."

Patrick shook his head. "They're here to ensure that you don't do anything... inadvisable."

"Like tearing your head off."

He tutted. "You may be wearing the big boy leader pants, but you're the same old Jill." Patrick took his feet off the desk. "I should've known that you wouldn't actually leave this stupid city. Did you know I've been looking for you all over the east coast? I knew you weren't in Leesburg. I spied on every team from here to Baltimore, tried to figure out which group of do-gooders was dumb enough to harbor you."

He shook his head. "My mistake. You were too in love with this rat hole to leave when I actually had the right to kill you—why would you leave after the library?" He leaned towards me, his eyebrows knit in faux concern. "As one leader to another, there's a fine line between bravery and stupidity. Find it."

I placed my hands on my hips. "You're threatening the lives of a thousand people just so you can taunt me?"

*"You're threatening the lives,"* he mimicked in falsetto. "I can't believe I ever talked like that. Man, I hate heroes."

Ember stepped next to me. "What do you want? Why here? Why now?"

Patrick leaned back, his hands folded behind his head. "You stopped by to see me last night, right? You wanted to fight? Well, here I am." At my expression, he grinned in boyish amusement. "Jill, you kicked down the door, moved furniture, and threw my books into the toilet. I know it was you. But actually, I'm not in the mood for a death match today. I'd rather make a deal."

The blood drained from my face; he'd killed people because of my decision to go back and challenge him. I cleared my throat. "Why would I ever make a deal with you?"

He smirked. "Because if you don't, everyone in that school, including Boulder Boy and Shorty, will die screaming while their skin melts off."

As much as I despised breathing the same air as him, he had me cornered. I sat on an empty desk. "Fine. Talk."

Patrick let out a long breath. "I suppose you think I hate you."

"You haven't given me any reason to think otherwise."

"Fair enough. But you should know, from the bottom of my cold, dead heart, that I don't. None of you are worth that."

I raised my eyebrows but said nothing.

He continued, "Sure, I did hate you all—*you* especially. You never could just shut up and do what you're told. But then I realized that none of it matters. Leadership doesn't matter. Saint Catherine doesn't matter."

"What do you mean, they don't matter?"

He slammed a hand on the desk. "None of it's *real*. I realized that, and I stopped hating you. In fact, I pity you."

"What's not real?"

"*Everything!*" Patrick's roar caused three girls in the back to burst into tears. Ember rushed over to comfort them, but I didn't budge. "The principles, the traits, heroism, villainy, morality, all that bull! None of it is real." He stared at something unseen. "It's all a lie," he murmured to himself.

The conversation was edging into dangerous territory; people who thought morality didn't exist were capable of anything.

"I've made the mistake of calling you crazy." I studied him, waiting for any sudden moves. "But you're not. You know right from wrong. You tried to teach us every night during the readings."

"Oh, please. The bedtime stories are the biggest joke of all. Don't you get it? It's all invented to keep us under their thumbs. The elders gave us the principles as something to aspire to, criminals as an enemy to unite against, and kept us stupid and starving so they could control us. They've been doing it for decades."

Patrick's conspiracy theory was easy enough to dismiss as the ravings of a lunatic, but one part caught my attention.

"They did keep us stupid," I admitted. "But I don't think it was to control us. The elders aren't evil. Whatever they did, they had our best interests at heart."

"Excuse me, lady, but my *father* is an elder. If anyone here is going to make judgments about them, it's me. You don't know even half the stuff they get up to."

I held up my hands. "Fine, that's fair." I needed to calm him down. "When did you start thinking all this?"

"The moment I saw our house. Do you actually believe that we're better heroes because we grew up in shacks without indoor plumbing?"

I opened my mouth to defend Garrett Williamson's decision, but shut it when I realized something: I agreed with Patrick. Cold slime sloshed in my stomach as I accepted the truth of what he was saying.

The principles were real, of course, but he'd pointed out the flaws in our education, and now he was highlighting another irrefutable flaw in our upbringing. I *liked* our house. I hadn't had chigger bites since I moved to Saint Catherine.

"You said you wanted to make a deal." My voice wavered a tiny bit.

He slouched back. "Yes. Like I said, I don't hate you. You and I are two pawns in someone else's game. I'm going to leave, and if you promise not to chase me, I promise I'll never cross your path again." He inclined his head towards me, his eyes almost sad. "You'll never have to see this 'ugly face' ever again. I gotta say, that kinda hurt."

In all my wildest imaginings of this moment, I never would've guessed that he'd offer to leave us alone. The chance at peace—true, honest peace—was tempting.

If he was gone, I could send my team out on patrols with the likelihood that they'd come back alive. We could live and move in the city without fearing invisible hands would push us in front of a car. We both wanted freedom, a new beginning. I hated to admit it, but Patrick was right: we were like each other in some ways.

But unlike Patrick, I believed in the principles. Unlike Patrick, I'd raised my right hand and sworn to uphold justice. Unlike Patrick, I cared about my team. And Patrick had hurt my team, my city, and me. I was going to see him in prison, or I was going to die trying.

Still, I wasn't going to *tell* him that while my teammates and hundreds of civilians were inside a gasoline-doused school with only one exit. This man had just declared to a room full of witnesses that he didn't believe in right and wrong.

In the distance, I heard Reid's loud voice direct students out of the school. I needed to stall just a little longer.

"Before I answer, I need to know something."

"Shoot."

"If you don't hate us, why have you been sending us those death threats?" Obviously they were from him.

He gave me a little confused look. "I haven't sent you any death threats." He raised his arms wide. "Death threats are a coward's way of scaring someone. As you can see, I'm a man of action."

Ember slipped into my mind. *He's telling the truth, Jill. And he doesn't know about Benjamin.*

"What about the gasoline and murders?"

"Those aren't threats. I needed to get your attention." He shrugged.

"And you don't care that you've killed a few dozen people just to get my attention."

"Nope."

"Even if I take your deal, how are you going to get out of here?" I kept my voice neutral. "I can hear ten helicopters above us, and you and I both know every cop in the city is on the scene."

"I'm perfectly happy to wait here until dark," he said coolly, putting his feet back on the desk.

"Or, you let the kids go, make a distraction, and then run," Ember countered, looking up from the three sniffling girls. "If you want, I'll contact Reid and tell him to do something flashy to draw everyone's eye."

Patrick's expression went from calm to leering as he gazed at Ember, his eyes lingering on her low neckline.

She froze. "Oh, knock it off, sicko."

"Or what? You'll sic a kitty cat on me?"

I stood up and stepped between them, shielding Ember from Patrick. "I'll thank you to not harass my teammates."

"Oh no," Ember whispered. "No, no, no." *Why did you have to move between us?*

Patrick's eyes gained a vicious gleam. "Look at you, defending weak little girls from big, bad men like me. That's precious."

My teeth ground together. "This is what a leader is supposed to do."

Patrick's face lit up with delight, his eyes glinting with excited malice. "Did Ember tell you about our little romantic moment before I found you in the library?"

I started to shake. "Yes. What about it?"

*Jill, he's trying to piss you off. Don't fall for it. This is his idea of fun. Calm down. You have to calm down.*

"That must've made you mad." A wicked grin was plastered to his face. "I bet you were chomping at the bit to come fight me and defend this slut's honor. But you never came. Maybe you changed your mind and thought she deserved it? Were you angry that she screamed and cried and told me where you were? *You* wouldn't have squealed on *her*. You're brave. She's a traitorous coward."

I had three knives. If I moved fast enough, one of them could hit a vital organ. Then again, maybe I didn't have to pierce something important. Even a flesh wound would distract him enough for me to get in close and break his neck, or strangle him. My fingers ached to be used; squeezing the life out of Patrick Campbell would be the most supremely satisfying kill I'd ever make.

*Jill, don't! He's trying to rile you up!*

"Get out," I whispered to Ember. "Help the guys."

Patrick chuckled. "Oh, I wouldn't go inside the school if I were you. I doubt Ember wants to see Reid's charred corpse." His eye twitched.

In the distance, I heard a hideous crackling *whoosh* from inside the gymnasium, and then the heartrending screams of students.

"*Leave!*" I shouted at Patrick, pointing to the door. "I'm letting you go! Just get out of here!" I'd kill him another day.

He laughed. "No. The deal's off. I just decided that as much as I want to never see you again, I want to see you try to stop me even more." He wiped a tear from his eye. "You're so much fun, Jill. Thank you." He inclined his head towards me, black humor spreading across his face. "Let's have a death match."

Sebastian lunged at Patrick and tackled him.

I sprinted the few feet between me and the tussling men. Patrick kicked Sebastian in the stomach, only to have me on top of him in the next second.

I brought my knife down towards Patrick's palm, but it flew out of my hand into the wall. Not willing to risk another knife becoming a projectile, I resorted to punches.

"Get them out!" I yelled to nobody in particular.

Out of the corner of my eye, Sebastian limped to the trailer door and opened it. Patrick made the door slam shut, knocking Sebastian backwards.

Patrick pushed me backwards into the desk, my head cracking against the hard wood.

Shaking it off, I grabbed a fallen paperweight and smashed it onto his thumb. He howled and slammed my head into the wood twice.

Once again I was struggling to fight him—telekinesis wasn't easily countered.

A flash of metal flew through the air, and then Patrick dropped on all fours with an anguished cry. Ember's blade stuck out of his shoulder.

"Damn, I was aiming for his heart." She unsheathed another knife hidden beneath her skirt.

Patrick's head jerked up, rage and shock battling for dominance. He looked from the knife to Ember and back again. "You little—"

"Call me a slut again. I dare you."

I kicked Patrick in the stomach.

Sebastian opened the door.

"You asked for it," Patrick growled.

A high mechanical screech combined with the heavy thud-thud-thud of helicopter rotors filled my ears, and the ceiling collapsed under a three-thousand-pound news helicopter falling through the roof.

Patrick and I were now separated from Ember and the huddled students by a mountainous explosion of metal and wood. The bent rotors were still spinning, slashing at the fuselage and spraying sparks that ignited leaking fuel.

Everything happened at once. Patrick pulled a twisted rotor blade towards us and telekinetically wrapped it around me, pinning my arms to my sides before I could react. Ember scrambled over the non-burning part of the wreckage, pulling students out. An explosion in the school rocked the trailer, followed by another explosion, and then another. People outside yelled in terror while helicopters crashed to the ground, onto the school, and into nearby buildings.

Patrick staggered to his feet and disappeared into the choking black smoke. After a minute I was able to escape from the rotor blade, wiggling free. The temperature inside the trailer was already rising.

"Ember! Where are you?" My eyes burned from the oily black smoke.

She coughed. "I'm by the door!"

The burning helicopter lay between the door and me. Could I move it out of the way? As if answering my question, the flames leapt higher, spreading to the ceiling.

"I'm going to go through the wall!"

Before she could reply, I pulled back my fist and punched through the thin wall of the trailer, which splintered easily. I grabbed the sides of the hole and started tearing, throwing every ounce of super strength into my escape. The wall fell away, leaving a hole large enough for me to push through. Gulping down cool, clean air, I fell onto the sidewalk outside the trailer.

A devastating scene lay before me.

Pillars of black smoke rose from downed helicopters all over the campus. Emergency vehicles had been flipped over with their occupants still inside, crushing civilians. The gym was engulfed in flames, which had spread to the main wing of the school. Dead and dying civilians were everywhere. Patrick was nowhere in sight.

I sprinted around to the front of the trailer and located Ember just inside the door. She was trying to remove the lone dead student from underneath the helicopter's fuselage, away from the fire.

I moved her aside and pulled the body out. It was Sebastian.

There was no time to mourn. "We have to get inside the school!" I yelled over the fire and screams. As I spoke, there was another explosion, followed by more terrified pleas from students. I didn't know how much fuel Patrick had dumped in the school, but I had to assume that the entire school was laced with accelerant.

Ember and I rushed to the nearest entrance, where a compact car was shoved nose-first in front of the double doors. With a loud yell of frustration, I shoved the car aside, the dead teenage driver's head banging against the window as it crashed to the ground.

As soon as I'd unblocked the door, a river of students gushed out, stampeding each other in their haste to flee. Ember and I could not get through.

Frantic, I scanned for another entrance. A large, upended pickup truck blocked a nearby window.

Steadying my breath, I began to push it over, straining from the effort. Ember rushed to my side with a small rock in her hand. As soon as there was a foot clear in front of the window, she smashed the rock against the glass, shattering it.

We squeezed through the broken glass into an empty classroom, the shards cutting at our arms and legs. We streaked through the classroom and into the hazy hallway, where terrified students still ran towards the exit, shirts pulled over their faces. The noxious smell of gasoline made my head swim.

"Where are the guys?" I yelled to Ember.

*Upstairs. Patrick blocked off an entire wing. They're trying to break through.*

We began the arduous, smoky journey against the mob, pushing and shoving students and teachers aside as we made our way towards a stairwell, any stairwell, to aid the rest of our team. When we neared the center of the school, I heard the monstrous crackling of flames.

In the main atrium we were forced to detour around a downed helicopter, which had caused another fire, though it burned much smaller because of the tile and stone materials.

The main stairwell was completely engulfed.

We ducked down a rear hallway and clambered over tables and chairs in the cafeteria, eventually finding a small side stairwell. We dashed up into the dense cloud of smoke, eyes burning, and skidded to a halt at the top of the stairs.

The entire second floor hallway was consumed by burning debris, like a hellish obstacle course that stretched the length of the school. Through the dark smoke I could see a pile of locker banks at the far end of the long hallway. They'd been torn from the walls and stacked haphazardly from floor to ceiling.

Above the muffled screams downstairs, the burning wood and stone, and crackling flames I could hear Reid shout to Marco and

Benjamin. They were behind the lockers, trying to make an escape route that would only lead to more fire.

An almost imperceptible creaking rose up from beneath my feet.

"*Tell them to get out!*" I screamed to Ember, who was kneeling on the floor to escape the smoke.

She nodded and closed her eyes, then jerked them open. "They're trapped in the hallway!"

I took my last breath of relatively clean air and began sprinting down the burning hallway, Ember's cries behind me, swallowed up by the creaking of the soon-to-collapse school. *Ember, go back the way we came!*

I'd never felt heat like that. Fingers of white-hot flame licked at my shins and arms, but I kept running. I smelled singed hair, not sure if it was my head, eyebrows, or arm hair that was burning. Maybe it was all three. Maybe my lungs were, too.

If it wasn't for my super speed, I would have collapsed in the hallway and died within minutes, but instead I slammed into the lockers. Reid yelled for the others to get back.

I pulled the lockers down, the scalding metal burning my hands. One by one the banks fell away until I could see the three shocked faces of my teammates. With one last burst of effort, I shoved the final locker banks aside.

There were no students behind my teammates; Patrick must have trapped them while they were doing a final sweep.

Before they could speak, I pointed behind me. "Ben, Marco, run. Reid, sorry, but—" I swept him up into my arms. "Go! Now!"

Wooden beams fell around us as we began our journey down the hallway. Benjamin disappeared in a blur, appearing at the other end a moment later, panting.

Marco raced down the hallway, not slowed by the heat, though I knew he couldn't last much longer than me.

Reid's extra weight on my top half threw me off balance, but eventually we made it to the other end. Benjamin touched all of us on the foreheads, and pain I wasn't aware of on my face, arms, and legs evaporated.

"Downstairs, down the hall, and through the cafeteria," I gasped, dropping Reid.

We ran down the steps and turned into the deserted hallway. We hadn't gone ten steps before a loud rumbling above us told me what I'd feared: we weren't going to make it out on time.

Reid shoved us to the ground as stone floor tiles flew up from beneath us.

The entire second floor collapsed. Thousands of tons of burning rock, steel, wood, wiring, and furniture fell on us at once with a deafening roar. The noise reverberated in my chest while Benjamin, Marco, and I huddled together in the dark around Reid's legs.

The roar stopped as quickly as it had started.

We were untouched, entombed in a small cocoon of stone tiles. The glow from Reid's eyes filled the space with enough light for me to see him kneeling, trembling from the effort of psychically holding up our protection. Sweat dripped off his chin.

All was silent for several long seconds. "Is everyone okay?" I whispered.

"We're fine," Benjamin whispered back. "Reid, can you use the tiles to push off the wreckage?"

"Why are you whispering?" Marco asked in a normal voice, holding up a ball of light. "We want people to hear us."

Reid took a deep breath, and the tiles began to push outwards, rays of sunlight breaking through their spaces. Wreckage fell away and within seconds we were standing in a cleared space of the destroyed school. The bones of the second floor were littered around us, smoldering and glowing.

"Where's Ember?" Reid asked, tense. He craned his neck and searched around us.

*I'm by the trailers and I'm unharmed.*

I sighed with relief, and we began to work our way through the destruction towards the trailers.

Parents and students swarmed the campus, calling out to each other and screaming when they stumbled upon the body of a loved one.

When we met up with Ember, she directed us towards survivors trapped in and under vehicles, but we also helped locate and remove bodies.

The first corpse I extracted was Captain Drummond's.

Over the next six hours, one hundred and seventy-eight bodies were recovered.

## 35

At twenty-one hundred we stumbled into the convent, sweaty and exhausted. I slammed the door behind us and bolted it, then sank to the floor and leaned against the door. My legs were shaking.

"Everyone, eat something and go to bed." I was too tired to sound authoritative. "At sunrise we're starting our search for Patrick. He's injured, so he can't have gone far. I wouldn't be surprised if he's still in the neighborhood." I punched the floor. "Kill him on sight."

I tilted my head back and closed my eyes. Today's earth-shattering Patrick versus Jillian "death match" would be in every newspaper across the country tomorrow...but a burning school and dead children would be in the picture, and the story would end with the psychopath getting away. This was not how I'd imagined our showdown.

Benjamin kneeled down and put his arm around my shoulders, lifting me up. His arm had several raw burns. "Let's all go to the kitchen and have some water first. I guarantee you we're all dehydrated."

I poured five glasses of water from the water pitcher in the fridge and passed them around, my trembling hands sloshing the water a few times.

While they drank, I studied my vague reflection in the water. Soot and blood speckled my face. My eyebrows were gone. Shaking my head, I gulped down my water, suddenly aware of how parched I was.

Marco broke the silence. "Jill, the storm is coming. We won't have time to search for Patrick."

"Then you guys can go help with the storm, and I'll search for him."

Marco slammed down his glass. "So you can get your ass kicked again?"

My own glass burst in my hands, flinging water and shards everywhere. "In case you haven't noticed, he needs to be put down," I hissed. "We can't afford to wait out the storm."

If *he'd* pulled out Captain Drummond's mangled remains from beneath a car, he wouldn't have been saying these words. If *he'd* had to tell a maimed Tatiana and her parents that Sebastian had died at fourteen years old, he wouldn't even consider waiting to go after Patrick.

"We have to!" Marco banged his fist on the table. Ember put her hand on his, but he waved her off. "Use some common sense for once!"

I rose out of my chair, heat flaring in my face. "You obviously have something to say, Marco, so say it."

He stood up. "You act like it's so simple, like you're ready to run off and fight Patrick, even though we've got a hurricane coming and you have no idea what you're going to do when you find him!"

My hands balled into fists. "We rarely have an idea of how we're going to take down other Supers. It's *always* a last-minute decision."

"No, that's just poor leadership. You and Patrick both have no idea how to lead. If you did, two hundred people wouldn't have died today."

Ember jumped up. "Marco! What's wrong with you?"

"You went and talked to him even though you knew nothing good could've come from that! Instead of helping with the rescues, you went and pissed him off even more!"

I took a deep breath. "Marco, you don't know what you're talking about. I didn't have a choice. As we saw, Patrick was perfectly willing to set the school on fire. I delayed his doing so by several minutes, allowing the three of you to get more people out than you would have."

Marco was trembling. "I know exactly what I'm talking about. You're a terrible leader. The second Patrick showed up, you ran off with Ember with no plan except to, what, talk him to death? Meanwhile, the three of us were running around in a burning building."

"Go to bed, Marco. You're tired."

"Don't talk to me like I'm a child!"

"I'll stop talking to you like you're a child when you stop acting like a child." I crossed my arms. "I stand by my decision. Patrick put us in a corner and that was the best option for everyone involved. He's shown us time and time again that he will kill innocent people."

"It was a stupid decision," he spat. "You went in there ready to *die*, with no thought of how that would affect anybody else."

"Marco, go cool off," Reid said, his voice a low rumble. Marco opened his mouth to argue, but Reid stood. "*Now*."

Marco stormed out.

I blinked at his retreating form, struggling to comprehend what had just happened. I knew Marco was tired and emotional—dozens of corpses of people one's age would make anybody emotional—but his outburst had been over the top. I hadn't seen attitude like that from him since we were kids. Marco was nearly eighteen, far too old for such displays.

"What's his problem?" I mumbled.

Ember mopped up the water. "Anger and fear are a bad combination. He's afraid you'll go run off and die trying to kill Patrick. And he doesn't even know about your trip to the house last night and its connection to today."

I rubbed my forehead. "I'm going to go talk to him, then go to bed.

We'll come up with tomorrow's plan tomorrow. There's no time for storm prep anymore, so we might have to play it by ear."

I walked up the stairs, rehearsing my possible opening lines. *I know you're upset with me and I want to fix it. We're heroes and this is what we do. I'll keep myself safe, I promise.*

"Jillian, wait," Benjamin said from the bottom of the stairs.

I turned and saw his worried face. Glancing once at Marco's door, I turned and walked down the stairs. "Yes?"

He stroked my hair. "Give Marco some space. Let him sleep on it. He's angry and humiliated right now, and we're all running on fumes."

I shook my head. "I don't want him being angry at me anymore. I can't stand when he's put out with me. I should talk to him."

"What if I said I needed a medic?"

"What?"

He gestured to the raw patch of skin on his arm.

"Oh!" I gently took his arm and examined the oozing, angry burns. "This needs attention." I took him by the hand and lead him down the hall to our new sick bay. Because of Benjamin, we hadn't needed to use it since moving in.

I grabbed a clear bottle of burn gel from a cardboard box full of first aid supplies and uncapped it, squeezing out a handful.

"Keep an eye on your burns," I said quietly, applying the gel to Benjamin, who sighed and closed his eyes. "I've seen burns turn nasty. Marco can tell you some stories." I removed a roll of bandages from the box and began to wind them around Benjamin's arm. "Not only has he caused burns, he used to be our medic. Then I met you."

"And then everything went to hell," he muttered.

I looked up in surprise. "What? No. Why would you say that?"

"Well, you met me, and then everything that happened, happened."

"Nah. You were the push I needed. But beating up Patrick? Taking over the team?" I tied the end of the bandage into a knot and fastened a clip to keep it in place. "I think I would've done that no matter who

I met that day in the café. But I'm glad it was you, and I hope you're glad it was you, too." I stroked his chin, enjoying the scruff there.

He captured my hand in his. "I am glad. So glad."

My voiced dropped to a whisper. "Benjamin?"

"Yes, sweetheart?"

"Am I a good leader?" My voice cracked with emotion.

He pulled me to him and touched his forehead to mine. "There were a few minutes today when the three of us were resigned to the fact that we were going to die, but you showed up and pulled down white-hot metal with your bare hands to get us out." His lips brushed mine. "It's an honor to serve under someone that courageous. God knows I'm not. I ran away from home and faked my death."

"You are courageous," I said, sniffing. "Your family is scary, but you're a superhero anyway."

We stood in the silence for a minute, listening to each other's breaths.

Finally, when I'd calmed down, I said, "I'm going to bed. You should too."

I walked upstairs and crawled into my sleeping bag.

I awoke at zero two thirty to the sound of civil defense sirens, eerie and echoing in the winds of Hurricane Ben.

## 36

"That's everything," Reid said, placing the last cardboard box in my closet.

The entire second floor of our home was littered with boxes and furniture, stowed there in case of flooding. Benjamin had endured a hurricane once and said we'd likely see some high water.

It was zero four, and though we were still exhausted from the previous day's activities, the roaring wind was enough to ensure we worked quickly.

I handed out ponchos. "Okay, guys, this is it. The church's entrance is one hundred meters from our door. I can see the best in the dark and Marco's got the light, so we're going to lead." I glanced out the window and took in the sight of rain flying sideways. "Let's make this fast."

We shouldered our backpacks and slipped on the ponchos, then trooped downstairs.

Before I turned the front door knob, I took a deep breath. "Brace yourselves."

I opened the door.

The howling wind swallowed up all other sounds, filling my ears with a constant scream. Small bits of debris flew through the air, a serious threat in the pre-dawn darkness. Nearby houses had already lost shingles, and a lone blue recycling bin tumbled down the street.

Thankfully, there was no flooding, but water had already started to pool around storm grates. A coastal city's water table was high enough; I didn't want to imagine what a storm such as this would do to the drainage system.

Marco raised an orb of light and we all joined hands, bending forward into the wall of wind. We were strong, but the storm was stronger.

Bit by bit we moved towards the church, which also functioned during the week as Sacred Heart Day School, and now as a city storm shelter. Eventually we stumbled onto the flagstones of the entryway, the building's wall blocking the wind.

Through the two sets of glass entryway doors, I saw Father Kokoski run to let us in. "Come in, come in! Thank God you're here. I was worried you'd try to stay in the convent."

Murmuring words of thanks, my team went inside. I was the last to go, and before I entered, I gave our home one last look. As I watched, a piece of roof tore off and was hurled into the darkness.

There was chaos in the shelter.

City employees were trying to organize at least two hundred citizens—families with children of all ages, homeless people, and even some college students. People were huddled in every available corner. Small children tore around the building, some screaming and crying that they were going to die. Others were systematically removing the pictures of students from the cork board, and another had knocked over the statue of the pretty lady in blue. Men yelled at each other while women huddled together, trying to soothe their families and each other.

Many of the items I remembered from my first visit were gone. The stand with pamphlets about sacraments had been replaced by a registration table. Beneath the grotesque decoration of the dying man hung a new sign pointing the way to Supply Distribution. Where the silver water dispenser had once sat were now boxes of blankets.

In the center of the room, the three city employee huddled together, their shoulders hunched as they spoke in low, tense voices.

We approached the city employees first and introduced ourselves, then offered our assistance. The city employee in charge, a harried woman named Juliet, nodded towards the yelling men.

"We have all the supplies we need. Our biggest problem is maintaining order. I've been squishing rumors since yesterday that we're running out of food. If word gets around that supplies are low, we'll have a riot on our hands. Can you help keep people calm?"

A man called Juliet's name and she hurried away. I gestured for my team to follow me to Father's office, which was empty.

I closed the door behind us. "Okay team, here's the plan. Reid, right now I want you to go break up any fights. Be scary. When you're done, report back to me and we'll work on storm surge barriers around the church. Ember, you're great with people our age, so hang around with the college students and let them know that everything is going to be okay. Benjamin, find anyone with injuries, do your thing. Introduce yourself to families especially, make sure parents know that you can heal. Marco, you're the best with kids, so round them up and do your magic. How are your energy stores?"

He scowled at me. "I'm full. I was working outside all day yesterday, remember?"

"Good. Don't use any of it unless you absolutely have to. We don't know the next time we'll see the sun."

Marco crossed his arms. "And what are *you* going to do?"

I brushed past his tone. "I'm going to go secure a place for us to sleep. Then I'll work on supply distribution with the city people so everyone gets what they need."

As they left Father's office, Ember touched my arm. *You want me to keep tabs on thoughts? I already heard someone thinking about stealing.*

I nodded. *If you overhear something really bad, come get me.*

She wandered towards a group of college students in UGSC hoodies. "Hi, guys! I'm Firelight."

I set out to find a place for my team to sleep and, when necessary, speak in private.

The classrooms were full, as were the storage rooms and kitchen. People lined every hallway.

The bathrooms were filled.

The social hall was packed.

Frustrated, I returned to the overcrowded gymnasium, which doubled as the main room in the storm shelter. I looked around. At that point I would've settled for a closet.

A narrow stairwell I'd never noticed before led to a small balcony overlooking the gym, no more than a few feet square, and a door. I walked up the stairwell and tried the doorknob, but it was locked. Glancing over my shoulder, I forced the lock and the door swung open to reveal a darkened room.

I saw immediately why the room hadn't been opened for shelter use: it was a weight training room, stuffed with large, heavy exercise equipment, no doubt for the older students to use during gym class. The shelter employees would have been unable to move the equipment and find a place for it on such short notice.

But I could move them. I pushed the treadmill and exercise bike to the side of the room with little effort, then carried the weights to a corner by another door labeled "Roof Access."

Though I was nearly six feet tall, the punching bag's hook was too far out of my reach to grab. Shrugging, I punched the bag so hard it detached from the ceiling and caught it.

An appreciative whistle came from the doorway.

"You are such an Amazon," Benjamin said, leaning against the frame. He grinned and held two water bottles. "Just how strong are you?"

I set the bag down by the weights and laughed. "I can bench press you and not break a sweat."

He tossed me a bottle. "We'll have to try that soon."

I joined him by the door and swatted him. "Down, boy." I took a sip and wiped my forehead. "When did it get so hot in here?"

Benjamin pointed to the overhead lights. "We're on generator power, I think. The air conditioning is off so the lights can stay on."

We stood on the balcony and surveyed the mass of people below us. In the far corner, a dozen children watched Marco while he molded clay, no doubt borrowed from the art room, and hardened it in his hands with his heat. He gave a tiny clay animal to a toddler, who promptly dropped it and began to sob. Marco picked her up and soothed her, a sight that warmed my heart.

In another corner, Ember chatted with a group of college students. She said something that made them all burst into loud laughter.

*You'll never be as helpful as they are. If the shelter floods, you can't do anything.*

I banished the insidious voice inside my head as quickly as it had come. I was tired and I was nervous. Of course the shelter wouldn't flood.

Benjamin turned to me. "I've healed every injury I could, and already people are calming down. The biggest task now is just riding out the storm. Water's starting to pool everywhere outside, and Reid is having trouble keeping the storm walls up because the ground is too saturated to work with. That's what I came up here to tell you. He's outside."

The hair on the back of my neck stood up. I let out a long breath. "Well, don't let anyone hear you say that. I'll go talk to Reid."

I made my way downstairs and determinedly ignored the niggling fears in my brain.

Yes, there would be *some* flooding, because there was always flooding in low-lying areas during hurricanes. But we could handle it. The storm surge barriers around the rivers and the oceanfront would hold, and the city would be fine. Tropical Storm Anastasia hadn't done any lasting damage, and neither would Hurricane Ben.

The *very* worst that could happen was that everyone was forced upstairs for a little while.

*There's not enough room for everyone upstairs.*

The wooden handrail cracked under my hand.

I collected my thoughts and headed towards the foyer, where I could see Reid leaning against the brick wall of the church and struggling to raise the earth for storm walls. Every time he lifted up the dirt, wind whipped much of it away. The rest collapsed on itself, little more than mud.

I pushed open the door, the storm's roar stunning me momentarily. "Come back inside! There's nothing you can do now!" I beckoned him in.

"Come see!" Reid yelled back, pointing towards the road.

I joined him in the front area, rain drops striking my skin with painful force. Tiny bits of rock and debris flew into my face.

"Look at the water!" he yelled.

I squinted at the street and gasped. The road, some thirty feet from the door, was under at least six inches of water.

Reid's eyes glowed white and another low wall rose up on the lawn, only to collapse. "I can't keep it back!"

Water splashed over the curb once, then twice. It was rising.

"Get inside!" I yelled, pushing him towards the door. He opened his mouth to argue. "That's an order, Reid!"

We sprinted back into the church, the doors slamming behind us so hard the glass bowed. We shivered and dripped onto the carpet for a few seconds while we got our bearings. "Get the team upstairs, above the gym," I said while I scanned for the city employees. "We're going to have to come up with a contingency plan."

He hurried off and I located Juliet, who was handing out boxed meals at a table near the gym. "We need to talk." I hoped the urgency came through without alarming the other civilians.

Juliet listened with grim understanding while I explained that situation outside the church. "So what's your plan?"

"The building has a second floor room, but it's... it's not big enough for two hundred people. After that, it's the roof." I couldn't see these people faring well on the roof while the storm raged around them.

Juliet pursed her lips and pulled a small radio out of her pocket. "This is an emergency two-way radio. I know that the Coast Guard was called in yesterday, so if it comes to that, you can reach them with it."

"Why are you giving this to me? It's yours." The small device was suddenly very heavy in my hand.

Juliet stared at a young woman singing to her baby. "Unless the water recedes, this is going to turn into a rescue operation. That's your area of expertise, not mine." She turned back to me, her eyes sad. "So far, everyone feels safe because your team is here. When the time comes, they might only keep calm because you're in charge of getting them to safety."

Juliet returned to her table, leaving me in the hallway with the radio I'd need to coordinate a joint Super-military rescue operation. I stared down at the black device, nausea rising in my stomach.

As much as I'd tried to be optimistic and think otherwise, I had to accept that I'd been deluding myself about the hurricane all day.

I leaned against the wall and my knees collapsed.

The church was going to flood. There wasn't enough room on the second floor for everyone. Rescue operations couldn't begin until the storm had passed—and it wasn't stopping anytime soon.

I closed my eyes against the reality of the moment, and all I could hear was the nonstop howling wind beyond the fragile brick walls.

*Patrick was a better leader than you. At least he'd know what to do.* The sinister thought snaked around me.

"Patrick was terrible," I mumbled to myself. But I could not stop the thoughts.

*You're so stupid, Jill. You were never good enough to be a leader. People are going to die because you wanted to prove something to the world. Your team will die. Reid should've taken over. He'd be a better leader than you. You can't even...*

The gentle tinkling of a bell in the chapel distracted me from my self-loathing, providing an unexpected, beautiful counterpoint to my ugly thoughts.

I opened my eyes and hugged my knees, then breathed in and out, willing my fear to leave my body.

*You can do this.* The still, small thought, so unlike my normal mental berating, washed over my mind like balm. I straightened a little. *Could* I do this?

No. Of course I couldn't help the civilians. I had nothing to offer them.

I laid my head on my knees. What was I thinking, pretending I was a leader of *anyone*? I'd tipped Patrick off that we were in town, and then I'd flubbed the mission at the school. *How* I'd flubbed it, I couldn't say, but it certainly didn't feel like a victory with hundreds of dead children and Patrick escaping.

And now I couldn't even stay on my feet to face a storm. I was huddled on the floor like a damned victim—of Patrick, of circumstance, of my own wretched ambition and pride.

I closed my eyes again. The physical sensation of sitting on the hard floor dredged up a memory of doing the same in the shed months before. I'd just run away from base camp and had been convinced that I'd hit rock bottom, that I had nothing left.

*That was a lie.* Benjamin's mental voice immediately struck back, my internal defender, as he'd been even before I'd defected.

In the shed I'd had the respect of my team, even though they weren't with me at the time. Marco had run away to find me. Ember and Reid had protected me at the library. They'd joined me, ignoring all warnings that my leading the team would ruin it. Despite my terrible behavior after we'd moved into the convent, they still trusted me and wanted to help me.

In that regard, I had more than Patrick had ever had. I had a team that was more than the sum of its parts, more than five superpowered people.

I had friends.

No, I had a family that loved me and was dedicated to helping me reach my full potential as a leader.

I slowly raised my head. I had everything to offer the people in the shelter.

I struggled to my feet and spotted the other four lingering by the entrance to the social hall. I concentrated on Ember, whose eyes widened.

She ran towards me. "What's wrong? What's happened?"

"I don't know how to save everyone. The water's rising and there's nowhere for them to go. I need your help." My voice, though low, was serious and strong, containing no fear.

The guys joined us and Ember repeated what I'd told her.

"We should probably talk about this where we can't be overheard," Marco said, eyeing three small children who were goggling at us a few feet away.

I agreed, and we walked into the gym and up the stairs to the weight room.

I pushed aside the weight rack with my foot and opened the door to the roof access. "This is the only second-floor room in the building. The stairs go to the roof, but that's not a better option at the moment, and I'm not sure the roof can even handle two hundred people on it."

Benjamin shook his head. "It can't, and this room can hold maybe fifty people."

I sank down on the punching bag, head in my hand. *Think, Jill. Think.*

We couldn't go up, and we couldn't go out. The building itself was solid, brick and stone. I doubted our wooden house next door was still standing, but the church was built like a rock.

Marco cracked his knuckles. I glanced up at his hands, and I saw streaks of clay on his fingers. I stood up and walked over to him, gently taking one of his hands in mine and examining it. "How much heat do you have left?"

"Um, a lot. Why?"

I smeared some of the clay on my finger and held it up. "Reid, Marco, you've got work to do. We're going to brick up every door and window in this place."

———

FLAGSTONES, bricks, and cement blocks flew from the walls and stone patio, directed by Reid into a ten-foot wall that completely covered the doorway of the church.

Reid's eyes glowed while he controlled the flying bits of rock, interlocking them as tightly as possible in preparation for the water that was encroaching on the church property. A foot of water lapped against the outside set of doors, leaking into the entryway between the sets. To hedge our bets, I'd told Reid to build the wall on the inside of the inner glass doors, letting the outside doors function as our first wall.

When the last brick fell into place, Reid stepped back and casually manipulated several buckets-full of mud, collected earlier, into the cracks.

When every space was filled, Marco walked forward, his hand outstretched. "Stand back. It's going to get a little warm over here."

My team retreated to the other side of the room, and then Marco unleashed a concentrated stream of heat onto the rocks. The mud hardened into a substance much stronger than dirt—it was glassy, almost like porcelain.

When he was done, Marco and Reid high-fived; the front door was the last door to be blocked. The church was now as protected as we could make it, with every window, door, and opening bricked and sealed shut.

I sat down against a wall and closed my eyes, the sounds of the shelter filling my ears.

Father Kokoski was talking to people in the chapel. Three children in a classroom down the hall laughed while they played a skipping game—I was surprised to realize that I'd played the same game as a child. Two young lovers were kissing in a nearby closet, whispering each other's names and murmuring words of love and appreciation. A father hushed his sons, who were playing a fighting game of superhero versus supervillain. The supervillain was winning.

I was proud of myself.

Sure, I'd had a dark moment in which I'd panicked, but I'd muddled through and come up with the best plan possible. I could hear deep water splashing against the walls of the school, but it wasn't inside. Nobody was going to drown on my watch.

The others eventually settled around me. Reid had secured boxed lunches for us from Juliet, and we ate our meals while chatting about rescue operations, clean up, and all that lay beyond. Benjamin suggested buying computers for everyone and enrolling us in long-distance classes.

A good-natured squabble broke out about which grade level we should start.

Outside, the water steadily rose, but Reid and Marco's walls held strong against the might of Hurricane Ben.

## 37

I walked down the dark corridor with a flashlight, peering into classrooms and offices where sleeping civilians lay on the floor. It was sometime after midnight, and my night watch shift had just started.

The shelter was finally quiet, allowing me to easily hear the endless water sounds from outside. I'd heard the wind all day long, but now that the brunt of the storm had passed, the flooding and constant rain mixed to make a plopping, flowing sound that would've been relaxing in other circumstances. Now it made me paranoid.

My team and the civilians could not hear what I could beyond the blocked windows: water flowing at least six feet deep. Half of the shelter was essentially underwater. As I walked through the atrium, I could hear the spooky swish-swish of water against thick glass, but I couldn't tell if the outer glass doors had held.

I roved around the church for hours inspecting every nook and cranny for leaks. I tiptoed through each room, over sleeping bodies, obsessively scanning for drips. I listened at each sealed window for the sound of cracking glass.

Finally, when I'd passed through the atrium for the tenth time without finding so much as a damp spot in the ceiling tiles, I admitted to myself that the plan had worked.

At zero two thirty I returned to the weight room, where my team was arranged in a small circle. I gently shook Ember, who was snuggled against Reid under a blanket.

"Hey lovebird," I whispered. "It's time for watch."

Ember opened her eyes and blinked at me. "Oh, boy," she groaned. She sat up. "Hey, the storm isn't as loud anymore."

"We'll probably get in touch with the military rescuers later today." I stifled a yawn and pulled a blanket over me, resisting the urge to copy Ember's idea and slide next to Benjamin. "Wake me up at zero five, please."

I laid my head on the floor and was asleep in seconds.

———

EMBER'S WAKE-UP shake came entirely too quickly.

I sat up with a groan and pushed my snarled hair out of my face, accepting a granola bar and an apple for breakfast. While I ate, she woke up the others, who moved with equal slowness.

Benjamin rubbed his neck. "God, I hate sleeping on the ground."

The rest of us snickered. "Be thankful there aren't timber rattlesnakes in here," Marco said. "There are a whole bunch in Chattahoochee camp."

"You're all lunatics, you know that?" He turned and looked at the roof access. "Hey, I can't hear the wind." He appeared at the door in the blink of an eye, pulled it open, and disappeared up the dark stairwell. "You guys gotta come see this!"

We followed behind. I was the last to step out onto the slick, pebble-covered roof.

The sunrise stretched its orange-gold rays over the watery expanse of Saint Catherine. Once a bustling city, it was now a vast lake punctuated by buildings and tree tops.

Downtown, a few miles to the east, was on slightly higher ground and so remained relatively dry. Old Town, where we were, was under eight feet of water—the flood came up to just below the roofline of the church's first floor. The church's flagpole stuck out of the flood like a bizarre lightning rod.

Around us stood the sunken homes of our neighbors, most of which were vacant. However, from our vantage point on the gym, I could see scattered individuals on rooftops here and there, too far away to identify.

Behind us were a few taller homes that were flooded, but still standing. Someone moved behind a curtain in the house nearest us, and I made a mental note to offer them relief supplies later.

Marco took off his shirt and closed his eyes, absorbing the sunlight with obvious pleasure. "Aw, man, I missed the sun."

Reid craned his neck to look at our left. "Well, the convent's gone. Shocker."

"Is it weird that I think it's almost pretty?" Ember asked.

Benjamin shook his head. "Nah, I think so too."

I pulled out the radio Juliet had given me. "You know what will be prettier? Two hundred people getting rescued." I switched on the radio and took a breath before pressing the red transmission button. "Mayday mayday mayday, this is registered superhero Battlecry, team number one four two seven, Saint Catherine, Georgia, requesting flood rescue assistance, over."

There was a long silence, and then:

"Confirmed, this is United States Coast Guard Cutter *Friedrich*. What is your location? Over."

---

FIFTEEN MINUTES LATER, I waved a burning emergency flare above my head, directing the orange-and-white helicopter to land on the larger lower roof. I scrambled down the rusty ladder and waved at the Coast Guardsman who'd jumped out. The draft from the helicopter churned the water and whipped my hair around my face. The smallest pebbles on the roof tumbled backwards, away from the helicopter.

"Are you Battlecry?" The Guardsman shouted above the din of the rotors.

"Yes!"

"The *Friedrich* sent me to coordinate with you! They're starting rescues and could use the help!"

We yelled back and forth for a few minutes, eventually agreeing to send Ember and Reid ahead to begin rescues, while I would stay with Marco and Benjamin at the shelter until everyone was out. A larger boat would come our way in a few hours, though he couldn't tell me when.

I hugged Ember and Reid, assuring them that we'd join them shortly.

Benjamin, Marco, and I watched in silence as the helicopter flew away.

When it had disappeared into the distance, I turned to Marco. "Benjamin and I are going to get in touch with some of the neighbors and offer assistance. Go inside and tell Juliet to keep calm and start preparing everyone for evacuation. We'll be inside in a little while."

Marco pulled a face. "Can't I help with finding people? I've been on babysitting duty this whole time. I want to *do* something."

I frowned. What *now*? "You helped seal up the building. And keeping order is not babysitting. It's the first step in reducing crime. You're the best one of us when it comes to interacting with civilians."

"Blah blah blah. You're making me work with kids because you think I am a kid."

"Marco, shut the hell and do your job!"

I loved my cousin, but Marco's attitude was out of line. I had to lay down the law. He was going to obey a simple order whether he liked it or not.

Throwing me a furious glare, he stomped off and up the ladder, disappearing onto the gym roof. The roof door slammed.

"He'll get over it," Benjamin said.

"Forget about it right now." I walked towards the part of the roof closest to the house with the occupant I'd seen. I scooped up some pebbles from the roof and tossed them at the window. "Hello! Is anyone there?"

Nobody appeared in the window, nor did I hear movement.

Benjamin took my hand in his. "Let's go back inside and help Marco. We can worry about the neighbors when the rescue boat shows up. If their house hasn't floated away by now, it won't."

I squeezed his hand. "Still interested in being a superhero after all of this?"

"Are you kidding? I can't wait to help with rescues. Do you think I'll go out with the helicopters or stay behind with the medical teams?"

I leaned towards him. "I think I'll attach you to the medical team and then find myself there with some exciting injury for you to heal."

He grinned. "Oh, really now? Like what?"

"Chapped lips."

Laughing, he scooped me up in his arms and kissed me. "We did it," he whispered. "Everyone's safe, and we're okay."

I winked. "Not bad for a team of rebels and a supervillain."

He pinched my bottom and I slapped his hand.

He laughed. "If you're going to still call me a supervillain, I'm going to do terrible things to earn the name."

Giggling, I dashed away from him, and he chased me towards the ladder to the gym roof. When I reached it, I put one hand on a rung and turned to blow him a kiss. "Time to be serious. Let's continue this epic battle later."

"That had better be a promise."

I grinned and turned to climb up the ladder. A horrific metallic screech made me jump back. The ladder pulled away from the bricks, rusted bolts popping out of place and raining down on us. It fell at our feet with an enormous crash, trapping us on the lower roof.

"What the hell?" I said, staring up at the gym roof. "How old was that ladder? Help me find another way up."

I glanced at Benjamin and froze. He was staring at something over my shoulder, undisguised horror on his face.

I turned, then took a step back.

Patrick floated down onto the roof from the neighboring house, his shirt damp and bloodstained. Though his face was white and taut with pain, he stared directly at Benjamin.

"Well, who do we have here?"

## 38

"You never told me you were courting, Jill."

Every muscle froze as Patrick took a step closer to us. I was hideously aware that we had nowhere to go. A fight with Patrick was becoming commonplace for me, but Benjamin was a non-combatant. He'd last two seconds against a trained killer like Patrick, injured or not.

I shoved Benjamin behind me into the bricks. "He's nobody. This fight is between us."

Patrick's lips twitched, but his stab wound prevented him from truly smiling. "I've seen you before," he croaked, studying Benjamin. "You were at the library." He looked back at me. "Nobody, huh? After you threw rocks at my window I watched you with him. Do you let every nobody grope you?"

I blushed, but my voice was steady when I spoke. "If you want to throw down the gauntlet, you're going to lose."

His ultimate goal was clear: threaten Benjamin to piss me off, and then seize the advantage when I went berserk. He'd pulled out that card several times, and it had always worked. He expected me to die defending Benjamin, and then he'd kill Benjamin.

But he was grievously injured, thanks to Ember. As I watched, he gasped and clutched his oozing shoulder. His knees shook. Revealing himself to us had been foolish. Was he so confident in the strength of his telekinesis alone? His powers were considerable, but he needed to focus on them to use them efficiently, and right now he was obviously in agony. He could pull down the ladder and carry himself through the air, but how would he fare in combat?

I needed to distract him more. He said he didn't believe in right and wrong—it was time to put that claim to the test.

I let my shoulders slump. "You're right, I lied. He's not nobody." I gave Benjamin my most sugary smile. "We're courting. Actually, we're dating." I wagered Patrick's definition of the word would carry all the implications it once had for me.

Patrick wheezed a laugh. "It figures that you'd abandon all propriety once you took over. Are you sleeping with Marco and Reid, too?"

"No, I'm not interested in superheroes. I prefer super*villains*." I stepped aside, as if displaying Benjamin. "His parents are the ones who broke into the bank in June. We've been seeing each other since that day, by the way."

"What are you doing?" Benjamin whispered, barely audible. Patrick was fifteen feet from us, so he wouldn't hear our exchange.

"Play along," I whispered back.

Benjamin stared at me, but recovered. "Hi, how're you doing? Benjamin Trent, criminal-for-hire, professional torturer, occasional murderer. I've heard all about you. In fact, the strengths and weaknesses of your team were one of the first conversations we had." He'd continued the conversation as though we'd planned it.

Benjamin threw his arm around my shoulder, and I kissed his hand, then looked at Patrick. "I bartered information about the team in exchange for... well, not *kisses*, if you know what I mean."

Patrick's face went from white to dark red. "You sold us out? You sold *me* out?"

I smirked. "Sold you out, betrayed you, turned traitor...yeah, I did. I told him all about you."

"I especially liked the story about what happened when Daddy

Campbell wouldn't let you marry that sexy redhead," Benjamin said, his voice like velvet. "Spanked you right in front of the whole camp, huh? Was Ember watching?"

"Shut up." Patrick's icy eyes flickered towards me. "I can't believe *you* betrayed me to one of them."

I raised my eyebrows. "Why do you care? Right and wrong don't exist."

"I care that a slut like you betrayed me for a piece of—"

I threw myself on top of Patrick.

The heel of my hand dug into his shoulder and he screamed, thrashing beneath me but unable to toss me off. Ember had already won my fight for me. I straddled him, one hand on his shoulder and the other slowly unsheathing the knife at my thigh.

"This is not going to be quick," I said quietly.

And it wouldn't. Patrick was going to suffer for what he'd put my team and me through. Every little moment of fear and loathing would be heaped on him before he died.

"You're psychotic," he spat. "Just kill me."

"No." I applied pressure to his wound. "You never killed me, you just tossed me into walls." I punched his shoulder. "You choked me." I dropped my knife and grabbed his windpipe, eliciting a wonderful gurgle from him. "You tormented and terrorized the people you were supposed to protect." I ground my hand into his shoulder, but his scream was cut off by the pressure on his throat.

A heavy blanket of vengeance descended on my mind. Deep down, beyond the rage and pain, a tiny voice reminded me that I had the right to kill him, but I could not justify torturing him. He'd tormented us, and mirroring his actions would be to lower myself to his level.

I ignored the voice.

I leaned in close enough to smell his breath as it wafted over my face. "What's it like, Patrick? How does it feel to have someone stronger than you cause you pain when you can't do anything about it? You feel small, don't you? You feel like a speck in the wind. You want someone to run to your side and save you." I brought down my fist on his unwounded shoulder, breaking it, savoring his agonized yell. "Well, guess what? Nobody's coming."

Behind me, I heard Benjamin slide down against the gym wall. He'd said the other supervillain children had mocked him for disliking violence; how would he feel about me once he saw what I was going to do to Patrick?

I cared less than I thought I would. My hatred of Patrick ran deeper than my desire for Benjamin's approval, though, to be fair, my hatred of Patrick ran deeper than most feelings of mine.

"So, how is this going to go?" I asked. "I rather like the idea of breaking your limbs and tossing you in the water, but I also like using my knives, and I've had so few chances to use them these days."

Panic flitted across his face. "Just kill me."

I laughed. "Where's the fun in that?"

"Jill, look out!" I heard Benjamin's warning at the same time I saw Patrick's arm move.

My knife, forgotten at my side, cut a jagged gash in my right arm. Dark blood gushed from the wound as Patrick threw me off of him.

Fun time was over, then.

The knife flew out of his hand and straight at my chest, but I twisted around, and it sailed past me into the water with a small splash.

I grabbed Patrick around his middle and threw him to the ground.

An invisible hand grabbed my collar and pulled me backwards, dragging my boots through the pebbles. He clambered to his feet and reached out a hand.

My throat constricted. I clawed at the invisible choking force, cursing his favorite tactic.

Benjamin slammed into Patrick, knocking him down again and breaking his chokehold.

I shoved Benjamin aside and began my final assault.

Fighting telekinesis was like trying to force two north poles of magnets together—my fists merely slid over the unseen force that repelled me. Only when one of my punches hit his shoulder did Patrick gasp, allowing me to get a decent punch in.

The force field dissolved completely.

A punch to the chest. His ribs broke, puncturing his lungs. He'd never yell threats of violence at my team again.

A blow to the upper thigh, and his pelvic bone cracked. He'd never kick me in the stomach after a beating, driving home how powerless I was to stop him.

Multiple hits to his soft middle, and I knew he was already bleeding internally. He'd never see another sunrise.

I finally stopped to catch my breath. Patrick was still conscious, but no longer moving. He gazed at me—through me—with an empty, broken expression.

"I hate you," I choked.

He said nothing.

"Fight back," I growled, pulling my fist back to punch him again. Blood from my arm dripped down my hand onto his body and mingled with his own. "Fight back!"

"He's down, Jillian," Benjamin whispered. "He'll be dead soon."

The late summer sun shone bright on the three of us, but a deep cold prickled at my skin. I'd beaten Patrick. My great enemy was dying in front of me, and when he was dead I would be free. We'd all be free. So why did I feel like I hadn't won?

I gripped the front of his shirt and shook him roughly. "Fight back!"

This couldn't be it. There had to be more to Patrick's death, something epic. "Fight back, dammit!"

Why had he come out to fight me? In his condition, the decision had amounted to little more than suicide. "*What's wrong with you?!*" I screamed. "Answer me!" I backhanded his face, but he said nothing.

Benjamin was at my side in an instant, pulling me away. "We have to go!"

"No! He'll escape! He'll—"

"No, we have to go! Jump in the water! Now!" He pointed to something across the water.

I looked to see what he was pointing at. In the distance, and rapidly approaching, was a small speedboat with three people in it. It wasn't a rescue boat.

I squinted. "Who are they?"

Benjamin's breathing quickened. "My family. Oh my God, it's my family." He grabbed my hand and my bleeding gash sealed itself. Benjamin searched frantically for an escape. "If we jump in the water now, we can... we can..."

He turned to me. His eyes, usually so full of laughter and strength, contained nothing but fear.

I squeezed his hand. "I'm right here. I won't let them do anything to you."

He shook his head and wiped his face with the back of his free hand. "You don't get it. *You* can't do anything to *them*."

The roar of the speedboat drowned out my reply. The boat pulled up to the roof, which was essentially a dock in the floodwaters.

At the helm was a tall, handsome, muscular man in his mid-twenties who bore a striking resemblance to Benjamin—Beau. The other two people were much older. The man, obviously Mr. Trent, was a vision of an older, dour Benjamin, tall and hazel-eyed. Mrs. Trent had softer features and wavy hair that spoke of Eleanor, though she and Benjamin shared the same mouth.

Benjamin stepped in front of me. "Mom, Dad, Beau. It's been a while." His voice was higher than normal.

His parents stepped off the boat and onto the roof. Benjamin pushed me backwards.

Mr. Trent gave his younger son a look of pure hatred. "Get in the boat, son." The order carried as much threat as any elder's. I shivered.

Mrs. Trent held up a hand. "Benny, we don't want to fight. We just want to talk."

Benjamin stiffened. "Put your hand down and I might believe you."

Mrs. Trent dropped her arm. "Honey, you can't possibly think I'd—"

"He's working with camp trash," Mr. Trent interrupted, staring beyond Benjamin at me. "Anything's possible now."

Trash? The man who'd dedicated his life to villainy was calling *me* trash? I wanted to respond, but for once I had the sense to keep my mouth shut.

"I'm not going with you," Benjamin said, his voice shaking. "So you can just get back in the boat and go home."

"Home's gone, idiot," Beau said from the boat. "Or did you not notice the flood?"

"Then go back to the Annapolis house. I don't care where you go. I'm not going with you, though."

Mrs. Trent's face went from sad to furious. "They're controlling you, aren't they? They want your healing power."

"No! I'm not being controlled!" Benjamin may have been trying to project authority, but his voice trembled.

His fear became mine—why did his family terrify him *so* much? I was a superhero, and I could handle supervillains, even if there were three. He knew something I didn't.

"Of course you're being controlled!" she shot back, balling her fists. "You're my son, and you would never betray your people for these pieces of—"

Mr. Trent held up a hand to his wife. "This is about the damn scholarship, isn't it?"

"No, Dad, listen—"

"Yes, it is. This is some bratty attempt to assert your independence because I didn't let you accept that damn scholarship to Columbia—"

"Old Dominion! *God*, Dad. Eleanor went to Columbia. Get your disappointing kids straight!"

"At least Eleanor never abandoned her family to work with the likes of *her*!" Mr. Trent roared, pointing at me.

Benjamin grabbed my hand, though to stay me or steady his own nerves I couldn't tell.

"Where is Eleanor?" Mrs. Trent asked, narrowing her eyes. "You left the house together."

I peeked over his shoulder. "I'll tell you what happened to Eleanor if you tell us how you found Benjamin."

Benjamin hissed at me to shut up.

Beau waved at me. "I knew my geek brother was alive when I saw the books on the floor of his bedroom that night." He shook his head. "You were in the closet, weren't you? Well, anyway, you shouldn't have told the Coast Guard where you were over the radio." He tapped his head. "I can hear it all." He leered at me. "I can see why you turned, Ben. You always picked ones with a decent rack." His leer turned vicious. "If I asked her about what you've been up to, do you think she'd talk?"

Benjamin bared his teeth at his brother. "You will *never*—"

"Did you get my letters? I sent six, but you never answered them." Beau was grinning from ear to ear—yet, somehow, his eyes were as flat and blank as a shark's.

Good gracious, he was creepy.

Mrs. Trent's head whipped back and forth between her sons. "You've been in contact? What's going on?"

"Thank you for explaining," I said, doing some quick thinking. So they'd been monitoring the frequencies. Were Ember and Reid safe? What about the people in the shelter below? I had no way to fight three supervillains by myself, and Benjamin was visibly shaking. We needed to get away from them.

Mrs. Trent crossed her arms. "What about Eleanor? Where's my daughter?"

I pointed to Patrick, who was still lying on the ground and breathing slowly. "He killed her at the library. I saw everything." For all I knew, Eleanor really was dead, but I wanted the heat off of the two of us.

Mrs. Trent calmly strode over to Patrick and placed a hand on his face. He flinched.

In the blink of an eye Patrick's face, neck, and upper chest collapsed into dust that scattered in the light breeze. Blood poured out of his ribcage, pooling thickly around his corpse. Mrs. Trent kicked his body to the edge and into the dark water where it bobbed slightly before sinking below the surface.

Benjamin and I backed up against the wall. My eyes were locked on the area of water where Patrick's corpse had sunk.

She turned to face me. "How are you controlling my son?"

I removed my shaking hand from my mouth. "I'm not. I swear."

Everyone on my team had killed people, but I'd never seen a death as horrible as Patrick's, nor someone kill another person so casually. Benjamin's terror of his parents started to make so much more sense. What did they do behind closed doors that made Benjamin think they'd turn their powers on him?

She took a step towards me. "You expect me to believe that my son would ever willingly betray his loving family for a stupid, back-woods girl like you?"

Benjamin took an unsteady breath and stepped forward. "No, I wouldn't expect you to believe it. But I would leave a family of murderers to serve beside a kind, smart, strong superhero and her equally admirable team."

Mrs. Trent rolled her eyes. "Really, Benjamin. Can you hear yourself?"

Mr. Trent studied us. "He can hear himself. So what's it going to be? Are you going to come with us quietly, or are things going to get ugly?"

Benjamin pushed me behind him again. "Define ugly."

"I drag you back to the boat and your mother erases her from existence."

I wrapped my arms around his torso. "I'll fight for you," I whispered.

"But you'll die," he whispered in return.

"Then I'll die for you."

He raised his chin and faced his parents. "I'm not going with you. But... but mom, it doesn't have to be like this."

Mrs. Trent gazed at her son, her previous fury turning to despair. "Henry..."

Mr. Trent gasped. "Janice, we can't let him stay! He's a threat to everyone, now. We have to do it."

"I can't kill my own son," Mrs. Trent whimpered. "He's my baby. He's my Benny."

Mr. Trent took his wife's hands in own and kissed them. "I'm sorry."

Mrs. Trent screamed and fell to the ground, twitching. Mr. Trent's hands crackled with electricity as he turned to us.

"Run!" Benjamin shouted, pulling me towards the edge.

Without pausing even for breath, I jumped into the floodwaters at the same time as Benjamin and surfaced a moment later with a gasp. The water churned, threatening to suck me under at any second. I grabbed Benjamin and swam with difficulty towards the church's flagpole. Benjamin and I clung to the metal pole and choked on the water we'd swallowed.

It only took a second for me to realize how much our situation hadn't improved.

Mr. Trent stood at the edge of the roof, shaking his head. "You can't escape me." He sounded almost sad.

"Dad! It doesn't have to end like this! Just leave!"

Mr. Trent raised his hand, electricity traveling up and down between his fingers. I knew that he could manufacture enough current to kill us in the water. The power of electricity in water had been one of the first subjects I'd learned about from a book, in the library, before I was even ready to admit that book learning had value.

Benjamin planted a desperate kiss on my lips. "I'm sorry."

I gave him my best smile.

Mr. Trent brought his hand towards the water.

An explosion of sound and searing heat nearly knocked us off the flag pole.

A rippling beam tore through Mr. Trent, vaporizing him where he stood, leaving nothing but a smoking pair of shoes with bits of ankle poking out. The roof beyond burst into flames. The water touched by the beam turned to steam in an instant, and even the water around us heated up to the temperature of bath water.

Marco stood high above us on the gym roof, white and yellow tendrils snaking out and away from his entire body, with his hand outstretched and his eyes glowing so brightly he truly appeared to be the sun titan Helios, beautiful and terrible.

He'd unleashed the full power of the sun.

A floating piece of furniture crashed into Benjamin and me, knocking us off the flag pole and into the swirling flood.

## 39

The swift-flowing water dragged us down into its murky brown depths, buffeting us against unseen objects and knocking the air out of my lungs. I kept an iron grip on Benjamin's hand. If I loosened it even a little, he'd slip away from me and drown in an instant.

I kicked as hard as I could and pulled us up into the sunlight, breaking the water's surface and desperately looking for something to latch onto. We were in the middle of the unofficial river, flowing rapidly towards the ocean. As I watched, a small house broke away from its foundation and joined our watery path to the Atlantic. All around us, families on rooftops waited to be rescued.

Benjamin sputtered and coughed. "C-c-can you swim towards a house?"

I nodded and towed him diagonally towards a solid-looking roof.

A submerged car slammed into us, tearing us apart. Benjamin disappeared underwater.

"Benjamin! *Benjamin!*" I took a breath, then sank under the water with my eyes open.

In the bubbly darkness, I spied flashes of pale skin mixed with cloth, bits of wood and debris, and a limp dog with a collar still around its neck. I surged towards the pale skin and reached out, but was met with only water.

I dove deeper, the wet silence pressing at me. Though my lungs burned, I absolutely could not surface, because I'd never find Benjamin again. I kicked, propelling myself forward to a glimmer of white, and closed my hand around Benjamin's wrist.

With a final burst of effort, I pulled him to the surface.

He sagged in my arms, unconscious. Fresh gashes from the collision with the car marred his arms, and his burn bandages were torn open. I hated to think what the filthy flood water would do to his wounds, but I couldn't dwell on future problems while drowning was a present threat.

A massive oak tree stood directly ahead, so I angled myself in such a way that I'd slam into the tree instead of Benjamin. *Three... two... one...*

All the air in my lungs was expelled when I hit the tree, but at least Benjamin hadn't hit it. I reached up and grabbed a limb, then pulled myself up with one arm while holding onto Benjamin with the other.

I gently draped him over another limb and inspected him. He was breathing, so I suspected his unconsciousness was from a thump to the head instead of drowning. After a few seconds, he coughed and dirty water gushed out of his mouth.

I settled back against the tree trunk and began to shiver.

Helicopters hummed in the distance. The flood flowed all around us, destroying my city from the ground up, but I couldn't get out of this tree to save anyone. Was Marco alright? Had he killed the rest of the Trents?

I thought of the shelter, submerged and vulnerable, and hoped Marco would know what to do. I hoped he knew I was sorry for yelling at him, and that he was so special to me.

I thought of my dead brother Gregory and hoped that wherever he was, he was proud of his big sister, who'd fought her leader and won, who'd lead her team against a storm and won, who'd faced her death without blinking and won.

I didn't think of Patrick except to wonder which luckless civilian would find his corpse, if anyone ever did.

I sat in the tree for an indeterminable amount of time, contemplating my past and future. Benjamin drifted in and out of consciousness. Every once in a while, he'd mumble something and jerk awake, but then his eyelids would flutter and he'd be still. Whenever this happened, I stroked his hair and placed tiny kisses on his clammy forehead.

When the sun was high overhead, I paused in my musings. The sound of helicopters in the distance, ever present, was growing louder.

I twisted around and pulled aside some branches, scanning the sky for orange and white. A small squadron of Coast Guard helicopters was flying our way. One by one, they broke off and went in their own directions, towards roofs bearing people, but the point leader approached the tree.

It slowed and hovered nearby, the wind creating small waves in the water, and then a small disk of hardened earth flew out bearing the most beautiful sight I'd ever seen: Reid.

He floated down next to the tree and held out his hands, the corners of his eyes crinkling in happiness. "Looks like you guys need a superhero."

I gingerly lifted Benjamin into Reid's arms. "Benjamin needs medical attention. I'm fine."

"Yeah, right." He shifted on the disk to let me on.

I jumped on and wrapped my arms around Reid's torso, struggling to stay upright in the draft.

We floated up into the helicopter's open doors. When we were safely inside, the disk disintegrated into dirt, which Reid directed into an orange bucket.

The co-pilot turned around in her chair.

"Ember!"

"Hiya. Sorry about the wait." She nodded at Benjamin. "The *Friedrich* has a complete medical bay. Benj... Mercury is going to be fine."

"Your teammate?" one of the Guardsmen asked Reid, mopping at Benjamin's bleeding arm.

"My brother. My other brother is at the shelter. We're going there next."

## 40

"So then I pointed at your brother and said that if he wanted to stay alive, he'd collect your mom and beat it."

Marco was solemn as he picked at a patch on Benjamin's scratchy wool blanket.

The five of us were in a tiny room aboard the USCGC *Friedrich*, crammed around Benjamin's bed. Benjamin sat propped up on pillows, multiple bandages on his arms, leg, and head.

Marco wouldn't meet Benjamin's eyes. "He got your mom and zoomed off in the boat. Then I went back inside until the rescue boat came."

"Why did you come out?" I asked. "I'm glad you did, though."

"I... I, um, came out to see where you guys were, and also to apologize for being a brat."

I hugged Marco. "I forgive you."

Marco frowned and finally met Benjamin's eyes. "And... I'm sorry I killed your dad. Can you forgive me, too?"

Benjamin's jaw dropped. "He was about to kill me and Jillian. You had no other choice."

But I saw a flicker of sadness in his eyes—he was hurting.

I put a hand on his shoulder. "Do you think we'll see your mom or brother again?"

"Hard to say. They'll be pissed, but Marco proved that our team isn't weak. If we see them again, it'll be a while from now. I wish I knew where Eleanor was, though. If she wasn't in the library, and she didn't go home to my family, then I guess she ran off. But where?"

"Back to the Rockies?" I suggested. "Maybe she'll take her boyfriend back. Dean, right? Maybe you'll have a brother-in-law soon."

"Or back to cleaning out casinos in Vegas?" Marco said. "She's Fortuna, isn't she? Jill and I read about her in the files."

"Ugh, yeah, she's *Fortuna*," Benjamin said, making air quotes around the codename. "That's the thing now, coming up with code-names like we're heroes or something. She's Fortuna, Beau is Cyber."

"What's yours?" Reid asked.

Benjamin sighed. "I never came up with one."

"Why not?" I asked, not quite believing him. It seemed to me that Benjamin would jump at the chance to give himself a heroic moniker.

"Because it would just have reminded me that I wasn't a super-hero. Like buying a car but not having a license."

"Well, Mercury, how do you like being a superhero now?" Reid asked. "You know the principles. You've dealt with a natural disaster, got beaten up and rescued from a tree, and now you're injured. You even fought supervillains. Sort of. The only thing you need now is an official uniform. We'll work on that."

Benjamin thought for a moment. "Is it weird that I love it?"

"Yes," we chorused.

We resumed swapping stories of rescues and near-misses. The *Friedrich* tossed and turned in the choppy ocean, but we were fine. Patrick was dead. The Trents were in retreat.

I watched the sun set through the porthole, thankful that my team had a place to sleep for the night. Tomorrow we'd continue what would be a long rescue and recovery mission with the Coast Guard. All of us, save Benjamin, would go back out into the ruined neighborhoods. Benjamin would stay behind with the medical team.

One by one, the others left for their own beds, until Benjamin and I were alone.

"How are you really doing?" I asked as I sat on the edge of his bed.

He hid his face in his hands. "My dad. My dad is dead." His voice broke.

I held Benjamin for several minutes while he mourned his father, and I found myself thinking about Patrick. I'd never shed a tear over him, but I couldn't make myself rejoice in his demise. Perhaps Benjamin thought of his father as a type of Patrick; a terrible leader, an almost-murderer, and an oppressor, but a relation and a part of his past all the same. I certainly had no warm feelings for my own father, but Benjamin clearly missed his own.

I rubbed his back. "Tell me about your father."

"Dad was horrible. I don't know why I'm so cut up about it. I should be happy he's gone."

"He was still your family. That means something."

"Being on your team means something more. You're my family now." He wiped his face with the back of his sleeve.

"So... am I like Eleanor, or am I like your wife?" I teased.

Benjamin started to laugh, then broke down again.

I chastised myself for bringing up Eleanor and pulled him into another hug. When he'd composed himself, I stroked his cheek. "We're all here for you, and if you want to talk about anything, I'd love to listen."

Benjamin sighed. "How are *you* doing? I mean, you basically beat Patrick to death back there. That kind of thing leaves a mark."

I examined my feelings. "I don't feel good, but I'm not sorry he's dead. I *am* sorry you had to see me like that, though. I... I went to a dark place. That was a different side of me."

"Is that the real you?"

"Absolutely not. You'll never see that part of me again."

He and I stared into each other's eyes for a few seconds, silent emotion passing between us.

His worry melted into something softer. "You know, I can think of one thing to be happy about."

"What's that, sweetie?"

"It's your birthday tomorrow. Since the piano is gone, I'll have to get you something else."

"Oh!" I'd completely forgotten that I was turning twenty-one the next day. I brushed my hair out of my face and feigned deep thought. "Well, hm. I'd like a fancy dress, a rope of pearls, a set of knives, a—"

Benjamin laughed and kissed my hand. "You may have to settle for a slice of sheet cake from the galley. But I can give you this." He leaned forward and kissed my lips. "Thank you for saving my life."

I stroked his cheek once, then stood. "Get some rest."

I walked out and shut the door behind me, then crossed the narrow passageway to my own stateroom.

Above the tiny sink hung a scratched mirror, and as I brushed my hair before bed, I studied my reflection.

Who was Jillian Johnson? An abused woman in need of saving? A rebellious upstart in need of discipline? A leader? A heroine?

I gave myself a small smile and turned away from the mirror.

# THREE MONTHS LATER

The doorbell rang. It was the first time it had rung since our headquarters had been rebuilt a month before.

I poked my head out of the bathroom, still in my towel after my bath. "Benjamin! Can you get that?"

He blurred past me and I heard the door open. Benjamin greeted someone, thanked them, and shut the door.

I walked downstairs, my towel wrapped around me, and he paused from opening the large cardboard box to stare at me. "Please tell me that's your new uniform."

"Go take a cold shower. These are *your* new uniforms." I recognized the logo of the company that the camp allies hired to make our uniforms. Benjamin and I had designed them a few weeks ago. They were the last shipment of new uniforms to arrive. I broke the tape on the box with no effort.

Inside the box were ten light gray tunics, each with a red cross embroidered on the right shoulder and the mythological Mercury's caduceus on the left. On the back was Benjamin's codename in bright red letters above another red cross. Underneath the tunics were ten pairs of sturdy khaki pants, a bulletproof vest, steel-soled boots, and a utility belt with many pouches. I hadn't put in a request for gloves like mine because Benjamin's healing power required bare hands.

"Suit up," I said, grinning. I carried the box upstairs for him and placed it on his bed, then went to my room to change.

My new uniform was similar to his, except my tunic was no longer black, but blue, my favorite color. I'd given my team an opportunity to change their names to whatever they wanted—our codenames having been given to us by Patrick—but nobody had wanted to change. I myself found that I liked being Battlecry, but I couldn't determine when my feelings about my codename had changed.

None of us wore masks anymore.

We met at the top of the stairs. Benjamin self-consciously tugged at his uniform. "The vest will take some getting used to," he said. "It's heavy."

"Not as heavy as the dead body you might be without it," I said, smoothing out a wrinkle on his sleeve. "You look hot, by the way."

He leaned in close. "Is that so?"

When we left our headquarters several minutes later, we walked past the church next door and waved to the schoolchildren at recess on the lawn.

The church had had some repairs from the fire Marco ignited, but besides that and a tiny bit of water damage, it was untouched. The church's financial board had unanimously voted to sell the convent's land to us for a dollar, and after a little finagling we'd received a new headquarters from the city. Construction, aided by five superpowered helpers, had taken a mere six weeks.

Down the block, James Oglethorpe High School stood half-constructed. Workmen labored at a steady pace to rebuild the school that had been burned out, then washed away three months before. Around the perimeter of the campus, nearly two hundred wooden crosses stuck out of the ground like a macabre fence. Each cross bore the name of a victim of that terrible day.

I paused at Sebastian Gonzales's and kissed my hand, then touched the cross. A few dozen crosses down, I did the same at Captain Hannah Drummond's.

Downtown, there were several new names and End of Watch dates on the city's fallen police officer memorial. They'd had to expand their existing one.

We strolled down shady streets to the Saint Catherine Central Library.

The stately building boasted three floors of books, computer rooms, conference rooms, reading rooms, and several dozen small displays dedicated to different subjects such as local history, current events, various countries, sports, and holidays. Thanksgiving was in a few weeks, so many displays offered picture books and history books about the pilgrims, fall-themed decorations, and cooking.

Reid sat in a large chair in the corner, engrossed in a cookbook titled *A Classic Vegan Thanksgiving*.

He looked up as we approached and put it down. "I'm thinking about trying my hand at some of the dishes," he explained when I picked up the glossy volume. "I'm making a totally vegan Thanksgiving dinner."

I laughed. "Well, it'll be memorable. Where is Ember?"

"Over here." Ember's sweet voice floated from behind a shelf marked Mental Health. She walked over with a large stack of books in her arms and dumped them on the table by Reid's chair. They were all about psychology and mental illness.

"Are you leaving my team for medical school?" I asked, faking wide-eyed horror.

"Hardly. I just want to learn more about the human mind, since I'm in it all the time." She waved at Benjamin. "Looking good, Merc."

"Where's Marco?" Benjamin asked, scanning for him.

Reid opened his book again. "Upstairs teaching kids how to knit. The regular storyteller guy had an asthma attack, so Marco swooped in to save the hour."

I leaned forward. "Since he's not here, now's a good time to ask: what are we doing for his birthday?" Marco would turn eighteen the next day.

Benjamin smirked. "Get him a pack of cigarettes and a porn rag. That's what Beau did for my eighteenth."

I ignored him. "I was thinking a bunch of knitting stuff, and maybe pizza."

I took a silent moment to remember our first time eating pizza, in the galley of the *Friedrich*. It had been an almost indecently pleasurable experience.

"Let's talk later, because here he comes," Benjamin said, pointing to Marco, who was walking down the stairwell.

Marco spied us and ran over.

"Hey, guys!" He plopped into a chair and sighed. "Fifteen five-year-olds and one pair of needles. Dang. I deserve an award."

I grabbed him and gave him a noogie. "Here's your award."

He yelped and squirmed away from me. "You're crazy, woman," he muttered, massaging his head but grinning.

A postal worker strode past us to the main circulation desk. Benjamin slapped a hand to his forehead. "I forgot!"

"What?" I asked. "Did you need to mail something?"

"No, we got letters. They were in the bottom of the box that came today." He pulled folded envelopes from his pocket. He gave us each an envelope bearing our full names in neat, typed lettering: Jillian Johnson, Marco St. James, Ember Harris, Reid Fischer. Benjamin didn't have an envelope.

We all stared at ours.

"It was bound to happen sometime," Reid said finally, tearing his open. "Let's get this over with."

I opened mine and removed the short letter. Benjamin read over my shoulder.

*Jillian Johnson (Battlecry),*

*You are hereby ordered to report to Chattahoochee Camp no later than 29 December to give testimony regarding the defection and the disappearance of Patrick Campbell (Atropos). Failure to appear by the appointed date will result in your immediate removal from public service and subsequent sanctioning by appropriate authorities.*

*Elder Thomas St. James*

I read the letter twice. Despite the letter's statement that we were being recalled to testify regarding Patrick, we all knew we were going to have to defend our own actions. I was in bigger trouble than any of them.

A flicker of fear burst to life in my chest. They'd waited until the storm was cleaned up, but our grace period was coming to a close.

Ember tore her letter into tiny pieces. "You are hereby ordered," she mimicked. "They're all invited to bite me. If they're going to pretend that this is about Patrick, then I can't wait to tell Elder Campbell what his son did. I hope the whole damn camp is there to hear the testimony."

Benjamin stared at her. "You're going back?"

I folded my letter and placed it in its envelope. "Of course we're going back."

He gawked at me. "What? Why?"

"Because it's a summons, which has to be obeyed." The flicker of fear flared. Feigning confidence, I lifted my head up. "Besides, what's the worst they can do to me?"

"Remove you from service," Ember said.

"Or brand your face," Reid added, shuddering.

"Or make you marry Matthew!" Marco covered his mouth with his hand. "Oh my God, they're going to make you marry Matthew, aren't they?"

Marco's suggestion provided the levity I needed, and the fear disappeared. "They won't remove me from service. I'm too highly trained and that would be a waste of a resource. I'll kill anyone who tries to brand me. And if for some weird reason they actually succeed in making me marry Matthew Dumont, that would be more of a punishment for him than for me."

Benjamin flexed his bicep. "Plus, I'll fight him." My calm assurances must have relaxed his worry, because he leaned over to Marco and whispered, "Could I take him?"

"He's just a shapeshifter," Marco whispered back. "I think you're safe."

"Knock it off, you two," I said with a laugh. "Next month, we'll all report to Chattahoochee and tell the elders exactly what happened.

They'll throw a fit, tell me I'm a stupid little girl, and then we'll leave. No big deal."

As I said the words, I privately vowed to repeat them to myself every day until I fully believed them. My fear was unfounded, an instinctual reaction that I'd one day shed like an old coat.

My team exchanged doubtful glances, but our conversation drifted back into lighter topics. We enjoyed the afternoon at the library, surrounded by the information we'd been denied for so long.

A little girl came up to us and thanked us for rescuing her big brother from a car wreck. A woman tripped while walking down the stairs, but Benjamin didn't have to heal any broken bones—he ran so fast to catch her that she never hit the ground.

When we left the library a few hours later, books in arms, I caught a glimpse of my reflection in the glass doors of the library.

I saw a happy young woman.

THE END

---

THANK you so much for reading *Battlecry*! If you enjoyed the novel, please leave a review on its Amazon page. Your review ratings will determine which series I prioritize, so please consider leaving a review.

I have included a sneak preview of *Battlecry*'s sequel, *Sentinel*, for your enjoyment. Read on!

# ACKNOWLEDGMENTS

No book is a solitary effort, and I'd be remiss to not give thanks where it is due.

First and foremost, I must thank God for blessing and guiding this entire process. Similarly, I must thank the countless people who've prayed for me, my book, and my career.

I must thank my husband Alex, who has been my biggest fan from day one. Thank you so much for letting me bounce a million ideas off of you, and talking me out of the dumber ones. You're the best content editor I could ever ask for. I love you.

All of my friends have been wonderfully supportive of my writing, but special acknowledgment goes to Sarah Gonzales. I'll never forget the day you read my first chapter and told me that I had a solid opening to a novel. There were times when I lived for your chapter notes. You're the best friend anyone could ever ask for.

A thousand thanks, and a few apologies, go out to Alex Edge, Danielle Snider, Alysia Rowe, Amber-Jean Hensey, and Ashlynn Peery. You listened to me go on about my book long before it was a reality—truly an act of charity.

My critiquers on Scribophile have been invaluable to me, especially: Alan Billing, Renee Harvey, Katie Acosta, and Ada Hardy. I *really* couldn't have done this without you guys. Similarly, thank you to the ladies of Enclave: Monika Holabird, Emily Gorman, Katie Bueche, and Ryann Muree. I'm so glad I'm doing this with you to cheer me on!

In a more abstract way, I must acknowledge the cadets and cadre of ODU's Monarch Battalion class of 2012. That was a wild four years, guys. The challenges and struggles of ROTC went directly into Jillian's story. I hope you're all doing well.

And finally, I must thank my mother, Virginia Hull Welch. No matter how many books I sell, how many fans I get, or what I write... deep down, I will always be the quintessential author's daughter, just trying to make mom proud with my scribbles.

# ABOUT THE AUTHOR

Emerald Dodge lives with her husband Alex and their two sons. Emerald and Alex enjoy playing with their children, date nights, hosting dinner parties for their friends, and watching movies. They are a Navy family and look forward to traveling around the nation and meeting new people. When she's not writing, Emerald likes to cook, bake, go to Mass, pray the rosary, and FaceTime with her relatives.

Her favorite social media platform for interacting with fans is Tumblr. Message her on her Tumblr page!

If you'd like to receive Emerald's newsletter, please sign up here.

# ABOUT SENTINEL BY EMERALD DODGE

When her team is betrayed by the people she trusts, Jillian turns her back on being a superhero.

Jillian's supposed to be the hero, and yet, her elders have her on trial as if she's a villain. If she's found guilty, she and her team face harsh punishment and destroyed futures. But when the betrayal and treachery of her elders leads her to flee in search of her missing boyfriend, she uncovers terrible information that makes her wonder if he is really who she thought he was.

Her quest for the truth leads her to a handsome militia leader who makes her question whether she's been fighting for the wrong side all along. Caught up in a secret war against the people who murdered her brother, Jillian will have to decide if she's really cut out to be a superhero, or if her loyalties lie elsewhere after all.

As Jillian's search for truth leads to a search for her inner self, she falls into a violent and tragic downward spiral that leaves many people dead. Jillian must face her elders head on and forge her own path in the history of superheroes, or find herself lost to the violence of the war. But denouncing superheroism as she knows it will mean taking on a century-old institution that will do anything—including commit murder—to stay in power.

EMERALD DODGE

THEY
SHOULD'VE
LEFT HER
ALONE.

BATTLECRY SERIES – BOOK 2

SENTINEL

# SENTINEL SNEAK PREVIEW

The lions had come out of nowhere.

One minute my team and I had been corralling skittish deer and chattering monkeys back into their enclosures, and then the next we were running for our lives from the Saint Catherine Animal Park's main attraction, the pride of five full-grown lions.

I'd seen them earlier as we'd canvassed the zoo with tranquilizer guns in hand; they'd been sleeping peacefully in the shadows of the enormous rocks that dotted their enclosure. None of us had thought to double check the bolt on their gate. After all, if the malicious wag who'd set the other animals loose had wanted to liberate the lions, the lions would've been freed.

But it seemed the ruckus from the other animals had woken the pride, and in short order we'd all been scattered across the zoo.

The pride had stopped chasing my teammates, apparently deciding I was the tastiest-looking prey. They herded me through the zoo's main entrance, over the turnstile, and across the street. My teammates had shouted my codename, Battlecry, a few times before they were distracted by other animals.

Now it was just the lions and me on the dark street, illuminated by the pre-dawn moon and Christmas lights from nearby yards.

I perched on top of a beat-up sedan and watched the pride slink towards me, their unblinking gazes never leaving my face. They were quiet, almost unnaturally so. My sensitive ears picked up the faint padding noises of their paws striking the pavement, but I heard no rumbling beginnings of growls, no snorted breaths, nothing.

Just the sound of five killing machines drawing closer.

The male, a magnificent beast at least six feet long, sauntered ahead of the others. Though I knew little about African fauna, I knew that lionesses were typically a pride's hunters. Why was the male leading?

The gentle breeze billowed their scent towards me. Beneath the musky, sweaty smell of cat lingered the unmistakable aroma of death. The lions had killed recently.

I drew my largest knife from its sheath on my thigh and held it up. "Firelight, tell them I'll kill them if they don't stop!"

Even if my telepathic teammate Firelight, whose real name was Ember, didn't hear my distinct words, she'd know to tune in.

Indeed, a second later, her wispy mental voice filled my head. *What's up, Jill?*

*Tell the lions I'll kill them if they don't stop.*

I felt Ember slip out of my mind, then back in. *I can't sense them. I couldn't reach them before, when they were chasing us. I thought it was because there was so much chaos. But I can't sense them at all. It's like there's nothing there.*

The hair on my arms stood up. Without Ember's ability to control animals, I had to rely on my powers alone to defeat the pride. Fast, strong, and agile as my powers made me, I was mortal and had faced death enough times to know when I needed to fold. This fight was better suited to Reid, my earth-moving second-in-command, or Marco, who could redirect the sun's heat and light.

However, they were still entangled with animals inside the zoo. I needed to make a decision, fast. My tranquilizer gun had been lost during the frantic scramble to safety, and for the first time in my life I found myself wishing superheroes were permitted to bear proper firearms.

The male stepped aside, and a lioness tensed to spring.

I took aim and hurled my knife. It sunk to the hilt between her eyes.

Instead of dropping, she bared her fangs. I might as well have thrown a kitchen sponge at her.

I leaped off the car and sprinted back towards the zoo's entrance, the image of my knife's hilt sticking out of the lioness' forehead seared into my mind. I'd fought some formidable enemies during my time as a superhero in Saint Catherine, but none of them would've survived a knife in their brain.

Whatever this situation was, it required a team effort. The zoo's entrance was just ten yards ahead—

One of the lions pounced, slamming me to the ground so quickly I couldn't even shriek. My nose broke from the force of the impact, and hot blood gushed out of my face while searing pain licked up my cheeks. Large paws on my shoulder blades pinned me down.

Ordinarily, I would've pulled out my shoulder knife and slashed at the lion's legs, but I doubted that it would do any good to a beast that could survive a knife between the eyes. All of my combat knowledge was founded upon the assumption that my opponent could die.

Suddenly, the lion standing on top of me stepped off. A rough tug on my hair bun lifted my head, forcing me to face the male.

I pushed myself up, my hands scraping painfully against the bloody pavement, and stared at the enormous cat. His white-rimmed eyes were vaguely cloudy, obscuring my pale-faced reflection. Was he blind?

The lion leaned in as if he were studying me. The stench of death and decay became overpowering. His jaws were inches from my face, and I wrinkled my nose at the smell seeping from him. What did the zoo keepers feed these things? And what was he doing?

To my right, one of the lionesses took the knife's hilt into her jaws and pulled it out of her sister's head. Instead of a spurting shower of blood, or even a steady flow, a single congealing drop of blood pooled at the bottom of the red slit left by the knife.

Realization sunk in.

I slowly leaned back from the dead lion in front of me.

"Who are you?" I whispered, my skin crawling. "Why are you controlling the lions?"

The carcasses were puppets. I'd never seen anything like this before, but I had no other way to explain how five dead lions were able to move and operate. Clearly some higher intelligence was behind their actions, but what was the goal? Why chase me down the street and knock me down, but not kill me?

As fascinatingly bizarre as the situation was, I could not ignore my gut feeling—the person controlling the lions meant me serious harm. I had two options: try to fight the lions and probably be mauled to death, or somehow alert my team that I needed backup and try to contact the puppet master in the meantime. Clearly he or she was waiting for something, or the lions would've killed me already. Instead, they stood around me in a circle, never taking their eyes off me.

As I weighed my options, the male gazed up at the zoo's entrance. There was a moment of silence, and then the five lions opened up their mouths and roared.

I clamped my hands over my ears, but couldn't help feel a twinge of hope. The roars would get my team's attention.

I planted my foot on the ground to push myself up, but the male swiped a paw at me, shredding my arm above the elbow. I gasped and doubled over while the other four lions moved in around me, low growls ripping out of their fangs. I pressed my hand to my arm and looked up, heat coursing through my cheeks.

I didn't care how many lions this unknown person was controlling —I wasn't going down easily.

*Jillian, what's going on?* Ember's concerned voice cut through my fury.

*Get the team and get out here now. Look for the lions.*

She slipped out of my mind and I glared into the white murkiness of the male's eyes, sensing he was the main avatar for whomever controlled them. "Come out and fight me yourself, coward."

The lion shook its head, its teeth bared in a hideous feline grin.

He raised a paw. There was a flash of fur, and pain exploded across my other arm. Blood dripped from my new wounds down to my elbow and pooled on the ground.

Without thinking, I grabbed a fistful of the lion's mane and jumped on him, leapfrog style. Before he could buck me off, I pulled my shoulder knife free, twisted around, and gouged one of his eyes.

In the corner of my vision, I saw a nearby chain-link fence at the edge of a small neighborhood playground. If I could make it there, I could climb it and leap onto a low residential roof to safety.

Without pausing for breath, I jumped off the lion and fled towards the fence, the pounding of paws close behind.

I made a wild, running leap onto the fence and clambered to the top, ten feet from the ground. The lions snapped and snarled below, but I was a good two feet out of their reach. Unwilling to risk falling while walking along the narrow rail of the fence, I gripped the metal and waited for help.

In the distance, Reid and Marco ran towards me. Ember and Benjamin, my fifth and final teammate, were not with them.

"Don't destroy them!" I yelled to the men. "Just trap them!" I didn't want to damage the connection to the person controlling them.

Reid's eyes glowed white, tiny pinpricks in the faint morning light. The ground rumbled and a depression appeared beneath the lions, sinking six, seven, eight feet below the surface of the street.

Before I could yell my thanks, the fence wobbled and collapsed. I crashed down eighteen feet in a painful heap of loose dirt, metal fence, and cold lion corpses.

I braced for the inevitable mauling.

It never came.

When I realized that I was still alive, I tested my limbs for breaks. Finding none, I pushed myself up and shoved away the portion of fence that had fallen in, still bleeding from my arms and nose.

The lions were limp and inanimate on the ground around me, no more dangerous than rag dolls. I dusted myself off and peered up at the edge of the pit above me.

Marco's light brown face appeared, amusement and worry

battling for dominance in his youthful features. Reid's significantly paler face appeared next to him.

Reid winced as he looked down at me. "I'm so sorry, Jill... Battlecry. Give me a second and I'll raise the pit again."

Reid's slip-up by almost calling me by my real name hinted at how upset he was. We were all more than used to the real-name-code-name flip flop in battle. Though we privately thought of and referred to each other by our real names, in battle Ember was Firelight, Marco was Helios, Reid was Tank, Benjamin was Mercury, and I was Battlecry.

I waved dismissively. "No, don't bother. I don't want to give them a chance to get free. Throw me a rope or something. I'd climb out myself, but my arms are busted."

Marco frowned. "Let me get that useless medic." He disappeared from the edge. "Hey, Mercury! Your girlfriend is bleeding to death! Get over here!"

Reid stifled a laugh. I put my hands on my hips. "Useless medic? What's he sore about?"

"Mercury threw a punch at one of the animals, but he hit Helios instead. It was the funniest thing I've seen all week."

"It was not," Marco snapped from somewhere unseen. "Firelight fights better than Mercury, I swear to God."

I heard someone—probably Ember—smack Marco.

A whooshing sound heralded the arrival of Benjamin. His lovely face appeared above me and he grinned crookedly. He extended a hand down. "You look like you need a medic. Tank, give her a little boost and I'll grab her." Beneath his humor lay the tenderness he reserved just for me.

I raised my hand to grab his, a real smile spreading across my lips.

A horrible growl from behind made me spin around.

There wasn't time to scream as four lions sprang, their teeth sinking into my arms, legs, sides...anything they could bite. My vision colored white, black, and red.

Agony, almost unreal in its intensity, seized my entire consciousness. It was hot, it was freezing, it was liquid and everywhere, it was needle-like and specific.

I was being torn to pieces.

Growls around me mixed with shouts above me, and then I was on the ground, the lightening sky mixing with swirls of purple, red, and green.

In the sky, a bright star twinkled like the crystal on the necklace Benjamin had given me two days before. It was such a lovely necklace, very... very....

I smelled cooking meat.

I heard the thud of boots hitting the ground.

Warm fingers grasped my cold ones.

Electricity surged through my hand and up my arm, down through my abdomen, and into my legs. Skin and muscle sewed itself together. Bones mended. Aches and pains evaporated, leaving wholeness in their wake.

My dull vision, formerly swimming with little dots, came into sharp focus, and I saw Benjamin kneeling next to me, cradling my hand to his cheek.

Marco, Ember, and Reid stood next to the severely burned lion bodies, no doubt Marco's doing. Ember looked nauseated.

I gave my head a little shake, droplets of blooding flying everywhere. "Thank you."

Benjamin didn't let go of my hand. "I thought the lions were dead. I don't understand how they just jumped up and attacked you." Painful confusion was in his eyes.

I pulled my hand free and stood, my shredded tunic hanging off me like rags. I beckoned the rest of my team to join me while I kneeled down next to the least-burnt carcass. Marco's blast of heat had scorched most of its fur off, revealing a tiny bullet hole in the skull I'd missed before.

I pointed to it. "They were dead when we arrived at the zoo. When we passed them earlier, I thought they were sleeping. Someone killed them and was controlling them like puppets, but I don't know how. Firelight said she couldn't hear anything in their minds."

Ember tapped her temple. "Well, yeah. If they were dead, there'd be no mind to hear. Whatever was controlling them isn't telepathic. Or at least, it's not like any telepathy I've ever encountered."

Wisps of dirt rose up from the ground and flew into Reid's palm, where they made beautiful, delicate little patterns. He wiggled his fingers, and the dirt clumped together to form small lion-shaped figures that prowled around his hand. "Maybe it's more like my power. I manipulate earth. This person might be able to manipulate dead tissue."

I had a sudden image of being attacked by a flying steak. Ember visibly fought a laugh.

Benjamin stared at the tiny dirt lions without blinking for several seconds. Finally, he looked at me. "Wasn't there a break in? Captain Nguyen said someone robbed the aviary, right?"

"Oh, right." In the morning's furor I'd forgotten that we'd been called in to investigate a far more mundane situation. "Tank, get us out of here."

Reid's eyes glowed soft white and the ground shook. The floor of the pit began to rise, and within seconds we were at street level again.

I nodded towards the zoo's entrance. "Mercury, Helios, Firelight, you go ahead. I'll stay behind with Tank to make sure the lions' bodies are secured so our tissue manipulator can't make a comeback."

"Got it," Benjamin said. "Come on, guys."

The three of them began to walk towards the entrance.

The sight of Benjamin's codename on his back filled me with awe. The five of us had come far in the last half year, but he'd come the farthest. As far as I knew, he was the only reformed supervillain that had ever served on a superhero team, and as he'd just demonstrated, he was arguably the most valuable one of us.

I took a moment to appreciate the emblems we'd chosen to sew onto the backs of our uniforms beneath our codenames, something no other team had ever done. Marco's dark purple tunic bore a stylized yellow sun. Ember's emerald green tunic sported a dog's paw print. Benjamin's gray tunic displayed the unmistakable sign of a medic: a red cross.

I turned to ask Reid if he could make some kind of earthen cage for the carcasses, but saw that he was examining his feet. "Hey, what's wrong?"

"The lions were able to maul you because I screwed up." He wouldn't meet my eyes. "I should've assumed the fence would fall in. That was an amateur mistake."

I carefully chose my reply. "Have I ever punished anyone on this team for mistakes in battle?"

"No, but—"

"You just said it: no." I put my hand on his shoulder. His muscles tensed, becoming as hard as the rocks he could move with his mind. "Reid, relax," I whispered. "I'm not Patrick. I'm not going to hurt you."

"I deserve—"

"We all deserve to go home and have breakfast." I gave him a little shake. "We're not doing the eye-for-an-eye thing, remember? If it makes you feel better, I'll let you do the dishes this morning, but for Pete's sake, forgive yourself. I'm fine. We're all fine."

"You almost died. I watched you get torn apart because I trapped you with lions."

"Of course I almost died. We're superheroes. We can't go a week without someone shooting at us or pulling knives on us. It comes with the territory. Stop hating yourself."

He gave me an unreadable glance but nodded once.

I pointed to the corpses. "Let's get the lions back inside the zoo. I doubt the zoo officials want them in the middle of the road."

He held up his hand and dirt from a nearby yard flew to the lions to form small, hard planks beneath them. The lions rose on their little platforms and followed us into the zoo.

Reid went ahead of me, allowing me to see the white-capped mountain on the back of his red tunic.

Once inside the zoo, stone cages sprung up around the bodies. Reid directed the cages to the lions' former enclosure, then dusted off his hands. We hurried towards the aviary, a low building decorated with a mural of brightly-colored parrots and other tropical birds.

Inside, the three others were huddled around a spot on the wall and running their hands over it. The bird house wasn't nearly as noisy as I expected it to be; the birds lived behind thick glass that muffled their calls.

"I know who we're dealing with," Benjamin said without preamble. "This was the Rowe twins."

"Who?" I recognized the surname, but I didn't know the individuals.

Benjamin dragged a finger down the wall again. The stone looked... weird. I was reminded of my favorite photo editing software on my phone, in which I could swirl and warp pictures. The bricks appeared as if someone had swirled them slightly, little curves and whorls appearing where there should've been straight lines of mortar and rock.

"The woman who broke into the aviary was Alysia Rowe. She's our age. She and I played together when we were kids, though I wouldn't call her an old friend. She coined the nickname 'Bleeding Heart Benjamin. When we were five or six she killed my pet frog because she thought it was funny when I cried."

I already hated her.

"What caused the swirling?" Marco asked.

"That's the calling card of her power. She walks through solid objects, but it's not a clean job." He pointed towards a pane of glass across the dim room. It was droopy and swirled in the middle. "She came for the Socorro doves. According to the plaque on the exhibit, they're extinct in the wild, so they must be extremely valuable." He ran a hand over the bricks again. "A hired thief. She's all grown up now."

"Any idea who hired her?" I asked.

Benjamin shrugged. "Could've been anybody. My family must've contracted with three dozen private parties over the years, and that's not counting the corporate accounts. I'm sure the Rowe family works for people I've never heard of. There are lots of rare bird collectors who would pay Alysia to steal the doves."

"Who's her twin?" I asked, studying the odd patterns on the wall.

Benjamin grimaced. "Will Rowe, my brother's best friend. We called him a necromancer. He can't manipulate human corpses, for some reason, but like you all saw today, animals are no problem for him. I suspected we were dealing with the twins when Reid mentioned tissue manipulation, but I didn't say anything because I wasn't sure. The swirls confirmed that it was Alysia, and I've never met anyone else who can do what Will can." He glanced at Ember. "I'd suggest you do a mental scan for him in one of the nearby houses, but no doubt he beat feet as soon as we went back into the zoo."

Marco gestured towards the Socorro dove exhibit. "Why did they set the animals free if this was a robbery?"

Benjamin ran a hand through his hair. "Yeah, um, about that. I can guarantee you that Mom has told everyone in my old circle that I defected to the heroes. I'm not sure, but I'm guessing Alysia and her brother did this just to be brats and cause problems for us. It's really not supervillain style to deliberately draw attention to our... their crimes. Not unless they're paid to be terrorists like my Uncle Mike usually is. You guys know him as The Destructor." Benjamin sighed. "I think we can expect a lot more stunts like this."

I pulled out my phone. "I'm calling Captain Nguyen. Tell him what you just told me. I'd like to see the frog killer and her brother behind bars, and if you're anticipating Super attacks, the police are going to want to know."

I dialed the police liaison and gave him the all clear. A few minutes later a squad of police officers arrived at the scene, flanked by zoo officials.

One of the zoo keepers dissolved into hysterics when he saw the dead lions, but upon seeing my shredded and bloodstained uniform, tearfully admitted that perhaps we'd had no choice. I didn't bother explaining the truth about their deaths.

Marco, Reid, and Ember gave their statements and left the bird house one by one. I stayed behind while Benjamin talked to Captain Nguyen about his suspicions regarding the twins' motives. The Captain nodded and took notes, grim-faced.

Finally, he flipped his notebook shut and pocketed it, then shook Benjamin's hand.

Benjamin joined me at the doorway. "Home? I'd kill for a shower."

I winked at him. "You couldn't kill someone even if they were trying to kill you. Bleeding Heart Benjamin, remember?"

Hurt flashed in his eyes.

I shook my head. "The difference between me and Alysia Rowe is that unlike her, I love that bleeding heart."

"You *love* it? That's some pretty heavy language, Miss Battlecry."

"Oh, stop. Let's not go there."

He chuckled and walked past me, and I took a deep breath before I followed. We joined our team by the zoo gates and walked down the sleepy residential streets of Saint Catherine towards our headquarters.

Half an hour later, we stumbled through the front door of our new headquarters. Without so much as taking off our boots, we trooped up the stairs, down the hall, and into our separate bedrooms.

I heard the sounds of four bodies falling into bed as I peeled off my destroyed uniform. My emblem, a five-pointed star containing the city's seal, was barely distinguishable beneath the bloodstains. I threw the rags in the garbage and crawled under my heavy quilt.

The last thing I saw before I went to sleep was my calendar hanging on the wall, and that day's date circled, with a little sad face drawn in the corner.

## END OF PREVIEW
### READ ON IN SENTINEL BY EMERALD DODGE
#### AVAILABLE ON AMAZON